THE ROWAN'S STONE

KILLIAN BLADE SERIES BOOK 2

STELLA BRIE

Cover Design: Mayflower Studio

Editing: Bookish Dreams Editing

Proofreading: Elemental Editing & Proofreading

 Created with Vellum

AUTHOR'S NOTE

This book is a Reverse Harem romance. The heroine does not have to choose between male interests. This book has a FMMMMM relationship. Recommended for 18+ due to mature content.

Playlist for all my books can be found on my YouTube channel - @authorstellabrie.

PLAYLIST

"MONSTERS" - FEAT. DEMI LOVATO AND BLACKBEAR

"GIRL WITH THE BAT "- FEAT. SHADOW BOXXER

"MY HEAD & MY HEART" - AVA MAX

"BACK TO YOU" - FEAT. SARAH DIAMOND

"RIOT GEAR" - MALAA & ABSTRAKT

"DANGEROUS" - KARDINAL OFFISHALL

"LITTLE BIT OF LOVE" - TOM BRENNAN

"THE UNIVERSE IS OURS" - HEADHUNTERZ & CRYSTAL

LAKE VS. REUNIFY FEAT. KIFI

"ALL IN'" - NITTI GRIPIT FEAT. JIMMY LEVY

"DANCING WITH THE DEVIL" - DEMI LOVATO

"WARRIOR" - ALUNA

"AFRAID" - NOISY

DEDICATION

To all the fantastic fans who loved The Rowan, you are truly awesome.

CHAPTER

ONE

ARDEN

It's silently mocking me. Taunting, in fact. No matter what question I ask, it gives me a blank stare and refuses to answer. Clearly, the spell requires certain parameters or terms to be met before releasing additional information, but I can't figure out how it's even working, much less what's required of me. I've asked it hundreds of questions in the last few hours, and I'm only stopping now because I'm thoroughly frustrated and my desire to crumble the parchment into a teeny tiny ball and throw it in the fire is almost overwhelming. Reluctantly, I lay the paper on the nightstand, forcing it out of my grasp for a while. I guess *find the journals* is all I'm going to get until I get to the next step. Whatever or wherever that may be.

Blunt fingers skim my naked back, causing me to shiver,

and I close my eyes, savoring the pleasurable sensation, my body still sensitive from earlier.

"When are Vargas and Solandis leaving?" Valerian asks quietly. His hand trails farther down my body, mapping its curves and valleys, leaving heat and desire in its wake.

"Tomorrow," I answer softly, already sad. "I'll miss them terribly, but it's not safe for them to stay too long. I'm just glad they were able to attend the ceremony and meet you and the rest of the cadre. I want them to know the life and people I've found here. I only wish I'd gotten a hold of Meri."

I called Meri to see if she could come by and meet them, only to repeatedly get her voicemail. Since I didn't want to leave a message that could be overheard, I simply told her to call me.

"They're certainly not what I expected, given their rank and titles," Valerian muses. "And they accepted me with only a little reservation."

I snort, then look at him incredulously. "Are you serious? Vargas fooled you easily. The King of Dragons mated to his daughter? Inside, he was squealing like a three-year-old girl getting her first pony. He even told me to be nice to you!" I howl with laughter.

"I don't think laughing at me qualifies as being nice," he growls before rolling me over onto my back and covering me with his massive, incredibly sexy and very naked body. "It means a lot to have Vargas and Solandis accept me as your mate." His eyes gleam with emotion from the demons of his past.

Sweeping his hair back from his brow, I stop laughing and assure him, "They do, I promise." Lifting my head, I nibble his pouty lips, kissing away his doubts and fears. "More importantly, I accept you as my mate." I continue nibbling and sucking lightly until I feel him relax. A sense of playfulness takes over, and I slide one hand between us and flutter my fingers against his side. When he squirms a little, I back off.

He drops his head to my neck and starts placing kisses along the side.

Turning my head to give him greater access, I slide my legs around and lock them behind his back. His lips hit a sensitive spot on my neck, and I gasp, unable to hold it in. Responding to me, he settles his body onto mine, and I can feel his desire returning.

I feel bad for a second, but sometimes he's entirely too serious. So I pounce, my fingers dancing around the ticklish spots on his sides.

He roars and jerks, trying to get away from me, but my legs hold him in place. "Arden!" he shouts, laughing, then gives in to the fun, turning the tables on me, and his fingers are merciless when they tickle me back.

I squirm, trying to get away from them, but I'm locked into my own trap. Laughing and crying, I call out, "Mercy!" but my voice is breathless, so he doesn't hear it the first time. "Mercy," I say louder. "I surrender."

Chuckling, he stops and wipes the tears from my cheeks. He gives me a big, boastful grin. "A bit of a miss on your strategy there."

Aligning my body with his, I arch into him. "Is it? I don't think so."

Dropping his mouth to my nipple, he flicks it with his tongue while he slides into me. With shallow dips in and out, I moan at the micro sensations spiraling out from my core and dig my heels into his thighs.

"Damn it, dragon," I curse. "Stop teasing me."

He chuckles, and I glare up at him. "I thought you wanted to play. Just trying to give my mate what she wants," he teases. "Are we done playing?"

"Valerian," I state firmly, "I want you, now."

Pushing all the way in until we're flush against each other, he stops and stares at me, his amber eyes flickering with sensuality and heat. Another slow pull, and he glides out, then back in, setting a languid pace, causing every nerve in my body to stand at attention.

My hands skim along his shoulders and back, feeling the ripple of movement as his body moves on top of mine, each muscle working in sync to the rhythm he's established. Sensation washes over me, and my breath catches. The pace is reflective of the slowly deepening nature of our relationship. His lips drop to capture mine in a languorous kiss, heightening the emotions sliding through me.

Our bubble is a cocoon, a buffer against the real world. We crawl toward the finish, taking time to savor the moment. My orgasm builds higher and higher, but still, I hold off, slow dancing on the edge, doing nothing to push us over, until suddenly, it's there and I free fall. My body clenches his tightly while powerful waves roll over me one after another. With a slight pulse, Valerian falls off the cliff alongside me.

His lips leave mine, and we stare at each other, saying nothing and everything at the same time.

Early the next morning, I wake to another piece of paper. Thankfully, this one isn't blank, and it isn't waiting for me to solve a riddle.

Will meet you in the training room—Valerian

His single-minded focus on training is as bad as Vargas'. After a quick stretch and shower, I dress in workout clothes, grab a banana, and head toward the training room.

When I open the doors, I hear Vargas sneer, "I thought you were the King of Dragons." He laughs uproariously before continuing, "Do you need me to slow down and let you catch up?"

My eyes widen when I hear Vargas' scorn. Slipping farther into the room, I move over to the wall and slide down quietly to sit beside Daire, who's watching the show.

"How long have they been sparring?" I whisper, staring at the two massive men circling each other about thirty feet away. Every few minutes, they blur into motion, which is quickly followed by the sounds of weapons striking and a loud curse or grunt as they miss or find their mark.

Daire leans over, placing his lips near my ear, and murmurs, "A couple of hours, at least. I haven't been this entertained in a long time. He's trying to make a good impression on Vargas." His low chuckle sends shivers down my spine.

I turn to glance at Daire, and his icy blue eyes are filled with laughter. This is not good. I give a long sigh. "Be ready to pull me out when this gets ugly," I instruct him.

Without waiting for his reply, I stand, throw my shoulders back, and stroll over to the two men facing each other. "Good morning, Vargas. Valerian. I know you two have been sparring for a while, but mind if I steal Vargas away? I'd like to have the chance to spar with him before he leaves." Giving them my best smile, I watch as they swallow their irritation at my intrusion.

Valerian picks up a towel and gives me a short nod. "Of course, Arden. I'll go watch with Daire." He strides off without looking at Vargas, anger and frustration beating at him.

"Tsk, tsk, my darling Arden," Vargas admonishes me. "The

dragon's been trying to win my respect all morning. But I have to tell you, I'm now doubting my previous high regard of him."

"Don't tsk me, Vargas," I reply sternly. "Valerian's holding back, and you know it."

Vargas frowns. "I know, damn it. I've been trying to goad him into a real fight all morning. Why won't he fight me?"

"I'm guessing he's a bit old-fashioned. You know, be nice and respectful to your mate's father," I answer. Drawing a pair of short swords, I bow to Vargas and take my fighting stance. "That's not the way to win your respect, though, is it?" With those words, I attack.

Vargas raises his swords up in time to meet mine, and it's a no-holds-barred match. Blood soon dots the floor around us, our swords nicking each other regularly. I don't worry about it too much. It's going to get worse before it gets better. A large grin splits my face, and Vargas gives me an evil grin back. Sparring with him is exhilarating.

His foot sweeps out to trip me, and I jump to avoid it, only to realize his sword is swinging toward my head. Arching, I let my head fall back, and the sword whistles an inch above me, slicing the air in half. I hear a bellow and several shouts from the wall. I'm guessing Daire and Valerian have been joined by one or two of the others, and they're not happy about Vargas' tactics, but I don't dare look.

Spying a rope off to the side, I quickly shift my attention back to Vargas, not wanting to clue him into my thoughts. Releasing a tendril of magic, I guide it toward the rope, instructing it to gather and coil into a circle. Simultaneously, I step back, away from the rope, allowing Vargas a chance to step forward, but before he gains his fighting stance, I cut in close and throw an elbow in his face, then bounce out again.

"Ha! I taught you that trick! I'd have thought you'd have

new ones for me," Vargas grumbles while rubbing his face. Shadows roll off him onto the floor and head toward me.

"Looks like the old ones still work," I taunt. "Where are your new moves, old man?"

My feet dance between the shadows, careful to avoid their grasp, while my gaze sweeps the floor. Out of the corner of my eye, I realize my trap is set. With a roar, I use a full-frontal attack to drive Vargas backwards. He grins, knowing I'm up to something now, but he's not sure what. I let off the attack and step sideways. He follows before driving me back a few steps. Then I charge again, this time bringing him within a foot of the rope.

Using my magic, I wrap the rope around his ankle, throw it over the beam above him, and hoist him in the air. In surprise, his sword swings out wildly, and the tip catches my thigh, slicing it open. Swinging back and forth above me, he laughs, knowing I'll have to take time to heal it, inadvertently giving him time to cut the rope and jump down. I step back until I'm not directly below him.

Fuck, fuck, fuck, that hurts, I cry silently.

Several loud shouts carry over to me from the side, and I hear running feet. Gritting my teeth against the pain, I paste on a smile and turn to Valerian right as he reaches me. Conjuring his favorite weapon, the claymore, I use magic to toss the massively heavy sword to him.

"Damn it, Vargas!" Valerian shouts, his hand instinctively coming up to catch the claymore. "What the hell were you thinking?" He reaches a hand toward my leg. "Let me see the wound, lass."

"No time," I shout, quickly hobbling past Valerian. "Vargas will be dropping in front of you in less than a second. Get ready!" I limp toward the wall to get a good seat for the show.

Daire steps in front of me. "Daire, what are you doing? I

need to sit down so I can heal my leg and watch this match. It's going to be epic." A clang sounds behind Daire, and I step to the side and turn to watch Vargas and Valerian battle it out.

Hands grab me from behind and hold me still, but I don't take my eyes off the two men in front of me. No longer dancing and sparring lightly with each other, Valerian's finally giving Vargas the match he deserves. This time, their match is silent, each of them laser focused on the other.

Heat caresses my leg, and I glance down to see Daire healing it.

"Thank you, Daire," I murmur, giving him a smile. Ever since he healed me the first time, after the assassination attempt at Santiago's, our relationship has been evolving. I haven't even seen a sneer or heard a snarl in a long while. "I'd planned to heal myself once I reached the wall."

"Next time, try not to get your damn leg almost cut off," he replies gruffly.

I laugh off his worry. "Over the years, I've received a lot worse in my skirmishes with Vargas, and he's received his fair share in return. And before you, I didn't have the luxury of healing myself without using potions, which seemingly took forever." I motion to my leg. "Hurry, you don't want to miss this." My eyes flick back to the two fighters.

Someone behind me snorts, and I glance over my shoulder to find Fallon. His hands are wrapped tightly around my shoulders, which is why tingles are running up and down my spine. "You threw a match on a field of gasoline. Believe me, Valerian's anger is going to take a while to burn out," he says curtly, his eyes glued to the two men fighting. A nerve jumps in his cheek.

My eyebrows rise, and I glance down to share my amusement with Daire, only to see the same simmering anger in his eyes. Shaking my head at them both, I wait until Daire's finished healing my leg before moving over to the wall. I may as well get comfortable.

THREE HOURS LATER, they finally stop to get a drink of water. Both are breathing heavily, blood and sweat coating their bodies, but large grins grace each of their faces. Finally!

"Well, darling, your plan worked." Solandis' melodious voice rings out, her tone conveying her amusement and approval of my actions. "Vargas, darling, we need to get going soon. Are you done?" While her words imply a question, she's really stating her intention to leave soon, with or without him.

I laugh. I've missed the games these two play with each other. Several heads turn toward us, a question in their eyes. "When Solandis is ready to go, she leaves. She's left Vargas and returned home, by herself, many times." Vargas chuckles and winks at Solandis.

While Vargas says goodbye to the others, I clasp Solandis' hand in mine. "It meant so much to me to have you at the ceremony, standing as my guardians. To be by my side, seeing my witch heritage unfold after all the years of secrets, was more than I could imagine. I guess we'll find out what it means to be the Rowan, witch of seven bloodlines, destiny of something, but we have some answers, and soon, we'll have more." I smile tearily at her. I'll miss having her here. "I wish you could stay longer. One day, when this is all over, we'll all meet at the house and you can spend time getting to know everyone better."

She pulls me into a tight hug. "I know you're in good

hands. Never forget how much I love you, darling. No matter what happens, I'm here for you."

"I love you," I reply, hugging her tightly.

"Where's my hug?" Vargas bellows.

I slide out of Solandis' arms and stand before him, wrinkling my nose. I wave my hands at the blood and sweat covering his body, using my magic to clean him up. Then I step into his arms. "I love you too. Take care of each other. I'll text often. Let us know if you find out anything."

After Solandis gives everyone a rare hug, they conjure a portal and leave.

Valerian comes up to me. "Thank you. I was handling him wrongly, and I couldn't understand why he was being such an asshole."

"He needed reassurance that you could handle whatever's coming our way," I explain softly. "Now he knows you can."

CHAPTER
TWO

THERON

My phone pings with an incoming text. I'm tempted to ignore it and continue with my delicious daydream, but of course, I don't. Picking it up, I see a text from Arden, asking if I have time to meet with her. Amusement ripples through me. I came to the garden to get away from her, to breathe without her delectable scent teasing me, to dream of roving hands and the slide of her towel as it falls to the ground, leaving me with a wet and naked Arden in my arms. The vision has teased me ever since I found her fresh from the shower in her room.

A second ping comes across with an apology for bothering me and a request to meet up later. Pursing my lips, I reply with my location and an invitation to join me.

Five minutes, she texts back.

Closing my eyes, I savor the grass beneath me, my bare feet

planted firmly, letting nature's elements seep into me from below while the sun shines down from above. Releasing a breath, I try to recapture the relaxed drowsiness of a second ago, but my body is tense in anticipation of her arrival.

The swoosh of the elevator doors opening fills the air, and seconds later, she stands beside me, her unique scent of strawberries and honeysuckle tickling my nose.

"Theron," she murmurs, her hesitancy to bother me apparent in her tone.

In a flash of movement, I sweep her legs out from under her before catching her in my arms. Lowering her to the ground beside me, I roll over and stare at her surprised face.

"Didn't Vargas teach you to expect the unexpected?" I tease her, my amusement apparent. My fingers brush the hair out of her eyes, and startled, I pause for a second. Usually hazel, they seem different, lighter, and a bit greener perhaps.

She stares at me intensely for a few seconds before laughter spills from her luscious pink lips. "He did," she replies. "I didn't expect it from you, I guess. You're usually in a suit and so proper, so...Fae. And I rarely see you sparring or doing physical things. Don't get me wrong, I like this side of you. It's a surprise, though." She shrugs. "I'm not disturbing you, am I?"

I jolt with surprise when I hear her description of me. I hadn't realized I'd never shown her more than the formal façade. I've definitely got some work to do.

"Always and never," I answer truthfully. Getting up on my knees, I lean over and trail my hands along her long legs to her feet. I slip off her shoes and plant her feet in the grass. She sighs in pleasure. At the sight of her lying in front of me, a bolt of desire makes my hands tighten on her ankles, but I force myself to relax.

She pulls her bottom lip in for a second, then tells me, "Before we get into anything else, I want to thank you for shaking Vargas' hand. It meant a lot to him and me. I've never seen another Fae shake his hand. Even Solandis' sister, the queen, won't embrace him."

"I learned a long time ago to measure a male by his actions, not his race, rank, or power. I know from personal experience how judgmental and unforgiving the Fae can be, even to their own." Memories cloud my voice as I reply. I lower myself to her side and stare at the sky. "I know Vargas to be worthy because of you. All the training and love he gave you is the highest recommendation of his character."

When she turns her head, mine also turns, as if it's tuned to her every movement. She smiles, her hand coming up to cup my jaw.

"Thank you. I got some of my best traits from Vargas," she responds. "He's fierce and loyal to those he loves and brutal to his enemies, but he takes time to laugh and enjoy life. He tells me to leave it all on the table and take the time to capture the moments, because those two things will later define the memories of my life. Given how long he's lived, I believe him."

Hmm, he's right, I muse. She lapses into silence, and I use the time to take in this moment with her. My eyes drop to her lips, and all I can think about is how they would feel against mine.

"Umm, do you realize you're glowing?" Arden asks tentatively.

"I'm the Lord of Summer's son," I tell her with a shrug, although it's not the whole truth. My desire for her is making me glow a bit brighter. "I usually dim the glow in favor of my winter side, but it gets tiring. If it bothers you, I can tone it down?"

"Absolutely not. The glow doesn't bother me, and it's nice to see you relaxed and less formal," she tells me. Biting her lip, she pauses for a second before continuing, "Why do you favor winter? If you don't want to tell me, that's fine. The few hybrid Fae I know seem to favor the light instead of the dark, but you chose the dark." She shrugs.

My gut churns, and I contemplate whether to answer. "My father never acknowledged me as his son. Not in the beginning, and not now. He prefers to act like I don't exist and often introduces his youngest son as his heir. In return, I rarely embrace my summer side and ignore him whenever I see him. It's been our *modus operandi* for centuries now." My mind plays a few scenes from my past where I hadn't ignored him, and I wince, not wanting to see the reminders.

Arden reaches over and entwines her fingers with mine, which brings me out of my internal spiral, and I give them a tight squeeze.

"I'm so sorry," she murmurs. "He's missed out on an incredible son. And I like both sides of you—the icy, arrogant side and this warm, more relaxed side."

Her easy acceptance washes over me like a warm breeze, and yet I say nothing.

"The sun feels incredible," she drawls a few minutes later, her body relaxed beside mine. "I can't remember the last time I've lain in the grass and soaked up its warmth. Things have been so hectic since I came here."

She's astute enough to realize my father's not a topic I want to discuss, and the change in subject is a welcome relief. One day, I'll explain more, but for now, this is enough. My eyes trace over her features, and I smile at the expression of pure bliss on her face. Seemingly not in a hurry for a discussion, she continues to lie there until she falls into a light sleep.

Closing my own eyes, I breathe in her delicious scent while my mind races with the novelty of her company. In all my years, I've never had the desire to be still and in the moment with someone. Even when I'm with the cadre, I'm always planning and working.

Her body rolls toward me, and she lays her head on my shoulder. The feeling of my arm pillowed between her sweet curves makes me groan. My body twitches with the need to take this to another level, a level I dream about often, but I control myself. For the first time in a long time, I'm tempted to throw caution to the wind, but I don't. My arrogance demands she chooses me without reservation, with lust and need, not friendship and comfort, riding her hard. So, I simmer and wait.

About twenty minutes later, I feel her stiffen against me when she wakes and finds herself in my arms. She stares at me, apprehension gracing her face.

"Umm...wow...I'm sorry. First, I interrupt your solitude, then I fall asleep on you. I was relaxed and warm from the sun. And I..." Her voice trails off.

As delightful as it is to see her flustered, I wave my free hand to ward off any explanations. "Why don't you tell me why you wanted to speak to me?"

Arden sighs. "Honestly, you're going to be surprised but very, very happy. Ecstatic, in fact," she muses. "It's something you've been waiting for me to do since I got here, and I think you need it. Like it physically pains you to not have it."

I tense, anticipation thrumming through my body. She licks her lips, and I hold my breath.

"We need a plan," she states decisively. "I know I've been winging it since I arrived, but I feel like there are so many things we need to do that some structure would probably be wise." She stops and stares at me, clearly waiting for an answer.

Disappointment wars with satisfaction. I definitely need something from her, but a plan was considerably further down on my wish list. Releasing her hand, I roll over onto my elbow and lean over her. *She's so beautiful.* Clearing my throat, I force myself to focus. "Of course. I've already been thinking about a few things to get us started. Why don't you tell me your thoughts first?"

Relief flashes across her face. "Great!" She lifts her hand and starts counting on her fingers. "One, we need to find the MacAllister journals, and the only place we know they lived is the Kingdom of Dragons. I have a feeling we will have to visit, but we don't have any information on the name of the matriarch. I don't want to search dozens of houses and, given the scene I experienced from the blood magic, it might be best to carefully plan our visit to Valerian's kingdom. Maybe we could search for information at Witchwood? It might save us valuable time. And I need to check in with the witches anyway. What do you think?"

"I agree. We should take advantage of our location and check Witchwood first. In addition, we need to check in with Caro and the council to see how they're handling things. I don't know what you want to do about the witches yet, but we should probably put a few things into place," I reply, sifting through the options in my head.

"Right," she agrees thoughtfully. "We also need to start figuring out the powers I inherited from my father. I was hoping if I was Fae, Solandis or yourself would have noticed something by now? Fae always recognize Fae, right?"

"Correct," I answer. I'm not sure whether to be relieved or upset about the fact she doesn't *feel* like a Fae to me. Shrugging, I push it aside. "Your powers have only been unbound for a couple of days, though. We'll start testing and see what happens. Once we know your heritage, we can figure out a teacher, and hopefully, this will lead us in the direction of your father. Last, but definitely not least, we need to find the assassins. Could they be related to your father, or is there an unknown player?"

Arden beams at me. "Fantastic, sounds like a plan. Do you want to go to Witchwood with me tomorrow?"

I scoff. "It's the beginning of a plan, but we need everyone's help. Why don't I start laying out the next steps, identifying each person's role and responsibilities, and you figure out what you want from the witches?"

A pained smile graces her lips. I'm guessing it's the thought of dealing with the witches. The sooner it's done, the better. If not, they'll sweep it under the rug and continue with their current agenda.

"Deal," she responds with a sigh. "Thank you, Theron. And thank you for letting me bother you." She raises her head and places a soft kiss on my lips.

My lips cling to hers, but in a breath, it's over. I stare down, tempted to show her the desire coursing through my veins, but I stop myself. With a groan, I roll onto my back.

She gives me a puzzled look, then stands and gathers her shoes. "I've got training with Valerian now, but I'll see you in the morning?"

I confirm and murmur goodbye. My hand curls in on itself instead of reaching out to stop her like it wants, and my head drops back to the grass in frustration. She needs a plan, but I'm beginning to think I need a plan too.

THREE

ARDEN

I'm browsing through my closet, trying to decide on what to wear to Witchwood, when my phone pings. My thumb slides across the screen, and a text and three hunky, shirtless guys with numerous tattoos stare back at me.

> Meri: So sorry I didn't get back to you. Been very, verrry busy. Proof is in the pic. And maybe a little bragging too. I mean, seriously…hot. Enough about me. What's up?

> Arden: Where did you find the luscious trio?

Meri: Picked them up last week. Or rather, they picked me up. They're triplets. Not identical, but close enough. Especially where it counts. LMAO! There is not enough willpower in this world that could have made me turn them down. And you know I have like literally no power, or willpower. *wink emoji*

Arden: *roll on the floor crying emoji* I'm learning this about you, but I don't blame you. I wanted you to meet Solandis and Vargas, though! Plus, I have TONS to tell you. Like heritage found, secrets revealed, you know... epic stuff!

Meri: Noooo, I wanted to meet them. I'm sorry. Please forgive me? *sad face emoji* and WTF? Epic? Are you being serious??

Arden: Forgiveness might require cupcakes. And wine. EPIC!

Meri: I'll pick up some wine and cupcakes and come right over.

Arden: Nope. I'm going to Witchwood with Theron. Tomorrow??

Meri: Witchwood, huh? Tomorrow. I'll be there!

Arden: XX Don't forget the wine and cupcakes. I mean it.

Putting the phone down, I laugh and shake my head, then turn back to my closet. No doubt Theron's dressed in his usual suit, but I'm not feeling formal today. Pulling a pair of dark jeans, a silk cami, and a blazer out of the closet, I throw them on the bed along with a pair of black riding boots. This outfit will work.

With a glance at my phone, I realize I'm running late. Throwing on the outfit, I head out the door and straight into the elevator. Theron's standing there with his arms crossed, waiting for me, his violet eyes firing with impatience and irritation.

"You're late," he drawls. "Punctuality is necessary to maintain order."

"Meri called," I retort and roll my eyes, my own irritation at his high-handed manner apparent. When I turn to tell him where he can shove his order, I'm stunned speechless. Theron's wearing jeans. Dark and pressed and a little fancier than most, but real, denim jeans.

Damn, he looks good, I observe silently.

He's paired it with a button-up shirt and blazer, so it's not completely informal, but it's not a suit. The polished perfection he exudes in a suit is a perfect match for his usual icy Fae demeanor. In jeans, he's still casually elegant, but it's as if the armor is gone and he's approachable and sexy. Utterly and completely sexy.

"And?" he prompts, nudging me to continue.

"Huh? And?" I mumble, jerking my head back toward the elevator doors. I've got to think about something else. And find my brain. Words would be good too. My eyes catch on the doors. Think about the doors. They're fascinating, right? Black, of course. And they have a seam between them. And they're smooth. They open.

"Arden?" He says my name impatiently. "What did Meri say?"

Meri? Oh, right. "She didn't say much. Told me she's been busy and was sorry she missed Solandis and Vargas. I invited her to come over tomorrow, so I can fill her in on everything," I tell him.

"Oh? What has she been doing lately?" Theron asks as the doors open.

"Triplets," I murmur, bolting through the door.

Theron insists on driving to Witchwood instead of using a portal. I don't mind. Watching his capable hands control the ferocious, matte black, metal monster we're riding in, at speeds that defy normal physics, makes me shiver with awareness.

"Where is everyone else?" I ask, knowing he has everyone's schedule memorized.

"Everyone's at The Abbey, except Daire, who had errands to run," he answers. "Why?"

"No reason," I reply with a shrug, not wanting to tell him I don't like how separate we live at The Abbey, where everyone goes their own way.

Shifting in my seat, I focus on him instead of the countryside. Although he's exhibiting his usual restrained self, he feels...edgier today. I'm not even sure I can describe it, but change surrounds him.

Maybe it's not him, though. After my last visit to Witchwood, I'm not exactly eager to return, and I'm certainly on edge. Pulling up to Witchwood, I turn to the door, startled to see Henry standing there.

"Good morning, Henry," I greet him when I step out of the car. "How on earth did you know we were here?"

"Good morning, Miss Arden," he replies warmly. "There's an alarm by the gates to alert me when we have visitors. Mrs. Pennington likes to be sure her guests are greeted promptly."

I hand him my phone. "I see. Well, I think you have enough on your plate without having to greet me at the door. Why don't you give me your cell number, and I'll call you when I'm coming?"

With a mischievous grin, he agrees, enters his number, and hands it back to me. "Would you like me to announce you?"

"If you must," I tell him. "I don't want you to get in trouble."

"True," he says, clearing his throat. "Let's head inside, and I'll find Mrs. Pennington."

When we step into the foyer, Henry heads off to find Caro. Standing with Theron, I can't help but think of past visits. None have been truly welcoming or pleasant. Even my first visit was more like an interrogation instead of a happy occasion, something else that needs to change in the future. New witches need to feel welcome from the beginning, not judged and accepted only after proving their worth.

Cassandra strides slowly down the stairs on our right. Stopping on the last step, she sneers in my direction. "Arden, what are you doing here? You should leave before my mother returns." She tosses her hair over her shoulder. "You know, it doesn't matter what the magic did in the ceremony, hybrids are not welcome in the coven. It would lead to chaos and an inability to predict or control new powers."

Anger burns through me at the exclusive rhetoric spewing from her mouth. I tamp down my reaction, knowing she's repeating Caro's bullshit, but I can't let it go without a warning. "My patience with you is almost nil, Cassandra, so quit while you're ahead. I'm already pissed at the stunt you pulled with Reyna, for which you still owe me an apology." My magic skates across hers lightly, and I find pretty powerful shields in place. Although I expect nothing less from Caro's daughter.

Her eyes narrow at my threat. "As if I'd ever apologize to you. And cut the threats, there's no way you're more powerful than me," she spits out, her resentment apparent in her tone. "My mother combed the archives for a long time to find any indication Santiago's bloodline mixed with the other bloodlines, and she found nothing. There's no way you have an affinity for all six bloodlines. We think it's an elaborate scheme you've devised with Santiago."

"You're right," I reply softly. Her face fills with satisfaction. "I'm a witch from all seven bloodlines." I turn to Theron and gesture to the hallway. "Let's go."

Fury fills her face for an instant before she attacks. Magic buzzes around my skin, searching for the tiniest opening, but my shields are impenetrable to the level of magic she's wielding. Her face hardens when she realizes her attack isn't working.

She clenches her fists and turns back to me. "It's not possible," she snarls, desperation in her voice. "I'm the most powerful witch. Pure. Not tinged with the blood of others." Magic spills out from her in every direction as she tries spell after spell, desperate to prove her statement.

I step forward and tuck a strand of hair behind her ear. Shocked, she stops bombarding me with spells. I decide to try and make her see clearer. "Getting past your shield is easy for me. Do you hear me? Easy. As a hybrid, not only do I have powers and strengths you lack, but my immortality boosts my magic in a way your 'purity' never can. You have a lot of magic, but if you don't rid yourself of the outdated exclusivity spouted by the coven, then you, your children, and children's children will continue to get weaker and weaker until their magic is gone."

"Get your hands off my daughter," Caro demands as she strides across the hall. Walking up to Cassandra, she pulls her chin up to check her face. "What did you do?"

"Excuse me?" I ask derisively. "As you know, your daughter drugged me and tried to bespell me into accepting a vampire's Mate Kiss. She also attacked me today. She's lucky I only gave her a dose of the truth," I bite out, irritation rising with Caro's threat. "A little humility and an apology would go a long way with me." I'm half joking when I say it, but acknowledging her mistakes will only help her recognize them in the future.

"My daughter doesn't have to apologize to you. You have no authority here," she snaps before turning to Cassandra. "Darling, why don't you go upstairs and get cleaned up? I'll send Henry up with some snacks, okay?"

Cassandra throws a smug look in my direction.

Frustrated with what Caro is teaching her, I step forward, deciding to push the issue. I step in front and block Cassandra's path. "Before you go upstairs, I'd like an apology." I stare at Caro and square my shoulders. "You're lucky I'm the one dealing with the situation and not the cadre, as they're within their rights to demand reparation. Cassandra broke the rules of sanctuary, which is something they don't take lightly. My toll is easy. I'm only asking for an apology." I glance at her speculatively. "But maybe the apology should come from you, Caro? If you gave her the order..."

Caro looks at Theron and frowns, then turns to Cassandra and huffs angrily. "Apologize, Cassandra."

Incredulity and fury flash across Cassandra's face. "But... you—" She stops speaking when Caro raises her hand and cuts her off. They stare at each other for several seconds until Cassandra turns to me, betrayal shining on her face. "Fine. I apologize for my behavior. Believe me, I won't do it again." She throws a nasty look Caro's way and steps around me to stomp back up the stairs.

I snort at Caro's stupidity.

"Excuse me?" Caro returns, her voice hard.

"We all know Cassandra takes her orders from you. You stood there and demanded she apologize for taking an action you ordered her to do instead of apologizing yourself. She will never forgive you, and any respect she had for you is at the very least damaged, and quite possibly gone entirely. It might be the best thing that ever happened to her. But you?" I shake my head. "You will regret this day forever."

Caro looks up the stairs, her eyes narrowed in thought, before turning back to me. "Why are you here?"

"To attend the council meeting, of course," I answer.

CHAPTER

FOUR

ARDEN

C aro marches down the hallway toward the room where the council meets, her heels clicking hard on the marble flooring as anger pours out of her.

"Henry, is the council chamber ready? Did the other members arrive?" she asks without slowing. "Please make sure we have plenty of refreshments for the session today."

Henry winks at me and replies, "Absolutely, Mrs. Pennington. The room is ready, the council members are waiting, and refreshments will be delivered shortly." He turns to us. "Do you need me to show you the way?"

"We're fine, Henry," I reply. "Please don't let us keep you."

He dips his chin and turns to follow behind her.

"Never a dull moment, Arden," Theron murmurs. "I assume you have something spectacular planned for the council?"

He holds up his arm, and I take it. "There are sure to be a few fireworks," I muse. I take a couple of deep breaths. Dismantling the status quo isn't going to be easy, but all witches deserve a voice, and if I don't do it, there's a chance no one will.

We walk into the council's chamber and take a seat while we wait for everyone else to get settled. There's one big change from the last time we toured this room. The new tapestry is hung on the wall for everyone to see. It's likely the council, or quite possibly the entire coven, has been obsessively studying it and comparing it to the tree they've seen the last few hundred years.

My eyes roam the audience and find Bianca, Reyna, and a few other familiar faces. Several witches stare at Theron and me, wearing frowns or tentative smiles on their faces. Others look at the council, pointedly ignoring us, not wanting to be seen fraternizing with the enemy. The council members themselves display varying reactions to our presence, from Santiago's smile to Nico Perrone's contemplative stare.

The council kicks off with minutes and updates from the previous meeting, which takes about thirty minutes. Boredom sets in. For Theron too, I guess, watching his fingers tap restlessly on his thighs. I smile. He's definitely more comfortable in my presence, but I'm sure he wouldn't want others to see his "tell." I slide my fingers through his, stilling and capturing them with one movement.

My fingers graze his muscular thigh encased in the rough denim, and I hear him inhale sharply. Not wanting to make him uncomfortable, I start to slide my hand from his, but his fingers tighten, trapping mine in place. I glance up at him, but he's staring at me, passion emblazoned on his face.

Licking my lips, I watch his eyes darken before his gaze drops to my mouth. He cocks his eyebrow a millimeter.

Leaning forward, I brush his ear with my lips while I whisper, "You might prefer those impeccably styled suits of yours..." I pause and nibble on his ear. "But I want you to know how much I love these new jeans."

He inhales sharply, and his hand tightens on mine.

A gavel thumping against wood startles me, and I lean back into my chair. Ignoring the witches for another minute, I stare intensely at Theron, wanting him to know I'm serious.

When the gavel pounds a second time, I turn my head to watch the proceedings. The council concludes its recount from the last meeting and opens for new business. Witches turn toward me, but I give them a bland smile in return. One by one, they stand at the podium and air grievances or submit new proposals to the council. Most of them are mundane. A few are worrisome, like witches reporting witches for having relationships with other supernaturals. I frown.

Santiago halts the proceedings. "The council needs to review recent evidence of our mixed heritage before we can assume any rules have been broken. The findings may influence a change to current laws. Until then, we will not hear any new fraternization cases."

The crowd murmurs and shifts restlessly. I smile and untangle my hand from Theron's.

"Are there any other open items?" Santiago glances at the crowd, then shifts his eyes to me.

When nobody answers, I stand and walk up to the podium. "Hello, my name is Arden, and I have several open items for the council." I pause. "First, I'd like to request a seventh seat be added to the council to represent the MacAllister branch. And as the only known surviving MacAllister witch, I demand to sit on that seat."

Whispers rise into a roar of voices when the witches hear my request. Necks crane to view the MacAllister leaves on the tapestry, while Caro bangs the gavel, mercilessly trying to restore order.

"There's always been six seats on the council. No more, no less," Caro states.

"Maybe, maybe not. If the tapestry displays seven bloodlines, the chances of the council having seven seats in the past is pretty high. It might have been lost to time, but now that we know there is a seventh bloodline, shouldn't we restore the council seat?" I respond confidently.

"We'll consider adding a seventh seat," she says dismissively. "Is that all?"

"Actually, I require an answer today," I reply. "It's my understanding that the council seats are given to the most powerful witches in the coven. Is that correct?"

Santiago's voice booms. "That's correct. If the witch has an affinity for the council seat's bloodline, the witch can challenge for the seat."

Smiling at him in thanks, I reply, "Thank you, Santiago. If the seventh seat is not established, then I'll have to challenge a council member for their current seat. Given my affinity with all six bloodlines, as proven by the council's own tests, I have the right to challenge for any seat on the council. What do you think, Caro? Should I challenge for your seat?"

This time, silence reigns supreme. Every witch holds their breath, waiting for Caro to answer my question.

An expression of pure rage covers her face. She opens her mouth, no doubt to deliver a blistering response, but Nico lays a hand on her arm, halting her intent. He leans over, whispering furiously in her ear. She shakes her head no several times. He keeps whispering. Closing her eyes, she finally gives him a jerky nod and agrees.

"I, Nico, motion to add a seventh seat to the council." His

voice rings out, stating his intentions. "Is there a second motion?"

Katarina Ivanov declares, "I second the motion."

"Motion carries to add the seventh seat," Caro responds, her voice strained. "But before we assign you to the seat, we would like to know if you have proof of your MacAllister heritage?"

"I only have my mother's word right now. I'm working on proof," I explain. "I'll either accept the seventh seat or challenge you for your seat, Caro. Which one do you prefer?"

Caro scans each person on the council to determine their agreement. Turning back to the audience and me, she bangs the gavel once before stating, "The seventh seat will be given to Arden as an interim measure. If no proof is forthcoming, we will reevaluate in the future."

Satisfaction and irritation fill me, but I decide to concede to the ruling for now. "Thank you. As a new council member, my second open item is to motion for An Lee to be seated on the council for bloodline four, replacing Adam Pennington." I turn and motion for An Lee to step to my side. "Or he can challenge for the seat. We all know he's more powerful than the current council member." I stare at Adam. Relief briefly flashes across his face before it settles back into its usual apathy. I almost feel sorry for him. As Caro's husband, he must be a big disappointment to her, and I'm sure he hears about it often.

"Absolutely not," Caro spits out.

"I second the motion for An Lee," Santiago says, overriding her. "Anyone else support this motion?"

Amelie, Katarina, and, surprisingly, Nico all agree to the motion. Caro's face is purple now. She glares at each person on the council, but to little effect. They quietly wait for her to bang the gavel and accept the defeat and motion. She doesn't move, silently protesting, until Nico takes the gavel out of her hand and accepts the motion on behalf of the council. An Lee turns to me and smiles. Caro's expression morphs into hatred and suspicion, her mind finally catching on to my plans.

In two moves, I've managed to kickstart a quiet revolution, and she knows it. The council wields the power of the coven, and Caro more than most. If I'm going to find a better way for all witches, the first thing I need to do is shift power away from her.

"Last, I motion for the removal of the 'pure' classification. I believe all witches should be allowed to test for affinity and placement in the coven. As the original tapestry shows, there isn't a single witch who is pure, not even you, Caro." I allow my voice to ring out loudly for this one. It's critical. We need to start changing the way we approach witches entering into the coven.

"I second the motion," Santiago states firmly.

There's silence from the other witches, but I expected it. This one will require a fundamental shift to their current way of life.

"I deny the motion," Amelie softly inserts. "I believe we need time to think about the repercussions of this change. I motion to table the discussion."

Not surprisingly, the rest of the council supports Amelie's motion. I incline my head and smile. I respect the need to cling to the familiar, but she's only buying time. I'm going to rip it all apart. I don't know how or when, but I refuse to be part of an exclusive coven and the inevitable destruction of witches and our magic.

CHAPTER
FIVE

ARDEN

With all the uproar at the council meeting, I completely forgot to request access to the archives. Running through the options, I send a quick text to Santiago. A minute later, I've got a startling reply. Apparently, a fire destroyed most of the early archives. I groan loudly. I guess it's not a complete surprise, given the hidden tapestry. I assume someone, possibly Gemma Perrone, went to a lot of trouble hiding the MacAllisters. Almost too well.

After discussing it via phone with Theron, he thinks we should still check Witchwood first. We'll shift our focus to correspondence or council meeting minutes, mundane pieces of history often overlooked by others. This means I'll have to arrange another trip to Witchwood to view the archives.

My phone pings, and I throw open the door to my room to find Meri standing there, her arms full of cupcakes and wine, with pitiful sad eyes and a quivering lip. I roll my eyes.

"Please, I know you're not in the least bit sorry," I tease, laughing at her antics. "But I'll take the cupcakes and wine." I reach out and grab those from her. "And I might give you some too, but it will require additional payment."

"Details of my nights with the triplets? Done!" She laughs and reaches for the wine.

I pull it out of her reach. "How about the scoop on you and Callyx?"

Meri freezes like a deer in headlights. She exhales and rolls her eyes to the ceiling. "Did he tell you we've met before? That bastard. He told me he'd keep it a secret."

My eyebrows rise at this piece of news. "You both told me when I introduced you. Neither of you can act worth a damn. It was all over your faces."

Relief flits across her eyes, and she shrugs. "Seeing him was a shock. It's really, really old news, but if that's the payment for cupcakes and wine, I'll pay it."

After pouring a glass of wine, I set it on the nightstand, grab two cupcakes, and plop down on the bed, my back to the headboard. "Get comfortable," I tell her and take a bite of the cupcake. It's chocolate with chocolate icing and completely decadent. I moan.

She toes off her shoes, grabs wine and cupcakes, then joins me. "Spill," she demands.

I decide to start at the beginning, like I did with Theron. She listens as I tell her about my mom, her seer ability, friendship with Solandis, her death, my obscure destiny, binding my powers, and all the rest of my background. I haven't even gotten to the stuff that's happened since I've been here, but I stop.

"Why are you stopping?" she screeches. "You're not going to give me a cliffy, are you?"

I give her a puzzled glance. "A cliffy?"

She sighs exasperatedly at me. "You know, leave me hanging on the edge?"

"I'm not giving you a cliffy, and I'm not stopping. I'm hungry for real food," I explain. Bouncing off the bed, I stride to the door. "Let's go downstairs and get something to eat." The empty bottle of wine catches my eye. "And some more wine."

Entering Syn's kitchen feels weird, like I'm trespassing on sacred territory, and his dominance hangs heavily in the air.

"Do you like grilled cheese?" I ask, motioning to the fridge. "Or do you want something else? I'm not much of a cook, but we can find something."

"Believe me, I'm not picky. Food is too precious to waste," she responds. She pauses, glances at me, her face blank, then heads out the door. "I'll go pick out some wine from the bar."

I freeze, her offhand remark more telling than any previous statement about her background. I hadn't realized she'd grown up poor and without food. It's such a rare occurrence in the supernatural world. Due to the longevity of immortality, most families are wealthy from centuries of accumulating money and land. And Meri is Fae. I don't know of one area in the land of the Fae where someone might go hungry. Even in the country, where the Fae live simpler lives, food is still plentiful.

Is she still poor? I think about the times we've spent together. She's bought drinks and food for us both many times and never said anything.

She comes back in the room and slowly puts a bottle of wine on the counter. Leaning her hip against it, she folds her arms over her chest. "Yes, I've gone without food. Sometimes because we were poor, and other times... Let's just say my guardian didn't like it when I rebelled." She shrugs, conveying her lack of concern. "I'm not poor now, and I can take care of myself and splurge on my friends. So no, you don't need to pay me for the wine and cupcakes. Feed me, and we're even." She stares defiantly at me.

"I'm sorry." My voice is soft when I reply. "You never talk about your past, so when I hear something significant, it throws me. And I've never heard of any Fae going without food."

She tenses, but answers my unasked question. "I didn't grow up in the land of the Fae. Far from it." She pauses before letting out a long sigh. "My guardian isn't Fae, she's a demon, a sorceress, and liked to move around a lot. If she found work, we had food. If I behaved, I was fed. From everything I've heard from you, I wasn't quite as lucky in the guardian lottery."

Digesting the words, both what she said and didn't say, I slide the finished sandwich onto the plate. "That sucks," I tell her truthfully. Putting the spatula down, I give her a pointed look. "I don't want our friendship to only be about me. It's about us both. And I want to hear all about you, good and bad. Okay?" I wait until she nods, albeit a bit unhappily. "And as far as guardians are concerned, I'm happy to share Solandis and Vargas with you. I'm sure they'll adopt you within seconds anyway."

She snorts in disbelief. "I'm not exactly the type of friend someone takes home with them."

"Ha! You're exactly our type but telling you won't convince you. When you meet Solandis and Vargas, you'll see," I reply. Holding up the plates, I motion to the chips with my chin. "One grilled cheese for you, and one for me. Grab those chips."

She trails behind me to the elevator. A minute later, we're in the garden.

Meri steps out, wonder on her face at the scene in front of

her. For once, she's speechless. I chuckle, knowing I must have done the same when Daire brought me here the first time.

"What in the world?" she exclaims, reaching down to touch the grass. "I never would have guessed this place had a garden. Dungeons, a couple red rooms of pain maybe, but definitely not a garden. I'd live up here." She spins around and around, laughing.

I choke out, "Red rooms of pain? What on earth are you talking about? And I didn't say we didn't have a dungeon. Who knows with the cadre? Knowing them, a dungeon is highly likely. But I'm not sure. They haven't taken me on a tour of the entire place. Yet."

She waves a hand. "Wow, you have been sheltered. You know, a sex room with lots and lots of toys? I'm quite sure Astor's got something like it around here. And why are you waiting for a tour? I'd have snooped in every corner after I moved in here."

"Some of us were raised with manners," I joke.

Her face is sad for a second. "Where are we eating?"

I jerk my chin to the grass on the left. "This is a great spot."

She conjures up a blanket and sits. "Mmm, it's such a rush to use your powers. Now give me a sandwich."

Handing her one of the plates, I plop beside her and inhale my sandwich. "Okay, where was I?"

While I don't tell her everything that's happened since I've arrived, I hit the highlights from my arrival until the placement ceremony. "The book you gave me was a huge help. I didn't realize it when I read it the first time, but after Valerian mentioned the MacAllisters, I realized there were seven families, not six. When I saw the original tapestry with six branches and a spell woven over the top of it, I realized someone had covered up the seventh one. Later, my mother's letter told me I was the Rowan, witch of all seven bloodlines, and my task is to find the MacAllisters'...history. Which helps me with the council too, because, according to Caro, I need to prove I'm a MacAllister to retain my current seat on the council." I roll my eyes, and she laughs.

I don't tell her about the blank paper and the journals. Some things feel too personal to share right now.

"Out of curiosity, where did you find the book?" An idea pops into my head as I ask.

Meri hesitates, then answers, "The dark Fae king's library is open to all Fae. It's one of the biggest libraries in existence, and my guardian often sends me there to find rare books for her. When I got a vision of your book, I recognized the location. Why?"

"I'm searching for more information on the MacAllisters and hoping the library can help," I reply absentmindedly, my brain busy adding this to the to-do list.

"The Rowan, huh?" she asks, tapping her finger on her chin. "What does that mean?"

"I only know it means I'm a witch of all seven bloodlines. Beyond that, I'm not sure. I'm hoping once I uncover more information about the MacAllisters, I'll understand," I reply. "Or maybe my father will know. If I can find him."

She sits quietly for a second, nose scrunched up, before letting out a large sigh. "Nothing. I tried to use your seer power to find the next step, and nothing appeared. Have you been able to tap into the power yet?"

"It's only been a couple of days, but no visions," I say with a huff, frustrated with the lack of change. "And my father's powers haven't manifested either." I lie back and stare at the blue sky.

She joins me. Closing her eyes, she raises her face to the sun, soaking it in. "You're right—this is epic," she drawls. Opening her eyes, she stares at me. "Don't rush it. Enjoy the moment. Here and now. Spend some time with the cadre. Destiny always finds a way to assert itself." Her face is solemn, as if she knows this firsthand. "Let's get to the good stuff. What's going on with you and the five, I repeat, *five* delicious men in your life?"

I throw a chip at her. "Seriously? I tell you epic things, and all you want to talk about is sex?"

"Sex, really? Who? I mean, I know Valerian, but who else? Tell me it's that yummy blond god, Daire." She sighs dramatically before continuing her interrogation. "Or did you go dark and fall into the shadows with the seductive Astor?"

"I haven't had sex with anyone but Valerian," I retort, then groan. "Astor and I are close, I think. But we're both enjoying this sexual dance, so neither of us are in a hurry. The rest?" I throw my hands in the air. *Arrgh.* I'm not good at these things. Theron's good looks and demeanor blew me away when I first met him. Then he became my rock, and I needed him in a different way. Now he's changing on me again. Daire was dating Solange when I met him and acted like a dick, so I kept my distance. But when he healed me, we started connecting, and even though he's given me no encouragement, I feel him watching me all the time. Fallon and I have a weird physical spark that happens whenever we touch, and he's incredibly attractive, but we haven't spent much time together. It feels...complicated.

Her mouth drops open before she starts laughing like a loon and literally rolls on the grass. "I was expecting at least two or three, but one?" She gasps. "You're living with one of the hottest and most powerful cadres in existence, and yet you haven't made one move on them?"

I consider her question. "The timing hasn't felt right. And honestly, I'm busy trying to figure out all of these other things, like who my father might be, and I guess I'm content to let things happen on their own." I don't want to admit I'm nervous. They've all become such a big part of my life, and while I want them, I'm not sure if it will screw things up. It would be different if it was only sex. But I like them too. Narrowing my eyes, I decide to throw her into the spotlight. "All right, we've talked all day about me. I'm dying to know what is up with you and Callyx. Your turn to spill."

Meri huffs and rolls onto her back to stare at the sky. Her countenance is dark. "Fine, I'll give you the condensed version. When I was younger, I ran away from home. With little food and no powers, I didn't get far. Some kids found me and took me in. They belonged to a pretty motley crew, running around, doing harmless things like pickpocketing, begging, and running errands for rich supernaturals. I ran with them for a few months. One day, they invited me to join their gang, and I didn't hesitate." She plucks at the grass for a minute, lost in the past.

"Unfortunately, I didn't realize my grace period was over. In reality, the gang worked for a shady demon, the kind you don't ever want to meet. He'd send us out on errands, dark requests designed to steal pieces of our soul, but we did them. I did them. Because you didn't want to disappoint him and there are worse things than death," she reflects, her voice monotone, expressing little emotion about this time in her life, but her fingers continued to yank on pieces of grass.

She takes a deep breath, as if the memories are suffocating her. "It was bad. Much worse than what I'd run away from," she explains, her voice raspy. "I spent a few years with them, unable to escape, until one day, I found a savior. The demon sent me to kill Callyx." She stops and laughs at the expression on my face. "Easy, tiger. Obviously, he's very much alive."

I slowly uncurl my fists. "I know he lives a dangerous life, but knowing it and hearing you tell me you were sent to assassinate him is tough to hear without wanting to kick your butt," I reply, my voice harsh with anger.

She pats my hand. "I get it. Thankfully, Callyx is a big boy, and he knows every fighting trick in the book. He laid me out in three minutes flat. Then he tied me up and scared the hell out of me with his shadows and glamours until I cried like a baby, confessing everything to him. He left for a few hours, and when he returned, he was carrying the head of the demon with him. He saved me."

Stunned, I look at her in horror. "Well, not quite the story I expected to hear. I thought you two had a one-night stand or dated or something." I sit up and stare down at her. "I'm glad you told me, and it makes me admire you both for what you've gone through. And..." I pause. "I'm so glad he saved you. If he hadn't, I wouldn't have you and that would be a damn shame.."

She laughs exactly as I intended and raises her glass. "Cheers to friends. And no, never, the chemistry isn't there. But I'm grateful, so very, very grateful. I was in rough shape when he saved me. Physically, mentally, and emotionally. The things I did to survive took a huge toll, but he didn't judge me. He listened while I told him every single heinous act I'd committed the last few years. It's tough to bare your soul, but he didn't judge." Her eyes are soft, looking back on the past. "The next day, he left to get us some food, and I left to go home. Partly because I felt so naked after spilling all my dirty deeds, but mainly because I realized you can't outrun destiny, so I went home to face it. We never saw each other again until you introduced us."

"Whoa, no wonder there was some serious tension between you two," I muse. "He must have been pissed when he returned and found you gone. His temper is almost as bad as Vargas' and he's very protective." She's biting her lip when I look over, so I grab her hand. "I'm sorry for everything you went through then and I suspect what you still go through. And no judging. I had an easy life compared to you." I pause, sensing some deep sinkholes in her past. "You know, if you ever want to talk about anything, I'm here. I mean it."

Meri nods solemnly. "Maybe. One day," she says softly, then gives a small chuckle and pours another glass of wine.

"Let's enjoy the sun and wine," I tell her, holding my glass up for her to clink. "To epic stories and friends who share a destiny."

CHAPTER
SIX

<u>THERON</u>

A rden leans against the bedroom door, her body glistening with water from her recent shower, her bottom lip pulled between her teeth. Her eyes stare into mine while she waits for me to signal my intent, but I refuse, staring impassively back at her, conveying little in return. With a flick, I dispense with her towel entirely, watching as her eyes darken with desire.

Leaning into her, I watch the pulse at her throat flutter and a light blush steal over her cheeks and the mounds of her breasts. Water seeps into my suit, molding us together intimately, but it's not enough. My hand trails down the curve of her hip to her knee, and I draw her leg around me and thrust closer. Her breath hitches.

"You have my complete and utter attention," I drawl huskily. My lips skim her throat to the pulse fluttering in the hollow, where I place a soft kiss. "And I intend to focus every bit of it on you. But you will not be in control, not even a little bit. Every piece of you will be mine, every whimper and moan the music in my symphony, every orgasm the crescendo in my concerto. Do you understand?"

She licks her lips and moves restlessly against me. "Yes, I understand," she whispers.

Satisfaction thrums through me. "Let's get started. Take off my clothes," I command.

Her hands reach up—

Piano riffs blare in my ear, my alarm interrupting the exquisite moment. Shutting off the phone, I curse and wipe a hand over my face. My hard cock throbs in agreement. Stifling the urge to go back to sleep, I grunt and get up to shower. At least I have the means to take care of one of my frustrations.

STEPPING INTO THE CONFERENCE ROOM, I nod with satisfaction at seeing everyone here. Valerian's sitting beside Arden, holding her hand, Astor across from him, while Daire and Fallon are seated on each end. I stand beside Astor and kick off the discussion.

"We're all here because Arden asked me to pull together a plan." I stop talking when I hear several groans. "Is there a problem?"

Daire stares at Arden with a pained look on his face. "Seriously, you asked him for a plan? You do realize you've unleashed a monster, right?" He shakes his head sadly at her.

She cocks her head and raises an eyebrow. "There's too

much to figure out, and I'm not sure where to start, so yes, I need his help to create a plan."

Astor scoffs at her. "Theron doesn't know the meaning of help, only control. He's a bossy motherfucker on his best day. We usually resist, but since you're the one asking for his help and, consequently, ours too, we're all handing him the keys to our lives until this is done. I probably won't be able to jerk off without getting his permission."

Valerian and Fallon only smile at Arden, while shaking their heads in agreement with Astor and Daire.

If rolling my eyes wasn't such a pedestrian gesture, I'd show them what I think of their antics. I give them a hard stare and continue, "Based on a list Arden and I drew up, we need to assign some tasks and get started. First, the MacAllisters. Arden's going to try and find any mention of the MacAllisters, and specifically, the MacAllister matriarch, in the archives at Witchwood. Unfortunately, sometime in the past, someone— we're guessing Gemma Perrone—started a fire, and the early archives were mostly destroyed. Arden's going to sift through the remaining records, including mundane items like council meeting notes, but it's doubtful she'll find much, if anything at all." I turn toward Valerian.

"Valerian, we know MacAllister witches lived in your village and throughout your kingdom. We're going to need to make arrangements to visit. How soon can you get this in place?" I ask.

He frowns. "There's no need for everyone to visit. I'll go and petition the elders for the information."

"I'll still need to visit. Some things might be hidden from dragons and only accessible to a witch, a MacAllister witch. If you could find out where they lived, it would help us narrow our search down to specific areas," Arden explains.

"You're not going to the Kingdom of Dragons, Arden. Did

you forget the part where you were stabbed? And I don't care if you're immortal. Right now, I'm barely even tolerated in my kingdom. Do you think bringing home a witch, who's also my mate, will make things any better? It will be akin to throwing gasoline on a roaring bonfire!" he fires back, his voice rising with every word until he's shouting.

Jerking her hand from his, she narrows her eyes and slowly stands and leans over to get in his face. "First of all, you might be my mate, but you do not tell me what to do. Second, fix it. You should have done it ages ago. Don't use me as another excuse to ignore your people. They deserve more than an absentee king. Your people need you. I need you. The cadre needs you. Find a way to fix it."

"This isn't something I can fix in a day," he snarls back at her. "It's going to take time."

"Time isn't a luxury we have much of at this moment. If we give the witches too much time, they'll hang themselves with their old ways, and I refuse to let that happen," she replies. "How about two weeks? One day to lay everything on the line, and thirteen days to fight your way to a solution? It's all I'm willing to give."

Frustrated, Valerian glares at her. He stands and peers down at her, frustration and anger warring for supremacy on his face. "You're *willing* to give me two weeks? How kind of you. It's my kingdom. You need my permission to enter."

"I highly doubt it. There are always pockets to slip in unnoticed." She smiles, anticipating the challenge. "Vargas and Callyx often spoke about the lack of security in obscure places. I'm sure one of them has been to your kingdom and can shed some insight."

Before Valerian can throttle her, I step into the discussion. "Valerian, she's right—she has little time. Find a way. You don't necessarily have to announce her as your mate, but we need to find the matriarch and your kingdom is our best lead."

He runs a hand through his hair, tugging on the ends in frustration. "Fine," he growls. "I'll try to find a location so we can narrow the search. Maybe we can find a way to slip her in for a visit and back out before anyone notices her."

"Great. Let's continue," I demand, waiting until they're both seated before I continue, "Meri told Arden she picked up the founding witches' book in the library of the dark Fae king. Only Fae can visit the library, which means I'll have to go and search for any additional mention of witches or the MacAllisters. Given the vastness of the library, it will probably take a week. I'll also check for any mention of the Rowan."

"Can we trust Meri's word?" Daire asks, his tone doubtful.

"Yes. She was only weird that one time, and it was because of Callyx. Long story, but apparently, they knew each other before I introduced them," Arden responds.

"My gut says there's more to her than she shows us, but I don't know her that well," he tells her. "If you believe in her, I'll take your word for it."

"Daire, based on our conversation earlier today, I know your father has requested your presence in the Underworld to handle a small uprising. While you're there, can you check the libraries in the Underworld? Also, before you leave, I'd like to ask you to use your First Vampire power to try and compel Arden. I know she's immune to other vampires, but given all vampires answer to you, I want to be absolutely positive she isn't part vampire or demon. Sound good?" I ask, steering the discussion back to the tasks at hand. After he agrees, I turn toward Astor.

Astor cocks an eyebrow at me, waiting for me to assign him a task. "All right, lay it on me."

"You and Fallon will be needed here to protect Arden,

which means I need you to accompany her when she visits Witchwood to search the archives." I keep my voice even but hard, knowing Witchwood is a trigger for him.

He stares blankly at me. "I'll happily protect Arden and her delicious body," he drawls suggestively, "but I can't promise to behave around Caro or Cassandra or the rest of those...witches."

Arden laughs at his response. His eyes cut to hers with a puzzled look, as if he's trying to figure out why she's so accepting of his nature.

"Arden, I'd like you to meet Fallon for training tomorrow. He's going to take over training from Valerian and test your powers, if that works?" I ask, waiting for her to agree, then I finish up. "That's it. We all have our assignments, and we'll regroup in two weeks."

Valerian stomps out, pissed at the plan and his part. Astor strolls over to watch Daire try to compel Arden. He communicates silently with Daire, and they laugh.

"Arden, I command you to kiss Astor." Daire's voice is husky when he states his demand.

For a second, she stands there staring at Astor's lips, a smile appears, then she slowly leans over and pulls him closer. His eyes widen at her actions, but his head remains still. She kisses him lightly, then pulls his bottom lip into her mouth to suck on. Gasping, he grabs her hips and pulls her closer. She wraps her arms around him and draws him into a scorching kiss, a carnal combination of sex and sensuality and inhibitions left at the door. His scent of burnt cedar and sex mixes with hers, turning the air into something decadent. He groans when the kiss slows, and she gradually peels her lips from his.

I exhale slowly to dissipate some of the need pounding inside of me and turn to Daire and Fallon, a question in my eyes. Daire's frowning, while Fallon is inscrutable as usual, but the heat in his eyes mirrors mine.

Daire's voice is rough with desire when he questions Arden. "What did you feel when you were compelled?"

"Oh, I wasn't compelled," Arden replies airily. "I just felt like teaching all of you a lesson in manners. I decide who I kiss or not. Compelling me to kiss Astor was a joke to you, but not to me. It's not a joke to you now either, is it? Get a little hot and bothered?" She smiles sweetly and strolls over to the door. "The good news...I'm not a vampire or a demon. As Prince of the Underworld, I imagine you can influence or at least sense both?" Leaning against the doorframe, she waits until Daire confirms. "Okay, then. What time are we meeting tomorrow?"

"Eight," Fallon answers. "In the garden."

"I'll see you at eight." She walks out the door. "Oh, and Astor, I like your shirt."

Astor flashes a pained smile, then turns to us.

"Completely worth it," I say, glancing at the others, who chuckle in agreement.

CHAPTER
SEVEN

N ature is at her best in the early morning. The light breaks from night to dawn, clear and bright, waking the world to a new day. The air is slightly chilled, but clean and crisp, untainted by the traffic of people and automobiles. In silence, she breathes, waiting for the rest of the world to join her.

I watch the sunrise while I sip my coffee in the garden, the solitude a welcome and rare respite from the pressures of my father and the duties of being a prince. Sometimes, I wish my father had another child for his unrelenting, often bitter, focus.

My thoughts drift from unpleasant to pleasant. Arden's certainly made a noticeable impact on the cadre. Adrift for a while, we'd needed a reminder of our purpose—to lend support and power to those standing alone or facing unreasonable odds. It was the whole reason we'd formed the cadre in the first place, and she gave it to us, not only in the form of a quest, but as a way to help someone with integrity, a rare trait. We'd been mired in our own separate lives for too long. Even if Arden had been a man, the impact to us would have been at the same level, albeit different, in bonds and friendship of a different sort. As a woman, she brings something extra and unique to each of us, and I wait with bated breath in anticipation of what she will be to me.

The doors swish open, and I glance at my watch, surprised to see it's eight o'clock. Standing, I stretch and meet her in the middle of the garden.

"Good morning, Arden," I greet her. She's dressed in her workout gear, but instead of her usual anticipation, she seems nervous.

Straightening her shoulders, she returns my greeting. "Good morning, Fallon. I assume we're going to test for Elven powers?"

"Yes. While there are a lot of races, most of them have derived from one of the main supernatural races—Elven, Fae, demon, dragon, angel, or shifter. Even vampires are created from demon and witch or human pairings, although Daire received a little something from Lucifer in his mix, given his father is also a fallen angel," I explain. "For you, we've ruled out demon, dragon, and Fae. Dragons are only born to dragon mothers, and while there might be the tiniest chance you're Fae, we think Theron would have recognized you. So we'll test for Elven power for a few days and move on to either angel, like a nephilim, or shifter if you're not Elven. Okay?"

She shifts restlessly on her feet and takes a deep breath. "Okay, let's do this."

Settling into a cross-legged position on the ground, I motion for her to join me. Once she does, I decide to start with the difference between witch magic and Elven magic. "If I tell you to create fire, what do you do?"

She snaps her fingers, and a flame appears. "I pull on the magic in my core and layer it with intent. Fire forms."

"Elves create magic from the compounds and elements in the Earth itself. For fire, we pull nitrogen, carbon dioxide, water vapor, and oxygen from the air, the plants, and the ground. We create using matter or energy," I explain. "We feel and use every bit of matter and energy around us, pulling and manipulating it for our purposes. Once done, we return it to the Earth."

"I'm not sure I understand. My fire is a light, and it burns. I create it and extinguish it. The magic returns to me," she says, puzzled.

"Fire's tough, because you're right—your fire takes on the properties of the elements, and therefore, is also real," I concede, then an idea pops into my head. "What about clothes? If you create clothes, what happens when your magic is blocked?"

"The clothes disappear, which is why most witches don't use magic to conjure clothing," she replies.

I nod in agreement. "Elven magic creates clothes from nature. Silk from a silkworm, cotton from a cotton plant, and so forth. Our clothes are organic, they don't rely on maintaining a magical link. Once created, they exist until we break them down and return the compounds to the Earth. We can pass them along to others, we can wear and wash them, because they are actual clothes.

"For the most part, Fae, elves, and witches all share similar magic. We can use the elements to create or cast spells, we have the ability to use telekinesis, we all have healers, we glamour or warp reality, and we can morph or change ourselves to some degree. Elves and Fae share a bit more because we're both tied to nature, and constructing energy with those elements is a common power. The main difference between Fae and elves is the Elven ability to animate. We can use matter and energy to give life to inanimate objects, like your Killian blades. They're both inanimate objects and sentient. While everyone of Elven descent can animate objects, they can't maintain or create something permanent. The Killian blades are unique in this aspect. It took a tremendous amount of power to create them and give them life."

"I heard the story of the Elven blacksmith who created the blades, but thought it was an embellished tale until I held one in my hand. It's sentient, all right. I can hear it speaking to me," she shares. "So how do we test my powers if they're so similar to yours?"

"I've never taught Elven magic to anyone, so I'm guessing here," I warn her. "We'll go back to the basics to see if you can feel and recognize the basic elements of the Earth first. Then we'll see if you can use them to create something without pulling on your witch magic."

I form a large drop of water in the air above my hand. "Let's see if you can sense specific energy or matter first. Close your eyes," I instruct, waiting until her eyes are closed before I continue, "Concentrate on the air in front of you. Can you feel the water in the air? A disturbance to the flow or a pinprick of energy? Breathe evenly, in and out. That's it. When you feel something, reach for it."

I hold the water in front of her. Her hand doesn't move, and a frown appears on her brow. She opens her eyes and shakes her head sadly. "I don't feel anything."

I close my fist and return the water to the Earth. Thinking back to my childhood, I try to remember someone teaching me the basics, but only the more advanced teachings come to mind. Rolling my shoulders, I admit defeat. "Don't get discouraged. I'm not sure if I'm starting this off correctly. I'm going to make a few phone calls, and we'll try again tomorrow, okay?"

"Okay," she replies, her voice full of frustration. "I know Fae have dark and light, but I haven't noticed much difference between the two. Are there any differences between dark elves and light elves? You're both, right?"

I still. "I'm both, although I only recognize my light Elven half, and I'm not aware of any differences," I say, trying to keep my answer brief. I reach toward the tree and pull a piece of wood from the branch above me, using energy to shape and mold it into a staff.

She gives me an inquisitive stare, and I tense. "I know you're not exclusive to the light because of Daire, Astor, and Theron. What's wrong with the dark elves?" she asks.

Not prepared for this discussion, I take a deep breath and try to maintain my calm. She's going to find out sooner or later anyway, and if I want her to know me, this is critical information. "They killed my mother." My throat tightens, as it does every time this subject comes up. "Because my mother loved my father, the light Elven king, and had a child with him, they killed her. Her sister is the Queen of Dark Elves, and in a fit of rage or jealousy, she murdered her." Bitterness and hatred pour out of me. I hate knowing her sister still lives, but my father made me swear an oath I wouldn't hunt her down or kill her.

Shocked, she blinks but doesn't say anything for a minute. "I'm sorry. As someone whose mother was murdered, I can relate a bit, but not fully. While I want answers and vengeance for her death, I didn't know her or have memories of her. Sometimes, it feels as if it happened to a friend or distant relative instead of my own mother. In my heart, Solandis is my mother." She places a hand on my arm. "If you ever want to tell me stories about her, I'd be happy to listen."

Stunned, I think about her words. I'd forgotten we had this in common. When I think of her mother, I think of Solandis as well. Would I have this bitterness if I'd had a mother figure? Have I let my father's rage become my own? Deciding to think about it later, I motion to my staff. "Why don't we spar for a second and get rid of some frustration?"

She cheers up immediately, and I laugh. It's rare to see a woman who loves fighting as much as she does. "Let's take it easy today, just light sparring. We can jump into it more tomorrow, okay?"

Instead of answering, she conjures her staff, takes a hard swing, and slams it into mine. The warrior in me responds, and the battle commences. I note tiny signs of weaknesses in her stance and grip, which we can tweak. She's trained her whole life and she's very, very good, but she's also relatively young. I've commanded my father's troops in battle many times over the last thousand plus years, and in my experience, the smallest of adjustments can change a warrior from trained to lethal. I'm looking forward to showing her. Stepping back, I hold a hand up.

"Let me prep the training room for tomorrow. We'll meet here first to test you for Elven powers, then we'll spar in that room. It's more equipped to absorb magic than the garden," I tell her. I return the staff to the tree. "Sound good?"

She gives me a determined expression and a nod, then stalks off, frustration apparent in every step. I blow out a deep breath. My gut says she's Elven, but I'm starting to wonder if it's only wishful thinking.

CHAPTER
EIGHT

E ver since the meeting the other day, Valerian and I have been arguing almost nonstop about the dragons. I recognize he's King of Dragons and knows his people better than I, but I also think it's past time he fixed his relationship with them. Be a king and present for your people or step down and let someone else lead.

Of course, he says it's more complicated than I realize, and in over a thousand years of ruling, the dragons have never asked to change the status quo. They like the way things stand. I remind him things have already changed because he has a new mate, who's a witch.

We've settled into a truce—he's going to think about it, and I'm going to back off and concentrate on the other stuff on my plate.

He's getting ready to leave, and I follow him up to the roof.

"Are you sure you don't want me to create a portal? Or get Astor to create one?"

Dropping his bag on the ground, he pulls me into his arms. "It's the dragon way to fly, and honestly, I don't get to do it often enough, especially for long distances. Flying into my kingdom allows me to assess the people and land from above, and it gives the dragon council time to prepare for my arrival." He tucks a lock of hair behind my ear. "I'll text you every day and call when I'm able to get some privacy. Concentrate on your training with Fallon and let me know if anything sparks on your father's powers, okay?" He swoops down and plants a hard, lingering kiss on my lips. "Take care, lass."

Taking his face in my hands, I stare into his amber eyes, which are filled with frustration, and sigh. "Have I told you how often I think about you?" His eyes fill with interest. My hands caress his hard jaw, and I smile up at him. "Every day. Something you've said or done pops into my mind, and I can't help but stop and smile. Whether we're training, in bed, or arguing, I'm happy. And regardless of whether or not you are king, you're mine, and I'll miss you." His eyes soften. "Be careful and watch your back." Pulling his head down, I give him a deep kiss, savoring his pouty lips and wicked tongue, until I hear him groan. Then, I release him. "And that's how you kiss your mate goodbye."

He laughs and yanks me into his arms for a bone crushing hug. "I'll remember that in the future."

Releasing me, he backs up about a hundred feet. The air shimmers for a few seconds before he transforms, and suddenly, a massive black dragon stands in his place. Standing completely still, I take in every detail. I've never seen a dragon up close, and I'm utterly fascinated and, if I'm being honest, a bit terrified.

He's huge, easily dwarfing me and the entire Abbey roof.

Gigantic, leathery scales ranging from the size of my head to the size of a school bus cover his body, while ridges run the length of his spine. His tail is so long, it hangs off the side of the building.

While his body is big, it's the teeth and eyes causing my throat to tighten in fear. He...smiles, and rows upon rows of razor-sharp teeth appear, big enough to make me the equivalent of a French fry in size. Amber eyes stare intelligently at me, glowing like jewels, but instead of sexy, it feels predatory and hungry. Very, very hungry.

Every ounce of me wants to take a step back, but I lock myself into place. *Never let a predator see your fear*, I remind myself. As a predator himself, Vargas drilled this into me at a young age, but it's tough when you're standing in front of a freaking dragon.

Valerian, or the dragon, huffs, as if amused by my reaction, before suddenly launching into the air. I'm sure he's having a good laugh at my expense and I'll hear about this later. I watch him fly away until he's a dark speck in the sky.

I'm going to miss that damn dragon. And our sparring. Damn it, I'll probably worry about him too, even though he's clearly a man who can take care of himself. Sighing, I turn around and find Astor waiting for me. Leaning against the wall, he's dressed all in black, his torn jeans and T-shirt molded tightly to his defined body, and of course, he's sporting a smirk.

"What are you doing here?" I ask, startled. I didn't even hear him come up behind me.

"Hello, gorgeous. Valerian wanted someone here in case you reacted badly to his dragon. You teetered a bit, but thankfully, kept your cool," he replies. "I knew you'd be fine. Not much seems to faze you, does it?"

I consider his comment. "I think it's because I've been sheltered. Instead of seeing or experiencing bad things directly, I heard about them in a calm, controlled manner by either Vargas or Solandis. Even Callyx kept the gruesome details to himself." *And apparently, other important details, like assassination attempts,* I think. "Plus, Vargas trained me to put aside emotions, assess the threat, then decide how to react."

"Now, that's an explanation I understand," Astor states. His hand grasps mine, and he pulls me into the elevator. "One down, two to go. Daire and Theron are ready to leave too."

When the elevator opens on the ground floor, Theron and Daire are dressed formally in impeccable suits, their presence commanding. Fallon is standing with them, dressed similar to Astor in dark jeans but with a black button-down. All three pairs of eyes turn toward me.

Theron assesses me quickly, then glances at Astor with a raised eyebrow.

"Cool as ice," he tells Theron.

A gleam of satisfaction crosses all of their faces.

I scoff and blow on my fingers. "Please, this isn't amateur hour." I give them a second to digest, then bust out laughing. "Seriously, I don't know how I managed to stand still. Every voice inside me was screaming to run far away from the gigantic beast getting ready to eat me. I had to lock my knees in place. He's terrifying."

They all laugh.

"It took us all a while to get used to him too," Fallon admits.

Theron steps in front of me. Raising my chin, he scans my features. "You have my cell. If you find anything, call me. I'll keep you informed and try to return quickly." He pauses, but with a quick glance at the others, he seems to scrap whatever he was going to say. "Don't take any unnecessary chances, Arden. I mean it." He drops a light kiss on my temple.

I've been dreading this moment. Theron's my rock, here for me every day since I arrived, and I'm not sure why, but the thought of him leaving is hitting me hard. He picks up his leather duffle and steps toward his portal, but I'm compelled to stop him. I pull him back to face me and straight into my arms. I hug him fiercely, and after a tense moment, he drops his bag and gathers me tightly into his arms. A few seconds later, I lean back and stare into his violet eyes. "I...will miss you."

His eyes tried to read mine, but I don't know how to convey what I'm feeling. It's so jumbled. "I'll miss you too, Arden." He steps back from my embrace, glances at the others, then disappears into his portal.

I look at Daire. "Tell your father I said hello, and let us know how things are going with the uprising." After years of living with Vargas, I know how quickly an uprising can turn ugly. Demons aren't known for using diplomacy to end things peacefully. "And text us. Me. I want to know you're safe. Please."

Daire's icy blue eyes darken, and with two blurred steps, he leans down and places a kiss on each cheek. "My fierce Arden, take care of yourself. And don't worry, I'm quite capable of managing a small uprising." A small, arrogant smile graces his lips.

When the portal of fire and magic opens, he steps back and leaves.

I bite my lip. The feeling of isolation is stronger without all of them here, and I've had enough isolation to last a lifetime or three. I walk over toward the other two.

Fallon and Astor have some type of silent conversation, then Astor puts an arm around me and gives me a squeeze. "Fallon and I would like to take you to dinner. Do you like seafood?"

I glance at Fallon in surprise. "I love seafood. Do I need to get dressed up for this excursion?"

Astor pushes me into the elevator. "First of all, it's a date. Second, you need to dress more casually. A good pair of jeans, a sweater, and a leather jacket would work. And boots. Meet us downstairs in about ten minutes."

Amused and excited, I reach my room and dress quickly, then rush back to the lobby. The elevator doors open, and the two men stand silhouetted against the dark backdrop of the club. I never noticed, but they both seem to favor black clothes a lot. Both are now sporting leather jackets, and they eye my attire with satisfaction.

"Are you going to tell me where we're going?" I ask, pulling on my jacket.

Astor pulls a helmet from his back and approaches me. "Don't you trust us?" He gives a low laugh.

"Fallon maybe, you...never," I lie, watching him wince when he feels the sting.

"We're going to have a little chat later about this new habit of lying you've developed, gorgeous. But for now, hold still so I can put this helmet on you," he demands curtly.

I smirk but hold still and let him place the helmet on my head. "Are we going riding? I haven't ridden in ages."

Fallon and Astor chuckle.

"We're going to ride to the coast and eat the best seafood in the world," Fallon's states in his naturally husky voice. "I don't know if you ride, but we don't have time to assess your skills. Why don't you ride with Astor on the way there and with me on the way back?"

My body tingles in anticipation of riding with the two of them. Like any woman in their right mind would turn down the offer. I shrug nonchalantly. "I've only been a passenger, so that works."

Astor leans toward me to tuck the strap into the helmet. "You can't fool me," a dark voice whispers. Glancing up, I see his incubus staring back at me. "I can't wait for you to wrap yourself around me."

Astor grabs my hand and pulls me toward the garage. I'd only been there once when Theron and I drove out to Witchwood. It's remarkable how many vehicles are stored in here. Of course, Astor's motorcycle is modern, sleek, and lethal. I glance over to Fallon and see him slinging his leg over a big black monster of a machine. I don't know much about motorcycles, but it will be interesting to ride on them both.

Astor slings his leg over, then steadies the bike while I sort of hop up behind him, scooting until I'm in place. It's a good thing I've got long legs. Widening my thighs to accommodate him, I slide in tight and wrap my arms around him. With a roar, the engine starts, rumbling beneath me. My thighs tighten on Astor, and I hear him chuckle.

The roar of Fallon's machine makes me turn to my left. He rolls up beside us, glances at me on the back, and cocks an eyebrow.

"Stop worrying," Astor growls back. "I'll be safe. Dinner says she's converted."

Fallon throws his head back and laughs. "You're on."

The challenge is thrown, and with a roar and a throttle, we take off like the hounds of hell are chasing us.

CHAPTER

NINE

ARDEN

Exhilaration steals my breath, and for the first time in days, I'm free and unencumbered. The destiny, my assassins, Cassandra, the council, and...everything weighing on my shoulders suddenly releases into the night air. I hadn't realized how much weight I'd been carrying until it was gone.

Astor pushes the bike to the max, and the thrill of the ride makes me feel like I'm standing on the edge of a cliff, the wind whipping through my hair, while I stare out at an abyss. My breath catches, and I can't help but laugh wildly.

The curvy, mountain road sweeps toward the sea, and we hurtle around its curves, racing to the finish, Fallon's beast following us the whole way.

At the bottom of the mountain, on a small cliff, a tiny

restaurant shines like a beacon. Astor throttles to a lower gear, and we coast into the parking lot.

Placing my hands on his shoulders, I slide down until my right foot hits the ground then swing my other leg off the back. I stretch and shake out my legs. My thighs tingle from the power of the bike and the proximity of Astor. Easing off my helmet, I release my hair and wait for him to do the same.

As soon as his helmet is off, I grab his jacket and jerk him toward me. I lay waste to his lips, devouring the taste of him, thanking him for the exhilarating ride. I break it off, my chest heaving for air, and lay my forehead against his. "That was incredible and so needed."

He closes his eyes for a second, then hugs me tight. "Let's go, gorgeous. I know you're hungry."

"Dinner's on me," Fallon's husky voice interjects from behind me. "Let's sit outside."

Nodding in agreement, I follow Fallon, who's striding over to a table near the edge of the patio. It's the perfect spot to watch the ocean and take in the night. The string lights above us give off a soft glow, creating the perfect ambiance. Glancing around, I notice several groups of people hanging out, laughing, and drinking.

The menu is extensive, filled with the promised seafood and, according to Fallon and Astor, everything's good. I order the grilled red snapper with crabmeat in a champagne beurre blanc sauce with a side of steamed vegetables. Fallon orders lobster, and Astor chooses the linguini with lobster and crab in a cream sauce, and he adds a crisp bottle of white wine for the table.

Leaning back with a sigh, I listen to the waves pound the shore below. "This place is fantastic. How did you two discover it?"

"On a ride, one afternoon, we came upon it. Over time,

we've brought the entire cadre here to enjoy it with us," Fallon answers.

"Does everyone ride?"

"We all have bikes, but only Astor and I ride together regularly. Theron's often too busy, Valerian would rather train, and Daire...used to spend a lot of his free time with Solange," Fallon states. "Although our lives and routines seem to be changing lately." He slides a glance at me.

"The thrill of the ride, the escape from everyday pressures, and the feeling of freedom, it can't be beat." I pause and smile at them both. "So, who's willing to teach me?"

Astor roars with laughter. "Definitely a convert." He snickers and looks at Fallon, who waves a hand. "Fallon should teach you. I don't have the patience and, according to him, I'm too reckless, so you should learn from someone who's the opposite."

I throw Fallon a dazzling smile. "Would you mind? We're going to be spending a lot of time together in the next couple of weeks. It would be easy to slip in another lesson or two." Tilting my head, I blink up at him and use the same pleading eyes I've used on Vargas in the past.

He gives a loud laugh and holds his hand in front of his eyes. "Stop. We can add a couple riding lessons to the plan."

Our food arrives, and I wait until the server leaves to reply. "I didn't realize the two of you were so close. I know the cadre is bonded, but it seems like everyone does their own thing?" While I wait for them to reply, I take a bite of my food and moan. I don't know if it's the freshness of the seafood or the night air, but this is the best fish I've ever eaten.

Fallon clears his throat, then lifts his shoulder. "We used to spend quite a bit of time together, but duties and responsibilities started taking center stage. It's only since you've been here that we've focused on something together. We're all close, but sometimes, our interests are different."

"Beyond interests, I get the feeling some of you know each other better," I murmur, reflecting on how they act around each other.

"We've shared different experiences together, and some of those have been particularly intense. It's shaped us, and our interactions probably reflect it," Fallon muses.

"Exactly," Astor chimes in. "For example, Valerian and I met when we were both stalking a group of warlocks who'd kidnapped a boy. The boy's mother had gone to the cadre asking for help. At the time, the cadre only consisted of Fallon, Theron, and Valerian. Fallon and Theron were following up on another case, which left Valerian to recover the boy."

He pauses to think for a second. "I was pretty much a waste of space at that point in my life. Drinking all day, fucking all night." He watches my face to see my reaction. I wince internally but keep my expression neutral. "Until the day they entered my favorite dive bar, talking about their plans to steal the boy's power, and I knew I couldn't walk away. I followed them. Later, when I was surveying their hideout, I noticed a dark, hulking mass picking them off one by one."

He grins. "That night, I decided to go introduce myself and see if we could join forces. I met Valerian, and together, we saved the boy. It was the first good deed of my entire life, and it was life-changing. I wanted more. Valerian brought me home, I started helping the cadre, and after a trial period, I eventually took their oath. I'm forever grateful to Valerian."

Pausing to savor a bite of my incredible food, I shake my head in amazement. "I can see why you and Valerian are close. Who started the cadre?"

Fallon murmurs, "I guess, technically, I did, almost fifteen hundred years ago. We didn't form a cadre bond until later, though. As a prince, I ran into a lot of people who needed help, but I couldn't always help them because of political reasons. It frustrated me. Cormal was a...contact of sorts. He reached out and offered to set up a separate identity for me in exchange for a favor. It was the perfect solution, so I agreed. When it began, I only helped one or two a month, but when word got out, it grew."

Fallon takes a long sip of his wine. "About four hundred years later, I met Valerian. A lost soul. He'd wandered into our kingdom in search of a greater purpose, and I knew exactly what he needed. Cormal helped create another identity for him. We eventually added Theron, Astor, and Daire, and created the Imperium Cadre. We found the sanctuary and applied to the Supernatural Council to be its guardians, and they approved. There's a lot to the story, but that's the gist of it."

Admiration sweeps through me. Very few people step out of their comfort zone to help others. I lay my hand over Fallon's and squeeze. "You don't find many members of royalty, or people with power, stepping out from their safe havens to help others. All of you are remarkable."

I want to know it all, but maybe another night. I yawn widely. "Sorry. I'm exhausted, and I'm sure they'd like to go home." I gesture to the staff sitting at a table in the corner. "Are you two ready to go?"

After thanking the owners, we head toward the bikes. Fallon gets on his beast and kick-starts it, then revs it a few times. Motioning to me, he leans forward while I get on the back. Thankfully, unlike Astor's, this seat is lower and easier to get on.

After getting comfortable, I lean forward and wrap my arms around him. Little sparks zing against my skin, and I gasp. Every time we touch, it's like holding a live wire. I inhale sharply and wait for it to settle. It does, a little, to something like a constant hum.

Astor's sharp eyes catch it all, and they gleam with envy and wonder. He takes off with a roar, leaving us to follow.

For the first few minutes, Fallon's careful, riding at moderate speed and taking the turns easy, until I tap him on the shoulder and point up. He laughs loudly and kicks it up about ten notches, then we're speeding after Astor. I laugh with joy.

Unfortunately, the ride home ends quickly. I peel myself from Fallon's bike and lean over to give him a kiss on the cheek. "Thank you for the ride and dinner," I say huskily, my body throbbing from the current between us. I stare into his bright green eyes for several seconds before turning to Astor.

"Are you going to Witchwood with me tomorrow?" I ask him.

Instead of answering right away, he sweeps me into his arms and stalks toward the elevator. "Tomorrow, yes, but right now, I'm kidnapping you and taking you to my lair," he says in a fake evil voice. "You'll be trapped, forced to cater to my every whim, your freedom a distant memory." He laughs wickedly.

Snickering, I relax in his arms. "Hmm, maybe a rain check? It's been a long day, and I'm exhausted."

He smiles seductively and licks his lips in memory. "It's a good thing you gave me a kiss yesterday. It was enough to feed me with magic for a day or two, so I think you're safe tonight. I can't vouch for tomorrow, though." His hands tighten around me. "I have to tell you, the kiss worried me for a second. Thankfully, it was a ruse and your other half isn't a demon or vampire. There's enough of us bastards walking around."

"I wouldn't mind. I'm quite fond of the demons in my life," I reply quietly.

He smiles at my statement before swinging the door open.

While I stayed in his room the night we went out with Meri, it still startles me. It's a room made for seduction with low lighting, sexy music playing softly in the background, divine smelling candles, and a bar filled with various bottles of alcohol. Low couches and soft pillows are scattered around the room, and a luxurious bed, piled high with more fluffy pillows and a cloud for a comforter, sits in the corner.

Exhaustion rolls over me. It's been an incredibly long day. Astor shoves a T-shirt and boxers at me and steers me to the bathroom. After changing and brushing my teeth, I crawl into his bed. A few minutes later, the bed dips behind me.

Astor gives a low laugh. "Sleep tight, my lovely little liar." He places a kiss on the soft curve of my neck, then gathers me in his arms. And it's the last thing I remember.

TEN

ARDEN

A ping wakes me the next morning. It's a text from Fallon, telling me his contact didn't get back to him and he's postponing the training until tomorrow. I send a quick reply, letting him know Astor and I will head to Witchwood earlier than planned, since we're not training today.

Astor groans and buries his head in my shoulder. "Tell them to fuck off," he growls.

Dropping my phone, I snuggle down into the covers and close my eyes, trying to fall back into the delicious dream I was having before the text woke me up. Scattered images float through my brain, but I can't grasp any of it. My brain is awake. I heave a sigh and realize I may as well get up, since I can't sleep. I'm pushing the covers back when Astor's arm clamps down hard across my body.

"Where do you think you're going?" he rumbles, his voice filled with sleep.

"I thought I'd get up and go work out since I can't fall back to sleep," I reply. "I didn't mean to wake you. You can go back to sleep."

"Or we can find better ways to fill our time," he tells me, pressing his hard body against mine. He opens his brown eyes and stares at me intently, waiting for an answer.

Already aching from my dream earlier, I know I want this. I want him. Our desire for each other has been burning brightly for weeks. And I could tell myself to wait, give us time to figure out the feelings part, but why? We're inevitable. Whether we rise high and fly or crash and burn, it doesn't matter. Sometimes, the only thing you can do is step forward. I murmur, "Yes."

Not wanting to be passive in my decision, I lean up and capture his lips in a kiss designed to set him ablaze. All the tantalizing teasing and buildup from the last few weeks is an inferno inside me, and I want him to feel it too. I pull back to suck on his bottom lip, giving him a second to breathe, then I take his mouth in another deep kiss, stealing the very breath I'd just given him.

He slips his hands under the T-shirt I'm wearing, making my heart pound and the ache in my body increase in anticipation of his hands on me. His fingers skim my sides, up and around, softly teasing but never touching the places I need.

I sit up and raise my arms, and he pulls the shirt over my head. Cupping the back of my neck, he eases me back down to the bed.

"You're so fucking beautiful," he rasps. He leans over to lavish my breasts with his lips and tongue, using tiny little licks and flicks to bring them to full attention. Once hard, he uses his firm lips to pull and suck on them, lightly at first, then harder and harder, making me gasp with need. It's not just his mouth, his hands are busy too, cupping, kneading, and playing with my breasts as if he can't get enough of them. Desire pools in my center, and my body moves restlessly under his.

His arousal builds with mine, and the air becomes charged with his special incubus magic, making me throb. Darkness surrounds us, but I don't look for the light, instead I embrace it, allowing myself to be sucked into the shadows with him. What is it about him that makes me want to dive into the unknown?

With a slight shift, I center myself under him. Bringing my legs up higher, I wrap them around his muscular body and rub against his hard cock in an attempt to alleviate the ache, but it's not enough. Needing to feel him skin to skin, I use magic to strip the rest of our clothes off, then I cradle him between my legs.

I sigh. The feel of his hard body against mine almost makes me want to stop to savor the physical feeling of the two of us together. It's that moment in time when the anticipation is at its peak, your body is pushing for more and your mind is engaged on the sensations bombarding you. Astoundingly, he feels...familiar. Remnants of my dream float through my mind like déjà vu.

Oblivious to my thoughts, he lifts his head and gives me a seductive smile. His brown eyes tell me he's in charge, but I also see flashes of black the longer I stare at him. The incubus is riding him hard. "You're so wet, it's tempting to slide right into you. But that would be too easy. I want you dripping for me, your body clenching with need and begging for your release."

I feel his cock twitch with his words and clasp him tighter

to me. Using a tendril of magic, I wrap it around his shaft and work my own magic. "Maybe I should make you beg?"

In retaliation, phantom hands grab my thighs and hold them apart, while shadows slither softly up my legs to my core and devour me. He drops his mouth to my breasts, and with his mouth sucking on my nipples and his shadows stroking my clit, my orgasm rolls over me, quick and strong but short, barely enough to take the edge off.

My body still aches for the feel of him inside me, but my hands ache to touch him. After a minute, I roll him over to his back. "My turn."

Surprised, he gives a low laugh and waves a hand over his body. "I'm all yours."

I straddle him and begin my assault. Starting with his ear, I nip his lobe softly and whisper, "I don't want you." A lie, obviously, but the sting of pain it generates works in my favor.

He hisses, then moans, pain and pleasure mixing together. "Minx, what's with the lying?"

"I told you in the lab. I'll tell you a white lie every day. And eventually, the little lies won't sting. You won't even feel them. It won't matter if it's Theron or a stranger. You'll be aware of the lie, but it will stop feeling like the lash of a thousand paper cuts," I explain softly. "Now where was I?"

His eyes burn and his voice is gruff when he replies, "I believe you were telling me how much you want me."

"I don't think so," I retort. My mouth returns to his ear, and I give him a light kiss. Rubbing my nose along his neck, I breathe in his scent, the tantalizing smell rolling through me. I place little kisses down his neck to his shoulder, where I bite him. Not too hard, just enough to stroke his desire. "Although I do, very much."

His stomach muscles contract. "Hmm, you're full of surprises," he rumbles.

"Shh, I'm trying to concentrate here," I remind him. My lips continue to trail over his body, lightly sucking and licking his nipples, tracing his abs with my tongue, placing open-mouthed kisses along his V until I get to the coveted prize. His thick cock stands proudly, waiting for my attention.

Grasping him firmly, I give him a few strokes, then take him into my mouth. *He tastes so good.* I slide his cock all the way out, lick my lips and his head, then take him deep into my mouth. Playing a bit, I hum a few bars, and he groans. Picking a tune with varying high and low tones, I slide him in and out, sucking and humming, changing my tone every few strokes, along with the pace.

My eyes flick to his, and I angle my head so he can see my mouth on his cock, my tongue licking his shaft and my cheeks hollowing from sucking on him. His eyes flicker and his hips buck.

"I want to fuck you," he says, his voice gravelly. His eyes are almost entirely black, and I realize he can't hold the incubus back anymore.

I slide him out of my mouth and give him one last lick before crawling up his body.

Straddling him, I feel his cock tease my entrance. I try to slide down onto him, but he refuses. He jerks up, lifts me, and places me on my hands and knees. Scooting up behind me, he places a hand on my back, and I glance over my shoulder. His face is inscrutable, making me frown, but I don't have time to question it. He lines up and thrusts into me hard, then stops. Clenching my body around his, I close my eyes to capture the feeling.

His finger swipes up the wetness dripping down the inside of my thigh. "You're dripping," he observes, satisfaction in his voice, and a wave of sexual magic wafts over me. "Are you ready to beg?" he asks as he starts thrusting in and out hard.

"Are you?" I counter. Using my magic, I caress his balls and the soft skin between his thighs.

In retaliation, his shadows capture my nipples, licking and sucking, and it feels exactly like his firm lips and tongue did earlier. He continues his hard strokes, never increasing or decreasing the pace.

My body burns for release, but I ignore it. My phantom hands move all over his body, seeking out his hot spots, driving him to the edge.

"Fuck, you play dirty," he breathes out. "Can you take more though?" His last bit of control vanishes, and he fucks me hard, his pace furious. "You feel so incredible, I want to stay inside you all day." Phantom fingers stroke my clit in time to his thrusts.

My body tightens, spiraling tighter and tighter, and when he pushes a strong wave of sexual magic toward me, I fall, my orgasm from earlier a butterfly kiss compared to the one crashing over me now. I moan and tighten around him, and in response, he quickens his pace until it's lightning fast. The magic flows over me faster too, and my body keeps coming, multiple orgasms ripping through me again and again until I can't take any more. "Enough, Astor. Please stop. Please come," I beg.

Hearing my plea, he comes, my words as powerful as the magic he used to heighten my response. He draws it back into himself. "Fuck me," he rasps as his hand grips my hip. "I've never had someone turn the tables on me. Kind of fucked with my head. Are you okay?" His chest heaving, he tries to catch his breath. Once he pulls out, I fall flat on the bed.

Breathing heavily myself, I mumble, "Better than okay. I feel incredible." I turn over and look at him. His red hair is dark with sweat, his body also coated with a light sheen. Sexy doesn't even begin to describe this man. I don't go deep, though, knowing it isn't the time. I simply relax and reply, "I'll stay in bed with you any day." I laugh and stretch. I'm going to be sore later.

He studies my face and relaxes. "Beds are good, but so are showers. Willing to shower with me?" His hand rubs a spot on my shoulder. "It appears you've got a smudge of dirt on your shoulder." At my nod, he picks me up and carries me into the bathroom.

AFTER A SMALL DEBATE, we decide to ride his bike to Witchwood. Astor felt it might make us more vulnerable to attacks, but I disagreed. An element of surprise and change in routine is never a bad thing. Although, I guess it won't be a complete surprise, because I texted Henry to notify him of our arrival.

I received a strange text in return. *Bring reinforcements.*

Biting the inside of my cheek, I worry bringing Astor might cause Caro to have a stroke, but I push it aside. They're going to have to get used to my family. I refuse to shun them in favor of the witches.

The large iron gates are closed when we arrive. With the sheer number of wards and spells guarding this place, there's never been a need to close the gates. I don't know if this is a political play from Caro or if there's an actual security concern.

We pull up to the house and get off the bike, Henry is waiting for us by the door. Slipping inside, we wait for him to join us.

Glancing around to make sure we're alone, I question him. "Why are the gates closed, Henry?"

"Miss Cassandra is gone. Mrs. Pennington believes she's

been kidnapped," he whispers. "Personally, I think she left on her own. Be very careful. Mrs. Pennington has been unstable since your last visit. Seems to think you're out to steal control of the witches' council." He clears his throat and calls out clearly, "Welcome, Miss Arden. How may I help you?" Winking at me, he tilts his head to indicate the hallway.

Taking my cue from him, I state my intentions loudly and clearly. "Hello, Henry. I'm here to search the archives. Can you show me the way?"

Caro's quick strides and the tap of her heels on the marble flooring signals her irritation well before we get a visual of her. She comes into view, and I can barely keep my expression intact. The controlled and impeccable façade of the past is gone, leaving this straggly remnant in its place. Previously sleek hair is frizzy and chaotic, her clothes are rumpled and askew, and her makeup is a few days old. But it's her physical appearance that's changed the most. Age lines bracket her mouth and forehead, and black circles lie heavily under her eyes.

"Did you kidnap my daughter?" she asks, her eyes pleading me to tell her I did, while her voice remains hard and accusing.

"I did not." I walk toward her, but she holds up hand to stop me. "But I'd be happy to help you search for her. When did you see her last?"

Her shoulders slump. "The night of the council meeting. She came to ask me if what you said was true. If immortality gave a witch the strength to wield greater power. I told you were lying, of course, but I know she didn't believe me." She swallows and closes her eyes. "I'm afraid. I've cultivated her need to be the most powerful witch, and I don't know what she's going to do now that she isn't. Cassandra's...laser focused when there's something she wants. Even I'm not able to persuade her differently. Can you help me find her before she does something irreversible?"

A tiny part of me wants to tell her no, but I can't. How do you say no to a mother searching for her daughter? "We'll help you," I say, gesturing to Astor, then myself. Astor vigorously shakes his head no, but I ignore him. "I assume you've tried the usual scrying and spell casting?" She scoffs. I guess that's her way of saying yes. "Great. Okay, let's try again. Maybe it will help if I boost your magic with mine."

Her eyes narrow in suspicion, and she stares intently at me, probably trying to figure out if this is a trick. Knowing she doesn't have a choice, she gives in. "Fine," she retorts. "Let's do this in the living room." She turns and walks over to the door on her right. "Are you coming?"

Astor turns to go, but I grab his arm.

"Wait," I plead. "I have to help her."

"Really?" he questions. "Why?"

"The same reason you helped that boy long ago," I reply softly. "Sometimes, you do the right thing."

Astor curses. "Fuck! Fine, but be careful. Put up a barrier. I don't want her taking more of your power than she should. And I'm staying close to you. If anything looks funny, I'm pulling you out. Got it?"

"Okay," I agree. Striding into the living room, I see Caro waiting for me on the couch, and I sit down and hold out my hand. "Ready?"

Caro eyes my hand like it's diseased. "Have you done this before?"

"No," I admit, "but I know the spell." Closing my eyes, I mentally create a six-foot concrete wall, cover it in steel, add spikes, and set it on fire. I don't want her anywhere near the core of my magic or my thoughts.

Astor strides over and stands near me, his body vibrating with anger, his hatred and suspicion of witches readily apparent.

Caro sneers at him and turns to me. "I'll open a conduit between us, and when you're ready, you can release your magic."

"No," Astor states emphatically. "Arden, you will open the conduit to her." He smiles darkly at Caro.

Her mouth tightens, and she motions toward me.

Astor's smart. If I open the conduit, I control it and can easily close it at any time. "Ready?" I ask before using my magic to open a conduit between us.

When we connect, she inhales sharply, and a euphoric expression crosses her face.

"Do you want me to say the location spell?" I rasp sharply, wanting her to focus.

"No, I've got it," she retorts. Clasping tightly to my hand, she closes her eyes and chants the spell. Her face is blank for a minute or two, then a smile of pure joy shines on her face. She stays like this for several minutes, her eyes moving rapidly behind her lids as if she's watching a movie. The smile slowly starts to fade, only to be replaced by a frown. Suddenly, her lips press together and hatred steals over her countenance, then she jerks and drops the conduit and my hand.

I raise my eyebrows toward Astor, and he shrugs. Caro remains motionless. After a minute, I place my hand on top of hers. "Caro, are you okay? Did you find Cassandra?"

She opens her eyes, and it's worse than I thought. Devastation wars with hatred in her eyes. Her mind must still be caught up in whatever she saw in the spell, because she stares right through me.

"What is it? Is she alive? Does she need help?" I race through questions, trying to figure out what to do next.

Caro straightens her shoulders, and her eyes find mine for the first time since she came out of the spell. "She's fine, alive, and, apparently, doesn't want to come home. There's a branch of our coven in the south, and she's staying there for a while." She pauses and inclines her head toward me. "She's got a powerful blocking spell in place, and I wouldn't have been able to see her if you hadn't helped me." Her lips purse. "Thank you."

"Are you sure you don't want to go talk to her? I...could go with you," I offer tentatively. There's something bothering me about her answer, but I can't quite put my finger on it.

She pats my hand. "It's fine. She'll come home when she's ready. Now, what did you want with the archives?"

"With your knowledge of the archives, you might be the best person to help us," I state, waiting for her to look at me. "Can you have Henry, or someone, pull any available correspondence or meeting notes from one thousand to fifteen hundred years ago? I know most of the archives were destroyed, but anything you can find will be great." I wait for her to agree.

She's looks uncomfortable for a second before she blurts out, "I've already gathered all the documents with the name MacAllister. I can have Henry send them to you."

Interesting, but not entirely unexpected. I wonder if she'd have been so forthcoming if we hadn't helped her. Probably not, but honestly, who cares? She's done us an unintended favor, and since we've also done the same for her, we're even.

"Great, I'd appreciate it," I reply. "If you need help with Cassandra, please let us know."

"I'm quite capable of managing my daughter," she returns snidely.

I grit my teeth but don't respond. Glancing at Astor, I motion to the door and stride out with him.

"Theron thinks my visits here are interesting. I wonder what he'll say about this one," I murmur softly, my mind whirling. "The good news is the first step is done, right? I wonder if she would have given them to us if we hadn't helped her."

Henry steps out of the living room. "I think it's better if you don't ask those questions. I'll box them up and get them to you tomorrow."

"Thank you, Henry. You're a saint." I place a kiss on his cheek to thank him.

He stills. "Far from it, but I'm trying to do better." Caro's voice sounds in the distance. He gives us a quick bow and walks toward the door. "I'm sure you can find the way out. Duty calls."

Heading outside, Astor and I walk over to the motorcycle parked in the driveway.

Picking up the helmet, he places it on my head and straps it on. "Lie," he whispers.

"Which part?" I wonder, thinking back to Caro's explanation. The sheer joy on her face tells me she definitely located Cassandra, but I'd bet a chest of gold Cassandra isn't staying with the coven.

Astor lifts a shoulder before getting on the bike. I hop on behind him, and we take off. I'm buried in my thoughts when Astor startles me. He lifts his hand and points to the side of the road. Running parallel to us is a wolf, but its gaze is too alert and intelligent to be anything but a shifter. I wonder if it's that asshole shifter I ran into at the club...or an assassin...or a spy. The possibilities seem to be endless.

Astor shouts back, "I'm going to create a portal to get us out of here. Hang on." A portal appears directly in front, and we shoot through it at top speed.

The garage appears, and we slip through the entrance into the safety of The Abbey, finally coming to a complete stop where we jump off.

Astor calls Fallon, who appears a second later. All three of us walk to the entrance and watch. A wolf, maybe the same wolf, walks by a few times but doesn't stop. The wards around sanctuary are so strong, I don't worry about it getting in, but I'd sure as hell like to know who's sending shifters after us.

"What the hell? As if we don't have enough to deal with. Seriously, who let the dogs out?" I smirk when Astor and Fallon look at me incredulously. "It's either laugh or kill right now. Personally, I'd like to hold off on the killing and see who sicced the wolves on me. Then we can kill them." I stride off, leaving the two of them in the garage.

THERON SENDS a group text to everyone later that evening.

> Theron: Shifters? Wolves? I leave for a day, and we've got wolves at the door?

> Arden: See, Theron's sense of humor is intact.

> Daire: When did Theron get a sense of humor?

> Valerian: This isn't funny, Arden.

> Theron: What did you two find out?

> What two?

> Fallon: Shifters claim to know nothing about it.

Astor: We've put up a reward for anyone with more information. We'll see who bites.

Arden: Ha! Good one.

Astor: ...

Arden: Changing subject. Maybe we should start a group text every night and update each other? I'll go first. Cassandra's missing. I helped Caro locate her. She's alive, but we're not sure where. Caro lied about her location. Wherever she is, Caro hates it. The good news is Caro did us a solid in return. Not on purpose, of course. She'd already pulled all the files mentioning MacAllister, and she asked Henry to send them to us tomorrow. Wasn't that sweet of her?

Theron: I wonder what she originally intended to do with the documents.

Arden: I shudder to think. Astor and I will work together to sift through them.

Astor: I will? Maybe I can help organize them for you.

Arden: Great, thanks.

Fallon: Nothing new on her other powers yet.

Valerian: Things are in an uproar here, which I expected, but nothing new to report.

Daire: The uprising is turning out to be bigger than we thought. Lucifer's spies are trying to find out what's going on. I did swing by the library and ask the archivist to search for information. Nothing yet.

Theron: Spoke to the archivist at the dark Fae library. Gave them a list. No other updates.

Arden: I'm exhausted. Dropping off.

Arden: ...

Arden: Night everyone.

I stare at the phone as everyone says goodnight. When my phone pings several times a few minutes later, I frown. Glancing down, I see separate goodnight messages from Theron, Daire, and Valerian. Guess they miss me too.

CHAPTER
ELEVEN

ARDEN

Fallon rings me early the next morning. "I've heard back from my contact, and they've given me some suggestions to test for Elven powers. Meet me in the lobby in fifteen minutes." He hangs up.

Groaning, I roll over and pull the pillow over my head for a minute. Exhaustion weighs on me, but I slowly steel my resolve and get up. After the usual morning routine, I dress in workout clothes, grab my phone and, at the last minute, grab a jacket. If we're meeting in the lobby, there's a strong chance we're leaving The Abbey, which is surprising, given our furry guard outside.

Nobody's in the lobby when I step out, but a tap on my phone reassures me that I'm right on time and Fallon is late. Too bad Theron's not here to see me. I laugh.

"What's so funny?" Fallon's voice is low as he strides up to me with a backpack in his hands. "I grabbed us a few waters and some breakfast. We'll be gone all morning. Are you ready?"

"Yes, let's go," I reply. My enthusiasm is low this morning. What if nothing happens? I didn't feel anything the first time we tried.

Fallon conjures a portal for us, and we step through it. When we come out the other side, we're in a forest, but not any I recognize.

"Where are we?" I ask. Studying the trees around me, I realize we're in a pretty young forest. The one near my old home backed up to the Wilds, a forest older than any other, full of dangerous creatures and wilding magic. The only known inhabitants are The Hunt, wielders of magic and riders of justice. Outside of supernatural law, they dispense and uphold the ancient laws governing all magic and magic practitioners. I've never seen them, but Vargas assures me they're real.

"A forest near one of my houses," he replies. Raising his hand to the left, he motions me in that direction. "There's a small pond nearby. According to my source, we need to be surrounded by natural elements, including water. I used to swim in the pond when I was a boy, so I know we're in a relatively safe area."

We walk a few hundred yards, until the trees stop and we're standing in front of a large pond and waterfall. It's peaceful. The steady sound of the waterfall cascading into the pond fills the air and the entire scene makes me want to lie down and be lazy for a while.

Fallon sets the bag on a large rock and takes off his jacket. "We'll start with the water. According to an old tutor, water is the most prolific and natural source on Earth, and the best one to use when learning or testing. Take off your jacket, and let's get started."

"Let's do this," I say, bouncing on my feet in anticipation.

With his magic, he creates a small hole and fills it with water from the pond. He sits down cross-legged beside it and sweeps a hand in front of him, so I sit and face him.

"First, we need to get a feel for the water. I'm going to pull a drop of water from this miniature pool. Cup your hands under the drop, and I'll cup my hands under yours. Then, I'll pull the water through your hands to mine. The idea is that you will feel the element when it moves through you, giving you a taste of its essence," he explains. He pulls a large drop of water from the pool, and it hovers in the air. He cups his hands under it and motions for me to do the same above his.

The water moves closer to my hands. I see it, but I don't feel the water. The only feeling is the slight current popping between his hands and mine. When the water hits my hands, it's cold, but it doesn't feel like anything but water—until he pulls it through my hands. When the water is inside my body, it feels different, like a foreign object.

The water is now between our cupped hands. "Try it again," I demand. When he pulls it up through my hands, I close my eyes. There's definitely an object passing through my hand, and I can feel it.

When I explain to him what I'm feeling, he smiles. "It's a start. Everything outside of your own energy and matter feels foreign. Its composition is different than yours. Even though your body contains water, its different than the water in the pond. Various other elements could be included in trace amounts. For example, the pond contains contaminants from the earth, like dead bugs, the atmosphere, and more. Let's repeat this experiment until you think you can recognize this water in other places."

Closing my eyes, I concentrate on the water—its texture, smell, and overall feel in my body and next to my skin. When I think I have it memorized, I give him a signal to move. The water moves above me, to the right, to the left, up, and down. My hands follow it easily. My chest feels tight, like something inside me is trying to connect.

"Keep your eyes closed and stand," he tells me. "Good, okay, follow the water."

We have more range to maneuver, and he takes advantage of it, slowly directing the water around the clearing. I follow, but when I feel a tug to my left, I frown. I can clearly feel the drop of water in front of me, so I open my eyes in confusion. The drop is where I thought it was...directly in front. Glancing to my left, I see nothing until I look down and find the hole filled with pond water.

Stunned, I glance from the hole to the drop. "I did it. I recognized the same water."

He pulls me into a hug and swings me around a few times, sparks lighting up between us. "And you didn't use any witch magic," he states confidently, letting my body slide slowly down his.

Mmm, definitely a warrior's body.

"How can you tell?" I ask skeptically.

"Witch magic has a different taste to it. Once you have a catalog of how the elements taste to you, you will recognize witch magic is unique," he replies. "Now, let's see if we can get you to stir the water in the miniature pool."

He steps over to the hole and swirls his hand over it. The water matches his movements, moving in a languid pace.

Closing my eyes to help me feel for the water, I wait until I can picture it, then I run my hand over it in circles. Opening my eyes, I frown when I don't see any corresponding movement. "What's going on?"

"You're acting like the water is sentient and knows to follow your hand," he answers. "Try to feel the water attached to your hand. Good, that's it. Now, move your hand, keeping the attachment in focus."

Sweat beads on my forehead, and my muscles start cramping. Ignoring them, I continue to hold my palm above the water until I feel it. Taking a small stream of water, I pull on it, while I move my hand in circles. This time, when I open my eyes, I see the water swirl below me.

"Okay, that's enough," Fallon states when he sees me sway. "Let's take a break and grab some water and a snack." Guiding me to the pond, he helps me sit down and pulls out our food and drinks.

Sitting on the bank, we listen to the waterfall and eat cheese and crackers. My left shoulder itches, and I twist to try and scratch it.

"Here, let me," he says, reaching over and scratching it for me. "Did I get it?"

"Yes, thank you," I reply. "I appreciate your help. Do you think this means I'm half Elven?"

"It's possible, but we can't know for sure until you exhibit other signs and can move beyond a drop of water. A lot of races are able to feel water, but not many can create water from the compounds itself. Only Fae and the Elven. The two are a lot alike, but the Fae cannot animate objects, which is the final test to confirm Elven heritage. It can also be helpful in determining the strength of the individual's power, based on how long the animated object retains its life," he explains.

His fingers reach over and grasp my chin, pulling my head toward him. "Another good sign will be if your eyes turn bright green, like mine. Theron thinks they're looking greener instead of their usual hazel, but I can't tell yet."

I stare into his green eyes. "I'd love to have eyes the color of yours. They're gorgeous. Anything would be better than the muddy brown green hazel color I've got now." They're especially beautiful with his dark hair and complexion, although his cheeks now display a tint of pink. "What do you like most about being Elven?"

He stares out into the distance. "I love nature. The beauty and harshness, the bounty it provides to all creatures, the explosion of birth and its counterpart, death, and the overall feeling of peace it brings. It's teeming with creatures, energy, matter, and new things every day. The elves are tied closely to her and she to us." His gaze is warm when his eyes flick to mine. "Sorry, I get carried away when it comes to nature. She's a lovely, fickle creature, but I love her."

"I understand," I reply, pondering his words. "I feel the same about fighting. It never feels old or static to me, since it presents me with new challenges every day."

"Speaking of training, remind me to show you a couple of tweaks on your grip and stance. I know some tiny improvements which could make a big difference in battle." He goes on to explain the tweaks he wants me to make, and I nod, barely listening. His hands move rapidly, demonstrating the difference in hand holds and why each one is important, while I watch, enthralled with this warrior side of him. His passion for the art of battle is sexy and nearly matches mine.

"Okay?" He waits for me to agree, then stands. "Let's try moving the water again."

We spend the next hour moving the water, not only in circles, but up in the air, into waves, jumping out of the pool, creating droplets that rain down on us, and more. I'm exhausted when we finish, but I feel something loosening in my chest.

"It's like learning to use a new muscle," I say on a groan and reach back to massage my neck. "I need a hot shower."

He turns me around until my back is to his front and begins to massage from my neck down. Tingles race up and down, but

I ignore them. "Mmm," I moan, feeling each knot and muscle release beneath his magical fingers. He takes his time, working all the way to my lower back. When he stops, I'm a puddle.

Leaning forward, he whispers in my ear, "Better?"

"Yes," I murmur, almost whimpering when he removes his hands.

He gathers our stuff and leads us to the clearing where we entered the forest.

Trudging behind him, I let out a huge sigh of relief when we reach it.

He laughs. "Using new magic always takes a bigger toll until your body gets used to it." He creates a portal and motions for me to go first before following.

"Thank you again for today. I'm looking forward to learning something new tomorrow," I say.

Grabbing the backpack, he takes off toward the kitchen. "You're welcome. See you tomorrow, Arden."

Arden: I moved water today without using witch power! But Fallon is not sure if I'm Elven yet. Could be Fae. We're narrowing it down, though.

Valerian: That's fantastic, Arden. Nothing to report here. Theron?

Arden: Valerian! You promised.

Valerian: ...

Valerian: Fine. It's worse than usual. With my visits so far apart, there are a couple of new challengers for king. The council doesn't feel they present any threat to me, but who knows? The council wants to speak to them first and try to get them to back down.

Arden: What do you mean new challengers for king? Other dragons can challenge for the right to be king?

Valerian: The crown is not passed down from father to son automatically. When a king passes, the most powerful dragons will challenge for the right to be king. Everyone knew I was the most powerful when I claimed the crown from my father or there would have been challengers. But with my infrequent visits, the young dragons aren't as aware. This happens every few hundred years, nothing to worry about.

Arden: I'm still going to worry. Who's next? Daire?

WHEN A TEXT DOESN'T APPEAR, I glance at my phone and notice Daire's not on the chat.

Arden: Anyone heard from Daire today?

Theron: He sent me a text earlier telling me it's a full rebellion, not an uprising. He'll be in touch soon. I'll go next. The archivist found a letter from the old dark Elven king to the dark Fae king, telling him of the MacAllister massacre. He mentions Valerian's father snapping and the resulting deaths, along with your rise to power, Valerian. He gives further details on how he thinks the rest of the witches rose up against the MacAllisters and the subsequent destruction of the entire MacAllister clan. What's interesting, though, is his last few sentences. He fears an outside force riled up the witches, driving them to destroy the MacAllisters. He cautions the dark Fae king to take precautions.

Arden: Do you think it's valid? Can we ask him for more information?

Theron: He died about twenty years after this letter, I think. I've petitioned to see the dark Fae king so I can ask him for his thoughts. In the meantime, we'll keep digging.

Astor: We received the boxes from Witchwood. There are thousands of documents, with different languages and from different time periods. Reading each one was frustrating, so I wrote a spell to translate all the variations into our modern language. Now I'm slowly scanning the documents into the computer. Once they're in the system, we'll be able to access them and search for answers.

Arden: That's fantastic! I'll come by tomorrow and take a look.

Astor: No, it's fine. It will take a few days to get them all into the system. Pretty boring right now.

Arden: Okay. Fallon and I will continue with the training. Goodnight, everyone.

I tap my phone against my chin. Something feels off with Astor. Is he avoiding me because we had sex? Valerian told me Astor hasn't ever been in a relationship, which is fine because we're still finding our way. But maybe he isn't even thinking in that direction? Regardless, I want to see the papers for myself, so I decide to go by there in the morning.

CHAPTER
TWELVE

DAIRE

As I lie on the cot, I feel my phone buzz and my stomach drops. Forcing myself to look, I pick it up and see it's a message from Arden, not the person I was dreading it to be from. Solange has been sending increasingly erratic texts for the last few days. Sometimes sweet and other times threatening, but it's the recent texts filled with manic words of death that worry me. Thankfully, Arden's message, while short and to the point, brings a smile to my tired face.

> Arden: I heard about the rebellion. Text me when you get a chance. I want to know you're okay.

> Daire: I'm good. Tired. I saw Vargas and Callyx today. They told me to tell you hello.

Arden: They're both there? This must be a pretty large rebellion. Vargas hasn't left Solandis alone since the last attack at our home. How is it going?

Daire: The group is organized and powerful, and they refuse to negotiate, which tells me they aren't interested in concessions, only winning. We're frustrated because the leader hasn't shown themselves yet, which means we're blindly making moves. But more infuriating than that is they seem to know our every move.

Arden: A mole?

Daire: Maybe. I think so, but Lucifer doesn't.

Arden: How's your father?

Daire: He's strategizing in another tent with Alain, Solange's father. They both seem pretty relaxed, but they've been in many battles with each other.

Arden: Get some sleep. Text me tomorrow and let me know you're okay.

Daire: I will. Goodnight, Arden.

My heart beat when I was texting with her. She eases the darkness inside of me, making me feel lighter and a little less weary. The tent door flaps back, and I jump to my feet, sword in hand.

Bright blue eyes widen in surprise, and my father chuckles. "Good to see you're still alert. We've got a long battle in front of us, but Alain and I have been working on a plan. We think you should take a contingent and maneuver behind the enemy. Then, when they engage us in battle, we can sandwich them between us, forcing them to surrender instead of fight. We'll map out the details, but that's the gist of it. When can you be ready to leave?"

Frowning, I consider the plan. "It would force us to cut our army in two, leaving you vulnerable which I'm sure would be noticed by the spies watching us."

"We thought about those challenges. We want you to leave the tents standing and fires burning. Place dummies throughout the camp to fool them. Have your soldiers sneak out a few at a time and regroup away from camp," he explains. "Alain and I used this tactic in another battle, and it worked brilliantly."

"All the more reason not to use it again," I argue. "What did Vargas and Callyx say about the plan?"

"I decided to tell you first so you could mobilize quickly," he replies angrily. Taking a deep breath, he explains his reasoning to me. "I want to try and save as many demons as possible. This is the best way to end the battle and achieve that goal. Other tactics are going to cause too many casualties, on their side and ours." He shoves his platinum blond hair back in frustration.

I look at my father and realize he still sees me as his young son and not the grown, experienced man I am, but now is not the time to address it. "Okay. I'll gather the men and head out. We'll call once we're in place. Should take us two days."

He clasps my arm against his and draws me in for a strong pat on the back. In surprise, I pat him on the back in return. Given he's not usually demonstrative, it's a sign he's worried. "Thanks. We'll get ready on our end and meet in the middle. I'll tell Alain." He strides toward the opening but stops to glance over his shoulder. "Be careful, Daire." And then he's gone.

Taking a deep breath, I slowly exhale. I know my father's seen a hell of a lot more battles than I, but something doesn't feel right. This tactic could work, but with new troops, not by splitting our current force in half. Before I gather the men, I decide to take to the sky to think.

Slipping into the shadows, I work my way to the forest beside the camp and pause to release my wings. Very few people know I have wings. My mother and Danica knew, but they're long gone. My father and the cadre are the only ones with the knowledge now. My father didn't want anyone to know I'd inherited any angel traits, because demons would have made my life hell. At first, I felt my secret alienated me from the other Underworld children, but I learned to cherish it because it's the one thing my father and I share.

They unfurl, the large, silky black wings barely discernible against the dark night, unless you knew where to find them. In sync, they beat restlessly, and I smile. Anticipating the rush of air and the feeling of freedom, I take off, shooting straight up. I go high, even farther than usual, to avoid the eagle eyes of the two camps. My wings catch on the air and I dip and whirl like a kid, but given how sounds carry in the night, I don't dare laugh. It's on the second dip when I see him—Alain's servant, traversing the forest alone. It's curious enough that I decide to follow.

He makes his way to the edge of the forest, where another man steps out, tall and commanding. He listens attentively before smiling and clapping Alain's servant on the back, who then turns and takes off in the direction of the camp, while the man fades back into the shadows. Puzzled, I look around for him, but I don't see him anywhere. He used the shadows to travel. The only other person I know that moves that way is Callyx.

I carefully fly to the side of the forest and descend. Heading back to the camp, I decide to check Callyx's tent. A few doors down from mine, it sits alone in the absence of light, menacing in its appearance.

"Callyx," I call out. The flap moves, and he appears at the door.

"Daire," he returns stiffly.

I'm guessing he's still a little pissed I held Arden's hand when I was dating Solange. Refraining from rolling my eyes, I gesture to the inside of his tent. "Can we talk? Privately?"

Without a word, he steps back, and with a wave of his hand, shadows fill the walls inside the tent, cutting off the sounds of the night. "Nobody can hear us now."

I question him on his whereabouts during the last hour. He narrows his eyes in anger but explains he hasn't left his tent recently.

"Why? What's going on, Daire?" he seethes.

"Can you prove it?" I ask firmly.

He shrugs. "I've been texting with Meri for the last hour, but I've been here," he says nonchalantly, as if he could care less whether I believe him or not. "What the hell is going on?"

I motion for him to give me his phone.

He hands it over reluctantly. "If you don't have a damn good reason for being an asshole, I'm going to kick your ass. Prince or not," he spits out.

Scanning through the texts, I see no interruption in the timeline. Certainly not the ten minutes needed to have a conversation with someone in the forest. I didn't see anyone text during the rendezvous. Tossing the phone back to him, I explain what's going on.

"Do you know of anyone who can draw and use the shadows like you do?" I query, foreboding making my stomach clench.

He stands and paces. "The only other demon with my ability was incarcerated a long time ago. Let me check on him."

Callyx shimmers out, riding the shadows in the same way the person in the forest did.

Texting instructions to my captain, I set our departure in motion. A few minutes later, Callyx returns, startling me with his soundless entrance.

Anger and confusion battle for supremacy. "He's gone, and that's not the worst of it. The prison is in an uproar. Several other nasty demons, caught by me or Vargas over the years, are also missing. These are the worst of the worst, demons with no code, no morals, and they thrive on killing. We need a plan, and we need Vargas."

Grabbing my arm, he steps into the shadows, dragging me along with him. A swirl of darkness surrounds me, while slithering shapes slide across my body, then we step out a minute later. I run my hands down my face and arms and growl at Callyx.

"Easy, we needed to get here quietly without anyone noticing," Callyx reminds me.

Insufferable bastard. I can't believe he and Arden grew up together.

Vargas is standing with his sword out, staring at us. Callyx gives him a code word to reassure him, and he lowers the sword to the bed. Callyx proceeds to bring him up to speed on the situation including the missing inmates. I add the battle instructions I received from my father earlier tonight.

Furious, he curses, but it's the worry on his face that makes me anxious. "Fucking fucker, betraying son of a bitch. Besides us and your father, the only other person who has access to that particular prison is Alain. It's keyed specifically to him and only him. If the prisoners are out, it means Alain is behind this rebellion and we're in deep shit. But why? He's been your father's best friend for thousands of years."

Seeing a map on the table, I stride over and study it. "We

need a plan. This is where we stand now with our enemies directly in front of us. Alain suggested I take my soldiers and come up behind the enemy to force them forward, but I have a better idea." Using the same plan, I add in unexpected forces. "I'll leave tonight, as if following orders, but I'll only take a small force of my soldiers with me, not half like he expects. My captain will remain behind to make sure the rest of the men stay hidden until it's time. He'll also set out the dummies to fool Alain. I'll pull together a larger army, but, Vargas, I'll need your help to get them down to the Underworld. Callyx, I want you to go back to the prison, pick anyone you think is redeemable, and offer them clemency in exchange for their allegiance to my father. Let them know they will be up against their previous inmates." Stopping, I survey the field of battle and lay out additional attack tactics. "What do you think?"

"I think your father's been greatly underestimating you for centuries," Vargas replies. "It might work. The element of surprise will be on our side, and with the additional forces, we should have even numbers. It's a chance, and sometimes, that's all you get."

Callyx nods his head in agreement. "This might take a while. The prisoners are not too fond of me," he admits, laughing at the danger. "Stop frowning, old man. I'll be back."

Vargas narrows his eyes. "Damn it, Callyx, don't be an idiot. And be careful."

Callyx salutes Vargas and shimmers out.

Smiling at Vargas, I give him last minute instructions. "If you need to get word to me, contact my captain. When we're ready to enter, I'll text you coordinates. If you have a few minutes to spare, take care of Alain's servant and anyone else you think might be on their side. I assume he'll have at least a few loyal guards with him, but the fewer traitors in this camp when it starts, the better." I wait for his agreement and stride out. Time to pull my army together.

THIRTEEN

ARDEN

Determined to check on Astor and get an update on the search for the MacAllisters, I stop by the lab early in the morning. Unlike my first visit, it's now a complete mess, with piles of paper scattered on every available surface. Astor's sitting on a stool near the computer, his head on his arms, sound asleep.

Bending over, I lift a piece of paper from a pile and find meeting notes from a council meeting held over twelve hundred years ago. A council leader, named Agnes MacAllister, made a motion to store the archives, including all correspondence and council meeting notes, at Witchwood, to make them available to the entire coven. The motion was passed.

Thank you, Agnes. If she hadn't, we wouldn't be here today. It also tells me there was a MacAllister on the council, and she likely held a seventh seat. It still doesn't prove my ancestry, but it's a start.

I pick up the next piece of paper in the pile, but before I can read it, Astor jerks it out of my hands and places it back on the pile. "Wait, I haven't read it yet," I protest.

"If you start moving papers around, you'll mess up my system," he complains, running a hand through his hair. "What are you doing here? I told you I'd give you an update once everything was scanned into the computer. As you can see, I'm not even halfway done. I'd hate to see how much the archives contained before the fire. This lot exceeded even my expectations. They kept records of every single fucking detail."

"This is a system?" I tease him, trying to lighten his dark mood. "How much is left to scan? Do you want some help? I've got twenty minutes before I need to meet Fallon." I raise up to give him a kiss, but he pulls away.

"It's fine. I've got everything covered," he mumbles, shuffling the papers into a precise pile. "Go to training and let everyone else take care of the details."

Narrowing my eyes, I tackle him head-on. "Is there a reason you don't want me to kiss you? What's going on, Astor? I'm happy to help. You were the one who volunteered to take the lead, but I can take it back." Anger bubbles up, but I push it down.

"Did I? I thought you corralled me into this project. I guess I did agree, though," he concedes, a resentful tone in his voice. He walks away to shuffle another stack of papers, his gaze fixed on the pile in front of him, before he continues, "Maybe it's best if we take a step back. You have a lot on your plate, learning new powers, trying to find your father, and helping the witches. And we're two very different people. I want the occasional romp, and you want...something else. And now because of you, I'm busy working on this project instead of my own experiments..."

My eyebrows shoot up. That was certainly fast. One night, and he's already backing away? Is this about us? Or the witches? Confused, I stare at him, hoping he will give me something more, but he avoids eye contact.

Locking my jaw, I clamp down on the emotions flowing through me until only anger remains. "You know, I can handle this project. And I'm sure Theron would help too. Why don't I clear all this out of here so you can work on your projects? Which piles have been scanned?" My hands tremble, but I shove them into my pockets before he can see them.

He points to the wall. "I've scanned every pile against the wall. You can file them away," he answers, his eyes darting to me in confusion.

"Every pile, from this corner to that one," I ask, pointing to each corner. When he nods, I lift the entire stack with magic. "To confirm, you have scanned this entire group?" He jerks his head in irritation at my questioning. "Great, I appreciate it." I murmur a quick spell, then flick my hand and set the entire group on fire. Ash flies everywhere, but I use a slight breeze to scoop it all up and place it in the trash. "Okay, I only have about ten minutes left. Can you walk around and point out the remaining piles that have been scanned?"

"What the hell are you doing?" he bellows, his hands pulling at his hair in agitation. "Those papers were priceless, historical documents. Caro's going to lose her mind."

I feel a twinge of guilt, but I ignore it. "I'm not concerned about Caro. She'll still have the documents, but they'll be in a much more accessible and user-friendly format. Thanks to you. Eight minutes. I don't want to be late to training. Can you please focus?"

"You were certainly concerned about helping Caro the

other day. You practically leapt to help her, trying to get in her good graces, and now you're on the council," he spits out, resentment in his voice. "And I won't let you destroy this history, even if I don't give two fucks about the witches."

Biting my cheek, I decide to forego the individual theatrics. After murmuring the same spell, I light every single pile on fire. Ash covers the entire room, along with Astor and me. Using my magic, I sweep up the ash, from the room and myself, but leave Astor covered in it. "Please send me the flash drives with the information you've scanned when you have a second. I've got training with Fallon now."

Standing there in shock, his jaw on the floor, he sputters incoherently while I walk out.

Anger burns like wildfire through my veins. After speaking with Valerian, I figured Astor would act weird after sex. But I guessed his reaction would be to treat it like a casual romp between friends, not back off entirely. I'd prepared myself for casual, not rejection. Thinking back on our interactions in the past, I know he has feelings for me. Unlike Theron, Astor isn't able to hide his emotions, but right now, I don't know how to deal with him. Taking several deep breaths, I try to shake off my worry and anger.

At some point, I'm going to have to go back and ask him which piles have been scanned, but for now, I let him believe I burned them to cinders.

FALLON'S WAITING for me in the lobby when I get out of the elevator. He takes one glance at the thundercloud on my face and raises an eyebrow. "Want to talk about it?"

"Nope," I reply, stopping to put on my jacket. "Let's go, please."

He eyes me warily but opens a portal. When we step out this time, we're in the same forest we previously used, then he motions me down the same path to the pond.

When we arrive at the pond, he drops the pack and steps up to water's edge. I follow and wait for instructions.

He raises his hands, palms toward the water, and the waterfall starts flowing backwards. Then the pond itself becomes a whirlpool with a deep hole in its center, swirling round and round before ultimately shifting into a large wave racing toward the shore and the place we're standing. Suddenly, the wave loses its momentum, like a puppet with its strings cut, and instead laps softly onto the shore.

"Your turn," he tells me. "Remember, you need to connect with the water in order to direct it." He steps back out of my line of sight.

Raising my hands, my mind spears toward the body of water and grabs hold. The water fights me, but I force the connection to my magic. Then I direct my will and the connection to the pond and command it to form a wave. In response, the water shoots into the air, forming a humongous wave around ten feet tall, and starts hurtling toward me and the shore.

Swallowing, I try to coax it into slowing down, but it's not listening. Using witch magic, I form a wall of water between the wave and me to act as a barrier. I turn back to the wave, trying everything to get it to listen and slow down, but it ignores me. Finally, it slams into the wall I created and stops, but the top portion flows over the wall in a wide arc and comes down on top of me, drenching me.

Fallon busts out laughing.

Spitting out pond water and wiping my eyes, I wave a hand

and use witch magic to dry off. Turning to him, I cross my arms and snarl, "Why didn't it listen to me?"

"You're dealing with nature. Nature's fickle. If you piss her off, you should expect some retaliation," he replies. "You need to lose the anger. Try to connect with nature like you do with Meri, as friends."

"I went by to see Astor before training," I blurt out. My anger isn't going to go away until I talk to someone about what happened. It must be Fallon's lucky day. I give him the short version. "I don't know what to think or do."

He digests the information. "You're right about the sex and feelings. I'm not sure he knows how to deal with them, which means he's likely going to compartmentalize and try to control the other areas of his life. Let him work through it on his own. If his feelings are real, he'll find a way back to you." He frowns at me. "Did you really burn the files?"

"Of course not. I used a spell to create duplicates and sent the originals to a pocket dimension where I store personal items. But he doesn't know I burned the duplicates, which is the point," I reply dryly.

His finger reaches out and tucks a wayward strand behind my ear. When his eyes turn to mine, they're serious and filled with disappointment. "I'm honestly amazed at how many times Astor has stepped foot into Witchwood since you arrived. He vowed a long time ago to never return. But he did it...for you. And every time he visits, his worst memories play on repeat and all he can see is his mother rejecting him in front of the coven. It was devastating enough the first time, but to watch it over and over is torture."

He lets me digest his words for a second or two.

"Helping the witches, in any way, is bound to trigger a lot of emotions in him, including a high degree of resentment. The council forced his mother to choose between them and him, and because she was ashamed she'd fallen for an incubus, she chose them," Fallon explains quietly. "I think you overreacted, but I also think you need to show Astor that he can be more open and honest with you and himself. Stand up for him, show him you care, and maybe he will allow himself to return those feelings."

Guilt and frustration mix together. I wish someone would have told me how severe his triggers were before I dragged him to Witchwood the first time, much less three times. I sigh. "Fuck. I didn't realize it was this bad. If I had, I'd never have asked him to go to Witchwood. I'll discuss it with him, then I'll back off and give him room to think about what he wants. Thanks. I needed to talk to someone, and with Theron gone, I'm glad you didn't mind."

He shrugs his broad shoulders. "I'm always here for you." He taps me on the nose. "Back to training. Try it again."

Turning back to the shore, I hold up my hands and focus on the water. With Fallon's words echoing in my head, I decide an apology might be in order, even if it feels silly. *Mother Nature, I'm sorry. I was angry and used my magic to force our connection. Can we try again?* The water slides up beside the connection and eases into it, and it feels necessary and right. Once connected, we repeat everything Fallon did previously. *Thank you.*

Ecstatic, I jump around to face Fallon. "I did it. What do you think?"

"You certainly did," he says, a broad grin on his face. "I guess I'm not too bad a teacher. We've got a long way to go, but we'll get there." His smile slips, and he brings his face closer to mine, like he wants to kiss me. The smell of earth and sunshine teases my senses. I reach up and loop my arms around his neck and pull him closer. He's staring into my eyes, and when I return his gaze, I get lost in his green depths. The tingling between us spikes with our proximity. "Theron's right, your eyes have flecks of green in them."

Wait, what? Embarrassed, I drop my arms from his neck and step back. Heat crawls from my neck to my face.

Swinging around, I stare at the pond. By the tingle at my back, I know he hasn't moved. Closing my eyes, I feel for his signature, like I did with the water. It stands out, a separate entity, but clearly defined. "Fallon, I can feel you. Kind of like I do when we touch, your energy is different from everything around it. Can you move around? Maybe back away? I want to see how far this goes."

Fallon takes a few steps back, but I can still feel him, so I motion for him to continue. A minute later, I turn with my eyes closed and point. Opening my eyes, I follow the end of my finger and see Fallon standing amongst the trees, about a hundred yards away. Excited, I laugh before closing my eyes again. "Move around, and farther out," I instruct him, wondering how this is possible.

No matter where he goes or how far he steps, I feel him. I wonder if it would work between walls or across the city.

Opening my eyes, I see the decision in his gaze to test this for himself. He closes his eyes, while I run from spot to spot, close, then farther away. No matter where I go, he finds me.

One second, he's far away, and the next he's up close. "This is amazing! I've never heard of this happening. Have you?"

His green eyes flicker, and he tilts his head to the side while he considers my question. "I haven't, but I'll ask my father." He pauses. "I'll be honest, your powers are responding similarly to Elven children. Even though you don't have green eyes or the ability to animate yet, my gut says you're Elven. It might take a while to learn everything though. Do you want to keep training?"

For the rest of the day, we work on pulling apart the

compounds of water. It's the first step to creating water. But it's tough to recognize the various elements, then use energy to combine them into a physical substance. Learning the compounds makes it feel less like magic and more like science, but I push myself to pay attention. Earlier today, when I was speaking with Mother Nature, I felt this ball of energy in my chest vibrate in response to our connection, and it felt magical and new.

CHAPTER
FOURTEEN

F allon and Arden walk into the lobby as I step out of the portal. They're both laughing and joking with each other. She's disheveled, probably from training, since Fallon is still immaculate, but it's her mental state that catches most of my attention. While obviously happy with the day, her eyes hold a twinge of sadness in them. I frown and step forward to get her attention.

"Daire!" she exclaims. "What are you doing here? Is everything okay? What's happening with the rebellion?"

Fallon narrows his eyes. "What do you need?" He's always been particularly intuitive, and the warrior in him misses few details.

I give him the condensed version. "Vargas, Callyx, and I figured out Alain's behind the rebellion. Given the power he yields as Lucifer's best friend and second-in-command, the chance of him succeeding is pretty high. I don't have much time, but I need your help. I've fooled him into thinking I'm headed to a designated place behind the enemy with my troops. Instead, I left most of my troops hidden in my father's camp, but now I need troops. Our enemy will be expecting us, but if I can arrive with additional forces, we might be able to crush them between the two armies. Alain's original 'plan,' but with my spin on it." I pause to gauge Fallon's reaction to my plan. He's more experienced in battle, given how often his father goes to war without the slightest provocation.

"It could work. Who are you planning on recruiting? I assume most demons are on one side or the other?" Fallon asks before he catches on. "I see. I assume you've already requested help from Theron and Valerian?" When I nod, he doesn't waste time. Calling a portal, he waits for me to give him the coordinates.

"We have a narrow window of surprise. If it takes too long to convince your father, we'll do without the support," I state. "We have to hit our timing."

Fallon glances at Arden and winks, his exhilaration with the upcoming battle easily apparent. "I'll see you soon." He steps into the portal, and it closes.

"Should I gather my stuff now?" she asks, bouncing from one foot to the other. Her anticipation of the battle similar to Fallon's, but with a hint of nervousness. "I need to gather a few things, including my armor, and I'll be ready to go. Maybe ten minutes?"

I still. The thought of her in battle with a horde of demons makes my throat clog with fear. And if she got killed because of me, it would be a thousand times worse than Danica. "Arden, this is going to be a brutal battle. We only have a slim chance of winning, and if we lose, the forfeiture is going to be staggering. I need to be able to lead my army with a clear head." I grasp her arms. "I know you can fight. Believe me. I'd easily put you in the ring against the most brutal fighter with confidence. Battle is different. It's bloody and filthy and full of desperate soldiers who will sell you to the enemy to save themselves. I don't want you to see battle. It changes you, hardens you. I'm begging you to stay behind."

"He's right." Astor's hard voice spills out from the shadowed corner. "Battle brings out the worst in every race. But for demons, it's an excuse to let their sadistic side run free. The battle frenzy gets so bad, they're likely to kill the enemy and turn on their own. It's a fucking bloodbath." Astor glances at her, then away. "I'm sure Valerian will also want you to stay here, where it's safe."

Confusion and anger wage war on her face. "Don't you need every fighter you can get? Not only can I physically defend myself, but I'm a powerful magic user. And I've got experie—"

I hold up my hand to stop her and glance at my watch. "Sorry. I don't have time to argue. Keep the wards up. We'll text you updates." I lean over and touch my lips to her cheek. With a deep breath, I lock the sweet smell of her into my memories and step back. "Be safe, Arden. Astor, are you ready?"

She frowns even more when Astor steps forward. Instead of his usual joking quips, Astor doesn't say anything to me or Arden. She stares at him sadly before giving us both a soft smile. "Be careful, please." It's the last thing we see before stepping into the portal.

When Astor and I step out of the portal, two distinct troops are waiting for us. Satisfaction and gratitude rise up at the sight before me. The cadre is powerful, not only because of our rank or powers, but because we command armies. Lethal warriors with collectively thousands of years of battles under our belt. And with the literal hell we're facing, we're going to need every ounce of skill and power we possess to win this battle.

Directly in front of me, Theron, with his icy demeanor, stands tall, in formfitting, black Fae armor made of an almost impenetrable fabric, conversing quietly with his second-in-command. Legions of winter Fae soldiers in similar attire stand at attention in precise lines behind him without a single expression on their faces, but their eyes move rapidly, missing nothing. His general tilts his head in respect and turns to address their troops. Theron strides to meet me in the middle of the field.

To the left of Theron's legions, Valerian's flight of dragons stands in clusters—men so big, they dwarf the Fae on their right by at least a foot, with fierce expressions and keenly watchful eyes. The various clusters exhibit different emotions. The oldest, most battle-hardened dragons are easiest to spot by their calculated indifference and the focus they're applying to their weapons. The youngest, with less battle experience, stand out with their spikes of excitement and nervousness. Most of the dragons are ready, but two distinct clusters catch my eyes. Instead of anticipation, contempt shadows their faces, mainly when they look at Valerian. They're big, battle ready men, which means they can back up the trouble they bring. I narrow my eyes. I guess I'll have to speak to this group of assholes before we head into battle. The last thing we need is internal conflict rising up on the battlefield from some cocky little shits who think they should be leading the dragons. I signal to Valerian to meet us in the middle.

A murmur arises from the dragons and the Fae when Fallon arrives with his father's league of Elven warriors. Fallon's warriors are elite soldiers, honed to be lethal from hundreds of battles over the years, and their almost mythical reputation proceeds them. Fallon himself has led them in battle for the last fifteen hundred years, and once the battle begins, they will annihilate everything in their path. They move like a single killing machine with a simple flick of Fallon's hand. Garrett, a brute of a man and second-in-command, steps to Fallon's side. They have a few words and clasp arms, then he returns to the Elven warriors, while Fallon walks over to meet us.

"I wasn't sure your father would agree to send troops," I admit, looking at Fallon. "He isn't my biggest fan."

"He's...not feeling well these days, so we try not to bother him with too many details," Fallon explains quietly, his eyes filled with turmoil. "Garrett and I agreed to make the call."

Nodding my appreciation, I scan the assembled troops and place the call to Vargas, who appears a second later.

"Is everyone ready? It would be best if Astor is on the ground when the troops come through. We don't want anyone to mistake their entry for an attack," he suggests.

Before he steps into the portal, Fallon calls out, "Where's Arden?"

Tensing, I glance at Valerian, Theron, and Fallon before I answer. "I asked her to stay behind. This battle is going to be brutal and bloody. I...we didn't want her anywhere near it." I flick a hand between Astor and me. "She agreed." My phone rings. It's Lucifer. I'll call him back when I'm in position. Silence greets me when I glance up. Vargas has a huge grin on his face, but I'm not sure what it means. The reactions from the others are mixed, but we don't have time to discuss. The phone rings again. Looking at Astor, I raise an eyebrow. "Go." He steps through the portal.

"Poor delusional bastard," Vargas murmurs to nobody and everybody. "I'll take the first group down to meet with Astor, then I'll come back for the second. Daire's taking the dragons in from the sky. But we have to hurry. Fae are up first."

When the Fae assemble in the middle of the field, Vargas waves an arm, and a huge portal appears before them. As one of Lucifer's trusted commanders, Vargas can lead whole armies into the Underworld. It's a special power only given to Vargas, Alain, and me. With timing being so critical, all three troops need to be in place within minutes of each other, which is why I enlisted Vargas' help.

Theron leads his legions into the portal. According to my battle plan, they'll be flanking the enemy on the right, and Fallon's warriors will mirror on the left. Astor, leading my small troop, will be center. The dragons will support all three from above. In a triangle formation, we'll move forward as one, herding the enemy into my father's soldiers and trapping them between us. They might surrender, but I doubt it. Demons fight viciously when cornered, and if they feel like they've got Alain's backing, they'll likely fight to the death. I wonder when he'll decide to join his army. According to Callyx, he's still with my father.

I open a large portal for the dragons. Whistling, I call for the minokawa. An ancient, gigantic bird-like creature, also called Eater of the Sun, flies through the portal. Golden and beautiful, it's easily the size of a dragon, with a razor-sharp beak and claws. The dragons collectively draw a breath and step back into a fighting stance, with some fanning out behind and in front of Valerian. I'm surprised but relieved. It's the first sign the dragons have shown of their willingness to protect their king.

"Before we go through, I want to make something clear. You are to leave your internal bullshit on this plane. It has no place on the battlefield, and I promise you, it will only get you killed. If either Valerian or I see you jeopardize any of our troops with your stupidity, we'll end you, and you'll never see home again. Got it?" I stare at each dragon in the two clusters I noticed earlier. One has the grace to be ashamed, but the other only displays defiance.

Valerian turns to his flight and commands, "Change to your dragons now. We go in from above." He changes swiftly into his dragon. Several dragons inhale sharply at his size, because even among them, he's the biggest. I watch the two clusters from earlier and notice one particular male scoffing at Valerian. This must be one of his new challengers. He's going to be a problem.

With a blur, I reach his side and take his throat in my hand. In this form, my strength is superior to his in every way. I hold him down and pull my sword. "I told you to leave the fucking shit at the door. Did you not hear me?" He wheezes, but I only squeeze harder. If he can breathe, my point isn't going to come across. Cutting off all air, I wait until he's turning blue. The other dragons move toward me, but Valerian steps in and cuts them off. "I can always tell when someone is too stupid to realize when they have it good. If it were up to me, I'd cut off your head now." He starts to slowly slide down, my grip the only thing holding him up. It's a sure sign he's about to stop breathing. It would be an ideal time to cut off his head. I peer up at Valerian. "Kill him?"

Valerian's amber eyes narrow on the man. He shakes his head no. I sigh. His generosity only puts the inevitable on hold. This one won't give up. He knows it, but Valerian is too stubborn to admit it. I release the asshole, and he falls to the ground, coughing and wheezing.

"Hurry up and fucking change! We need to go now," I growl, pissed off at this delay. I mount the minokawa and watch the rest of them shift. When they're all ready, including the asshole, I open the portal and wave for them to enter, Valerian leading the charge. I follow up behind them and close the portal. We descend toward the flat rocky ground below us. The troops on the ground look up when we fall into place above them.

Astor will lead my troops, and I'll command everyone from this vantage point until the battle starts. We brought everyone in about twenty miles out to remain undetected, but we'll soon be on the outskirts of the battlefield. My mind drifts to Arden for a brief second, content to know she's safe at The Abbey.

CHAPTER
FIFTEEN

ARDEN

As soon as the portal closes behind Daire and Astor, I run to my room to get my armor and weapons. Tearing into the closet, I pull out my armor. It was originally Solandis' armor, given to her by the light Fae queen, but she rarely goes to battle and handed it down to me. Made of lightweight, nearly impenetrable fabric, it molds to the wearer, protecting every inch of them. This suit even has a hood I can pull over my head to protect every inch, even my eyes. Stripping down, I pull the suit on and activate the magical shield I added to it. Between the fabric and my magic, I should be able to deflect most spells and dampen the impact of any weapons.

My hands shake a little, but I ignore them, focusing instead on the final touches. I add a weapons' holster to my back for my swords, as well as a couple of thigh holsters for two guns.

One shoots tranquilizers and the other regular bullets. Sometimes, if you don't know how to kill something, putting it to sleep is better than nothing, and these babies work fast.

Rolling my hair into a smooth bun, I pin it down, pull the hood on, then roll it down to cover my entire face. No need to let anyone see me. Plus, it gives me an advantage when enemies turn to face me and find no facial features. Anything to give me an extra second in battle.

If Daire had let me finish my sentence, I'd have told him I'd been in battle. Only a few times, but probably more than most of the enemy. I think it's sweet he wants to protect me. I do. He's right—battle is brutal. The first time Vargas took me to battle in the Underworld, I fought hard, and after we won, I went to my tent and cried for hours. It shook me. Blood, limbs, and bodies everywhere. The destruction. The killing. The brutality. And it took me another fifteen years before I could summon the courage to go with Vargas to my second battle, then the next and so forth.

I like fighting, but battle is different. Some aspects appeal to me—the sheer numbers, challenging fighters, the chaos, and the feeling you're fighting for something instead of just fighting. But the deaths and gore wear on you.

I didn't ask to go to battle. Vargas insisted. We don't know what this destiny of mine holds, but he tried to prepare me for everything. And not for the first time, I'm thankful for the experience, especially now, because it means I can help Daire. And Vargas and Callyx. I pick up the phone and text Vargas. Thirty seconds later, I'm stepping out of the portal into an army camp.

Turning in a circle, I eye the chaos around me. Tents are pitched everywhere, and from the beautiful to the grotesque, demons and creatures surround me, rushing around, shouting orders, and pulling on armor and weapons. Some leap on beasts waiting nearby and take off. Others shift into dangerous beasts, snapping and growling, before rushing to the front line. When a hand reaches out and grabs my arm, I lash out.

"Fuck, Arden, stop. It's me," Callyx grits out. "Why the fuck are you here? I couldn't believe it when Vargas texted me to come get you. This one's going to be bad. Really bad." He swipes his blond hair out of his eyes. "Come on. Stay close to me and my men." He takes off swiftly, dragging me behind him, until I jerk my arm out of his hand.

"The... He knows I have a lot of family here, and I couldn't stay behind when I could help," I state, being purposely vague in case anyone is listening.

Callyx sighs exasperatedly. "I know, but your family can take care of themselves." He waits to see if I'm going to argue, but I don't.

Several pairs of eyes follow me when I pass by. Conscious of the body-hugging suit, I step closer to Callyx. When their eyes drift to him, they quickly decide to look at anything but the two of us. I smile behind the hood.

We reach the tent, and Callyx waves me to a seat. "I'm going next door to change. Don't leave." He steps to the flap. "Please."

Once he's out, I head to the table in the center of the room where I see the map. Callyx and Vargas usually have a copy in their tent to familiarize themselves with the terrain and surrounding areas. My eyes widen in surprise when I see the battlefield.

The enemy is slightly below us, in a valley between two mountain ranges. The valley is huge, but given the markers on the map, so are their numbers. They fill the valley from front to back and side to side.

Lucifer's camp, where I'm standing, is on a large hill above them, giving us a slight advantage. But there's also a forested mountain behind us, so our topographical advantage is slim. And, of course, our numbers are fewer. I wonder how many troops are coming in with Daire and the others? Sensing a presence behind me, I turn.

Alain stands in the opening—Lucifer's best friend, and I guess Solange's father, although I only knew him as the former growing up. He's a handsome man, or demon, although he's in human form at the moment. But the façade is a pretty cover for the predator lurking beneath the surface. Solandis never liked him and made Vargas swear to never invite him to our home.

"Solandis?" he asks hesitantly, eyeing my suit. His eyes dart around, looking for Callyx or Vargas before coming back to me.

The hood protects my identity, and right now, being Solandis might be a good thing. Holding my hand out, princess style, I decide to mimic her usual greeting, making sure to keep my voice low and perfectly modulated. "Good evening, Alain. It's so nice to see you, even if it is under these dreadful circumstances. Callyx and Vargas stepped out for a second. Can I assist you?"

Alain pauses and peers at me intently before taking my hand and placing a kiss on it. I squeeze his hand in return. A bead of nervous sweat rolls down my neck, making me thankful I'm hidden behind the hood. "No, no. Please tell Vargas I need to see him when he returns." He takes a step back, still looking carefully around the room, until he finally decides everything's okay and walks out. Alain is more cautious than I expected, and his gut is probably telling him something's amiss, but not once does he glance at me, which is interesting. It tells me he doesn't see Solandis as a threat.

Callyx steps into the tent about a minute later, wearing his demon form. Exponentially larger and taller than his usual huge self, he screams lethal predator. Shadows curl around his ebony skin and horns until only his face and eyes show. He's truly the poster child for nightmares in this state. The shadow under the bed. I shiver. His monstrous nostrils flare, and he raises an eyebrow.

"Hello, my darling son," I greet him, giving him a clue. "Alain stopped by to speak to Vargas. Do you know where he might be?" I raise my mask so I can communicate silently with him. Tilting my head to the side, I wait until his shadows line the wall before continuing, "He's ready for battle, armed to the teeth, and I don't think he planned on having a friendly chat with Vargas."

"Fuck," he spits out. "Okay, we need to leave and get to Lucifer's side. I don't know what Alain's planning, but if he's trying to take out Vargas before the battle, he's going to try a coup here first." He glances to the map with longing, then turns toward the chest in the corner. He pulls out several weapons, including a sword, a huge double-barreled gun, several smaller knives, and a multitude of pouches, which he straps onto his belt. He places the sword in the holster on his back and the knives in various places within easy reach. Carrying the gun, he steps toward the entrance and motions for me to follow.

He is one scary motherfucker, I think. I rarely get to see him in this form, but I always feel a sense of pride when I do. Not everyone has a big brother like mine.

He takes several turns toward the back of the camp until we stand in front of a luxurious tent. Demons guarding the entrance bow their heads to Callyx but glance suspiciously at me. "Solandis and Callyx to see Lucifer. Is he inside?" The guard cocks his head to the side, listening to a voice only he can hear, then waves us in.

Lucifer's bent over a map when we enter. Although he has several forms, he's currently wearing his human form, beautiful and blond, tall and physically perfect. As an angel, he must have been incandescent. Daire's the spitting image of him. Although Lucifer's hair is slightly longer and shaggier, and his clothing more casual. But it's not his appearance that always startles me, it's the pure power he exudes. Power that screams top of the food chain. Lucifer glances up when we enter and does a double take when he sees me.

I poke Callyx in the back. He gives Lucifer a bow. "Sorry to barge in on you, Lucifer. My mother wanted to say hello. I hope it's okay?" He glances to Alain on Lucifer's right, and dips his head in deference to him too.

Lucifer steps forward and pulls me in close to give me a kiss on each cheek. "Hello, my sweet Arden," he whispers in a voice only I can hear. Raising his voice, he answers Callyx. "Of course, Callyx. I'd have been upset if she hadn't come by. It's so good to see you, Solandis. Why don't you two stay awhile? It's just Alain and I here. And where's Vargas?"

Using Solandis' low voice, I reply softly, "Thank you, darling Lucifer. He stepped out a while ago, but I haven't seen him. I must confess we didn't stop by just to say hi, but we're hoping to catch up with Vargas when he arrives." Giving a low tinkling laugh, I gesture to my outfit. "I hope you don't mind the outfit. I don't want anyone to know I'm here."

His eyes dart to Callyx and me a few times, trying to figure out what's going on. "Not at all. Please excuse me, I'm really busy, but there are refreshments on the table over there," he tells me, stepping back to the map. Callyx walks over to stand at his side. Soon, all three are discussing battle strategy.

Surreptitiously, I sit and cross one leg over the other to block anyone's view of my hands. Pulling out my phone, I send a text to Vargas and Daire.

Arden: With Lucifer. Alain came asking for Vargas. Unfriendly visit. Good thing you aren't here. Callyx and I thought it best to stay by Lucifer's side. Alain's planning to lead his troops into the fight from here.

Vargas: Bastard. Be very careful. Alain's not stupid. What did Lucifer say when you showed up?

Arden: I'm wearing my armor. I'm Solandis.

Daire: WHAT THE HELL ARE YOU DOING? I thought we agreed you would stay behind where it's safe!

Arden: Helping my family. Lucifer's surrounded by guards. I'm pretty safe right now.

Hearing footsteps, I quickly slip my phone between my legs and eye my manicure. I dip my head and lightly file the side of my nail. A shadow comes up beside me, and I glance up. Alain's standing there, looking down at my lap. I ignore him and hold my hand up to peer at my nails in the light. He gets a glass of water from the table beside me and walks away. I pull my phone out and allow my hastily conjured nail file to disappear.

Arden: Alain wants Lucifer to take a special force to the right of the enemy and push them into the middle of the valley. He's insisting. Lucifer disagrees. Wait. Callyx volunteered to do it. Alain frustrated. Should I stay with Lucifer or go with Callyx?

Vargas: Lucifer.

Daire: You should go to The Abbey.

Arden: I'm staying with Lucifer. Text later.

I slide my phone into a hidden pocket and stand to grab a glass of water.

Damn it, I can't drink without raising my hood, I curse silently. I glance around the tent and decide to step outside and find a restroom. Portable, of course. Once there, I rip off the hood and take a couple of deep breaths. I drink down the entire glass of water and use the restroom. Putting the hood back on, I step outside and run into Alain.

"Please excuse me, Alain," I murmur. Walking around him, I stroll back to Lucifer's tent. When I get to the entrance, I'm so tempted to glance back, but I don't.

Sitting down at the same seat, I stare at the enemy camp below us and whisper a few prayers to the goddess.

CHAPTER
SIXTEEN

<u>DAIRE</u>

The phone rings, and I pick it up. "We're in place," I tell Lucifer. I need to tell him of Alain's treachery, but I haven't been able to get him alone. According to Arden, Alain's decided to stay in Lucifer's camp and remain glued to his side. *Arden*, I snarl. I want to call and tell Lucifer to watch over her, but I can't with Alain nearby. Anger rises up, but I force my thoughts away from her to concentrate on the conversation. "What time do you want us to move forward?"

"We'll be ready in an hour," he replies. "Watch for the burst. Don't be late." He pauses. "Be careful." The line goes dead.

We've paused our troops behind the mountain line to hide them until it's time. Theron, Valerian, Fallon, Astor, Vargas, and I stand around the map in the center of the hastily pitched tent serving as our field headquarters. "All right. In about forty minutes, we need to charge forward. It will take us ten minutes to get over the mountain and engage the enemy. Unfortunately, they'll see us coming, but if we can get in position early, we might be able to turn their attention toward us and away from my father's troops, giving him a slight advantage."

"We might have an advantage for us too," Valerian interjects. "Theron and I have been working together to mimic Callyx. After I push my shadows into the valley, Theron can glamour them to seem like the forest. It's not foolproof and we can't hold it long, but ten minutes will give us time to get over the mountain and into the valley before they see us."

Astounded, I glance at Theron, and he nods in agreement. "Do it. Any amount of time will help." If we can get within attacking distance without them seeing us, it could change the outcome of this battle. Remembering Arden's text, I look over to Vargas. "Alain's up to something. I guarantee Callyx is going to find something nasty when he leads those troops. He'll need your help."

Respect and relief shine in Vargas' eyes. Clapping me on the shoulder, he grunts, "Thanks." He gathers his weapons and walks to the opening. "You should know Arden's been in a few battles. She's good. Quick on her feet. Calm and collected." He pauses. "I'd deny this in a heartbeat, but between her and Callyx, I'd pick her every time. She's not reckless, never feels the heat of the battle." He walks out, leaving me to ponder his words.

I realize the cadre isn't aware she's here, so I fill them in. I scrutinize their faces and realize we're all worried about her. But Valerian, Theron, and surprisingly, Fallon believe she has a right to decide for herself, and since she made the decision to be here, we should support her. But I can't. The idea of her in battle makes me want to rage at something.

"Let it go, Daire," Theron advises me. "We need you to focus. In thirty minutes, we push forward. We know the signals and our orders. It's time." He also claps me on the shoulder. "See you on the field."

Fallon falls in line behind Theron. "My warriors are ready and at your command."

Valerian, Astor, and I walk outside and join our troops. If Valerian and Theron can hide us from the enemy on the ground, we'll wait to take to the skies. Getting over the mountain range unseen is more important.

THIRTY MINUTES LATER, we stand on the precipice of battle. One by one, our enemies turn to face us, but find nothing. Beasts sniff the air. Flying creatures with leathery wings drift toward us in the sky. Demons in soldier formation move restlessly. They can sense we're here, but they can't see us, yet. The shadows start thinning, and I signal to Valerian and Theron to lift the veil.

I give a warrior's roar and hear it echo across the valley, from vampire to Fae to Elven to dragon. Even the minokawa screams, heralding our readiness for battle, as we leap into the air and I drive her straight into the middle of the enemy soldiers. Dragons follow me in V formation. The enemy scatters, throwing themselves right and left to get out of my way, unintentionally creating an almost perfect line straight down the middle, exactly as I planned.

Dividing them allows us to attack them from multiple directions. We flood the middle and the sides, while attacking them from several fronts on the ground. In the sky, we provide cover wherever necessary, but mainly in the middle to support Astor and the troop he's commanding for me and because holding the middle is critical.

In the distance, I see a burst of light, and Lucifer's army pours from the hillside into the valley. The enemy turns to fight this new front by forming a hard wall on the front line, stopping the rest of Lucifer's army from entering the valley. Now it's even more critical that we spread this line up the middle and give them a chance to enter the field.

Signaling to Valerian, I lead several of his clusters up the middle, using fire, ice, and shadows, plus the viciousness of the minokawa to help clear our path. As I reach the hill, I salute my father and turn back. The surprise on his face brings me an immense feeling of satisfaction, but I don't dwell on it. To my father's left, I spot Arden, and to his right, Alain's furious face. Suddenly, I'm glad she's there. At the very least, she can warn my father of his traitor.

The minokawa screams when a lance buries itself in her neck. I glance to the ridge and spot Alain's second-in-command grinning with pride. I ignore him for now, but the bastard's dead. I glide her toward the back of the battle and hop off. Using my bare hands, I grip the lance, pull it from her neck, then heal her wound. She takes off with a screech of anger, flying low, flattening any demon stupid enough to get in front of her. When she reaches the front line, she arrows toward Alain's second-in-command and plucks him off the ridge. All I hear are his screams when she devours him.

Using vampiric speed, I catch up to Astor and the rest of my troops. Drawing my sword, I enter the thick of the battle. Astor's on my right, using his mastery of shadows to strangle and blind demons right and left. For the few that get through, he uses potions or magic to disable them, leaving many of them screaming for mercy.

With my speed, I cut through a line of demons in two seconds, only to find another right behind the first. This is battle, unending and relentless, where you kill ten only to find a hundred in their place. Around Astor and me, the area fills up with demons in various stages of dismemberment and death, their screams of pain barely heard over the deafening roar of battle and the dragons above.

I crane my neck to look up and spot Valerian fighting with a wyvern, the creature significantly smaller but fast. Valerian gets tired of swatting it away and finally encases it in ice and lets gravity drag it down, where it shatters on the battlefield. He moves on to the next enemy waiting to challenge him. Several dragons nearby pause to watch him with astonishment, and I chuckle. They're either newbies who've never fought with him, or they've simply forgotten he's King of Dragons for a reason. A few clusters watch him with pride, happy to be fighting by their king's side again. I glance to the left, at the one who thinks he can still beat him. Apparently, the asshole believes he has a chance. I laugh loudly.

Demons in front of me start backing away. Word is getting out now—the Prince of the Underworld is in this battle. Either they'll back away from Lucifer's son, or they'll challenge me. I set my stance and prepare for the challengers, but before the first one gets to me, a loud boom sounds to my left. I turn and watch in horror as the mountain comes tumbling down, exactly where Fallon and his men are standing.

Looking up, I signal to Valerian, and he drops down to pick me up. We head straight for the cloud of dust rising from the field. From the air, all we see are bits of trees, rock, and dirt everywhere, but not a single Elven warrior. The demons surge forward, but Valerian lets loose a ton of fire, burning the entire first line instantly, which buys us time. Thinking fast, I consider asking Valerian to go back and get Astor, but I'm not sure what he can do. Normally, Fallon is the one with the magic to deal with nature. There's only one other possibility. I look to the hill and pick up my phone, while Valerian continues to hold off the demon horde in front of us.

CHAPTER
SEVENTEEN

ARDEN

The view from the hill is chaos. Instead of one army meeting the other, the field has been broken into groups, thanks to Daire. When he came up the middle of the battlefield, riding the massive golden bird, he looked magnificent, his fierce countenance a warning for anyone standing in his path. After saluting his father, the bird took a hit, and he rode off to deal with it. We haven't seen him since, but it's all Lucifer can talk about.

Alain, on the other hand, might actually have an apoplectic fit soon. His face is purple with anger, which would be comical if I weren't worried about him snapping. He's dangerous when calm, but in a rage, he's capable of mass destruction, literally. He's known for his natural disasters.

I've been quietly standing to the side, watching the armies in the back, my hands clenched so tightly that all the feeling left them long ago, constantly reminding myself they all know how to fight. As a distraction, I've started to watch the soldiers standing nearby, hoping to categorize them as ally or enemy. Typically, the guards are pretty stoic, but little tells are quickly giving away their allegiance. When one of our troops wins a skirmish, you can see which guard is quietly rooting for Lucifer. Either by the sneer on their face or the clench of their fist, these nonverbal cues tell me if they're an ally or the enemy. It's not foolproof, but unfortunately, in battle, you're guilty until proven innocent. Better to be wrong than sorry.

A loud boom fills the air, and I scream as the mountain comes roaring down in a landslide of trees, rocks, and dirt, directly on top of Fallon and his men. I glance at Lucifer, and he's staring at them in horror too. Alain is smirking.

My phone pings. It's a text from Daire.

> Daire: I need you. We can't find Fallon and his men.
>
> Arden: On my way.

Glancing at Lucifer, I motion him over to the side. Alain's suspicious eyes follow us, but he doesn't dare step closer and give away his position.

I pull Lucifer into a hug and kiss his cheek, whispering as quietly as I can. "Beware your disciple, for he stands at your right hand and calls you rabbi, while placing a kiss upon you in front of the crowd." I step back, not daring look to his right, while Lucifer stiffens and glares at me. His disbelief and subsequent glare assure me he understood the message. Hopefully, Alain won't make a move until I get back. "I've got to go. I'll try to get back soon, but if I don't, please be careful. Daire needs his father." I open a portal and step through.

When it opens at the other end of the field, I find Daire

running around with his vampires, trying to clear the debris. He strides over to me, his hands running agitatedly through his hair, dirt covering him from head to toe. "We're removing the debris as fast as we can, but it keeps shifting. Is there any way you can lift the earth away from them?"

I eye the mountain in front of me. It's much bigger in person, and I'm not sure I can lift the entire thing without making it worse. Plus, there might be some kind of spell holding it in place. I pace, thinking and listing my options. "I can do large chunks, but I can't lift it all away at once. And if I make the mountain disappear, everything in it will disappear too, including Fallon and his men. I can try to figure out some sort of exchange like dirt for feathers, but thousands of pounds of anything is still heavy." I place my hands on the top of my head, thinking quickly through the options. "First, I need to use a counter spell to..."

Suddenly, I feel a tingle directly in front of me. It's faint, but I know it's Fallon. I feel him, about fifty yards away. Scrambling over the debris, I point to the area. "Dig here. We'll get Fallon out first. He's got the strongest connection with nature, and he'll be the biggest help to get the rest of his men out."

Daire eyes me with skepticism. "How do you know where he's at?"

"We can feel each other," I reply. Waving a hand, I lift a huge chunk of debris and shift it to the side gently. I don't know if any of the chunks contain Fallon's soldiers, and I don't want to take a chance I'll hurt them.

Working in sections, we make our way foot by foot to where Fallon is located. Finally, we're close. Using a soft wind, I scatter the dirt in front of me, carefully removing it inch by inch, until suddenly, I see a hand. I place mine against his and feel some type of membrane between us. I tap his hand to let him know we're here and use a spell and my hands to push the remaining dirt to the sides, like a curtain parting for the sun.

Daire and I peer through the membrane and gape at the sight in front of us. Fallon and all of his men are holding up the mountain above them with Elven power. When the mountain came tumbling down, they must have formed this barrier between it and them. In awe of the sheer collective power to move mountains, I watch while they cluster together and shift toward Fallon. The mountain above us groans.

Cutting through the membrane, they slide out one by one, maintaining their hold on the mountain, until the last one remaining is Fallon. He slides out, and they all strain to let it down gently. Once it's down, they all slump to the ground, including Fallon.

Daire starts shouting for his men to get them water, but they're engaged in keeping the demons off our backs. Fighting ferociously about ten feet behind us, Valerian and another dragon at their sides, they valiantly hold back the horde.

I motion for Daire to join them. "I'll get them water. Go," I tell him, knowing the battle needs him more right now. He strides off, leaving me with hundreds of men and little water nearby. I rapidly consider my options. I'm not skilled enough to create water yet, which means I need to find a source of water. Opening the portal to the pond where I've been training, I close my eyes and ask Mother Nature for her help. After connecting, water starts flowing directly from the pond to each of the men lying nearby. They drink thirstily, then splash water over their faces and bodies to get the layers of sand and rock off.

I run over to Fallon, who hasn't moved. When I get to him, I realize he's devastated. "What is it? Are you okay? Drink some water." He shakes his head no, but I ignore him. Using the stream of water, I wash his hair and face off. When he looks up, I direct the stream to his hands, and he drinks.

"Garrett didn't make it." He shakes his head, tears forming in his eyes when he tells me. "A demon came out of nowhere and grabbed him before we could get the shield up. He pushed me forward and went down."

Remembering how we felt when we thought Fallon and all his men were lost to the mountain, I realize there could be a chance. "You don't know that for sure. We thought you lost, and here you are. Where did you see him go down?" I stand up and pull him up with me.

Gah, it's like moving an elephant.

Motioning for all the men to stand up, I hold on to Fallon's hand. "Concentrate on him. You know him. Try to feel for him like you do me." He stares at me incredulously. "What do you have to lose?"

The men crowd around Fallon, reaching out a finger or a hand to touch him, lending him their power to help find Garrett. The buzzing grows, and static electricity fills the air between us. Fallon's face is scrunched up, concentrating.

Slowly, his hand raises, and he points to the right. "I think he's that way."

We run to the area he pointed. "How far do you think?" I yell.

"Forty feet, maybe?" he replies excitedly. Using their power, the men begin to lift the debris from the area, slowly revealing a body on the ground, wrapped in a small cocoon. "Garrett!"

The Elven man lifts his head, and relief flashes in his eyes. Once they've broken the seal, they get him water to drink and try to sit him up. Several large gashes cover his body, and he's very pale.

He claps Fallon on the back. "I knew you wouldn't let me

down, son." He coughs and leans over. A deep gash in his chest spurts blood. When he sees Fallon eyeing it, he spits out, "Poisoned blade. I'm not healing."

Stepping forward, I try to heal him, but the poison is resistant.

Fallon's face whitens, and he opens a portal. Summoning one of his younger soldiers for help, they get Garrett on his feet. "Get him to ground and have my father call on Mother Nature for her assistance. Don't let him die."

When the portal closes, he turns to me and pulls me into his arms. His large hand cups the back of my head, and his muscular body wraps itself around me. "Thank you. The men, Garrett, they're my brothers. We would have suffocated and died a thousand times before someone could get to us," he says gruffly. He draws back and cups my face between his two hands, then leans down and drops the softest, most heartfelt kiss on my lips.

When he pulls back this time, his green eyes reflect an ocean of emotion, but he slowly removes his hands. Giving a large whistle, his warriors file into place. In sync, they all turn to me and bow, gratitude shining in their eyes. Fallon gives another signal with his hand, and they head back into the battle, leaving me standing there alone with my fingers on my lips.

My body is trembling from an overload of adrenaline and emotion, but slowly, the sounds of battle permeate my bubble, making me aware of how vulnerable I am. Shaking off the nerves, I glance around and notice I'm in a circle of Daire's protection. Relieved, I wave my hand and motion to the hill. Daire nods. Having seen Valerian, Daire, and Fallon, I'm so tempted to go check on Astor and Theron, and Callyx and Vargas, but I don't. Daire needs me to be there for his father, and that's what I'm going to do.

EIGHTEEN

ARDEN

Returning to Lucifer's side, I notice quite a few more guards around us, but I don't know if they're friend or foe. I slide to the side to get a better vantage point to observe the new guards, placing myself a couple of feet closer to Lucifer.

He raises an eyebrow and flicks his eyes to the field.

I give him a discreet thumbs-up, and he returns it with a hard nod. I guess he's still a wee bit angry with me. Nobody likes the messenger who brings bad news. And a traitor who's been your best friend for thousands of years? Maybe he believes me and maybe he doesn't, but as a ruler, he has to at least give it consideration. The repercussions for ignoring a traitor in Alain's position would be devastating.

Watching the guard's fist clench in front of me, I follow his eyesight directly down the middle of the battlefield, where

Astor fights valiantly against another magic user. It's hard to tell from this far away, but probably a sorcerer or sorceress, common to the Underworld. The skies above them are filled with the color of magic—spells and counter spells. Astor quickly defeats his opponent, but he doesn't rest for a second, simply choosing the next one and engaging quickly. I so badly want to join him. Instead, I turn back to the guard and memorize his face. *Foe*, I mark him.

A large arc appears in the sky to the right side of the battlefield, exactly where Callyx and Vargas are fighting. The arc slowly evolves into a portal. The deafening roar of the battle ceases as all eyes turn to it. Peering through the opening to the other side, an army lies waiting to enter the battle, but not like any army I've ever seen. Row upon row of creatures stand ready to enter. Dark, expressionless, and fucking scary, they make the denizens of the Underworld seem like pansies. Tensing, I look to Lucifer for information, but he's turned away from me, scanning the battlefield. He stills when he spots something to his left on the hill nearby.

Glancing back at the portal, I watch several creatures slip through the opening. *Fuck, this isn't good.* Suddenly, the enemy stops fighting us and turns to help us fight the creatures entering from the portal. You know it's bad when your enemy is suddenly your ally. We need to close this fucking portal!

Horrified, I'm unable to take my eyes off the scene. As I'm staring, I see the edges of the portal wavering and possibly shrinking. It's got to be Vargas, but it's so fucking slow, too many of those creatures are pouring into our side.

Where is Daire? I scan the back of the battlefield, but I don't see him. When I turn to my left, I notice Lucifer is also gone. *Fuck! Where did he go?*

I shoot off a text to Daire, telling him to get up to the front and help Vargas get this portal closed or we're all going to be fucked.

I turn in a circle until I see a guard I can trust. Or at least I think I can trust. Hopefully, my powers of observation are working. Sliding quietly up to him, I murmur, "Where's Lucifer?"

Without taking his eyes off the portal, he leans down. "Why should I tell you?"

Pulling the Killian blade, I slide it between his thighs. "Because I'm here as his honored guest. And because I'll cut off your dick if you don't help me find him. You can go with me, but we need to hurry!" My gut's churning, along with my intuition. "I think he's in trouble."

The guard gives me a measured look and must find me sincere, because he decides to help. I sigh with relief. I really didn't want to hurt him. He taps the guy next to him on the shoulder and motions for him to follow, then heads off toward the left side of the camp—in the same direction Lucifer was looking earlier.

One of Alain's personal guards gives us a suspicious glance when we pass him and decides to investigate. Pretending like I don't see him, I cup my breasts and plump them up, then run my hands down the sides of my body before grabbing onto the bicep of the guard in front of me. Walking beside him, I add an extra wiggle into my hips. Alain's guard slows but doesn't stop. Damn it, I'd hoped my ruse would work. I guess we'll have to do this the hard way.

"Stop, we've got company," I whisper to the guard in front. I slide around the corner of the tent and motion for the two guards to keep walking. Drawing my sword, I wait.

Alain's guard walks by a minute later. He doesn't see me in the shadows, and I wait until he's past, then hit him hard on the head with the pommel of my sword. He crumples to the ground, and the two guards eye me warily.

"He's a traitor," I explain quietly. "Let's go."

The guards communicate silently with each other, but they don't turn back. When we come to a small ridge, the first guard points to the left. When I get to the edge, I follow his finger and see Lucifer fighting with Alain. I also see several men sneaking up on his back. The guards beside me pull their swords, but I hold up a hand. We need to get closer. I think I can put us directly between Lucifer and the attackers. I step back until the men on the ridge have disappeared from view, hoping if I can't see them, they can't see me. I open a portal and motion for the two guards to follow me.

When I open the portal, we're standing in front of the enemy, exactly where I'd targeted. The rune at my throat flares in warning, but I'm already moving. We engage quickly, and it only takes a few minutes to kill them. Turning in a circle, I notice Alain's men sneaking up from several sides, not just this one. Pulling my other sword, I motion for Lucifer's guards to spread out.

The first group tops the hill and smile when they see me. The only thing standing between them and Lucifer is a woman. While they can't see my face, thanks to the suit molded to my body, they can obviously tell I'm female. Apparently, they follow the same school of thought as most demons —a woman is not a threat. It's my turn to smile, even if they can't see it.

"Hello, boys. Decided to join the party? I have to tell you...it pretty much sucks. No booze, no yummy appetizers, no flirty men, and it's missing my friend Meri. Believe me, you don't know how to party until you party with that girl. Although," I babble, distracting them with my chatter while I decide which one to take out first. He's perfect, and I direct my gaze to him.

"I don't think you're her type. She likes them to be sexy as fuck, and you obviously didn't inherit the good looks gene. Ugly parents, huh? Sucks to be you."

His sword slams into mine. Finally. I thought I'd have to beg him to fight me. I pivot and, with two strokes, cut off his head and step over to the next guard, who is standing there in shock. My sword swings through the air, and his head rolls to the ground.

Feeling a disturbance at my back, I duck and slide to the side, bringing my sword up to meet the next swing. It reverberates, and I step back to assess this new threat. "Well, you're a big boy. Ugly too. Does Alain only like the ugly ones? Probably thinks you make him prettier." He is one big, ugly motherfucker, and based on his grip and stance, he knows how to fight. Thank fuck.

He attacks, fast and furious, focusing everything on a purely physical fight. I zing a tendril of magic at him and find good wards. But does he have magic? Running up the side of a rock, I use the second away from the constant hammering of his sword to conjure up a ball of witchfire. When I come down, I fling it at him. It sizzles against his shield, creating a fairly sizable hole in it. His eyes dart to it, but he makes no move to repair it. It's not a sure sign, but if he had magic, I doubt he'd leave himself so exposed.

His eyes flicker, and my rune flares as I catch a whiff of something raunchy behind me. I shove the pointy end of my sword under my elbow and hear a squelch when it finds its target. Quickly, I pull it out and swing up to catch the sword of the guard in front of me. Dancing to the side, I maneuver until I can see the threat behind me. Another guard presses a hand to his side, waiting for it to heal. Damn immortals. If you don't cut off their heads, they regenerate. And some are so bad, you have to cut off their heads and burn them to make sure they're dead.

An idea comes to mind. I ease back and cast my magic toward the guard I just stabbed. With a twirl, I put on a burst of speed and come up behind him. Or myself. With a quick glamour spell, the big guy takes the bait. Thinking it's me standing in front of him, he swings and chops off his buddy's head. When it falls to the ground and the glamour fades, he realizes it's a trick, but it's already too late. His head follows it a second later.

Lucifer's guards are doing pretty well themselves. Both have dispatched several enemy guards, and they're engaged with the last two now. I eyeball the portal and notice it's half the size it was originally. Fewer creatures are slipping through, and those that do quickly find themselves dead.

When the final two enemy guards are dead, we move in closer to Alain and Lucifer.

"Why?" Lucifer's voice is raw, bleeding from the betrayal of his closest friend as he questions Alain. "We've been friends for thousands of years. Why suddenly throw it all away? Tell me, you bastard!" Lucifer draws his sword across Alain's stomach. Not deep enough for guts to spill out, but it takes Alain a few seconds to heal.

An idea pops into my head. Using a simple magic spell, I amplify their voices until the entire battlefield can hear.

"You didn't hold up your end of the bargain!" Alain yells, his sword swinging through the air to connect with Lucifer's. "From the day you conquered the Underworld, I was your loyal servant. Finally, a fitting king to be our ruler. No weaknesses. A machine purely dedicated to fucking over the world. It was your motto and mission rolled into one, and it was beautiful. Underworld had never seen better days—mayhem, wealth, and power. We were rolling in it, and after years of serving, you rewarded my loyalty with your friendship and made me your second-in-command. Together, we became invincible. For over two thousand years, we were ruthless and nothing could stop us, but then you ruined it! Instead of fucking the witch and moving on, you fell in love, like a human, a weakling! The great King of the Underworld brought to his knees by basic human emotion," he sneers and spits on the ground. No longer fighting, he's standing there raging at Lucifer, years of pent-up anger and betrayal spewing out of him. "And like all humans, she got pregnant. Daire was born, then Danica, and all you wanted was to play happy fucking families. You stopped giving a shit about this magnificent empire we'd built." His face is ugly, hatred twisting his features into a grotesque caricature.

"I tried to ignore them, but surprisingly, I discovered I liked Daire. He was immortal, not like his mother and sister, and magnificent. A new species for the Underworld—a vampire! Maybe a son wouldn't be so bad, after all," he reflects, as if Daire was his. "In fact, the more I thought about it, I realized this could be the opportunity of a lifetime. We could be more than friends. We could be family. Once I adjusted to the idea, I realized I needed a daughter. For twenty years, I searched, until one day, I found this beautiful baby girl vampire, the absolute perfect match for Daire.

"I'm a bastard, but even I could see how devastated you were when Danica died, then the witch a few years later. I knew you needed time to grieve, so as your friend, I stepped back and spent my days grooming Solange to be everything Daire desired while I waited for you to pick up the reins. Finally, you did, but instead of the beautiful monster of the past, you became this pathetic shell championing free will and striving to find balance with the greater good. Every single moment I'd spent as your servant and friend was wasted, and not once did you consider how I'd feel. I helped you build this empire, and you wanted to make it...less, in every way. I couldn't stand it." His voice is raw when he recounts his devastation. "So when she came knocking twelve hundred years ago, offering me the throne, I accepted."

Changing to his beast form, he renews his attack against Lucifer. Towering over him, he waits for Lucifer to shed his skin, but it's in vain. Lucifer stays in his human form. Whether he means it as an insult or if he has another reason, I don't know.

Except for those busy with closing the portal, the battlefield is silent, all eyes upon these two, watching the brutal fight with fascination. Their knowledge of each other's fighting habits means they both have to work hard to make a mark on the other. Alain is giving it everything he's got and manages to land a few deep hits on Lucifer, but nothing incapacitating, not even for a moment. Soon, it becomes readily apparent to all—Lucifer's holding back. I've known it from the beginning, because I've seen his power and I've never seen anyone match it. Alain knew it too, which is why it was only a tactic to buy some time until the creatures could get through the portal.

Lucifer shakes his head. "Who promised to put you on the throne?" He ignores the rest of Alain's ramblings to focus on the one fact he deems important, and his restraint suddenly makes sense. "You said 'she' a second ago. Who are you talking about?"

Alain checks the portal, sees it's closed, and drops his sword. Defeated, he laughs maniacally. "Fuck it. That bitch never helped me anyway. I'll tell you if you let me live."

"No," Lucifer replies, his voice full of pain. "You could tell me as payment for the friendship we shared for thousands of years. I know it wasn't all a façade."

A dark defeated laugh escapes Alain. "Fuck, you're a real pain in my ass." He runs a hand over his face. "But you're right,

I owe you. A little over twelve hundred years ago, the Prime came knocking on several doors, including mine, offering deals left and right. She offered me the ultimate prize—King of the Underworld. If I got rid of you, she'd support my reign, and if I didn't...well, you know the old threat, except she's powerful enough to back it up." He sighs. "And let's be honest, I wanted to be king, so I took the deal. Since then, I've done everything I could to undermine you. I stirred up your enemies, caused a wedge between you and your son, broke treaties with our allies, and so much more. The things I did in your name...well, let's just say your reputation as a cruel, unforgiving bastard is cemented for all time. And yet, I couldn't find a way to bring you down." His expression reflects his own disappointment in his failures.

I freeze. *Prime?* The poem on the second piece of parchment mentioned the Prime. I didn't realize it was a person.

"Who's the current Prime?" Lucifer is laser focused when he asks.

"You're going to laugh. It's the—" An almost transparent hand snatches Alain by the neck and starts dragging him toward a dark hole literally appearing out of nowhere on the ground. He claws at the hand, trying to get it to release him. Lucifer dives forward, but his hand passes right through the phantom's wrist, and he can't prevent it from taking Alain. Alain mouths one last thing, then he's gone.

Shaking, I pull off my hood and stare at the hole. The same thing happened to the assassin who broke into our home when Solandis started to question him.

What the hell is going on? Who is the Prime? And why is the person behind my attempted assassinations after Lucifer too?

CHAPTER
NINETEEN

Satisfaction courses through me when I see the battle turn in our favor. The enemy is thinning, and without true leadership, losing its focus. Enemy forces are showing signs of fatigue, and the pile of bodies is growing. Whistling to the rest of the cadre, we tighten the lines and prepare ourselves for one last push. I assess our troops and find them fighting and launching attacks with almost the same energy as when they started. We have our own small pile of bodies, but far fewer than the enemy. It helps when the fighter next to you has your back.

Raising my arm to give the signal, I feel my phone buzz. Knowing Arden wouldn't text unless it was important, I pull it up.

Arden: To your left. Huge portal opening. Gigantic army of black creatures waiting to enter. Vargas can't close it by himself. He needs you. Lucifer's gone. Going to find him.

I'd seen a bright arc on the left, but thought it was a bomb or magical skirmish, not a portal. And, if I'm not mistaken, a portal to another world, one filled with creatures of death, whose only focus is finding food to eat, which is whatever or whoever is in its path. We'd had a few of them slip through barriers into the Underworld in the past, and they'd decimated entire populations.

Signaling to Valerian, I explain my plan for the last push and hand the reins of leadership to him. I motion for Astor and a few of my best fighters to follow me to the portal. If Alain's holding it open, it's going to take my full concentration to close it, which means I'll be vulnerable for several minutes. I need them to watch my back until it's done.

I whistle for the minokawa, and it kindly gives us a ride. Thirty seconds later, we land near the portal, where the overwhelming smell of blood and gore hits my nose, and I grimace. Usually after the first hour of battle, a vampire becomes immune to the smell. Something must be causing it to be worse than usual. Scanning the area, I notice the ground is littered with bodies from both sides of the war, but the smell isn't originating from them. No, it's caused by the rivers of blood and mounds of fresh body parts by the portal—body parts with huge teeth marks on them. Dread churns in my stomach. We've got to get this portal closed, fast!

With Astor and my men following, I head toward the center of the portal. When we reach the middle, I'm astonished by the sight in front of me. Vargas stands in a circle of protection, working on the portal, while Callyx and several other large, feral-looking demons fight to keep the creatures off him.

Callyx blinks a few times, then shouts, "It's about fucking time your princely ass got here. Took your sweet time. Playing soldier again, huh?"

"I'm not sure I'm needed, since it looks like you've got things covered. And I'm not here to help you. If it wasn't for Vargas, I'd happily leave your ass here to be a snack," I growl at him. I can't believe he's Arden's brother. No wonder she's so damn headstrong. "Vargas, I'll close from the left, and you work on the right. We'll meet in the middle. Let's hope to hell someone takes out Alain."

Astor creates a stronger ward around both Vargas and me. Once cocooned, we pool our powers and work toward closing the portal. Slowly, it starts shrinking, but not fast enough, as several creatures slip through the opening. One is tough to kill. Several, and we're dead. I brace myself for their impact, but suddenly, I see Alain's army step up beside us to fight the creatures. Apparently, nobody wants these creatures in the Underworld. Relieved, I focus on closing the portal.

We've got it halfway closed when I start hearing Lucifer's and Alain's voices rising behind me. I guess Lucifer knows about his betrayal. The portal would have given it away. Besides Lucifer, only Vargas, Alain, and myself have the power to open a portal large enough for an army.

Alain's control of the portal rises and falls while he fights Lucifer. When it falls, Vargas and I double up our efforts and gain significant ground. We're straining to close the last few feet when Alain's power drops and it slams closed.

Vargas slumps to the ground, his body alternating between his demon form and his human form, showing his depleted power state. Callyx moves to stand over him, protecting him from anyone approaching, but none do. The battle is over.

I turn around just in time to see something drag Alain's body into a hole. Astonished, I blink and glance at Lucifer.

Fear for his safety rises, and I grab Astor and signal for my men to follow. We use our vampiric speed to get across the battlefield to him. When we get closer, I spot Arden standing at his side, frozen, her gaze locked on the spot where Alain disappeared.

I motion to Valerian to get the cadre. He turns and heads to the back of the now quiet battlefield, which I notice isn't that far. We'd taken more ground than I'd thought.

A blur on my left catches my eye. It's a vampire, heading toward Lucifer and Arden at full speed. I roar and point. Both look around, but they can't see what I'm seeing because they're up on a ridge. My eyes dart around for a solution, but even Valerian is too far away to reach her now.

Astor taps my arm, his eyes on Arden, and shouts, "You need to let me go or you'll never make it."

Realizing he's right, I let go of his arm. I hear him curse, but I don't turn back. Without Astor, I pick up speed, pushing myself hard, but I'm still too far away. I'm not going to make it.

The blur tops the ridge, grabs Arden, hits her hard on the head, and throws her so high into the air, I can barely see her. For a split second, I pause, my mind sifting through the options, but my body has already made the decision and is turning to help Arden. My wings break free, and with the power of wind, I arrow forward and catch her mid-flight. I pull her tightly into my arms, needing to feel her against me.

"I've got you," I murmur. "It's okay. You're okay," I croon softly to her, adrenaline coursing through my body. My body curves protectively around her, while my wings flap softly, allowing us to hover in one spot. I pass my hand over her head and heal the spot where Solange hit her.

"Daire?" she gasps, flinging her arms around my neck and squeezing me tight. "What the hell is going on? One minute, I'm standing there watching something drag Alain into the ground, and the next, I'm flying through the air." She eyes my wings. "And you can fly? Where did you get the pretty wings?"

Chuckling, I drop my head to her neck and breathe in the mouthwatering mixture of her unique scent. My lips skim her cheek before settling a hard kiss on her lips. "And thank the fuck I have wings. I've never been so happy to be able to fly in my life. But let's get one thing straight—they're magnificent, not pretty. Picked up a bit of something extra from my father's genes." Looking around, I turn to face the ridge. "We need to get to Lucifer, but we'll talk later."

Making a hard turn in the air, we fly back to Lucifer. The roar of the crowd watching below makes me nervous. I guess my secret's out now. Glancing down at Arden in my arms, I don't regret it. She wouldn't have died, but it would have hurt like hell and there's no way I'd allow that to happen.

We glide onto the ridge and land where we see Lucifer patting a sobbing Solange, who's kneeling on the ground next to where Alain disappeared. Tears roll down Lucifer's face too. They're united in their grief for a man they both loved, so I stand back with Arden, respecting the moment.

Solange raises her head to find me standing nearby, and her unstable mind flips from grief to hatred to bewilderment in a nanosecond. "It's your fault," she accuses before continuing, "I don't understand. Why couldn't you just love me? I did everything I was supposed to do. I spent hours learning all your likes and dislikes, from food to sex. Every single kernel of information we could scrounge or buy from servants to lovers, we used it to mold me into your perfect match. I stood by for years while you treated me like a little sister, until finally, you woke up and saw the woman and not a girl. Everything was perfect. We were perfect. Until she came along." She points to Arden without looking at her. "And then you walked away as if I were nothing." Her hands curl into claws. "Now he's gone. My father, the only person who loved me." She slowly stands, and I tense, ready to defend Arden.

"But you're going to pay," she continues in a singsong voice. She glances from Arden and me to the cadre standing behind me, and finally, to Lucifer. "You're all going to pay. The Prime doesn't allow anyone to get in her way." A deranged sort of laugh escapes her.

Lucifer grips her arms. "Tell me, you fool. I can protect you," he urges.

She shakes her head, an expression of sadness on her face. "Nobody can protect me," she replies softly. "Not even you." With a few steps, she stands on the same ground where Alain disappeared. "I wonder if I'll see my father. You want to know who the Prime is..." The same phantom hand reaches up and grabs Solange's ankle. "But I want her to win." And with those final words, she's gone.

Arden is standing in my arms, shaking. She reaches up and grabs my hand as if it's the anchor keeping her from falling apart. Alarmed, I look over to the cadre. I've never seen Arden fearful of anything. "It's okay, she's gone." I squeeze her hand tightly. "She'll never bother us again."

After waving a hand to cut off the amplifier, she whispers, "This is the third time I've seen someone disappear in a hole because of a damn phantom hand. I don't want to be next."

CHAPTER
TWENTY

<u>ARDEN</u>

Although I whispered it to Daire, Lucifer clearly hears me and stalks over. "What do you know about the..." He stops and glances around before continuing, "The person? Who was the first person you saw disappear?"

"Perhaps The Abbey would be the best place for this discussion," Theron suggests quietly by my side. "The wards and protections given to sanctuary were established by a primal source long ago."

Realizing we have little protection here, I agree with Theron's suggestion.

Lucifer dips his head in agreement, then pulls me into his arms for a hug. "Thank you, Arden, for your warning." His voice is raw and full of anguish. "I'd have never believed it from anyone else, but you've never lied to me. Not even as a child."

"I'm so sorry," I say inadequately. I can't even imagine

having a friend for thousands of years, much less a betrayal of this magnitude. After all, Meri is my first friend.

He pats me on the shoulder, then sweeps past to pull Daire into his arms. "You were magnificent. If you and your cadre hadn't brought reinforcements, we would have lost the battle and Alain would have won. The strategy you deployed was brilliant," he praises. He points to the battlefield, and I watch them walk over and view the destruction. The enemy army is subdued, with Lucifer and the cadre's forces rounding them up.

A flash of black teases my peripheral vision, and I turn to face Theron. Shocked, I scan every inch of him. Gone is the impeccably dressed, icy Fae lord. Instead, a fierce warrior stands in front of me. Wearing Fae armor similar to mine, every inch of his tall muscular body, including his powerful shoulders, is showcased in the fabric molded tightly to his body. Instead of his phone, his hand holds a magnificent sword made of the purest blue ice, and if that's not surprising enough, more weapons are strapped in various places across his body.

When I inspect him, my breath catches. His blond hair lies carelessly disheveled, he's wearing a couple days of scruff on his face, and his violet eyes are stormy and staring intensely at me. I'm not sure I'll ever see him in the same light again.

Clearing my throat, I reach up and push back the few tendrils of hair escaping my bun. "Theron," I murmur huskily.

One large step, and he's standing directly in front of me, gripping my hips, while his violet eyes sweep over me. "Arden," he returns gruffly, his usually modulated voice trapped in whatever emotion he's currently feeling.

Feeling a tap on my shoulder, I glance up to find Fallon behind me. He squeezes my shoulders, and I lean back. After saving his life today, my emotions are pretty heightened around him right now. Touching him reassures me he's alive and not buried under the damn mountain. I shiver, and both him and Theron move in closer.

Looking into Theron's violet eyes, I watch them darken into a deep purple, and for the first time, I contemplate what he would be like in bed. I lick my suddenly dry lips, and an almost imperceptible smirk appears on his lips.

Valerian comes striding up beside the three of us with his hands clenched. Theron and Fallon step back, and he sweeps me into his massive arms and closes them tightly around me.

Boneless, I let him hold me up. "Whoa, my fierce dragon. I'm okay. I barely saw any action today," I remind him. I cup his jaw, forcing him to look at me. "But you were truly magnificent, and I saw where you and Theron used shadows and Fae glamour. Callyx is going to be strutting like a peacock because you used his idea." I notice a couple of shadows in his eyes, and if I take a guess, I'd say the dragons were the cause. "The dragons performed well, and it probably did them a world of good to see you as a warrior and king." I stand on my tiptoes and kiss him, my lips lingering on his soft pouty ones for a brief second.

A roar sounds off to my left, and Valerian stiffens. He withdraws from my arms and walks to the edge of the ridge to stare at the dragons in the field.

"Hello, gorgeous," Astor says from behind me. "I'm not surprised you ignored our request to stay home, but I'm a lucky man to be staring at you here on the edge of this ugly battlefield."

I turn around and face him. "Astor," I murmur, taking in the fatigue on his face. He was all over the place in this battle, fighting fiercely, and I'm sure his magic is low. I'm relieved to see he's okay and willing to talk to me. I see several cuts on his hands and arms, which must have been deep if they're not healed yet. I run my hands over them, healing each one. "I'm so sorry. For everything. I shouldn't have taken you to Witchwood or asked you to watch me help your enemy." I reach out and tangle my fingers with his. "And I know you don't believe me right now, but family is the most important thing to me and you're part of it. It doesn't matter what happens, you will always be family. Always."

He's staring intently at me, so I know he hears the truth.

"I appreciate the work you did, and I want you to know I didn't burn those papers. They're safe. I'll work with Theron when we get back to figure the rest out." Tears clog my throat, creating a lump, forcing me to swallow several times while I try to find the words to set him free. I've been drawn to him since the day we met. His darkness and *laissez-faire* approach to life captivate me, but it is his intelligence and unexpectedly fierce loyalty to the cadre that makes me want the man behind the façade.

My hands clench and unclench as if they can feel him slipping away. "And...if what happened between us needs to stay simple, it can, but it will need to be the only time. I feel something for you, and it wouldn't take much for it to grow deeper." I couldn't let him walk away without knowing he means more to me. His brown eyes are full of an emotion I can't read. I lean over and kiss him on the cheek. "I love your green eyes." Chuckling, I watch as he winces at the tiny lie, then I walk off to find the soothing comfort of Daire's company.

WE STAY in the Underworld for a week, helping Lucifer clean up the battlefield and organize his court. He pardons most of the enemy, knowing they were merely pawns in Alain's quest for power, as well as a few of the allies Callyx pulled from the prison. He executes others when their sworn allegiance proves to be insincere, thanks to Astor's rune. Finally, he names Vargas his second-in-command, which brings tears to my eyes.

When we leave, he hitches a portal back to The Abbey with us.

Once we've all rested for a couple of days, we gather in the VIP lounge, whiskeys in hand. I sit on the couch, Theron and Valerian sit on either side, and Lucifer sits across from me with Daire by his side, while Astor and Fallon sit on each end.

My hands tighten on the glass while my leg bounces up and down. I decide to walk through my experience first. "As you are all aware, right before I came to The Abbey to ask for Theron's assistance, we were attacked by assassins in our home. They carried the last Killian blade with them, which was my signal to come here," I remind them. "But something odd happened during the attack. After Solandis and I defeated them, we managed to capture one of the assassins, a demon. When Solandis started to question the demon to find out who sent him, a phantom hand reached into our pocket dimension and yanked him into a hole the exact same way it did with Alain. It terrified Solandis and me. Solandis is extremely powerful, our home well protected with wards and spells, and she'd never have thought someone could breach it so easily. She thinks it's either a blood spell or a powerful geas activated with specific triggers."

Lucifer frowns thoughtfully. "It could be. Did your assassin say the...name?" he questions, not wanting to speak the word Prime aloud.

I try to think back to the exact conversation. "We asked him to reveal his source, and he explained it would be his death. Suddenly, his body stiffened and he panicked. He opened his mouth to speak, but the hand cut off his air and he didn't get the words out. Then he was gone." I shiver, remembering the feeling of helplessness.

Taking a drink of whiskey to calm my nerves, I remember Alain's last moment. "Did you understand Alain's last word? I couldn't tell, but I'm not the best lip reader."

Lucifer closes his eyes but shakes his head sadly. "I'm not sure. Right now, I can't think about it without losing myself to my emotions, but I'll keep trying."

"And what do you know about the person? Or the name?" I press, knowing he has some knowledge. "Maybe we should call it 'Primary' to prevent us from accidentally saying the wrong name?"

He sits there for a minute, staring intensely at each of us as if weighing our ability to hold a secret. I get the feeling he shares little with outsiders. "A few thousand years ago, I wanted more power, and an old demon jokingly told me the only way to get more power was to become the...Primary. I became fascinated with this unknown entity, and while I found several mentions of it in the archives, I could never find out how to find or how to become it," Lucifer explains. "I put it aside for a while. Then, about twelve hundred years ago, I felt a shift in the universe. At first, I thought it was because my grief was finally lessening and I was rejoining the world, but the feeling wouldn't go away. I felt this immense pressure to redress the imbalance, but I wasn't sure what I needed to do or how. I searched for answers in my personal archives, and when I did, I noticed all the documents I had on the Primary were missing. No matter who I asked, nobody had even heard of the Primary, nor did they know anything about the imbalance. I negotiated with several leaders to search their libraries to see if they had answers, and that's when I discovered some of their archives had been destroyed or were missing as well. Not just records relating to the Primary. Pieces of history had disappeared. Someone went to a lot of effort to destroy or rewrite the past."

"A portion of the witches' archives were destroyed by a fire during the same timeframe. I thought it was Gemma Perrone, the seer, but now I wonder," I tell him. "So approximately twelve hundred years ago, the Primary was making deals left and right. Archives disappeared or were destroyed, eliminating documented knowledge of the Primary and the history during that time period, and you felt a shift in the universe," I summarize, listing the key points from our discussion. "Fast forward to present day, and the source of my attempted assassinations seems to be the Primary." I groan and give a half-hearted laugh. "Well, that's not scary as hell." Valerian must think so too, because he curls his arm around me and squeezes tight. "What do I have to do with it?"

Theron leans forward, his gaze intent, and reminds me, "The MacAllister massacre also happened a little over twelve hundred years ago. Up until that time, the witches were powerful, outnumbering almost all of the races. Only the Fae and demons had larger populations, but we also bear few children. Eventually, the witches would have become the largest group. The massacre immediately decimated their numbers. It also inadvertently put them on the path to lesser power." He glances over to Valerian. "Valerian became King of Dragons, and twenty years later, the old dark Elven king died without heirs. Another family took up the reins of power. There was definitely a monumental change in power around the same time period, but I don't understand the imbalance. Light and dark still existed for each race."

Lucifer's eyes are narrowed while he thinks about the additional facts Theron added to the mix. "I'm not sure, but there has to be something we're missing."

Theron nods. "We've only checked the official libraries, but maybe someone's personal library will have answers. We could send inquiries to our networks. Tell them we're searching for any records from a thousand to fifteen hundred years ago. We don't need to tell them why." Theron furiously sends off a few texts.

Lucifer agrees and picks up his phone to shoot the same inquiry to his network.

Theron stops texting. "Valerian, we need to speed up our visit to your kingdom. Find a way to resolve your issues this week."

Valerian scowls but agrees.

Lucifer stands and stretches. "I'll continue to need Daire's help for the next week to get things settled, but I'll let you know if anyone gets back to me. Astor, you're welcome to come back with us. I could use your help to weed out the liars in my court."

Astor looks up in surprise. "I can come for a day or two, but I have something important to settle here." He turns his gaze toward me, trying to silently communicate something, but I'm not sure I understand.

Hope makes my heart race, but I don't let it take flight. Hearing it, Daire's icy blue eyes dart to mine, and he raises an eyebrow. I smile to reassure him, and he dips his chin in acknowledgement, but I can see him wondering what caused it.

I smile at Astor. "Before you go, would you mind walking Theron and I through the work you completed on the documents? We need to find a name before we go to Valerian's kingdom," I remind him, waiting for his agreement.

My thoughts turn to the Primary, and I shiver, thinking about the power behind the person. Who the hell am I up against? And why?

161

My phone pings, and I jump. Raising it up, I see a text from Astor.

> Astor: I'm sorry. I've been trying to say those words to you for over a week. Don't give up on me. I may not know what to do, but I know walking away isn't the answer. I want more. More mornings in bed, more of your bad jokes, more pain from your sweet little lies, more days spent riding the wind with you wrapped around me. Is it enough?

> Arden: It's enough. I won't miss you. Hurry home.

TWENTY-ONE

FALLON

A rden walks into the lobby the next morning, bleary-eyed and yawning, like she barely slept last night. I know I didn't. Between dreams of the mountain crushing my men and me and thoughts of her, I haven't been able to get a full night's sleep since before the battle. Slipping on her jacket, she mumbles something about coffee and heads to the kitchen. A minute later, she's back, thermos gripped in one hand and a banana in the other.

"Sorry, I didn't sleep well last night," she murmurs, cocking her head to the side. "You look like you didn't either."

"I didn't," I reply curtly, not wanting to discuss it. "Are you ready?"

She lifts her coffee as if to silently say *let's go*.

Opening a portal, I take her to our training area in the woods. I set down the backpack with our waters and snacks and give her a few minutes to eat her banana and drink some coffee. I've already had two cups this morning while watching the sunrise in the garden, or I'd probably be out of it myself.

"Want to talk about it?" I ask softly.

"Nothing to talk about really. I kept dreaming about the vision I had when I used the blood magic. Nothing like getting stabbed over and over to make you scared to fall asleep," she replies darkly, her hand absently rubbing a spot on her chest. "Strangely, the vision is changing." She frowns.

That's weird. I make a note to text Astor later and see if this is normal. I don't remember his visions changing after the ritual. "Are you good to train?"

She nods her head in agreement and finishes her coffee. "Okay, let's do this." Dropping the thermos beside the backpack, she waits for me to give her instructions.

"When we were on the battlefield, looking for Garrett, I felt something happening to me. Not only could I feel you, but I could sense every single one of my men. Their...essence, I think. Ever since I met you, I've felt you, but it was the first time I've ever felt others. I'd like to experiment with it today, if you don't mind?" I pause and wait for her to answer.

She taps a finger to her mouth. "I've been thinking about it too. I know Solandis' sister, the queen, can feel the Fae. She even knows which ones are light Fae versus dark Fae. As a prince, maybe this is an inherited power?"

"Exactly," I reply, relieved to hear my thoughts echoed. "My father can do the same. What if I'm getting a new power? If I can recognize elves, maybe I can confirm whether or not you are Elven. I'm not sure where to start, but I was able to track Garrett once everyone touched me." I sit down cross-legged on the ground and motion for her to do the same across from me.

Once she's seated, I raise my hands and wait until she does

as well, then I lace my fingers through hers. Sparks zing between our joined hands, and we both take deep calming breaths while we wait for it to settle down. When it's more of a constant hum instead of a live wire, we're ready.

"I'm going to close my eyes and see if I can feel you," I tell her.

"Okay."

My eyes drift closed, and I feel her instantly, physically of course, but also something else inside of her calls to me. I find a golden ball of power surrounding her soul, but it doesn't feel familiar, and I realize it must be her witch power. But no matter where I search, I don't find any other source of power.

Opening my eyes, I find her staring at me anxiously. "I don't know. When we were searching for Garrett, I could feel something inside of you and the others. I can feel you, but I can't recognize anything Elven."

Her shoulders drop. Then she raises her head, her eyes shining with excitement. "What if I use my new power to call the water to me? Maybe it needs to be active before you can feel it?"

"It's worth a try," I muse, then close my eyes. After finding her, I wait for the water to connect, and when it does, I feel its essence too. "I can feel you and the water connected to you, but that's it."

When I open my eyes, I see the water above her hand.

"Okay. Let's think about this for a second. When we were on the battlefield, I was trying to find Garrett, and you touched me. Suddenly, I could focus better. Then each one of my men touched me, and I could feel them individually and their power too..." I pause and think about it for a second. "What if I need to be using my power first?" I could call my father and ask him, but he's been angry with me since the battle. "We'll try one more thing. If it doesn't work, I'll wait and call an old tutor. We can always switch and train your power the rest of the day."

"Sounds good." Agreeing, she lets go of my hand.

She stretches, and I cough to hide my groan. The leggings and sports bra she's wearing for training are very formfitting, perfectly showing off her athletic body. Ever since I held her on the battlefield, I constantly feel the imprint of her body against mine. Dreams of the mountain crushing me and my men aren't the only reason I'm not sleeping these days.

Turning around, I adjust myself and head toward the pond. Raising my hands, I turn them palms out toward the water. "Ready?" I wait until she steps up beside me and lays her hand on my back. The smell of honeysuckle, strawberries, and coffee drifts up, and I take a deep breath in appreciation. I flick a hand, raising the water twenty feet in the air, and close my eyes. Then I feel it—her power channeling into me, supporting my power. Unlike my men, her power is faint, only a small stream.

"I can feel your power," I tell her excitedly. "I'm going to try and find its source." This time, I follow the stream of power from me to a small dark mass, entwined like a ball of yarn, inside of her. Instead of a solid core of power, individual ropes of power lie tangled up in each other. I pluck at a string to see if I can unravel it. After a bit of resistance, it finally loosens and unravels from the larger ball. I reach for another, then another, pulling and unwinding over and over again, determined to get to the core. My body starts to feel shaky, but I don't stop. Finally, I've got it completely unraveled. The ropes disappear, and in its place is a small green sphere. Elated, I marvel at it. This is what I felt the other day. It was stronger and larger in my men, but it's the same. My body sways, and I hear Arden cussing. Reluctantly, I follow her stream of power back to my own body. When I open my eyes, I smile and lower my hands, allowing the water to crash into the pond, just in time too. Darkness sweeps over me, and I'm out.

Water keeps dripping on my face, and when I reach up to wipe it away, several more drops hit me. I frown. *Am I sleeping outside?* I hear someone muttering and cussing and realize I'm not alone. Peeling open one eye, I blink to find myself lying on the ground beside the pond. Someone taps my cheek several times.

"What the fuck, Fallon? Come on. Don't make me drag your big carcass all the way through the portal to The Abbey. You probably weigh as much as Valerian, and I don't want to strain my back." She continues to spew a litany of words.

"I do not weigh as much as the damn dragon," I spit out, offended by the idea. I open the other eye. "He's a beast." I snap both eyes up and find her leaning over me with a worried expression on her face. Satisfaction thrums through me when I see beautiful, bright green eyes staring back at me, and my body sings with happiness. "We did it."

She stares at me with confusion. "Did you hit your head when you fell? I didn't think to check." She uses her fingers to map the back of my head. "I don't feel a lump. How many fingers am I holding up?" She waves four fingers in my face.

"Four, and I'm not hurt," I answer impatiently. I try to conjure a mirror, but shards of pain slice through my head and I groan. Burnout, something I haven't experienced since I was a child. "Okay, maybe I'm a little hurt. We need a mirror."

With a snap of her fingers, I feel her witch power surge and a mirror sits in the palm of her hand. Without lifting my head, I carefully pick it up and turn it toward her. "Look in the mirror, Arden."

She rolls her eyes and gazes into it, then she stills, shock coursing through her at the sight of her bright green eyes.

Tears fill her eyes and spill over her cheeks. "I'm Elven? Really?"

"Yes. When I found your power, it was still bound and resembled a big ball of yarn. I picked up a strand and unwound it, then another and another. It took me a while to unravel, but once I did, I could see your Elven power," I explain. "It's pretty small right now, especially compared to your witch power, but it will grow as you learn more." I use my thumb to wipe the tears from her face. "Are you okay?"

"I'm part Elven," she repeats. "My father is Elven." Her hand trembles as she continues to hold the mirror up.

"I'm probably going to need you to go get Theron," I tell her. "I've never experienced burnout this bad, and it hurts to even move my head."

"It's fine. I was trying to get you to wake up and respond to me," she explains, waving a hand and returning the mirror to the ether. After scratching her left shoulder, she waves her fingers toward me. "Let me see if I can get rid of your headache, then I'll use a levitating spell to get you through the portal and back to The Abbey. I'll even tuck you into bed."

I huff. "Now I understand why Valerian's always pulling his hair out."

She laughs and leans over to place her hands on my head.

When I feel her chest press into mine, I groan. *Now I understand why Valerian's always smiling too.*

She raises up and smooths a hand over my hair. "Feel better?" she asks. When I confirm, she smiles. Leaning down, she places a soft kiss on my lips. "Thank you, Fallon. You don't know what it means to finally know what I am—witch and Elven. And I know I'll one day find my father, all because of you." She stands, and I feel myself rising in the air. "Now let's go home."

CHAPTER
TWENTY-TWO

S lowly waking, I hear someone breathing to my right, but I don't open my eyes. Using my magic, I scan the room and come to rest on the person beside the bed. It's Arden, but what is she doing in here? The last thing I remember is her levitating me back through the portal to The Abbey. I open my eyes to find my room dark and glance at the clock, which reads four a.m. *I slept twelve hours?*

Confused, I slide my gaze over to Arden. She's slumped down in an upholstered chair next to the bed, a blanket covering her. I stretch and groan softly. My body is still sore from the burnout yesterday. She stirs and opens her eyes.

"Hi," she says sleepily. "How are you feeling?"

"Sore, but I'll recover. Did you sleep here all night?" I'm shocked I'm even asking this question. I don't think I've ever

169

had anyone stay up with me all night. Not even my nannies when I was little. Certainly, never my father.

She ducks her head and plays with the edge of the blanket. "It's fine. Callyx used to come home injured, and he didn't want Solandis to know. So I'd stay up with him. I didn't know what to do for burnout, though. I asked Theron, and he said to let you sleep. When do you think your magic will come back?"

"It's already coming back, but it will take a couple of days to reach a hundred percent," I murmur. She mumbles something and snuggles down into the blanket. There's no way she's comfortable in that chair. I slide out of bed and pick her up.

"What are you doing? I can walk back to my room," she assures me.

After sleeping for twelve hours, I know I'm not getting any more sleep. I place her in the spot where I was sleeping and pull the covers up over her. She stares up at me from my bed, with her tousled hair and sweet smile, and the temptation proves to be too much. Groaning, I lean down and capture her lips with mine, but when my lips touch hers, I know one kiss isn't going to be enough. Gripping her head between my hands, I kiss her over and over, my passion rising with each stroke of my tongue. Feeling her curves against my chest, my hands twitch with the need to explore every inch of her, but I rein in my desire.

When her passion meets mine, I hear her moan and she dives into me, stoking the fire even further and testing my control. With each deep kiss, I memorize the feel of her lips against mine and the taste of her passion, but I hold tightly to my control. She moves restlessly in the bed, and I pull back. When I look down, her swollen lips make me smile with satisfaction, but the dark circles under her eyes reinforces my decision.

"I'd love to stay here kissing you, but I know you've been up all night. So I'm going to work out..." I pause and mentally add a cold shower to my list. "Then I'll have coffee in the garden and watch the sunrise. If you get up later, come join me."

She smiles and snuggles down into the bed, and within seconds, she's asleep. I place a soft kiss on her forehead and head out.

I'M DRINKING coffee in the garden and watching the sunrise when I hear the elevator doors open. I grin and check over my shoulder, only to encounter Theron's violet eyes, not the bright green ones I expected. My smile drops.

"Expecting someone else, were we?" Theron jeers softly. "My company used to be good enough for you, but I've been replaced by a delectable witch who I'm pretty sure has put a spell on us all."

Chuckling, I lift my hand and point to the table next to me, where two mugs sit—one for Arden and one for the insufferable Fae next to me. "I believe that's your mug, correct?"

He strolls over and pours a cup of coffee and grabs the chair next to me. Propping his elegant, polished shoes on the railing, he stares out at the sunrise with me.

"I offered to stay with you or to take shifts, but she refused. Said it was the least she could do after you helped her discover her Elven heritage. Honestly, though, I could see more in her expression." He takes a sip of coffee and sighs. "Her eyes shocked me yesterday, even though we all felt she had to be

Fae or Elven. I'd gotten so used to her hazel ones, it was almost like looking at another person."

I also take a sip and glance over at one of my oldest friends. "Are you upset to find she's Elven?" I cautiously ask.

"No, I guess it's marginally better than some of the alternatives," he jokes, making me snort. "It might make it easier to find her father too. And she seemed content yesterday, as if knowing her heritage helped ease some of her fears." He shares a smile with me. "Where is she now?"

"I left her sleeping in my bed." My voice is a tiny bit smug when I reply. "She looked pretty damn good in it."

He groans and finishes his coffee. "I can only imagine, you bastard. I'm going to get some paperwork done. Why don't we take her to dinner tonight?"

"That sounds good. The Italian place on Broadway? Café Nonna's?" I suggest. He waves a hand in agreement and walks off. I glance at my watch. I've got about ten minutes before I have to head down and call my father. I relax back in my chair and think about the woman in my bed.

Ten minutes later, I'm on the phone with my father, barely holding on to my patience.

"My sources haven't been able to find anything on the assassination attempts, but the only forces able to withstand pressure from me are Fae, demon, or those dark Elven bastards. It's probably them. You know they don't give a damn who they kill," he snarls.

My own fists clench. This is the single point on which my father and I agree wholeheartedly. Our hatred for the dark elves, especially the royal fuckers leading them, is absolute. They killed my mother for consorting with my father and left her in the land between our two kingdoms.

Given our recent assistance with the battle in the Underworld, Lucifer's got his own men searching for any demon with insider knowledge of Arden's assassination attempts and the Primary behind them.

We have to hope Solandis can make some inquiries with the Fae, and Theron too, but I'm not sure how we will reach the dark elves. Maybe Cormal might have an idea, since he seems to have contacts on both sides. Honestly, his contacts rival my father's in some instances, and in the bowels of criminal society, his are probably better.

I don't mention the Primary to my father. It would be too difficult to explain over the phone, and the code name makes it even more difficult. Plus, I'm not sure he would be able to keep the information to himself. He's been...off lately.

"What's with this girl?" my father asks, inserting the question smoothly into the conversation, as if he could care less. "You seem to be quite taken with this witch. She's not your mate, is she?"

I ponder the question for a second. "She's not only a witch, she's Elven." I pause to let it percolate in his brain. "I don't know if she's my mate. She's Valerian's mate, and the rest of us are trying to figure it out. How do I know if she's my mate? How did you know my mother was your mate?"

His voice gruff, he replies, "You just know. I can't explain it. I've got to go. Bring her home for me to meet soon. That's an order, Fallon." He hangs up.

I exhale loudly. Conversations with him are always difficult, but he seemed worse today. I hoped he would find something, but I guess even he has his limits. My biggest concern is his order to bring her home. He never wants to meet my friends, which tells me he's worried she's my mate.

LATER IN THE EVENING, I'm standing in the lobby with Theron while we wait for Arden to come down. I tug on the collar of my shirt and straighten the sleeves on my jacket. How Theron wears these things day in and day out, I'll never know. A boa constrictor would feel less restrictive.

"Stop tugging on the suit," Theron demands. "Did you find out anything new from your father on the assassinations?"

I repeat our conversation to Theron. "Something felt off with him today, and he seemed inordinately interested in Arden." I move my head side to side to crack my neck.

He stiffens. "Why do you think he wants to meet her?" I can see his brain running through the possibilities. "You know he's strutted every light Elven female in front of you since the day you were born, and you never found your mate. Maybe he's worried she will ruin his grand plans."

I want to argue with him, but it's futile because I agree. "I'll handle him."

The elevator doors open, and Arden steps out in a short black dress, her long legs on display and her feet encased in strappy silver heels. Easily as tall as Theron, she strides confidently toward us like an Amazonian warrior. She's magnificent. When she stops in front of us, I get a whiff of her scent, but instead of her usual honeysuckle and strawberries, she's switched it out for something more decadent. Maybe champagne and strawberries? My eyes drop to her lips, and I silently groan, wishing it was just the two of us.

"Ready to go?" Theron asks huskily, stepping in front of me to hold his arm out for Arden, which she takes as if she's done it a thousand times. "I hope Italian is okay?"

If she'd said no, he would've whipped out his phone and made another reservation in a heartbeat. I snort, and she gives me a puzzled glance.

"I love Italian," she assures him. "You both look so incredible, I'll be the envy of every woman tonight." She laughs lightly. "Good thing I'm a witch."

My eyebrows raise, and I roar with laughter. She just subtly threatened to take care of any threats from other women. I almost wish a woman would be brave enough to flirt with us so I could see her in action.

Theron's eyes are smiling, but he gives us a mock frown. "This is a proper restaurant. Both of you heathens need to restrain yourselves. Now, I don't want to be late. Let's go." He lifts an eyebrow toward me. "Are you driving? My car won't fit both of you." Ha, as if I'd let him drive Arden and leave me here.

"Already pulled it up to the front of the garage," I answer smugly. His mouth compresses into a thin line. He hates when I outmaneuver him. "Arden rides up front."

We head to the luxury SUV idling in the garage. Theron escorts her to the passenger side and assists her into the vehicle, while I slide into the driver's side. I glance over Arden's head, raising my eyebrows, and he smirks back at me. Damn, he's upped his game.

We're pulling out of the garage when Arden suddenly twists to the side. A wolf stands at the entrance to the alley beside the garage. "I swear it's the same wolf who followed us home from Witchwood." She turns to Theron. "Have you found anything more about their involvement in this whole mess? It doesn't seem to fit with everything else going on."

Theron pulls up his phone and snaps a picture. "I heard back from several of the pack alphas and each one swore none of their wolves had been sent to watch us, but I'm still waiting on a few to get back to me." He taps quickly on his phone. "I'll send them another message reminding them who is asking."

"It doesn't make sense. Unlike other supernaturals, the shifters, especially the wolves, rarely involve themselves in the politics or wars of others. They tend to keep to themselves," she says, her hands tapping rapidly on the seat as she thinks about the possibilities.

I reach out, taking her hand, and the familiar electricity courses between us. "Let's put it aside for tonight. We'll put more pressure on the wolves tomorrow and figure it out. Don't worry." My thumb caresses the back of her hand, and she relaxes.

"If you can spare some time from training tomorrow, I'd like to start working through the rest of the files from Witchwood. Astor gave me a list of the ones that need to be scanned. If you can write a spell to get them in the system, I can start searching through the computer for specific correspondence in the period before and after the massacre," Theron says absentmindedly, his gaze on his phone. He's in full planning mode right now.

Arden swivels her head around to glance at him. She replies, "Of course, that's a great idea. We need to get the name of the matriarch and start scouting locations. Although I haven't heard from Valerian on whether he's been successful with getting me entry into the kingdom."

"We should be ready to go when he gives the green light," Theron states. "We likely won't get a second chance."

I pull up to the valet and hand him the keys. Theron is already at Arden's door, having stepped in front of the doorman to prevent him from assisting her out of the vehicle. I give a low laugh, but I agree. I don't like the idea of other men touching her either. Stepping up to her right, we escort her into the restaurant.

The hostess leads us to a private table in the back. I survey the entry and exit points and tilt my head toward Theron. He discreetly points to the additional security he hired for the evening. It's reassuring to have backup, but I don't relax. We still haven't figured out how the assassins keep finding her.

When Astor and I took her to the seaside restaurant, he laid a false trail away from The Abbey before we ever left and maintained a shield around us the whole time.

Arden lays her hand on top of mine. "Relax. We still have to live our lives. Besides, I created a shield around the restaurant when we arrived. It will provide us with advance warning if anyone tries to break through it." She turns and picks up her menu.

Theron's eyes crinkle with amusement and admiration. She thinks like a warrior. None of us relax, but we can at least pretend for a little while.

The server places our bottle of wine on the table. Theron sniffs, tastes, and finally gives a sharp nod of approval. The server pours us each a glass.

"Mmm, this is so good," Arden states after taking a sip. "So tell me, how did you two meet?"

I glance at Theron and he shrugs, but his fingers tap restlessly on the table. She reaches over and laces her fingers through his. "You don't have to tell me."

Before I can open my mouth, Theron takes over. "We met at the Gathering of the Light. As you know, the previous winner crowns the next. I'd won it the previous time, and it was required I show up and do my duty. What nobody realized was how far I'd gone downhill in the hundred years since I won. I was a complete wastrel. After arriving at the ceremony, still reeking of alcohol from the previous night, I stumbled my way up the stairs and placed the crown on Fallon's head. When I started to sway, he put his arm around me and proceeded to hold me up through the entire ceremony. After it was over, he invited me out and plied me with more drink until I spilled my sob story, then the bastard decided to save me. He kidnapped me, sobered me up, and told me I should be using my resources to save others instead of wasting them. It took him about a month to convince me, but he's damn persuasive when he wants to be. I finally gave in just to shut him up." He lifts his glass in a silent toast to me. "He's probably the best damn person I know."

Arden's shocked, but she quickly recovers. "I can't imagine what would be bad enough to make you choose to be a wastrel, but I'm damn glad you chose to stop being one." She takes a sip of wine. "And you're all the best of the best as far as I'm concerned."

Theron's face flashes with a look of relief, and it's my turn to send him a smug smile. She's right—it was his choice all along, and I only pushed him to make a decision. The way she handled it was brilliant and exactly what he needed to hear.

She raises her glass. "To three of the best champions of the Gathering of the Light."

Startled, I consider her words. "Three?"

"Of course," she replies, a touch arrogantly. "Solandis wouldn't have it any other way." She laughs. "Seriously, it was the toughest physical thing I've ever had to endure. I didn't think I'd make it to the end. The only thing that kept me going was having to tell Solandis I lost. Thankfully, I won and got this nifty warning tattoo as my prize."

"Ahh, the work of Rivan," I murmur and raise my glass to clink theirs. "To the three champions."

"Maybe we should make Daire and Astor enter and win," she says mischievously. "Remind me to ask them when this is all over."

Theron and I laugh. "Daire would probably do it, but not Astor."

"Care to wager?" she challenges confidently.

We stare at her sparkling green eyes and beautiful face and shake our heads no. We're not stupid.

The rest of the evening goes by surprisingly fast, and before I know it, we're walking back into The Abbey. It was like this the first time too. It doesn't seem to matter whether it's Astor or Theron with me—she's equally relaxed with all of us. The only tension I've seen lately is between her and Astor, but I'm hoping they find their way through it.

She reaches up and pulls Theron into her arms for a hug, thanking him for the dinner. Seeing the two of them together, I can't help but move closer. My eyes meet his, and I realize he's balanced on a knife-edge, his need for her driving him crazy. Gripping her waist, he pushes her back toward me, and I inhale sharply when I feel her soft curves line up with my body.

He brings her hand up to his mouth and places a kiss in the center of her palm. Dropping his hands to her waist, he turns her around to face me. When his eyes meet mine, they're demanding, and I can't help but shake my head at his willingness to be tortured.

"Thank you for dinner," Arden murmurs.

Reaching up, she places a soft kiss on my lips, but instead of letting it end, I tilt my head and capture her soft lips with mine. Nibbling a little, I wait until she relaxes, then I deepen the kiss, stroking her tongue with mine until I hear her moan.

Theron takes a half step back, but she places her hands on top of his, holding him behind her. I start to pull back, but she steps forward and pulls my tongue into her mouth, deepening our kiss while simultaneously pulling Theron in tighter against her. The three of us are locked together, her softness teasing both of us, each shift in movement taking me to the edge of my control.

A minute or three later, she draws back and pulls away from us. She glances from Theron to me and back. "Thank you both for an incredible kiss," she rasps. Smoothing her hands down her dress, she backs away until she's in the elevator. "Goodnight."

When the doors close, I drawl, "She's one hell of a kisser." I look over at Theron, my eyes simultaneously condemning him for being a fool and encouraging him to stop holding so tightly to his control. "Goodnight." Whistling, I stroll off, searching for a drink to take the edge off.

CHAPTER

TWENTY-THREE

ARDEN

I drag myself into Astor's lab the next morning, where Theron waits for me. The nightly dreams are killing me. I spent all last night fighting dragons and having vivid memories of Valerian's black beast and a brown one. I must be more worried than I realized about this upcoming visit.

Entering the lab, I find it empty. Astor could only remember which papers had been scanned based on where they lay in his lab, so we need to recreate his piles again. With a spell, I bring the files back to the same spot. Once they're in place, Theron points to each pile and a new spell scans them all into the computer. Once they're done, I pack them away in the same boxes they arrived in and close the lids.

Theron is at the computer, a paper in one hand and mouse in the other, following the instructions Astor wrote down. A program comes up with a search box, waiting for his command.

"This is going to take a while," he states quietly. "Why don't I call you when I get the search results narrowed down to a more consumable level?" He's typing various terms into the search box and doesn't look up.

I reach back and scratch the back of my shoulder. "Okay, if you're sure?" I wait until he agrees. "I have something I've been wanting to do for a while. Text when you need me."

Excitedly, I head toward Daire's room. This is the perfect time to pull together my surprise. When I enter the dark, dimly lit room, I shudder. Turning on all the lights so I can see, I eye the black walls with distaste. I know where I'm starting first.

I'm going to paint the walls an edgy blue color called Stunning, which I ordered from a paint store nearby. It's the perfect medium blue, not too dark or light, but modern and luxurious feeling. It reminded me of Daire when I saw it, and it will make a good base for the other blues and greys I intend to add to the room. I wave my hand to get the paintbrushes started and move on to the couch.

I've hidden the new furniture in an empty room near mine, so it's pretty easy to swap everything out. The hideous black leather couch is the first to go, and I replace it with a long, soft grey couch perfect for lounging. Hopefully, it will fit his tall body. I want him to feel like he can take a nap on it, or just sit and relax. Throwing a couple of pillows in various shades of blue, grey, and white on it, along with a soft blanket, I step back and smile.

I replace the rest of the black furniture with new furniture in a light grey wood. The bed gets made up in pillows and bedding similar to the colors on the couch. All his clothes and stuff are placed back in the drawers. And while I'm tempted, I don't snoop. Although, I did accidentally find pictures of his mom, dad, and Danica stored away in his previous nightstand. With new chrome frames, I place them where he can see them before he goes to sleep.

Last, I remove all the black rugs and replace them with lighter grey ones. Thankfully, the wood flooring underneath is gorgeous.

My phone pings. It's Theron. Stepping to the door, I study the room for anything I might have missed. The walls are bare, but I think art is too personal to choose for someone else. The room is sophisticated and luxurious, but inviting and sexy too. It says Daire to me, and if he doesn't like it, it's easy to change. Only takes an afternoon.

My phone pings again before I can get to the lab. I roll my eyes but don't reply, since I'm almost there anyway.

"I'm here, so stop texting me," I say exasperatedly, waving the blank parchment and my mother's letter in the air. "I stopped to get these. Maybe it will deign to speak to me this time."

Theron peers at the clock on the wall. "I texted you twenty minutes ago. Where have you been?"

"Working on a surprise for Daire," I retort. "And I'm sorry I'm late." I walk over and peek at the screen on the computer. "Agnes? You think she's the matriarch?"

He turns around to face the monitor. "A surprise for Daire, huh? He doesn't like surprises. Maybe you should have asked him first?" he comments.

I bite my lip. Maybe I should have, but honestly, I couldn't stand going in his room and I don't think he could either. "If he doesn't like it, I'll help him change it. Now please tell me what you found?"

He types a few commands into the computer and shows

me the results. "Once we had our discussion the other day, I decided to start my search during the time period of the massacre. Not surprisingly, there's no correspondence for the years immediately prior or following the incident, so I went back ten years. Once I had a starting point, I read each document. They were all written by the same person—Agnes MacAllister. Once I had a name, I pulled all correspondence related to her and found her first letter to the council, which was sent about forty years prior. She identified herself as the matriarch of the MacAllisters and head of bloodline seven, and asked to be instated to her seat on the council. I'm guessing they agreed, because there are council meeting notes with her name on them."

My fingers are tingling with excitement. To be this close to the next step feels unreal. Holding the blank parchment up in front of us, I query, "Is Agnes MacAllister the matriarch?"

No.

Frustrated, I think about it for a second, then realize I should have been more specific. "Was Agnes MacAllister the matriarch during the time of the MacAllister massacre?" I hold my breath and wait for it to answer.

Yes.

One more answer, please, pretty please. "Did Agnes MacAllister live in the Kingdom of Dragons?" Crossing my fingers, I hold my breath again.

Yes.

"Yes!" I shout and begin dancing around the room. "We have a verified lead." I turn to smile at Theron and notice he's on his phone. Grabbing it out of his hand, I continue dancing around the room. "Dance with me!"

Theron snags me around the waist and pulls my body flush with his. He stares down at me, and slowly, his impassive face stretches into a...smile. A real, full-blown smile. My heart literally stops beating in my chest. He's smiling. For me. Stunned, my hand reaches up and traces his smile. *Absolute perfection.* When it starts to fade, I shake my head no. "Wait, I haven't captured this moment yet." He starts smiling again, and I reach up and snap his photo quickly. I smile. "Thank you. I'll always have this photo to remember this moment."

"We don't know if we can find her yet," he reminds me.

"What? No...I wanted a photo to remember the first time you smiled at me." I cup his jaw, even though the smile is gone now. "I was speechless there for a second."

Pink tinges his features while his gaze lingers on my lips, and time stops for a brief moment. He slides his hand up the side of my body and down the arm hanging at my side, making me arch into him, and he inhales sharply. I feel his hand caressing mine, then he leans down and drops a kiss on the corner of my mouth before he steps back.

Clearing his throat, he brings his phone up and shoots off a text to someone. He must have grabbed it from my hand when I thought he was caressing it.

"Seriously? I thought—" I stop talking. Damn man blows hot and cold. I stare at the phone in his hand, not wanting to see his impassive face. "Never mind. I'll go pack."

Putting the phone in his pocket, he pulls my body back into his. "Arden, stop. I don't want something rushed when we're up against the clock. I want every minute I can steal. So when you're ready for everything I have to give you, tell me, give me the words, but be very sure, Arden. The part of me that yearns for you isn't the icy, controlled version standing in front of you. It's consuming and raw, and once unleashed, I won't be denied. I'll claim every single inch of you." Even his voice is full of hunger. "Maybe we have time for a small demonstration."

And with those words, he lays waste to my lips. His kiss is consuming and raw and powerful, full of everything he stated and more. He opens himself up and gives me a glimpse of the passion he's holding for me, and I fall into it, into him, surrendering myself.

Even though I know he's hanging onto his control by a thread, I want him to know he's not alone. Weeks of tantalizing torture and brief moments have been driving me crazy, and I meet his kiss with the need clamoring inside of me, claiming him in return.

Groaning, he pulls back and rubs a thumb over my lips. His violet eyes are dark and stormy, like he's in the thick of battle. For me. Swallowing, I read the absolute truth in his eyes and know it's only a matter of time.

"You'll have your words, Theron," I assure him, my voice husky with desire. "Soon. Even if we have to steal away to a secret place where the world can't find us." His eyes light up with my words. "I'm going to get packed." Leaving him in the lab, I manage to walk to my room before sliding to the floor in a puddle.

"Damn, he packs a punch."

Valerian calls Theron about an hour later. The council approved our visit, or I should say *my* visit. They are not aware Valerian and I are mates, only that a witch is searching for her history. Valerian and a dragon elder will meet us in the morning, then we have two days to find what we need, and that's it.

I'm standing at the foot of my bed with my bag open, wondering what I should pack. I decide to pack workout clothes that can double as an outfit. Tennis shoes and hiking boots. Jeans and a few sweaters. Plus, the usual essentials. I lay the parchment paper and my mother's letter beside the bag, so I don't forget it. Skimming the room, I spot the Killian blades and pick them up to put them in there too. When my hand closes around them, they...sigh. They feel different than they did before, and I wonder if it's because my Elven power is unlocked. Maybe when we look for my father, I can research the blades. Going back to packing, I try to decide which final things to add. Toiletries, of course. I wonder if I should pack my armor.

Someone knocks on the door. "Come in," I call out. Hearing the door open, I turn around and see Meri standing there. Squealing, I drag her into a big hug. With the battle and my Elven training, I hadn't seen in her a couple of weeks.

"Ommph, mfmmf," she mumbles. "Trying to breathe here."

I apologize and release her with a laugh. "I forget how tiny you are sometimes. What are you doing here?"

"Well, when the mountain won't come to you..." she begins, but when she sees my eyes, she freaks out. "What the hell? You're Elven? Tell me you're wearing contacts. I wanted you to be Fae like me," she wails.

I hold up a hand. "Stop, no mountains." When she frowns, I explain about the battle and the mountain coming down on Fallon and his men. "It was frightening to watch them all disappear in one fell swoop. I can't even hear the word without wanting to throw up."

"You were in battle, in the Underworld, and you didn't think to call me?" she yells. "What if something had happened to you? I might not have active powers, but I'm sure I could have stolen some from somebody. And I know how to fight, ask Callyx. I'm kind of pissed and jealous right now. It's a weird combination. Tell me more, and maybe I'll forgive you."

I tell her almost everything, including the part about the Primary, although I don't tell her the Primary is behind my assassination attempts. It's worth the risk. She seems to have a huge network of people, maybe even some dodgy ones from her past, who might have some knowledge to share.

Her eyes are wide and worried. "I may have someone I can ask," she offers hesitantly. "She's dark and will probably try to take advantage of the situation, but she also knows a hell of a lot more than what's in the history books. Still want me to check with her?"

My gut churns, but I have a feeling only those vested in the outcome are going to know the answers. "Go ahead. Can you tell your friend you overheard the cadre talking about the battle and wondered what Alain meant? I'm sure most of the Underworld has heard about it since I broadcasted Alain and Lucifer's fight to the entire battlefield. It's not a secret or anything."

"Good idea," she says thoughtfully. "You're not running off to another battle, are you? If so, you better take me with you." When she glances at my eyes, she whimpers. "And Elven, seriously?"

Rolling my eyes at her demanding tone, I explain the rest. "Fallon helped unlock my Elven powers when we were training together." I don't want to share his new power with anyone. It's not my secret to tell. "And I'm not going to battle. We found the MacAllisters, and I'm going to go and see what I can dig up. Hopefully, there's a paper or something I can show to Caro to prove my heritage. If not, I'll have to fight for her seat on the council," I reply. "But the best part is I get to see Valerian's home, since it's in the Kingdom of Dragons."

She trails a hand on the edge of the bag. "That's wonderful!

I hope you find the proof you need. But if you find something, promise me you'll get Theron to video Caro's expression when you show it to her. Deal?"

I laugh. "Maybe." Looking around, I realize almost everything's in the bag.

She twirls her finger in the air. "Now, let's get back to the moment when Daire sprouted wings and saved you. I think that's the best part of the whole damn thing. Who knew the First Vampire had wings? And silky black ones too. I bet it shocked everyone."

I hold up a finger. "One second, I've got to get my makeup and armor." Moving into the bathroom, I grab my toiletries and the Fae armor I handwashed and hung on the rod earlier in the week.

When I come back in the bedroom, I see Meri snapping pictures of the parchment and my mother's letter. Frowning, I quietly step back into the bathroom. Standing still, my mind races. Why would she want a picture of those items? I'm not worried about the parchment, since it's blank, but I try to remember what I told her about my mother's letter. Not everything, I'm sure.

"Did you get lost in there? Fall in the toilet? Portal out to another battle and leave me here?" She throws question after question at me.

I step out of the bathroom. "Sorry, I couldn't find my extra bottle of shampoo." Stuffing the toiletries into the bag, I turn to her. "Everything's okay with you, right? You know if you need anything, you can come to me."

"Promise?" she says, a tinge of desperation in her voice, then laughs and waves it off.

"I promise," I reply.

It's getting late, so I close up the bag and give her a hug

goodbye. My gut says she's in trouble, but I can't help her if she won't ask for it.

Lying in bed later, I pick up the phone and complete my nightly ritual of sending a text to Astor. *Theron says you're late all the time.* He'll probably laugh at this one since he's on time almost as obsessively as Theron. I wonder if the lies are working.

CHAPTER
TWENTY-FOUR

ARDEN

Early the next morning, I head down to the lobby in zombie mode again, where Theron is already waiting, of course. I drop my bag at his feet and keep strolling. I'm not going anywhere until I get coffee and breakfast. I hear him call my name, but I refuse to answer. My phone says I have five minutes, and I need every single one of them.

When I walk back to the lobby four and a half minutes later, Fallon's standing with Theron. "Thirty seconds to spare," I report cheerfully. Taking a sip of my coffee, I let out an appreciative moan. "Well, let's go."

Fallon grins and shakes his head at my antics. "One day, you're going to push him too far." He pulls me into his side and picks up my bag. "Theron's going first. You're going through with me, just in case someone's waiting for us."

I wink at Theron, feeling confident this morning after our

talk yesterday. He huffs and steps into the portal. A second later, a ping sounds on Fallon's phone. "All right" —he grabs my hand— "we're up."

On the other side, I'm surprised to see several people waiting for us. Besides Theron, Daire, Astor, and Valerian, a couple of large men, likely dragons, also stand nearby. They seem young by dragon standards but it's hard to tell, and they're dressed casually. I skip over them for now and focus on the grey-haired woman with piercing blue eyes, standing regally beside them. This must be the elder dragon. It's always such a shock to see a supernatural with grey hair, because it means they are positively ancient. Too bad it's not polite to ask. She's the oldest supernatural I've ever seen in person.

The atmosphere is tense while she stands there studying me. Instead of giving my usual polite smile, I bow my head in deference to her status and keep my face serious. I want her to know how much this search means to me. It's not a lark. "Hello, I'm Arden. Thank you for taking the time out of your day to show us the way. Heritage is important, and when it's hidden from you, it becomes more precious than gold. I'm here to find out who I am."

Her eyes glint with appreciation. "Fine manners for a witch. And you're right—heritage is important. Yours more than most. I'm Glynnis. Agnes told me you would show up one day. I was starting to wonder if she'd lost her marbles, but I guess I'll have to apologize to my old friend when I see her." She cackles and taps the two men on the arms. "She's not going to attack me. Go stand on the hill or something." As if waiting for her signal, their eyes flicker from her to me to Valerian, then they leave to stand on a nearby hill.

Raising my eyebrows, I shoot her a mischievous smile. "You must teach me that trick. I usually have to resort to violence to make stubborn dragons listen." I wink at Valerian, and instead of laughing, he tenses. *Right, I forgot, we barely know each other.* I want to roll my eyes. If it had been me, I'd have told the dragons we were mates. Hiding it only makes it worse, like it's wrong. I prefer to believe and trust in the Fates. They know a hell of a lot more than I do.

She gives a hearty laugh. "I can only imagine. Been like that since he was a boy. Come along. We've got a fair hike in front of us."

After putting on my hiking boots, we set off with the cadre and the two dragons following us. According to her, we're about ten miles away. I offer to open a portal, but she refuses, assuring me it's best to go in quietly. Good thing we all work out regularly, and I'm doubly glad Daire offered to carry my bag. I glance back at him and grin. He smiles in return.

It's an absolutely beautiful walk through craggy hills and deep green grass, with the occasional blue loch popping up every couple of miles or so. The air is so crisp and clean, I breathe in deeply every chance I get.

Glynnis is a talker, and the sheer amount of knowledge she's accumulated is astounding. She tells me stories about how the land used to be filled with MacAllisters and dragons. Equally powerful in their own way, they provided complementary services and protected each other. Few supernaturals dared to cross into the Kingdom of Dragons, which allowed the witches to live in relative peace here for a long time, and with such strong magic users living on their lands, the wars plaguing dragons for much of their history dwindled.

"Do you know what happened that day?" I ask tentatively, not wanting to bring up bad memories or break the peace between us.

She dips her chin in sadness and stares off in the distance. "Aye, it was terrible. I've never seen anything like it. First the old king goes mad, killing one of Agnes' daughters, her granddaughter, Moira, and everyone else in their immediate family. Then, in the middle of the night, magic crossed into our lands, seeking out every last MacAllister witch, including Agnes, and killed them all. The worst part of it was, we didn't even get a chance to bury them or remember them in any way. There were no bodies, no belongings. The magic erased every trace of them. In that moment, they ceased to exist."

Valerian had been listening intently. "Wait, why didn't I know? I never heard a word about the massacre. And who is Agnes? My father killed Moira's family."

She gazes up at him. "Most dragons only remember the death of her granddaughter Moira and the rest of the immediate family because your father and his men killed them, not magic. But the witches killed by the magic, almost nobody remembers them. Agnes gave me a charm a long time ago and made me promise to wear it for the rest of my life," she explains, pulling out a thin leather strap with a medallion on the end of it. "She said it was the only way to remember her. I thought it was a joke, until I realized very few could remember the MacAllisters, and only those given charms, like me." She studies me. "She knew what was coming, didn't she?"

"Yes, a seer told her," I explain, telling her about Gemma and her visions. "It's why I'm here today, to start piecing together the remnants of the past."

She stops and points at a nearby tree. "The rowan blooms here all year round. Agnes planted it to help me find the path. She used to say, 'The Rowan will seek the rowan. All you have to do is show her the way.' You'll find a set of steps at the base of the tree which will lead you down into a cave. A spell surrounds the cave and tree. Only a MacAllister can enter until you invite the others. I'm going to sit with my grandsons." She waves a hand to the two men who have been following us.

"They're fine-looking men, don't you think? You wouldn't be single, now would you?"

I hear several grumbles behind me. Ignoring them, I answer, "I thought witches and dragons were taboo?"

"There's some opposition, it's true. But you're not just a witch, are you?" She peers into my bright green eyes. "And if a dragon was lucky enough to find themselves a mate like you, they'd be a damn fool not to claim you. My grandsons are not stupid dragons."

I laugh, but honestly, I agree. "Thank you. I'm honored, but I'm also taken, sort of."

She shakes her head. "A woman should know without a shadow of a doubt when she's no longer single." Pivoting on her heel, she starts walking toward her grandsons but stops and stares at the cadre. "Damn fools, all of you. Especially you, boy." She jabs a finger in Valerian's direction and sighs. "I thought we'd finally landed ourselves a smart king. Guess not." Her grandsons come over and grab her by the arms, hurrying her away from us.

I laugh at her antics, but I'm the only one. They're all scowling, except Astor. He seems to be in deep thought. I decide to ignore them.

Walking toward the rowan, I feel the air change when I hit the spell marking the boundary. I take a step back. "Stop here. The spell covers a pretty large area. Glynnis said a MacAllister must enter the cave first, then I can invite you inside. I'll come back for you guys."

They protest loudly, but they know it's the only way. I step over the boundary and head to the base of the tree. When I get within a couple of feet, stairs appear, going down into a dark cave in the ground. Pausing, I create a sphere of witchfire in the palm of one hand, and in the other, I grip my sword. With a deep breath, I descend into the darkness. Cobwebs catch in my hair and on my skin, making me shiver. Blood and gore don't bother me, but bugs and spiders... I hate them.

When I get to the bottom, a torch sits in a holder by the entrance. I sheathe my sword and use regular fire to light it. Deciding to keep the ball of witchfire, I cautiously make my way forward. About ten feet into the first cave, a second cave appears. Where the first cave was small, dark, and narrow, this cave is significantly larger and taller. I find several torches along the wall, and with magic, I guide the fire from the first torch to the others, lighting them all. My eyes dart from corner to corner, but I don't see any threats. The air is musty and still, as if it hasn't been disturbed in a long time. Extinguishing the witchfire, I walk closer to the middle of the room.

The two caves seem natural, as if they've stood here since the dawn of time. Agnes didn't create them, but their location underground, hidden from all, was certainly ideal. Made of dark grey stone, the walls are smooth in places, indicating water ran through here eons ago, but they've been dry a long time, based on the amount of dirt on the floor.

The second cave feels more like a chamber. It's roughly a large circle, with rock benches lining the walls, where I assume witches sat for their ceremonies. Walking to the center, I find a pentagram engraved deeply into the floor, cut from the very rock itself.

You could probably fit thirty or forty witches around the outside of the circle and maybe another ten close to the pentagram. I wonder if there's a pentagram at Witchwood? I'd bet money on it. I'll have to ask Henry.

Loud shouts break into my thoughts. Hurrying back up the stairs, I pause at the threshold. "As a MacAllister, I invite the Imperium Cadre to enter." Buzzing pierces my skin for a second, then the spell clears. I pop up at the base of the tree and wave them over.

When we're all in the cave, I motion to the next. "There's a larger ceremonial chamber here, but I haven't found anything else yet."

Astor whistles and heads to the back.

I follow. We need a spell to reveal what's hidden, but which one? I hurry over to Daire. "Do you have my bag?"

He hands it over and I open it, then dig through until I find the parchment.

Holding it up, I cross my fingers, hoping this works because if not, I don't have any idea what to do next. "Are the MacAllister journals in this location?"

Yes.

"Do you have a reveal spell for the MacAllister journals?"

No.

Frustrated, I blow a hair out of my eyes. "What do I need to do to make the MacAllister journals reveal themselves to me?"

Use that which makes you unique.

"Use your blood," Astor murmurs, reading the parchment over my shoulder. He waves a hand toward the pentagram. "Place a few drops in the center."

I hand him the parchment and dig a Killian blade out of my bag. Walking to the center of the pentagram, I glance at Astor, and he confidently nods. I wince as I slice my palm. Closing my hand into a fist, I squeeze until blood drips through my fingers and onto the floor. I don't know how many drops are needed, but I don't want to have to do it again.

The blood is absorbed into the floor immediately, and a second later, the pentagram lights up and the air buzzes with magic. I try to step out of the circle, but I can't. Uneasy, I can only wait for the spell to activate. The cadre stands outside the circle, surrounding me, with tense expressions on their faces and their hands held loosely at their sides, ready for anything.

The wall on the far side of the chamber starts rolling

back, the rock grinding loudly against the floor and ceiling for several minutes until it finally stops. The minute the pentagram goes dark, Astor picks me up and carries me outside the circle. More hands reach over and pull me several feet away from the pentagram. Looking up into Daire's icy blue eyes, I notice his unease with the situation and give him a hug.

"I could do with a little less drama," I say, only half joking. "I'm guessing they're hiding more than a bunch of old journals."

Astor walks over to the recently revealed chamber and peers into it. "You would be right. Come see."

Daire refuses to let go of me, so together, we walk over to join Astor. At the entrance, we stop and stare at the contents in the hidden chamber. Gleaming wooden chests, about five feet wide and three feet tall, sit side by side, untouched by time or dirt, as if they were placed here only hours ago.

"There must be ten chests in here," I murmur, not wanting to break the quiet atmosphere. "I wonder what they contain."

"We don't have a lot of time before it's dark. We could scan through a few of them today and come back tomorrow?" Theron suggests, his practical nature and need for a plan taking over.

I'm already shaking my head no. "I'm not leaving until it's all out of here. Who knows if the spell activates only once? And with the barriers down, would I be able to recreate the spell to get them back up? It's too precarious." I glance at them. "We have two days, right? I suggest we send Glynnis and her grand-sons home, and camp out here until we've gone through every-thing. Then we load it up and send it back to The Abbey via a portal."

"I agree," Astor interjects. "This is old magic, and the spells are unique to this situation and this place. It's too unpredictable. We need to stay and get this done. It's probably our only shot." He smiles when I shoot him my silent thanks.

Theron grimaces, and Valerian closes his eyes in resignation.

Daire volunteers to get us supplies, water, and food to camp out, and Fallon offers to help him.

Theron and Astor discuss the best process to open and catalog every chest, then proceed to reorganize the space to make it the most efficient.

Walking over to Valerian, I squeeze his arm. "I'm sorry. I know you didn't want us to stay long, but we can't leave. Let's go talk to Glynnis."

He gives a long sigh and pulls me into his arms. "I'm beginning to believe I'm a stupid dragon, lass. I should have told them the truth and dealt with it upfront. Now we're stuck here, and I can only hope we get everything done and get out in time. After this, I'm going to change a few things around here, starting with the council. I've been holding off the changes for centuries, but it's time." He leans down and gives me a lingering kiss. "And I'm going to tell everyone you're mine. I've missed you so damn much. I feel like we haven't gotten to spend much time together lately."

"You'd better," I retort. "Or you're going to spend the next thousand years sleeping by yourself." My hand cups his jaw, and I run a thumb across the dark circles under his eyes. "And I missed you too."

He stares at me in horror and raises his hands. "I surrender." He gives me another kiss. "Let's go chat with Glynnis."

When we get outside, we notice it's almost dark. Glynnis and her grandsons meet us in the middle of the field. "I think Agnes managed to save a lot of the MacAllister history. Their story will be told and their history read." I grab her hand. "Without you, this would have all been lost to time and magic.

I can't thank you enough for wearing the medallion and showing me the way. Agnes truly had a best friend in you."

Tears roll down her face. "Maybe she can rest now, and I can remember the happier times we spent together." She looks around for the rest of our group. "Are you going to stay here?"

Valerian steps up. "We need to get everything out of the cave, but it's going to take us a couple of days. If you wouldn't mind holding off on your report to the council until we're done, I'd be grateful to you and your family." He waits for her to answer.

"Those damn busybodies? Hell, it would be a pleasure," she replies. "Are you ever going to do something about them?" Her grandsons try to drag her off, but she waves them away.

"Yes, ma'am," Valerian agrees wryly. "It's a great time for change."

She pulls me in for a hug. "Good. And you take care of this mate of yours."

"Yes, ma'am," Valerian repeats.

Valerian takes my elbow and pulls me to the side of the field while we watch Glynnis and her grandsons change into dragons and fly away.

"I like her," I state firmly. "You should put her on the council. I also like the deference her grandsons gave to you. Maybe they can join your guard." I leave him standing there, contemplating my words.

TWENTY-FIVE

ARDEN

Astor and Theron are waiting impatiently for me when I get back to the cave. I'd normally roll my eyes, but I'm eager to start opening the chests. They've dragged the first one out of the chamber, but they haven't opened it yet.

"I'm assuming this requires a MacAllister witch to open it," I state absentmindedly, my attention on the chest. "But I don't see a latch." Running my hands along the edges, I search for a latch but don't find one. Puzzled, I glance at Astor.

He gives me a grim smile. "More precisely, it requires your MacAllister blood to open it," he states. "From what I've observed, the MacAllisters used blood magic to secure this entire site. Every single spell. It's odd, since most witches abhor the practice, and yet the MacAllisters must have used it regularly to be advanced level practitioners. I wonder if this is why you have such a strong reaction to blood magic. I haven't quite figured it out yet, but my gut says the answers are here somewhere."

The last time I used blood magic, I couldn't get myself out of the vision. Fallon had to bring me out of the darkness. I'm not sure it's something I want to embrace. Besides, I have enough on my plate trying to learn how to use my new Elven powers.

Using the Killian blade again, I slice my hand and hold it over an old stone bowl Astor found in the corner. Hopefully, this will be enough for us to open all of the chests. After healing the cut, I take the bowl, dip my finger into the blood, and swipe it across the chest. With a hiss, the seal breaks and the top lifts up.

We crowd around the chest to see the contents. This one seems to be filled with journals. Theron and Astor pull a few out of the chest and notice different names on them. Astor starts reading the one in his hand, while Theron and I dig through the rest to find Agnes' journals.

"This one is from a matriarch named Cylla, who lived about two thousand years ago. The journal contains everything from her time period—spells, population of MacAllister witches, daily life, and the overall evolution of the witches. It's pretty fascinating, but given how much we found at Witchwood, not surprising. Witches seem to want to write everything down," Astor muses darkly.

We set up a system. I walk by and swipe my blood on the chest, Astor and Theron dig through it, and when done, Valerian moves it to the first cave. It's a tedious process, but necessary.

After the journals, we find several chests filled with heirlooms and jewelry. As I run my hands over the items, tears fill my eyes. All of these families are gone, and while their names and a few of their artifacts have been preserved, their personalities and individual stories have been lost forever, gone with the magic that took their lives.

"Astor, what do you think about the magic that killed and erased the MacAllisters? It doesn't sound like witch magic to me." I tap my finger on the chest while my thoughts spill out. "Do you think it's blood magic?"

"It would take too much from the castor to weave a blood spell of this magnitude," he replies, his eyes gleaming while he ponders the magical puzzle. "The magic killed hundreds of people, erased memories, made belongings and bodies disappear, and it did it all in one night. It would have taken more power than I could ever imagine. I wonder if it was one person or a hundred."

"That's an interesting thought," I remark, thinking about the tapestry at Witchwood. "If all the witches from the other six branches pulled their power together, would it be enough to cast several simultaneous spells? It's the only thing I can think might fit."

"Possibly, but the sheer organization and timing would have to be perfect," he says absentmindedly. "I think I've found something."

Hurrying over to the chest he's kneeling in front of, I notice a smaller chest placed within the larger one. On the top of this chest is a rowan tree. Using my blood, I swipe a finger over it. Expecting the hiss of the seal breaking, I'm confused when I don't hear anything.

"Try again," Astor suggests.

After adding the blood a second time, we wait, but still, nothing happens. Setting the bowl on the floor, I pass my hands over the edges of the chest. Nothing.

Theron suddenly reaches out and grabs my wrist. He holds it over the chest, and we hear a click. My mind picks up on his thoughts, and I turn my wrist over to look at the tattoo of the rowan tree I received the night of the placement ceremony. It wasn't only a tattoo to mark me as the Rowan, but also a key to opening this chest, which means this chest is important.

Excitedly, I lift the lid and find a treasure trove of unusual and familiar items. In the center of the chest lies a small black box. It's about four inches wide and four inches tall. When I open it, a dark grey stone sits on a blood-red silk cushion. Puzzled, I tentatively reach out a finger to touch the stone, but nothing happens. I hand it off to Astor to examine.

We hear a shuffling at the entrance to the cave, and we all pause. A minute later, Daire and Fallon come in with several backpacks and a chest of food and water. After setting it down, they cross over to where we're all huddled around this smaller chest.

"What have you found so far?" Daire asks quietly.

"Thanks for going to get supplies. We're making great progress. We've found matriarch journals from several eras, some heirlooms and jewelry, and a chest full of small painted portraits," I reply. "And this intriguing little chest which could only be opened with my rowan tattoo." My voice is high with excitement. "We're going through it now. The only thing I've pulled out of there so far is a stone." I motion for Astor to show them and go back to the chest.

A silver box catches my eye, and I pull it out next. Inside, I find a silver bowl and knife, both engraved with the name "MacAllister," a quill, and parchment paper. "It's a set of tools used for blood magic. I guess you were right, Astor. They must have practiced pretty heavily to have an expensive set like this one."

Below the silver box, I find a leather-bound journal with the name "Agnes MacAllister" engraved on the front. My hands tingle when I pick it up. This must be the journal I was meant to find. I want so badly to rip it open and start reading, but we need to get through the rest of these items and the remaining chests. I hand if off to Valerian this time, and he gives me a relieved smile. I know he was worried this was a wild goose chase.

I search through the chest, but it's the only journal. I know the parchment said, "Find the journals," but I don't see another one, and I don't think it was talking about the journals from the earlier eras.

My hands reach eagerly for the final item in the small chest. It's a huge, leather-bound grimoire with the name "MacAllister" embossed in gold on the top. I pull it out and set it in my lap. My trembling hands run over the soft leather and embossed name reverently. This is my heritage.

Forming a sphere of light above me, I open it. On the first page, there's a beautiful, painted illustration of a woman and a dragon. The rich colors and gold leaf tell their ancient story. The woman stands in the foreground, wearing simple clothing from an era long ago. Her long, blonde hair flows wildly around her beautiful face, while golden light surrounds her hands. Below her in script is the name "Caledonia." A large red dragon curls around her protectively from behind, rich red fire blowing from his snout, with the name "Ewan" written above his tail. To the right of them both is a rowan tree, its red berries in full bloom.

This must be the first MacAllister witch and her mate.

Turning the page carefully, I find the beginnings of a family tree with Caledonia and Ewan at the top. Their children and grandchildren are listed on the page. Turning to the next page, the family tree gets smaller as more and more children are born. New branches are formed. On the third page, the tree changes to columns. Rows upon rows of names along with their parents, birth dates, marriages, and deaths. There must be hundreds of pages. Flipping through them, I get to the end and there, in a damp cave in the middle of the Kingdom of Dragons, I find the last entry in the grimoire. Arden MacAllister, born to Gia Perrone, father blank, the date of my birth, and a blank space for date of death. Here is the proof of my MacAllister heritage, proof I matter in the world of witches. My fingers trace over my name.

If I'm in here, then my father, who I inherited my MacAllister blood from, should be listed directly above me, but the three lines above me are blank. I flip back a couple of pages and find every line filled in with a name. I start to flip back when a name jumps out at me—Agnes MacAllister. It lists her birth, parents, and the date of her death, the same date of death listed for hundreds of names. I shake my head at the loss.

The rest of the grimoire is filled with spells written in various languages throughout the ages. Every generation seemed to add more spells. Most of the spells use witch magic, but there's an entire section dedicated to blood magic. I point it out to Astor and hand him the grimoire, which he buries his nose in and walks off.

Setting aside the small chest, we quickly get through the remaining chests. Standing at the back, I scan all the opened chests. I don't know what I'm going to do with everything, but I know it should be shared with all witches. Everyone needs to know the history of the MacAllisters and their fate, even if it turns out the other witches were responsible for the massacre.

TWENTY-SIX

ARDEN

After finally eating dinner and sleeping for a few hours, we're up at the crack of dawn to get the chests loaded and through the portal. Valerian wants us—or rather me—out of here as soon as possible, but when I wake, I know it's not going to happen.

Once the chests are packed, I seal them with my blood so they can carry them through the portal one at a time. I hurry to get the backpacks and the cooler and set them in the cave for Fallon to grab, which he does while I do a final walk-through. Looking around the large chamber to make sure we haven't missed anything, I spot a letter sitting on the bench. When I pick it up, I see it's addressed to me and, remarkably, in my mother's handwriting. Puzzled, I stare at it, trying to figure out how it got in here, when I hear my name.

Stuffing it in my jacket pocket, I head out of the cave. When

I get to the entrance, I cast a simple spell to repel intruders. There's no need for anything complex, since we've already removed the contents. Turning around, I find big men and bigger dragons waiting for me.

My eyes dart around to find the cadre. Relieved, I see them standing near the portal, weapons in their hands. None of them seem happy, but Valerian looks murderous. His normally amber eyes are gleaming with gold, telling me his control is thin and his dragon is close to the surface.

Pulling a sword, I saunter toward them. When a man steps in front of me, I point my sword at him. "I wouldn't do that if I were you," I warn him loudly, wanting to be sure everyone hears me. "See this pointy thing? It's not a decoration. I know how to use it, and if you take another step, I'll use it on you." I give the sword a few experts spins, just in case he's more of a visual learner.

Of course, he doesn't listen. I exhale loudly. Chuckling, he reaches forward and grabs my sword arm. Before he clamps down, I toss the sword to my left hand and run it through him. With a loud bellow, he falls to the ground. I lay the point of the sword under his chin and lift his head. "If you ever lay a hand on me again, you won't live to regret it." He's still bellowing when I walk away, and he's not the only one. All of sudden, everyone is shouting.

With a roar, Valerian shuts everyone up. "Enough! As your king, I demand an answer. Who's given you the authority to detain me and my guests?" He narrows in on the guy in front, who I'm guessing is the leader of this little group.

"The council requests the presence of you and your guests," the guy sneers, his tone making it obvious it's not a request. "If you refuse, we're authorized to forcibly detain all of you."

Valerian's anger intensifies, and I realize he's about to lose control. The rest of the cadre isn't doing any better. Every single one of them is poised to fight for their freedom. Normally, I'd be right there beside them, but I realized late last night my restless dreams from the last few weeks were not dreams after all—they were glimpses of the future. My seer powers are awakening, and in those visions, I see the same vision I received when I used the blood magic, then I see more.

"Valerian, sweetheart." I almost snicker at the sweet sound of my voice calling his name, but I think it's probably the only thing that will jolt him out of his rage. "It's time." The entire cadre stares at me like I've lost my mind.

"Time?" he says gravelly, his voice almost lost to his dragon.

"Yes, to go to the ceremonial chamber," I reply sweetly.

His face pales. "What?" He starts shaking his head. "No!" His resounding no is repeated by each of the cadre.

"How the hell did you know where we were taking you?" the guy in front asks me.

"Hello, I'm a witch," I remind him, sarcasm dripping from my tongue. Normally, I wouldn't be so rude, but I don't like his attitude toward Valerian, his king. I turn back to the cadre and Valerian. "Did everything get back safely?" Astor gives me a thumbs-up. His eyes are speculative, wondering what I'm doing. "How are we getting to this chamber?"

The guy in front steps forward. "You can ride with me. The rest can grab a ride with Valerian or walk."

"Over your dead body," Valerian snarls at him.

"I agree with your king," I state firmly, emphasizing Valerian's title. "We'll take a portal. You can come with us or fly back, but we're not going with you." I hold my breath, waiting to see what he'll do. If he's smart, he'll take my offer.

He confers with a few of the other men, and they move

toward us. The cadre meets them head-on. Holding up his hands, he motions to me. "We'll take your portal."

"It will probably have to be someone else's portal. I've never been to the chamber, and I don't like to land somewhere blind," I correct him. It's not entirely true, but I don't want to be the first one out of the portal, nor do I want someone I distrust at my back. Turning to the cadre, I raise an eyebrow.

With fierce frowns on their faces, they step forward and surround me. Astor creates a portal to the chamber, but before we can step through, the dragons insert themselves into our group. One tries to stand behind me, but Daire picks him up by the shoulders and throws him to the side. I step back, eliminating the space between Daire and me, and he wraps an arm around my waist. The dragon snarls and reinserts himself in front of me.

We all get through the portal without too much snarling and shoving and come out the other side to mass chaos. Everyone in the kingdom seems to be here.

Unlike the simple countryside we just left, we're now in the heart of Valerian's kingdom—the city where a majority of the population lives and home to the king and council. Eyes wide, I spin around, trying to capture a glimpse of everything around me. Unlike the city surrounding The Abbey, where everything is steel, glass, and concrete, these buildings are mostly stone. Newer, more modern buildings sit nestled amongst older buildings, but all of them are made from the same light stone. I wonder if it's natural to the land here.

Someone bumps into me, and Daire pulls me closer to him. It's hard to walk in this crowd, but we slowly make our way towards the large grey domed building in front of us. This must be the ceremonial chamber, but I won't know for sure until I see the inside. Our escorts clear a path, and we're finally able to get to the door.

Filing into the chamber, I wait for my eyes to adjust to the dark. I hear a lot of shouting and look to the back of the room to find the source. My eyes finally adjust and I see the raised platform in the back of the hall and shiver. It's the same one from my dreams.

Several men are arguing loudly, but when Valerian steps up to the dais, they instantly shut up. I don't blame them. Right now, Valerian looks like he's going to kill anyone who steps in his way, and so do the three men following him. I'm not sure the dragons were thinking this through when they requested the presence of their royal guests. One would be bad enough, but to have to deal with an Elven, a Fae, and the demons? I shudder. Someone needs a class in political strategy.

I follow everyone up to the platform. *This feels about right*, I think. Glancing at the walls, I turn in a circle, making sure everything is the same. When my eyes land on the tapestry with Valerian's coat of arms, I compare it with my vision and take a tiny step to the left.

The crowd fills the chamber. Someone starts up a chant, yelling, "Kill the witch! Kill the witch!" I almost smile, but fear is making my heart race. It's one thing to see this in a dream and another to be here in person, knowing you are going to be stabbed. Actually, knowing you are going to *let* someone stab you might be worse. Taking a few deep breaths, I remind myself I'm immortal and kick off the sequence of events.

"Astor," I say, calling him over to me. Slipping the Killian blade out of my thigh holster, I hand it to him. When his hand closes around it, I look him in the eye. "Remember my vision where you stabbed me?"

He glances down at the blade, blanches, and tries to shove it back into my hands. "Arden, I'm not stabbing you. Take the damn blade."

Out of the corner of my eye, I see a blond head moving.

"Astor, if you don't stab me, I'll stab myself," I warn him. I use our sharing spell to send a vision of his hand raised with the knife. "Fine, I'll stab myself." I reach for the knife.

With a twitch, I see my enemy in place. The protection rune at my throat flares in warning. Astor raises his hand to get the knife out of my reach, and I turn slightly to the left. Just in time to catch the blade directly in my chest. *Bullseye.*

Staggering back, I feel my knees start to buckle. Numbness begins to spread over my body. Fear clogs my throat. I know I'm immortal, but I haven't put the theory to the ultimate test until now. I reach up to pull out the dagger, but it's too slippery for me to grasp.

A massive roar shakes the rafters, and Valerian drops to his knees beside me. "My fierce dragon, it's okay." I grasp his hand and place it on the dagger. "I'm immortal, remember? Now, pull this damn blade out of me, and don't let Daire heal me. They need to see I'm immortal." My voice fades, and the light starts to dim. My breathing becomes labored, but he still doesn't move. He's roaring, locked in some past only he can see. Theron grabs him by the shoulders and jerks him to the side. My eyes close.

I hear someone call my name and peel my eyes open. Astor's smiling face comes into view. I feel a tug and glance down to see him removing the dagger from my chest. I frown in return. "Gorgeous, you scared the literal hell out of me. I'm not even sure I'm a demon anymore. And when we're home again, we're going to have a long talk. About us. You see, I refuse to let you go." He smooths my hair back from my face and sighs. "I'm betting you have a plan here. Your actions certainly shut the crowd up. Of course right now, they think they've killed you, but once you pop up, I'm going to grab some popcorn and enjoy the show."

I lie there listening to his babbling while the wound slowly knits back together. Anyone listening would think he was completely calm, cool, and collected, but if they were close, they would see his hands shaking. I'm glad. Feels good to know he cares.

I shift to the left a bit. *Damn, it hurts.* I'm partially paralyzed by the pain. I'd forgotten what it felt like to heal without potions or Daire.

Speaking of Daire, I smell his luxurious cologne right before I see his icy blue eyes. "I'm not happy with you, Arden. In fact, you could say I'm pretty pissed off."

"I'm sorry," I whisper. "I'm kind of new to the whole seer thing. I wasn't sure if telling someone would change the path, and therefore, the outcome. Honestly, if this doesn't work, I'm going to be pretty pissed off myself. This hurts."

His mouth tightens. "I can't fucking stand to see you in pain."

I grab his hand. "I know you think I'm being blasé, but I hear you. It's not okay for me to put myself in danger and expect you to stand by." I pause. "And it's not okay for you to put yourself in danger and expect me to stand by." I let my comment sink in for a moment. "I'll make sure to keep you in the loop in the future, if you do the same."

Anger wars with understanding. Sighing, he kisses me and stands, joining the men yelling above me. Valerian's roaring at the two men in his face. I hear the word "kill" and "mate." *I guess the cat is out of the bag now. Mission number one accomplished.*

I probe my chest and find the hole closed. In another ten minutes, I should be good as new. Turning over, I get to my knees and elbows. The crowd gasps. Gritting my teeth, I make it to my feet and flip off the crowd. Instead of "kill the witch," all I hear now are murmurs and whispers—except for the person cackling in the back of the crowd. I bet that's Glynnis.

I'd smile, but it would probably appear pretty gruesome right now.

The man who threw the dagger into my chest is standing with his arms crossed, smiling smugly at the man beside him. Brothers, maybe, since they have similar sandy blond hair, thick necks, and stocky bodies. Swiping his dagger off the floor, I ignore the stab of pain, and using the most exaggerated swagger I can manage, I saunter over to him. The smug smile slips from his face when he realizes I'm alive.

Remembering the battle, I murmur my amplify spell. We should be more transparent with each other and the people. You know, so there's absolutely zero chance of backstabbing. "I'm not exactly sure why you're so smug. Killing me from twenty feet away with a throwing dagger has got to be the most cowardly thing I've ever seen someone do, and you want to brag about it? I'd want to hide in shame." Almost the entire chamber is silent, except for the cussing coming from the cadre. Well, actually, I think Astor's laughing.

"Are all dragons so afraid of a witch they can't face her in battle, or just you? Wait, don't answer. I have a few more questions, not only for you, but for every damn dragon here." I hear a few grumblings from the crowd and step to the side to see them. "Do they not teach you to value things like integrity and character? What about honor?"

Picking out a few familiar faces, I continue with my point. "During the last battle in the Underworld, I saw a fearless leader" —I smile at Valerian— "and his fierce dragons. Warriors who faced danger without flinching, giving their absolute best in a head-to-head battle with demons and other creatures of the Underworld, bravely representing the dragon race and making their king proud."

The warriors in the crowd puff up with every word.

"Not only did you fight well together, but you fought hand-in-hand with Elves, Fae, warlocks, vampires, and demons without an ounce of prejudice." I flash them my saddest face and shake my head. "Then, I, a witch and *mate to your king*, come to visit you in your house, and you do *nothing* when someone throws a dagger in my chest? I have to tell you, I'm disappointed. If it weren't for the battle, I would think you had *no honor*." I watch those same warriors' faces drop in shame.

"If I weren't immortal..." I stop to let them whisper for a minute. "Yes, I said immortal. If I weren't immortal, I'd be dead, and your king would be heartbroken. Again. Is that what you want?" I took some liberty with the heartbroken part, but it worked. The crowd is silent, and I turn back to the asshole beside me. I hold the dagger out and drop it on the floor. "Think you have enough balls to take me on directly? I challenge you to a fight of mercy."

The two men in front of Valerian start shouting, "She can't challenge him. It's against the law. We will not permit it."

I ignore them for a minute, solely focusing on Valerian. His face is impassive. I walk up and stand before him. "You are one of the most honorable men I know. The thousands of supernaturals you helped over the last twelve hundred years, not for reward or glory but because they needed it, tells me you have honor. Yes, there were mistakes made in the past, but you have more than paid your dues and your kingdom should reflect you and the ideals you uphold. Stop being benevolent and demand they step up. You deserve to have dragons with honor guarding your kingdom. Honor is non-negotiable."

I glance at the rest of the cadre and see them nodding their heads in agreement. When I look up at Valerian, his amber eyes are smoldering. He yanks me up into his arms and proceeds to kiss the hell out of me, in front of everyone. Ending the kiss, he holds me tightly. "You're right—honor is non-negotiable. It's time I stopped feeling guilty. Although, I wish you had avoided the dagger instead of using it to prove your point. I almost lost my mind."

I pat his cheek. "I understand. I did try to get you to listen a few weeks ago, but you were being stubborn," I remind him, my tone teasing. "I hope I don't have to resort to such drastic measures in the future." I cast a thumb behind me. "Who are the two assholes yelling in my ear?"

He laughs. "The council leaders. Do you want me to handle them?"

I shrug. "Let's see what they have to say."

He puts me down, and I turn around and hold up my hand. "Stop shouting. I'm kind of irritable after being stabbed. And do you always talk to your king this way? What's the problem?"

The two sputter for a minute. "Witch, you—"

"My name is Arden. Why is challenging someone against the law?" I say, interrupting him. I doubt they're going to give me a chance to talk later.

They communicate silently for a minute, then one steps forward to be their spokesperson. "Arden, I'm August," he grits out. "It's against the law for women to fight."

"Seriously?" I throw a cross look over my shoulder at Valerian. We're going to fix a few other things around here, including the backward mentality of the male dragons. "Why is it against the law?"

"Because you're a woman, and our women don't fight. Male dragons are protectors, and our females are caregivers," he explains, his voice filled with exasperation.

"I see." I shake my head in disappointment. "Well, I'm not a dragon, and therefore, I do not fall under your jurisdiction. I appreciate you taking the time to explain it to me." I peek over his shoulder and see the coward whispering to the man beside him. "You ready to defend yourself?"

When he sneers at me, I take it as a yes. "Here are the rules," I begin. A hand grabs my arm, and I raise an eyebrow.

The cadre steps forward. Valerian grabs the hand and bends it completely backwards until the man screams. "I did not give you permission to touch my mate, did I?" After sufficient groveling, he throws him off the dais. There's the badass dragon I know and love. I stop. Damn it. I'll worry about it later.

"Okay, here are the rules. No magic. I repeat, no magic. No shifting. We fight in human form. Pick your weapon," I tell him.

"Sword," he replies smugly.

"Sword it is. I'll see you on the battlefield, coward." I shut off the amplifier and peel the bloody shirt away from my chest. "I need a shower and a place to change clothes." The cadre is standing in front of me with their arms crossed. "And obviously, we need to talk."

TWENTY-SEVEN

VALERIAN

Until Arden's speech, I hadn't realized I've let guilt rule my decisions and my people rule me using guilt. Dragons are known for their honor and their straightforward approach to conflict, but instead of handling their dissent directly, I thrust Arden and the cadre into a perilous situation that resulted in her getting stabbed and a challenge of mercy.

Dropping my head into my hands, I try to get the pictures of her dying out of my mind, but it's on replay. Every time I see it, my heart is yanked from my chest and I can't breathe. Like the rest of the cadre, I'm angry at her for not telling us, but should we be? I don't know how her seer visions work and neither does she right now, but there must be a better way to get around them. Then I remember her mother's sacrifices based on her visions of Arden, and I wonder if they have much choice.

Instead of killing that asshole right away, I stood there arguing with the council. I snort. Another matter I need to handle right away. The current council has gained too much power, creating a dictatorship while leaving little room for growth and change. When this is over, we're holding new elections for those positions. Let the people decide who they want to serve them, and a few of those seats better be held by women, or I'm going to catch hell. A hand claps me on the shoulder.

"Don't be too hard on yourself," Fallon advises, sitting down beside me. Out of all the cadre, he's the most likely to understand because of his duties to his kingdom. "It's a thin line between responsibility for your kingdom and responsibility for the people in it. They don't always mean the same thing and can often be in conflict with each other. It's only important you learn and adapt."

"I'll probably stay here for a couple of weeks while everyone else returns to The Abbey." I'm silent for a minute, thinking about the work I need to do. "Her eyes shocked me when I saw her, but they look good on her. How's the training going?"

"Slowly, but it's new magic and it will take time. She's a fast learner, so that will help," he replies. "Are you sure she can beat this dragon?" His eyes are intent and serious when they land on me, needing reassurance she can come out of this challenge intact.

"Easily," I assure him. "Now, if it were the brother, I'd be more worried. He's a nasty piece of work and the biggest dissenter in my ranks. The main thing we need to watch out for is cheating. Arden pegged him accurately—he's a coward."

STANDING on the edge of the field, I stand behind Arden with my hands on her shoulders. Even though I reassured Fallon earlier, I find myself a wee bit nervous about the battle, and my hands tighten.

"Take it easy, big guy," she says, pulling away from my hands. "Tell me about him."

Thankfully, I've been watching him and his brother the last few weeks. "He's strong, with a long reach and propensity for tackling his opponents. He's not bad with a sword, but he's unpredictable, which makes him dangerous. His inferiority complex and his temper are his biggest weaknesses, both of which you can turn in your favor." I turn her to face me. "Try not to get stabbed again today. I don't think I'll survive a second time."

Her startling green eyes look at me softly. "I'll do my best." She hands the hood of her armor to me and struts out into the field, a warrior and a damn fine woman. My heart swells with pride.

When the battle begins, she uses the first ten minutes to lay a false trail, and he eats it up. She allows him to showboat while she dances around him, only engaging enough to test his response before retreating. He starts to get cocky, paying less attention to her and more attention to the crowd, until it bites him in the ass. The next time he turns to bow to the crowd, she whips her sword up and swats him on the butt.

The crowd roars with laughter, but they're not laughing a minute later. He whips around and attacks her, but she knows his moves now, while he's taken little time to learn hers, and she uses it to her advantage. With each new move, blood appears on his body until he's covered in red from all the slices she's made on him. Still, he doesn't call for mercy.

Arden glances at me in frustration when she realizes she'll have to catch him in a death hold in order to get him to surrender. His pride won't let him concede defeat to her, a woman and mate to the king he hates. She becomes a blur, moving around him, slicing his legs and arms repeatedly until he gets frustrated and leaps toward her, trying to tackle her to the ground, but she steps to the side. Before he can get up, she places the sword at his neck.

"Mercy or death," she says, her voice ringing out clearly. The crowd is silent while they wait for his answer.

"Mercy," he spits out with fists clenched at his sides.

She slowly backs away and lowers her sword, but not her guard. He isn't the type to surrender, and she knows it now.

With a roar, he shifts to his dragon and charges her. The cadre runs up beside me, ready to intervene, but I know we can't, and I know she can defeat him.

Fire shoots out of his mouth, but she stands there with her shield intact and not a single flame touches her. Using witchfire, she returns his fire with a volley of her own, searing him down to the bone.

"Damn it, I don't want to have to kill you," she screams at him, but he doesn't listen.

Surprisingly, the crowd is strangely silent. The lack of honor he displayed when he shifted to his dragon turned them against him. When he scans the crowd for approval, they stand and turn their backs on him. It's the worst insult you can give to a dragon, and it's the last straw.

With one last roar, he lays a stream of fire on her, and she hunkers down, waiting him out. When he takes a breath, she throws one large ball of witchfire at him, and it burns through his scales and incinerates his heart instantly. He turns to ash, and a second later, he's gone.

An anguished roar comes from the far end of the field, and in a flash, his brother is charging her. Like me, he can wield all three powers, and he's aiming all three at Arden.

"Daire!" I shout. Knowing he will grab Arden, I run toward the rampaging dragon, shifting on the fly. A blur paces alongside me, grabbing Arden out of the path of the dragon just in time.

The dragon roars with frustration when he finds Arden gone. He looks at me, and hesitates, but I can see the moment he makes up his mind to take me out. He's been waiting a long time for this opportunity, but I've been trying to avoid it, hoping he would take a different course. I didn't want to kill another dragon, but Arden was right today—honor is non-negotiable, and he has none.

With the roar of kings, I let him make the first move. He decides to use shadow and ice, instead of fire like his brother. He's used to fighting dragons who don't have the three powers, and it shows. Ice appears beneath my feet, but with a little heat, I melt it easily. His shadows slither across, trying to find vulnerable spots within my scales, but my shadows are there to meet them, shredding them instantly. I whip my body around and use my tail like a sword, striking him across the face, and before he can regroup, I crash into him and hold him close. Bringing my talons up, I heat them with my flame until they're forged iron spikes, and I strike hard and fast, ripping his heart out of his chest. With my flame, it burns to a crisp, and he falls to the ground in a pile of ash. The entire battle took five minutes.

Shifting back to human form, I look up at my people in the stands. "Anyone else want to challenge for king today?" I shout, giving them time to come forward.

None do. I can't say I'm surprised. It's precisely the reason I ended the battle quickly.

"There's a lot of change coming to this kingdom. For far too long, I've let things slide, but no more. We're going to find our way forward with honor and integrity. Every law will be thoroughly examined, and together, we will vote on whether to keep it, change it, or abolish it. Obviously, I'll be abolishing the law against women fighting. I'm sure my mate will agree." The crowd cheers. "Starting tomorrow, we're holding elections for new council seats. The seats will be open to both men and women. If you want to be considered, add your name to the ballot. Every seat will be open." I stare at the two men who argued with me earlier. "And make no mistake, I'm King of Dragons, no one else. You answer to me."

My gaze finds Arden's, and she smiles, holds up two fingers, and mouths, "I'm so proud of you."

For the first time since I took the crown, I'm finally confident I'm the best ruler for this kingdom, not anybody else, and I'm looking forward to the changes coming.

Who knew this day would turn out like it did. Tilting my head, I think about her new seer abilities and her earlier comments. Maybe she did.

STANDING under the hot spray of the shower, I let the water wash away the dirt and grime from my body. Two dragons, gone and buried. Everything in me wants to feel guilty for not addressing the situation before today, but I refuse to let it get a grip on me. Guilt is the reason I ended up on this path in the first place. If I expect the people to change, I must as well, which means assigning the blame to the ones who made their own choices, but it's a hard habit to break.

The shower door opening startles me out of my thoughts. My eyes snap open and find Arden waiting for me. She's breathtaking, from the fire in her eyes, to the flush gracing the tops of her breasts, down to the long legs I can't wait to feel wrapped tightly around me. I pull her into the shower and shut the door.

"This is a damn fine surprise, lass," I say gruffly, loving her spontaneity.

"Mmm, I've missed you," she informs me, running her hands over my shoulders. "Looks like you were almost finished, though?"

"There's not a damn thing that could get me out of this shower now," I tell her. "Let me take care of you."

Switching places, I place her under the spray and grab the soap. Lathering my hands, I slowly wash every inch of her body. The soft glide of my slippery hands is mesmerizing, and her silky-smooth skin tempts me too much. After the first path over her entire body, I begin again, but this time, my mouth follows my hands on their journey. Skimming her neck with my lips, I lick and suck, paying close attention to several spots I know are triggers. My hands continue their soapy caress on her breasts as my slick palms rub her nipples lightly until she gasps and arches into my hands, wanting more. My hands close on the plump mounds, cupping and kneading them.

Kneeling, I grip her hips and turn her to wash the soap from her breasts before turning her back around so I can capture them in my mouth. My lips are firm, grasping her nipples, alternately sucking the hard buds into my mouth or running my tongue over them to flatten or flick as I please. I make sure I pay equal attention to each one, and hearing her moans makes me hard as a rock.

Fuck, she's beautiful. And mine.

Soaping my hands up again, I run them over her sweet ass, kneading each cheek, then down the back of her legs and back up on the inside. Even when she thrusts her hips forward, I ignore her unspoken request and continue repeating the same path.

When I feel her fingers lace through my hair and give it a hard tug, I cup her knee and pull one leg over my shoulder so I can move my mouth from her breasts down her stomach to the nub between her folds. My tongue begins flicking back and forth, waiting for the exact moment when her body tells me it's ready for more. Her hips thrusts forward, and she opens wider. Capturing her more firmly, my mouth begins sucking and licking, while my fingers plunge into her sweet warmth.

Her hand grips my head, pulling me in tighter, and her sweet moans fill the air. Adding another finger, I curl it up and find the ridged spot guaranteed to bring her over the edge. A few more strokes, and suddenly, I feel her convulsing around my fingers. While waiting for the tremors to stop, I place soft kisses on her stomach.

A few minutes later, I stand, and she pulls me in for a deep kiss. Worshipping her mouth with mine, I kiss her deeply, never letting up. Picking her up, I wait until she wraps her legs around me before turning and placing her back against the tiles. My cock nestles tightly between her folds, and I slide it back and forth, then ease into her, but I don't thrust. Pulling my mouth from hers, I wait for her eyes to find mine.

"Don't you ever willingly let anyone hurt you again," I demand, my voice fierce and raw as the images from earlier race through my mind—her fall to the floor, the knife buried to the hilt, and the endless river of blood pouring out of her chest. "Not for me, or anyone else. Promise me."

Her voice is husky when she gives me her word. "I promise."

Sliding in and out, I stare into her eyes and tell her, "I need you. Not this kingdom, not the people, not the crown. You. I'll do everything in my power to keep you safe, no matter your destiny or the enemies we face, because I refuse to live without you. Do you understand?" My voice is gruff but serious, needing her to know she's not expendable. Not to me.

"I understand," she murmurs. "I love you too."

The dragon in me roars at her words, and my hips thrust into her over and over. When she begins to come again, I give her the words back. "I love you, Arden." Then I follow her, coming hard within her sweet body.

TWENTY-EIGHT

Striding through The Abbey, I stop at the bar to grab a bottle of blood. Noticing we're low on stock, I send a quick text to Theron to ask him to reorder. Typically, Maya would manage everything pertaining to the bar, but with everyone still on sabbatical, it falls to Theron. Picking up a glass as well, I head upstairs.

The Abbey is quiet without anyone else here. After watching the battles today, I'd gotten a text from Lucifer asking me to check on a possible rumor he'd heard about a dark sorceress who was also searching for information on the Primary.

When I arrived in the Underworld city where she lived, I found the area to be full of criminals and demon families living in extreme poverty. A few buildings were standing, some with meager food supplies and necessities, but the people were living in shacks and tents nearby instead of homes or apartments. Disturbed, I sent Lucifer pictures, admonishing him for their conditions, but he was shocked too. Apparently, this region was Alain's responsibility, and none of the resources made it to the people. Furious, he decided to visit himself and find out what's going on.

Surprisingly, I couldn't find out whether the rumor was true or not. Getting information out of anyone seemed near impossible. Any time the word "sorceress" was mentioned, the demon I was questioning would suddenly be unable to speak. Apparently, a powerful geas prevented them from giving her up. I texted the info to Lucifer, and he decided to add it to his list, so I headed home.

When I get to the door of my bedroom, I stop and breathe in deeply. The smell of strawberries and honeysuckle lingers in the air. It's still pretty strong, which means Arden visited me recently. Frowning, I can't think of why she would come to my room. She knew I was in the Underworld prior to our visit to Valerian's kingdom.

Opening the door, I pause in the threshold and inhale. Her scent is even stronger in here, and I groan. Sleeping is going to be near impossible tonight, since my mind will be busy picturing her in my bed. Turning on the light, I almost drop the bottle of blood on the floor, which would be an incredible shame, considering all the old black rugs have been replaced with beautiful light grey ones. My eyes flick up, and I'm stunned. The entire room has been redecorated.

Standing in the doorway, I feel the light airiness of the room. The depressive dark dungeon of the past is gone, and now, it's inviting and warm. The excessive black furnishings have been replaced with blues, greys, and whites. Even the walls are an incredible shade of blue, not too dark or light.

Bemused, my eyes flit from one spot to another, unable to

decide where to look first. Setting the bottle and glass on a nearby table, I make my way to the large grey couch and sit. Sighing with pleasure, I sink back into the cushions and run my hands over the soft texture. It's incredibly comfortable and deep, and not too stuffy. Eyeing the length, I swing my legs up and lie end to end. From my head to my feet, I fit. It's almost as if it were made exactly for me. A few soft pillows and a blanket complete the comfortable cocoon.

The décor is minimal, but all the fabrics and textures give it a luxurious feeling, and the colors blend well to create an atmosphere of total relaxation. Standing, I make my way over to the bed. She replaced everything, from the bed itself to the mattress. I can smell the newness of it. My fingers caress the pillows and comforter, finding the texture soft and pliant. Stretching out on the bed, I can't help but picture her lying beside me.

A wink of silver catches the corner of my eye. Glancing over, I see three silver frames with the pictures I'd hidden in my nightstand. My breath catches at seeing Danica's and my mother's smiles. Solange always hated those pictures, so I'd kept them in the drawer in order to avoid another argument. But Arden's placement of these pictures in beautiful new frames means a lot, and I can see them from practically everywhere in the room.

I'm literally speechless. I can't remember the last time someone surprised me or did something for me without expecting anything in return. My heart beats, and I can't help but be warmed by the sound. Wishing she was here to share this with me, I pick up the phone to text her, but put it down. It's late, and I don't want to wake her or interrupt her time with Valerian.

The only odd thing is the bare walls. I'm glad she didn't add the harsh pieces Solange had chosen, but I'm surprised she didn't add any new art. Grinning widely, I decide to use it to my advantage.

Walking over to the bottle, I pour myself a glass of fine A+ and sink down into my new couch. I grab my tablet and start searching for places for our date.

CHAPTER
TWENTY-NINE

ARDEN

Yawning widely, I step up to the portal, drop my bag, and plop down on top of it to wait for the others. After a delicious but emotional night spent with Valerian, I'm exhausted. All I want to do is go home and relax for at least a day or two. But I'm going to miss Valerian. He's staying for a week or two to kick off the changes, including the new elections.

Picking up my phone to check the time, I blink when I see I'm ten minutes early. No wonder I'm the only one here. This is all Theron's fault. I like being on time. Not early because you have to wait for others, and not late because...well, Solandis wouldn't have tolerated it. Bad manners.

When a cup of coffee appears in front of me, I look up in surprise. Theron's standing above me, holding coffee and a banana. Taking them from him, I take a sip and moan. "This

231

should feel like a reward, but it kind of feels like strategy. I don't care, though, I'll take it," I jokingly tell him. Although he is a planner, so I wouldn't put it past him.

"Ready to go? I know you must be dying to know what's in the journal," he remarks, his phone already in his hand as he prepares for his day.

"Shit!" It slips out louder than I intended. Scrambling up, I hand him my cup of coffee, then kneel back down. Pulling my bag to me, I start digging through it. Taking everything on top out, I get to the bottom where I wrapped my bloody clothes in a plastic bag. It's gross to take them home to destroy, but after seeing what blood magic can do, there's no way I'm ever leaving my blood for anyone to find. Snatching up the jacket, I shove my hand into the pocket and pull out the letter. The edges are a little darker from my blood, but most of it is intact and relief pours through me.

"Is that your mother's letter or the parchment?" Theron asks, squatting down to help me put my things back in the bag.

"I think it might be a new letter from my mother, but I'm not sure. When I went back through the MacAllister chamber to make sure we had everything, it was sitting on the bench," I tell him. "It's my mother's handwriting on the outside, but I didn't have a chance to read it, yet."

"Read what?" Astor calls out as he approaches us.

Theron explains while I add everything back to my bag.

"Are you going to read it now?" he asks.

"No, later," I reply. Biting my lip, I realize we don't have a lounge where I can relax and go through everything. They each have couches in their rooms, so they never needed one, but my room is too small. Besides, they should stop living separately. "Is there a comfy lounging place in The Abbey? Somewhere where we could all hang out together?"

Surprised, Theron tilts his head and considers me. "There's

not, but The Abbey accommodates our wishes. One can be created pretty easily. If you want one, I can do it when we arrive, but you'll have to find couches and stuff for it. Preferably organic fabrics for Fallon and me. Will that work?" When I agree, he makes a note on his phone.

"Can you put in a fireplace? And a bar area where we could get drinks and snacks?" I try to think of anything else I can ask him to add, but nothing comes to mind. "Thanks, Theron. Maybe we can all meet there this evening and hang out? I'm going to read this letter and the MacAllister journal."

Astor eyes me speculatively. "I'll join you. I'd like to study the MacAllister grimoire, if you don't mind?"

"Are you sure? We resolved our last witch issue, and I don't want to create a new one," I ask, frowning. "Think about it. Regardless, I'd love to have you join me." Glancing around, I realize I don't see anyone else. "Where are Fallon and Daire?"

"Fallon needed to go see his father, and Daire left last night to run an errand," Theron explains. "Ready?"

Excited about the new lounge, I smile, ready to get back. Vargas, Solandis, and I used to hang out at home all the time. Callyx too, when he was around. I miss it.

AFTER AN AFTERNOON OF RUSHING AROUND, I stop and study the room with satisfaction. Besides the two large couches in the room, there are several comfy chairs scattered throughout, a large table by the bar area for food or games or whatever, ottomans by the fireplace, and a ton of soft pillows and blankets. It's everything we could possibly need to lounge.

Exhausted, I head to my room and pop into the shower,

then dress in leggings, a long shirt, and socks, perfect lounging clothes. Grabbing the small chest with the rowan tree on the lid, I make my way to our new lounge and set it down on the coffee table.

After grabbing a water, I pick a corner on the sofa, grab a blanket, and settle in with the letter and the journal. Of course, I'm reading the letter first.

My darling Arden,

In my visions, your green eyes shine brightly now, which means the path to discovering your Elven heritage is right around the corner. And if you're reading this letter, you've found your MacAllister heritage as well. They are two important pieces of your father's lineage.

When your father and I met, we didn't know it was destiny. We simply fell in love. I thought I was falling in love with an Elven male, which was hard enough, given the coven's views on exclusivity and purity of blood. I didn't care. I was willing to leave the coven for him, but after I became pregnant with you, things changed quickly.

He had to confess his greatest secrets, because they would now impact your safety. The first secret he revealed was his MacAllister heritage. He explained his entire family had been living under a false name with a fictitious background for twelve hundred years. When he revealed he was also a witch of an unheard seventh bloodline, I wanted to scream and rail against the Fates. His bloodline, combined with my six, meant you were the Rowan, witch of seven bloodlines. Gemma left me a letter telling me about the Rowan, a witch of seven bloodlines and the key to saving our race. I just hadn't realized my child would be the one chosen for this destiny. I started preparing and planning immediately to give you the best chance of fulfilling your destiny. My visions helped me see the possibilities and pitfalls, and I took steps accordingly.

When Agnes left her final journal for you, along with the history of the MacAllisters, she only had one piece of a much larger puzzle. There are two more journals. It's time to find your father, as he has the second journal. It's his grandmother's, and it tells of her life after she left the MacAllisters. As you step foot on the path to find your father, you'll find your Elven heritage and his second secret. Only those you trust with your life should know this truth.

Your father also holds a clue to the location of the third journal, the one written by me. It will contain my final words to you. Until then, be safe, and tell your father I'm counting the days.

All my love,
Your mother, Gia Perrone

Tears roll down my cheeks. My emotions are all over the place when I finish reading the letter. More secrets. More journals. It's frustrating, but it's her story punching me in the gut. I can't imagine falling in love and getting pregnant, only to have it ripped away. I didn't know whether to cry tears of joy or tears of sorrow when she mentioned my green eyes. She could see me in her visions. I can't even imagine how it must have felt knowing she wouldn't be there in person. I'd been feeling pretty good about my seer ability after things turned out well in the Kingdom of Dragons, but after reading this letter, I'm not sure I want it.

Astor saunters into the lounge, his eyes checking everything out, and announces, "This just became my favorite place in the whole building. It's fantastic." He frowns when I don't respond. "What's wrong, gorgeous?" He sits down on the edge of the sofa and sweeps my hair from my face. His expression grows dark when he sees my tears. "Who do I have to kill? Tell me and it's done."

"Who are you killing now?" Daire taunts Astor as he enters the room and whistles. "This place is incredible. Kind of reminds me of another recently remodeled room." He peeks over Astor's shoulder, and his face is thunderous when he sees my tears. "What the hell?" He pulls Astor up to face him. "Did you make her cry?"

Astor shoves him back. "Get off me. She was crying when I came into the room. I was trying to find out who I needed to kill. Do you mind?"

"Stop," I croak out and reach behind me for a tissue. After wiping my face, I hand the letter to Astor and Daire for them to read. A second later, Theron enters, and they give it to him.

Daire leans over and picks me up, then he turns and sits back down with me in his lap. As soon as I feel comforting arms around me, my tears flow faster.

"Cry all you want. I'm not going anywhere," he assures me. He tucks the blanket in tight around me and holds me, letting me douse his silk shirt with my tears.

"I wish Solandis was here," I whisper. "She always has the right words to make me feel better. But this feels good too."

His arms tighten around me. "I know what it feels like to live without your mother. We all do, actually. Although technically, Theron's mother is alive, she's been absent his whole life. Any time you want to talk about it, you can pick any one of us, and we'd be happy to listen."

His voice aches with his own sadness. Laying my head back, I stare into his icy blue eyes. "Would you tell me about your mother?"

Fallon comes in, and his brow furrows when he sees me in Daire's lap with red, puffy eyes. When he opens his mouth, Theron pulls him aside and hands him the letter. I swivel back to Daire, who's staring into the past.

He lights up. "It's been a long time since someone asked me about her. I loved her very much, and when I talk about her, she comes to life again." He pauses to gather his thoughts. "She had the most beautiful soul, and she exuded life. People were drawn to her because her happiness made them feel good. It was almost tangible, and it made you want to reach out and touch her to see if a little bit of her could rub off on you. As a healer, she was incredible and always knew the right spell or word to make someone better. When I was learning to heal, she would tell me to be open to my magic, let it tell me what to do. She was this bohemian spirit who only wanted to share herself with the world." He laughs. "She was the complete opposite of my father, which is why he worshipped her. We all did."

He goes on to tell me stories about his family growing up. Until Danica died, they lived and loved fiercely, but after she died, they all quietly fell apart. "My mother's light dimmed, but it didn't go out. She continued to help others, but her heart was broken and you could see it. When she was dying, she told me not to be sad. She was happy to be mortal because she couldn't bear the thought of Danica being alone."

I swipe at the tears rolling down my face. "It's the most beautiful story I've ever heard," I murmur. "She sounds wonderful."

"She was," he agrees, shifting me around to grab another tissue. "And I know someone else who's wonderful too." He looks at me pointedly. "Why did you redecorate my room?"

"Do you like it?" I ask, biting the inside of my cheek while I wait for him to answer.

"I love it, and I can't thank you enough. It's the best surprise I've been given in a long, long time," he answers, his eyes full of emotion. "Why?"

I shrug. "I couldn't bear the thought of you in that cold, dark room devoid of any of your personality. You needed somewhere to relax and get away from the world, a place that felt like you." I play with his fingers for a second before deciding to take a chance with the truth. "And honestly, I didn't want one iota of Solange anywhere in The Abbey and certainly not in your room."

His eyes lock with mine, and they gleam with satisfaction. "Would you let me take you to dinner?" he asks, his gaze intense.

Butterflies somersault in my stomach. "Yes," I reply huskily.

He lifts my chin, and his mouth is firm when it captures my lips, sealing the deal.

CHAPTER
THIRTY

<u>ARDEN</u>

A few minutes later, I scoot back into the corner of the couch and grab the journal, leaving my legs in Daire's lap. Occasionally, he runs his hands over them, almost absentmindedly, while he gives Fallon and Theron updates on the changes Lucifer is making in the Underworld.

Astor asked to see the grimoire again, and after he swore it wouldn't cause any issues between the two of us, I handed it to him. He's now in a chair in the corner with his head buried in the pages.

Taking a deep breath, I open the journal. The first page states, "Agnes MacAllister, Matriarch of the MacAllister Witches," with the beginning and end date of her reign. Quick math tells me she led them for almost fifty years.

On the second page, it says, "The Beginning," and includes a story.

Of dragon's flame and witches' blood, the MacAllisters were born. We were the first humans to discover our potential for magic and call ourselves witches. In the beginning, we marveled at our ability to create fire and water and to heal with a whisper of power and a chant. Until one day, when a maiden witch fell in love with a dragon—a human in love with an immortal. Desperate for her own immortality, the witch conducted many experiments, all of which failed to produce the desired outcome. The quest seemed doomed... until the day she created the stone.

Using flame and blood, she'd created a source of power that unexpectedly fueled her magic and made her powers grow exponentially. When her children were born, even stronger than her, she fed their blood to the stone and the rowan tree was born. Separate from the stone, it connected the MacAllister witches to each other, collectively making them stronger, but the original source of their power remained with the stone.

A sacred tree, the rowan sought other humans with the potential for magic, and when those witches mated with supernaturals from other races, they became strong new branches on the tree. Separate from the MacAllisters, these witches brought with them new and different powers based on their mates, and some even bore immortal children with powers stronger than their parents.

The original maiden, in her elderly years, sought to connect all of the branches and witches. Pulling a thorn from the tree, she promised them greater power. They each swore an oath and gave their blood, tying themselves to the other witches and, unbeknownst to all, to the stone that replenished their magic. Collectively, they were now greater and their powers were stronger.

But as more and more witches were born, they too pulled from the source, and the stone began to turn dark, while they became weak. The MacAllisters realized the original magic was dwindling.

If we didn't find a way to renew the spell, witch magic would revert to the most basic of powers.

Several MacAllisters were mated to dragons and, using the original spell, we sacrificed blood and flame to the stone, over and over. With our regular donations, the stone began to glow again and witch magic flourished. Witches became one of the most powerful races, our services sought by both supernaturals and humans.

Then the witches began to shun other supernaturals, including their mates and children. They wanted a pure race, untainted by others. Overnight, the bloodlines pruned their branches of all immortal children, and without their ties to the rowan and its stone, the witch powers in these children died out or became minimal. Horrified, we tried to tell them how the supernaturals and their immortality made us collectively stronger, but greed and envy ruled, and they refused to listen.

Distancing ourselves from the rest of the bloodlines, the MacAllisters continued to mate with dragons, and consequently, our branch remained strong, making us the most powerful witches in the coven. We continued to feed flame and blood to the stone, knowing they were all benefitting from the source, but we didn't know how to separate the other branches from the rowan tree or the stone itself.

When the other bloodlines mated with humans, the number of witches increased dramatically, as humans weren't plagued by the infertility challenges faced by many immortals. But while they grew plentiful, their powers remained about the same. Children acquired new powers if they mated with other bloodlines, but their level of power changed minimally over the years.

It has remained this way for hundreds of years—the MacAllisters fueling the stone with flame and blood, the rowan connecting all witches, and the stone replenishing their magic. Never did we reveal the secret of the stone and the rowan tree.

The story ends, and I sit there stunned, my mind barely able to comprehend the magnitude of what I just read. Picking up the journal, I read it again and again. It rings true—the witches are still using the rowan's thorn to tie themselves together. The exclusivity born centuries ago is ingrained into their very bones, and yet, they know nothing. They only know their power is getting weaker. The truth behind this is partly because of their refusal to mate with other supernaturals and let hybrid children into the coven, and partly because the stone hasn't received its sacrifice since the massacre twelve hundred years ago.

When I saw the stone in the cave, it definitely wasn't glowing. I wonder what would happen if I added a drop of blood? It might not power it, but it could give it a boost. I set the thought aside and pick up the journal. Turning the page, I find a letter from Agnes to me.

To the Rowan, witch of all seven bloodlines,

I can't imagine what you will think of the MacAllisters after reading the story. As the matriarch of the clan, I want to share our struggles with you.

Many, many times over the years, we sent delegates to the council, begging them to change their minds about witches with mixed heritages, encouraging them to accept every witch, not just those of pure blood. Every time, they refused to countenance the very idea.

We frequently debated whether or not to tell them of the stone, but we feared what they would do with the knowledge. Would they demand we hand over the stone? In our hands, we all benefitted from the sacrifice, even if they weren't aware of the source of their power or our direct contribution to it. If the stone were to fall into their hands, we feared for the continuation of the MacAllisters. Although stronger, we were fewer in number. Still, every time a new matriarch came to power, we would debate and reassess the situation. Each time, we failed to find the courage or the confidence to share our knowledge.

When I came to power, I went to the council to judge for myself, and what I saw concerned me greatly. Even I, a powerful witch, was viewed and judged with disdain because our bloodline still consorted and mated with dragons. Resolved to keep our secret, I returned home.

But during my only visit, I met Gemma Perrone, and apparently, this triggered an avalanche of visions—visions that would change the course of the MacAllisters forever.

Gemma came to me a couple of years later to share those visions and to ask for my help. Her visions had shown her the stone, and she knew if all MacAllisters perished, so would the source of witch magic everywhere. At first, I refused. If we were to fall, then why should I care about the very ones who would murder us?

She stayed with me for a year, and I came to

trust in her and her visions, but that isn't what changed my mind. As the matriarch, I visited with MacAllisters every day, helping in whatever way they needed. Every time I looked at them, the knowledge they would cease to exist in a year burned a hole in my heart, and even though I wanted to, I couldn't share it with them. The consequences for that path were too severe, as shown by one of Gemma's visions, with a war between witches and supernaturals and thousands of deaths being the most likely outcome.

What finally changed my mind was the way of our death. We all die, but to erase our very existence from this earth, to make it so nobody would remember us, mourn us, or carry our stories forward, made me furious. As the matriarch, I couldn't bear it. The MacAllisters have been in this world for over two thousand years, but in one night, someone would steal our souls and entire heritage? I refused to let it happen. If I followed Gemma's suggestion and saved one person, someday, we would be remembered, and the prophesied Rowan, witch of seven bloodlines, would be the one to tell our story and carry forth our heritage.

Gemma and I planned, and where needed, we pulled in outsiders to assist. If you're reading this journal, then I'm sure you've met my dear friend, Glynnis. I knew she would honor my wishes and wear the medallion her entire life, not only to remember me and my kin, but to show the Rowan the path.

When it came time to choose the MacAllister witch to save, the decision had to be left up to fate. Gemma and I chose five young MacAllister witches to flee before the massacre, all of them female and orphans with no families. We knew women had a better chance of blending in and finding shelter. Their children would take their fathers' surnames, but secretly, they would have MacAllister blood. When they set off, I cried because I knew only one would make it and the others were simply decoys. It is another burden to carry to my grave.

Gemma and I parted ways shortly after, as she had other things to do to ensure the survival of our line, like hide the original Rowan tapestry and leave messages and clues for the future. When she left, I knew my time was short, and I had to finish my remaining tasks quickly.

Using blood magic, I created all the necessary spells to secure our legacy and filled the hidden chamber with chests containing our history. At the last minute, I added our grimoire, although I did put a spell on it to cover up any MacAllisters born between my time and yours as a precaution.

With a few days remaining, the only thing left

to do is add this journal and my final words. The stone is now in your hands, along with the responsibility that goes with it. Many MacAllisters and their mates served to fuel the power in the stone. One mate pairing will not do it, and if the witches are still practicing exclusivity, they will not have enough power left to give to the stone either. You will have to find another way. It will take both your blood and a great burst of power to fuel it again, but Gemma assures me you will find the solution. My only caution is to not follow in our footsteps. Once it's fueled, do not hide the secret of the stone. Share it.

When you share our story, please do so with kindness and grace. The MacAllister witches lived, we were fierce, and we created a powerful legacy. Don't let us be forgotten.

Agnes, Matriarch of the MacAllisters

Fiona MacAllister

Aileen MacAllister

Catriona MacAllister

Lara MacAllister

Sima MacAllister

Tracing the five names in front of me, I wonder which one is my ancestor. As to the rest of the journal, it will take time to digest. I'll probably read it a hundred times before I can begin to comprehend it and all of its nuances. If I'm to tell their story,

I want it to be rich and full like their lives.

When I started my journey to find my destiny, I hadn't realized the legacy I'd be inheriting along with it. I hoped it would be something worthy of my mother's death, and it is. To have the chance to save witches everywhere, it's powerful and worth one person's life. But hundreds of MacAllisters? A whole legacy almost lost? I'm not sure witches are worthy of such sacrifice, myself included. Would I give up my powers to save them, absolutely yes, but it's too late, and now I can only honor their sacrifice by continuing on this path and by telling their story.

As the Rowan, I know what I need to do now, but I don't know how I'm going to do it. According to Gemma, I'll find a way to power the stone, but once it's powered, what will I do with it? The witches are the same today as they were in Agnes' time. Simply fueling the stone will only allow them to maintain the status quo until the stone's power dwindles completely. I sigh and rub my temples. Another problem for another day.

The next step is to find my ancestor, and hopefully, my father and the second journal. "Theron," I murmur, not wanting to startle him. When he turns his head, I stretch over and hand him the journal. "There are five names listed at the bottom of the journal. We need to research them and find which one of them is my ancestor, but we need to do so quietly and without using the MacAllister last name. Do you have anyone in your network who can assist? We can probably narrow it down to unknown witches entering Elven territory around twelve hundred years ago."

He ponders the question for a second. "I may have a way to find them myself if I can get access to the tax records. Back then, every person living in a territory was recorded in a ledger to make sure they paid taxes. If we have first names and an approximate time period, I can narrow it down within a few days." He motions to the journal. "Do you mind if I read it?"

Waving my hand at them all, I shake my head. "Please, you can all read it. I'm going to bed. My head's killing me from the emotional and informational overload." They all glance at each other, their faces mirroring their concern, then crowd around Theron. "Goodnight."

THIRTY-ONE

ARDEN

The next day, I'm feeling flattened by the knowledge swimming in my brain and the emotion filling my heart. Every step I take on this journey leads me to another discovery, and if it weren't for the strength of the cadre and my family supporting me, I'd have run away, even if it was just for a moment.

Picking up my phone, I decide to text Meri. She'd sent me a couple of texts the last few days, but I hadn't answered because I'd felt odd since I saw her taking pictures of the parchment and my letter. I still don't know what to think about it, but maybe she was tapping into my seer powers or something.

Arden: Hey. Miss you. What are you doing?

I really miss working in The Abbey, waiting tables with her, and being surrounded by supernaturals of all races. It was fun and way too short. I yearn for those simple days, but my instincts tell me all of our lives are changing and nothing will ever be the same.

My phone pings, and I tap on it.

Meri: Running all over the place for my guardian. She's got a few ideas on the Primary. You seem to have caught her complete attention. Honestly, I'm not sure that's a good thing. How was your visit?

Arden: We found the MacAllisters and a grimoire with my name in it. I can finally prove to Caro I'm from a seventh bloodline. *winking emoji with tongue out* Or sort of the first bloodline. It's complicated. Now I'm searching for my Elven ancestor. I wanted to check in to see how you're doing.

Meri: Well, I could use a good lay to release all this stress, but I don't see that happening any time soon. Got to go, Cormal's getting pissed. Text you later.

Arden: *Heart emoji*

Cormal? The same friend of Fallon's? Meri knows the criminal king of the supernatural? My gut churns with worry. I don't want to see her fall into the wrong hands like she did with the demon gang, certainly not to help me. Answers will come whether we want them to or not. It's destiny and fate, right?

Jumping out of bed, I shower and dress in the usual workout clothes. *Damn, I forgot to tell Meri about the blond god, as she calls Daire, asking me out.* Grabbing my phone, I shoot off a quick text with my scoop and head off to the lobby to meet Fallon for training.

My phone pings. Her response is a drool face emoji, followed by a fire emoji and an eggplant emoji. I think it's probably the tamest thing she could say, and I laugh.

"What's so funny?" Fallon asks, startling me. When I look over my shoulder, he flushes, and I know he saw Meri's text.

Suppressing a laugh, I follow him through to the other side. "Meri." I don't say anything else, but he eyes me with speculation.

I know he's wondering if Meri and I were texting about him, but I decide to let him wonder. Dropping my phone near his backpack, I stretch and let my eyes wander over his large, warrior physique. For training, he's wearing dark grey loose pants and a black T-shirt molded to his abs and biceps, both items emphasizing his best traits. Swallowing, I try to move my focus from his body to his mouth—err, to what he's saying.

"I've been thinking about our training. Sometimes, magic is about learning how to be familiar with the way it's called. During our last session, could you feel me call the water when you were connected?" When he hears me say yes, he inclines his head. "Let's try something different today. We'll stay connected to each other the whole time. I'll use my power to do something, make a flower grow for example, and you will then try to repeat it using your power. What do you think?"

I think you should kiss me and touch me, and we should forget about training today. Sighing, I force myself to pay attention and answer. "I think witch magic is so much easier, but I'm game."

He scrutinizes me for a second, as if he knows what I'm thinking, then grabs my hand and pulls me closer. "You're too far away for this to work. We need to stay together." Lacing his fingers through mine, he pulls me over to a wilting flower on the ground. Using his Elven powers, he feeds the flower, making it perk up. He motions to the wilted flower next to it and turns to me.

Gripping his hand, I mimic him, but instead of the whole flower, one petal perks up. "Arrgh," I grunt out.

"Try again," he suggests quietly. "This time, I'll feed you a little bit of my power."

When I repeat the task, I feel a push of power from him into me, and this time, the entire flower perks up. "So I guess my power's pretty low, huh?" I'm disappointed. When you're used to being powerful, being weak sucks. I'm so tempted to rely on my witch magic, but I know it's important to learn these powers too.

"It takes time," he reminds me. "You've had over three hundred years of practicing to be a witch. You've only had access to your Elven powers for a couple of weeks. Let's try a few more things."

Every time we do a task, he has to push his power into me to help me accomplish it, making my entire body fill with his power and his essence for a split second. It's making my insides buzz with energy, until I feel like a live wire. Sweat coats my face, and I rub my arm across my forehead to clear it off.

"One more, and we'll take a break," he cajoles. His eyes are like green flames when they dart toward me. I wonder if my power is giving him a buzz too. "Maybe something a little bigger." His eyes race around the area surrounding us until he spots a twig. Picking it up, he places it on top of a nearby boulder.

"We're going to animate the stick. Just for a second," he informs me. Power rushes out, encapsulating the little stick like a cloud, then dissipates. The stick is still lying on the boulder, when suddenly, it bends in half like it's sitting up. One of its branches waves at us, then it lies down again and stills.

I've seen a lot of incredible things as a witch, but nothing like the animated stick. My jaw drops, and I stare at him in astonishment.

His face is animated. "Pretty incredible, don't you think?"

"It is, but I'm not sure I'm going to be able to do it," I say hesitantly.

When we connect this time, I push a stream of power toward the stick, but nothing happens until Fallon pushes power through me. I inhale sharply, and my teeth start to chatter. That is a lot of power. The cloud forms and dissipates like his, then the stick follows the same routine, but I barely see it.

"Fallon!" I cry. My body's overloaded with his magic right now, and I don't know what to do.

Seeing my distress, he grabs my head between his large hands and forces me to look at him. "I've got you, it's okay. Take a deep breath. I'm going to deepen our connection and slowly pull the excess magic out of you," he explains. "Ready?"

All I can do is blink my agreement. Within seconds, our connection is stronger and deeper, melding the two of us into one. Our hearts and breaths are in sync, and together, we stand motionless while he pulls power from me, then disperses it into the air around us. The deep connection is the most intimate experience I've ever had with another. His thoughts and power flow through me, along with images from his life, while mine flow through to him.

God, she's beautiful and so strong. Steady, not too fast, almost done.

Blushing, I close my eyes and savor the connection, but there's an element missing. Opening my eyes, I lick my lips and stare at him intensely, trying to convey what I want without having to speak the words.

He moves his hand from the side of my head to the back of my neck. Pulling my head back, his eyes silently ask for permission, and I give it. He lowers his head and kisses me deeply and firmly, like he's been kissing me his entire life and knows exactly what I want. Unhurried, he takes his time, his mouth capturing mine again and again. I loop my arms around his neck and moan, surrendering to him, while all sense of time and space is lost.

"More," I cry, needing more of him and to release the last of this energy.

Without saying anything, his hand dips into the waistband of my leggings and cups me tightly, but it's not enough. I thrust up silently, telling him I need him to take me over the edge. He runs a finger along my seam before finally sliding into me.

Moaning, I pick up my leg and bring it up around his hip to give him greater access. He slides two fingers inside me and brings his thumb up to my nub. While his fingers plunge in and out, his thumb rubs circles, and ripples of pleasure spread out from my center.

"Fallon," I gasp, gripping his shirt.

"I've got you, sweetheart," he assures me.

Feeling my body coil tighter and tighter, I bite my lip. Heat keeps building and building, until I can't contain it anymore and my body explodes. Squeezing my eyes shut, I give a low moan and ride each wave until they finally subside.

Opening my eyes, I search his bright green ones, and a blush spreads over my chest and face. His eyes are serious and full of emotion. Leaning down, he captures my lips again, but this time, his kiss is hard and hungry.

The last of the power is pulled from my body, and the connection lightens. He pulls back and stops kissing me, but his long arms reach out and wrap around me, giving me a full body hug while we catch our breath.

"Damn, you're beautiful. That was one hell of a kiss, and I

barely refrained from joining you as I felt you come undone through the connection," he admits huskily. "But more than the physical, I could see flashes of your life, hear your thoughts, and experience your emotions. I almost didn't know where you left off and I began. It felt good and...right."

I pull back from his embrace. "It's strange the way I know you now. Not the basic stuff like your green eyes and sexy mouth," I say, lightly tracing his lips with my fingers, then I drop my hand and tap his chest, "but the heart of you—your beliefs, the loyalty you feel for Garrett and your men, and the heartbreak over your mother's death." I take a deep breath and shudder, remembering the dark abyss I'd found in him. "And the absolute hatred you have for the dark elves." I don't even know what to say about it.

He grips my hand. "And I know you—the innocent way you view the world, the fierce love you hold for your family, and the dedication to finding your destiny and making all the sacrifices mean something. If this is what it means, I want it. And I want you to be a part of my life. I want to show you my kingdom and introduce you to Garrett and my men."

My eyes search his, and I see the serious intent burning in them. "I want it too," I drawl slowly, "but I have to speak to Valerian first." I reach a hand behind me and scratch my shoulder. It's itching something fierce. I wonder if I've brushed up against poison ivy or something.

"I understand," he states, his thumb rubbing over my hand. "We've got time. Garrett said to give you a kiss for helping to save his life. Do you think this qualifies?" He chuckles.

"Not even close," I rasp, wanting more of him. Pulling him closer, I wrap my arms around him and lift my chin.

THIRTY-TWO

ARDEN

Strolling into the lounge the next morning, I find Astor relaxing on the couch with his nose buried in the MacAllister grimoire and the usual dark shadows surrounding him. With the fire roaring in the fireplace, the shadows appear like they're dancing around him.

"Find anything interesting?" I sink down onto the couch beside him and lean over to see what he's reading. I subtly inhale the scent of him and squirm.

"A lot." His eyes are lit up with excitement as he lifts his head to reply. "For instance, I found the spell to replenish the stone." He flips to a page marked with a piece of paper. Tilting the book, he points, but instead of the spell written down, the page depicts the same red dragon and blonde witch from the first page—the original MacAllister couple. The written portion of the spell is intricately woven into the illustration showing how to merge the flame and blood. Interestingly, there are several smaller illustrations and spells hidden throughout the image as well.

"It's incredible," I breathe, looking at it in wonder. "The journal mentioned I'd have to conduct this spell and give it a burst of power. Thank you for finding this for me." I read through the spell. "And I think the replenishment spell is relatively straightforward, although I have no idea where I'm going to get more power." My eyes dart to his for confirmation and find him assessing the page.

"I believe so," he says distractedly, "but I want to study it further before we attempt the spell." His fingers trace some of the cleverly hidden words and spells.

Raising my eyebrow at his comment, I wonder if he realizes he just said "we."

"That's not all I found," he drawls, flipping to another marker. He tilts the book for me to read the page.

The entire page is dedicated to explaining the MacAllisters' affinity for blood magic. Their essential power is rooted in this affinity. It started with the creation of the stone itself, then slowly evolved to become their primary power, and they became masters at wielding it.

"More than half the book contains spells for blood magic," he explains. "This is why you reacted so strongly the first time you tried it. There are spells in here I've never even heard of or tried. When you want to wield it again, you'll need to start small and build up a tolerance, but your heritage is blood magic." Shutting the book, he lays it carefully on the table in front of the couch.

Remembering the power of the blood, I shiver. It worked, but it also felt like I was pulled under a tidal wave. "I'm not sure," I tell him hesitantly, "but if I do, I want you by my side to help me."

Relief and something else flashes in his eyes. "I want to be by your side," he admits, his voice hoarse with emotion. Turning to face me, he continues, "The need to kiss you is overwhelming. When I saw you fall with a dagger in your heart, it was like I splintered into a million pieces. My mind comprehended your immortality, but my heart felt like it was being ripped out of my chest. Every time I close my eyes to sleep, it replays over and over in my head." He gives a harsh laugh. "And I can't breathe anymore."

Indecision racks me. My first instinct is to say yes, hell yes, and ease his pain. But if I kiss him, am I making a foolish decision I'll regret later? Is he having a knee-jerk reaction to the situation or real feelings?

"I'm not sure..." The words come out of my mouth before I even realize I've said them, but I refuse to take them back.

He shakes his head and gives a harsh laugh. "I'm such a fool. At the battle, I felt such joy when I saw you, and yet I couldn't find the words to prevent you from walking away. It never occurred to me that leaving you is already an impossibility. I'm ruined for anyone else. It's you and only you. When I see you with one of the others, I burn, not with envy, but with regret."

I cup his cheek with my hand and stare into his dark chocolate brown eyes. "I've been drawn to you since the moment I met you outside the kitchen. An incredibly sexy and smart man, with a wicked level of power and a delicious dark side? How could I resist?" His incubus flashes in for a second. "But I need you to be absolutely sure, and I need to feel confident it's real. I won't kiss you today, but I'll open the door. It's up to you to show me how you feel, not just tell me."

A devilish grin spreads across his face. "Gorgeous, you won't regret it." By the look in his eyes, he's already plotting his next move.

"I hope not," I reply, "or I may stab you in the heart." Then I leave him sitting alone in the lounge.

AFTER SPENDING an hour on my hair and makeup, I stand in front of my closet chewing my lip, trying to figure out what to wear on my date with Daire. He's always dressed impeccably in luxurious clothing, and as I assess my options, I realize nothing works. I haven't had time to replenish my wardrobe after the hotel incident, and I have two, maybe three options and no time to shop. I could create something with magic, but it's always such a risk.

Hearing a knock on the door, I adjust my towel before I walk over and open it. Theron is standing there, holding a box in his hands. His jaw drops and his eyes turn stormy and wild when he gets a glimpse of me.

He thrusts the box at me. "Daire sent you a present," he states hoarsely. After I take the gift, his finger drifts up and skates along the tops of my breasts. "The sight of you in a towel tests the limits of my control, but given it's Daire's night, I'll leave without tasting." Rolling his shoulders, he gives me one of his tiny smirks and gets in the elevator.

Shaking my head, I close the door and put the box on the bed. After lifting the lid, I reach in and pull out a navy-blue jumpsuit. I hold it up to my body and assess the picture in the mirror to make sure it fits. With my height, it's tough to find clothes, especially pants that reach my ankles, but it looks like it will fit.

Tossing the towel on the bed, I step into underwear and a bra before pulling on the jumpsuit. The pants fit perfectly, from my ankles to my waist, however when I pull the top up, I realize it's not going to work with a bra. With a deep V in the front and thin straps crisscrossing in the back, I'll have to go without a bra, so I slip it off and pull the top back up.

It's perfect. I turn from side to side in front of the mirror, loving how it emphasizes my height. The jumpsuit skims my long body like a dream, and the soft material caressing my almost naked body gives it a decadent feeling I didn't expect. Slipping on my silver strappy heels, I grab my phone, then start pacing. My nerves are too unsettled to sit.

CHAPTER
THIRTY-THREE

ARDEN

At exactly seven o'clock, there's a knock on the door. When I open it this time, Daire is standing there in a navy suit, the exact color of my jumpsuit, with an icy blue tie. "Hello, handsome. I'm impressed. Nobody has ever bought me an outfit." My words are cool and calm, but inside, I'm jittery.

When we enter the elevator, he steps close and takes a deep breath. "You smell incredibly sinful and delicious, as always, and you look beautiful." The deep timbre of his voice causes shivers to run up my spine.

Mmm, smooth. Too smooth? "This elevator ride is significantly better than our first one," I toss out. "You know, the one where you were kind of a dick."

He gives a low whistle and a wicked smile. "I don't recall being that bad."

261

"You were," I assure him. "I finally get to meet my crush, and with one elevator ride, the picture changed from hero to arrogant jerk with a sneer a mile long." I sweep my hair back from my shoulder. "I'm not entirely sure how we got from there to here. I suppose once you lost the sneer and the superior attitude, I liked the guy underneath."

He stares at me in fascination before laughing. "Old habits are not going to work with you, are they?"

"Would you want them to?" I retort, before stepping out into the lobby. "Now if you can be your true self, we can leave. The man I want isn't the same one Solange dated."

Sliding a hand behind my back, he steers me to the garage. "I think you're going to love our date tonight." With a mysterious and lighthearted grin, he leads me to the luxurious SUV parked in the garage.

Twenty minutes later, we're seated at a table in the middle of an art gallery. Various paintings grace the white walls, each one showcased perfectly. "I hope you don't mind, but I thought we could dine and discuss the paintings on the wall. I want to hear your thoughts on whether they will fit with the design in my new room."

Interesting and entirely unexpected—I like it. "I'll give you points for originality and catering to my interests," I tease him. "I didn't add any art to your walls because it's such a personal choice. It needs to speak to the person living in the space."

"I agree. I picked these paintings earlier today because each one appeals to me in a different way, and since I'm hoping you will spend time relaxing in my room in the future, I want your opinion." He throws this casually into the conversation, but when I stare into his eyes, I realize he's very serious.

Settling back, I pick up the glass of wine in front of me and take a long drink. If I'm honest, I'd love to relax in his room with him and do other decadent things. Just thinking about the possibilities makes me shiver, and judging by the carnal look in his eyes, he is wondering too.

Looking for a way to ease the tension, I glance down at the table and notice he's drinking from a different bottle. "Are you not drinking the same wine?"

"No, mine is a rare AB negative, hundred-year vintage, if I'm not mistaken," he drawls, watching my reaction.

"Do you always drink procured blood?" I ask, fascinated with the idea of aging blood like wine. I know we serve it at The Abbey, but I've never asked any of the vampires about it.

He lifts a shoulder. "Some blood is hard to find, and by ordering it, I can make sure I have a good supply available for when I desire it."

"So, you don't always need it?" I ask, diving deeper into the subject. I want to know about this part of him.

"Need, want..." he muses, taking a drink. "You don't always need coffee or food, but you want it. Although you can't live without food and water. It's no different for me."

"What about taking blood directly from someone?" My heart races as I ask this question, but I don't look away.

His gaze drops to the pulse fluttering at the base of my throat, and his icy blue eyes seem like flames. "When a vampire takes from your vein, the act briefly creates a path between the two of you, intensifying your emotions and opening the door to your mind. Sometimes, it goes both ways, and a vampire opens the door to their own. Regardless, it's extremely intimate." He watches my tongue lick my suddenly dry lips. "Your blood smells mouthwateringly delicious, and even before we met, I wanted a taste. Does this bother you?" He stares intently, waiting for my answer.

"No," I rasp, desire making my voice hoarse. I hold his gaze, wanting him to see the truth.

Heat flares between us and for several seconds, we sit and

stare at each other. Our server arrives, breaking the tension, and Daire relaxes back in his chair and informs him we're ready for our dinner. Lifting a hand towards one of the paintings, he changes the topic to something a bit less explosive. While we eat and talk, the tension eases between us, becoming a low simmer.

Studying each painting, we discuss the things we like and don't like about each one until we narrow our picks to two— an abstract picture in various shades of blues and blacks which reminds him of flying at night, and a gorgeous painting of a cottage by the water that brings back memories of his mother.

When the gallery manager comes by, he points to the two paintings, and they wrap them up and load them in the vehicle.

"Dinner was incredible," I drawl slowly, "and the atmosphere equally impressive."

"And the company?" he inserts smoothly.

"Intriguing," I reply sassily, but truthfully.

"I'll take every crumb I can get," he jokes. "Want to come help me hang my paintings?"

I snort. "With such a smooth pickup line, how can I resist?"

Once we're back at The Abbey and in his room, I'm surprised at the touches he's already added to personalize it. There's a stunning vase, a bronze statue, and a silver organic shaped bowl. We hang the abstract "night sky" painting over the bed, and the cottage canvas in the lounge area.

"It's stunning," I tell him.

"Mmm, I completely agree." I turn to find him studying me and can't help but blush.

Grabbing a jacket from the closet, he slides each of my arms through the sleeves. It's too big, but he doesn't give me a chance to question it. In a blur, he picks me up, and a second later, we're on the roof.

Strolling to the edge, I take in the nearby city with its lights shimmering for miles. "It's beautiful."

He turns me around to face him. "Would you like to see it from another angle?" His wings snap out behind him.

For a second, I can't speak. He's magnificent, with his golden perfection framed against the backdrop of his black silky wings. Now that's a painting, but I'd want it in my room, not his. "Yes," I agree huskily.

He swings me up in his arms, and in a heart pounding second, we're high in the air. My arms cling to him tightly at first, but as we cruise over the city, swerving in and out of the skyscrapers, a sense of exhilaration takes over. Throwing back my arms, I let go of everything and ride the night air with my dark prince, knowing he won't let me go.

I shiver slightly from the cold, and he takes us back to the roof of The Abbey immediately.

Setting me down, he wraps his hand around my neck and places his thumb on the pulse beating rapidly at the base of my throat. "And the company?" he asks, repeating his earlier question.

"Exhilarating," I answer breathlessly. "The wings are a game changer. You might be able to reach hero status again."

"You're impossible," he growls out. Stepping in close, he swoops down and captures my lips in a scorching kiss, his mouth dominating mine with unreserved passion. Fingers slide into my hair, gripping firmly, while he shows me the stars.

Moaning, I reach up and clasp him tightly to me, wanting to give everything back to him in return. But I want to take too. I whimper, wanting to dive into his blue fire and revel in it. Turning my head for some air, he moves from my lips to my neck. He skims his teeth lightly down my neck, and I moan, knowing he wants to drink, but he only places a small kiss on my pulse.

Breathing heavily, he steps back and pulls in his wings. His hand grasps mine, and he places a kiss in the center of my palm before laying it on his chest, where I feel a beat. "Will you join me in my room?"

"If I can stop by the lounge for a minute, yes," I reply, and a puzzled expression crosses his face, but he agrees.

In a blur, we're in the lounge. I want to laugh at his impatience, but out of the corner of my eye, I notice Theron is slumped down into the couch, fast asleep. Stepping away from Daire, I carefully pull Theron's phone from his hand, place it on the coffee table, and slip off his vest and shoes. Daire helps me ease him down into the sofa, and I cover him with the throw. My hand aches to sweep his hair back, but seeing the dark circles under his eyes, I refrain.

A minute later, Daire sets me down in his room. Taking off his coat, I hand it back to him to hang up. I wander around his room, picking up items, only to set them down a second later. For some reason, my nerves are lit up. Glancing over my shoulder, I notice Daire leaning against the wall, his icy blue eyes intent and hooded.

"Ever since I walked into my new room, I've been picturing you in it." His voice is husky, convincing me of his sincerity. "You've been here twice tonight...more than I'd hoped. I might be pushing my luck."

For some reason, his open declaration calms me. Sauntering over to him, I breathe in his natural scent and his luxurious cologne, and the sexy combination fires up the passion simmering inside of me. Placing my palms on his chest, I slip his suit jacket off his shoulders and place it on a nearby chair. When I return, he's still, watching my every move like a predator who's getting ready to pounce. My palms smooth over his silk shirt and the muscular body hiding beneath it.

"I'm here now," I remind him. Leaning my body into his, I kiss his neck several times then move to his jaw, but when I reach up to capture his lips, I find myself flat on the sofa with him lying next to me.

"I'm truly a lucky man," he murmurs, his voice rough with need. Slanting his mouth over mine, he picks up right where we left off. His kiss is demanding as he strokes and sucks, and I can't help but return it with equal fervor. He plunges into each kiss, taking fiercely, until I'm lost in the sensations bombarding me.

Turning my body, I grip his shoulders with my hands but encounter a barrier. Using my magic, I strip him of his shirt. When they return, my hands encounter smooth skin and his hard body, and I sigh. Skimming his body, I map every inch, not stopping until I find a smooth piece of skin on his lower stomach. I run my nails across it, and he twitches and moans.

With my hands on his bare skin, his kiss gets rougher. Pulling back slightly, he tips my chin to the side and skims his teeth against my neck. Lifting his head up, he rasps, "Are you sure you want me to taste you?"

My heart is beating fast, but not in fear. I want this kind of kiss from him. "Yes, I'm absolutely sure." My answer is firm and clear, leaving him without doubt.

He groans and trails a finger down my cleavage. "It's more intimate here," he whispers, stopping on the inside of my left breast, by my heart.

When I nod, he picks me up and sits down on the sofa with

me in his lap. When I'm straddling him, he tightens his arms around me and gives me a deep, languorous kiss, filled with heat. His hand tugs on my hair, pulling my head back, and he places kisses along my neck. Lingering on each individual pulse point, he makes me breathless with anticipation as I wonder what it will feel like when he sinks his teeth into me.

His fingers hook the straps of my jumpsuit and pull down the top. "You're so beautiful," he says, leaving my mouth to lavish attention on each of my breasts. When I moan, he uses his firm lips to suck hard on my nipples, and I shift restlessly on top of him.

Grinding down, I rock back and forth, needing more. With my hands on his shoulders, I arch my back and move against his hard body.

He moans and thrusts up to meet my core. In a flash, he bites, sinking his teeth into the side of my breast.

There's a pinprick of pain, then an avalanche of sensations rushes through me. Desire floods my body, and I come hard. He grunts, and his body jerks against mine. Holding tightly to him, I inhale sharply when the desire is replaced with images of me and a kaleidoscope of emotions. Anger, fear, sadness, wonder, hurt, and of course, desire—all for and about me. He's been hiding a lot behind his deceptively calm exterior. Breathing heavily, I ride out the intense wave, finally coming down a few minutes later to find him staring at me. I glance down and notice the tiny holes on the side of my breast.

His eyes reflect a strange mixture of satisfaction and apprehension. Grabbing the throw on the couch, he pulls it around my shoulders. "Did you know my heart beats when you're around? The rest of the time, it might as well be a rock in my chest. I don't even know if it's involuntary or if I subconsciously will it to happen, but I like it because it reminds me of my human half." He trails his finger across my lips. "The taste of you lingers on my lips and tongue, and I know one taste is never going to be enough." His finger slides down and circles his bite. "Thank you for my incredible surprise. I would love for you to sleep here with me tonight and share it with me."

Tilting my head, I consider his words. "I felt it beat earlier, but I didn't realize it was a rare occurrence. I like the fact that a piece of you only responds to me." Reaching up to cup his jaw, I lean forward and swipe my tongue across his bottom lip. "Mmm...I taste us, and I would love to stay with you."

A wicked smile graces his face. "I can't wait to see you in my bed."

CHAPTER

THIRTY-FOUR

THERON

When I wake early the next morning, I realize I'm on the couch in the lounge. Puzzled, I lie there for a moment, trying to figure out when I took my waistcoat and shoes off. I can't recall, but things are usually blurry when I get caught up in researching something. Standing, I stretch a few times and grab my phone off the table. Based on what I found last night, we have three possible leads, but only two of them have a significantly higher chance of being the right one.

After grabbing some coffee, I head up to shower and change. If I can check one of the leads this morning and rule it out, we'll be pretty close to finding Arden's ancestor. If it was later, I'd take Astor with me, but he's not a morning person, and I don't like dealing with him when he's irritable. Valerian is still away, and Fallon left to check on his father, which leaves me with Daire. Shooting off a text, I ask him to meet me in the lobby in fifteen minutes.

Of course when I get to the lobby, he's not there, but he's not technically late either. Scrolling through the information on my phone, I take the extra two minutes to make sure I have it memorized, since technology doesn't always work the same in the land of the Fae. I hear a whistle, then a blur goes by me, headed toward the kitchen. Twenty seconds later, he comes to a stop in front of me, holding a cup of coffee.

Giving him my best impassive stare, I scrutinize him carefully. When he grins, I realize I've never seen him this relaxed. "You're cheerful this morning. I thought for sure you'd give me hell for getting you up this early. What's going on with you?"

"A tall blonde with legs for miles, who's one of the best warriors I've ever seen and smells utterly delicious," he replies with an arched eyebrow. "Our date last night? Thanks for delivering the present for me. It fit her beautifully."

The date. I can't believe I'd forgotten, or maybe I can. When I heard him ask her to dinner, I could only sit there and gnash my teeth. I don't mind if she goes on a date with Daire, but I'd been planning on asking her out myself. Frustration eats at me. It always feels like something or someone gets in the way.

Pushing away the negative thoughts, I feign casual interest. "Oh? Where did you take her? The new place on the east side?" He usually keeps up with the newest restaurant openings.

"First, I took her to an art gallery, where I had dinner set up for us. Then we came back and I took her flying," he replies before taking a sip of coffee.

That's interesting. And a good sign. I stare at him in fascination. He never takes anyone flying. "I can't believe Arden wanted to hang out in your dungeon," I remark dryly. "You're a lucky bastard." I'm sure he can probably hear the envy in my voice, but I can't help it.

His eyebrows rise in surprise. "You don't know?"

"Know what?" I ask irritably.

"Arden redecorated my entire room in all these different shades of blue. She got rid of all the old furniture and brought in new, comfortable stuff. It blew me away," he admits, describing all the various changes. "It's luxurious but comfortable."

This must have been the surprise she worked on before we left for the Kingdom of Dragons. "If it's anything like the lounge, I'm sure it's fantastic," I say shortly. "We've got to get going if we're going to make it back in time for the meeting this afternoon."

"What meeting?" he asks, then grimaces when he hears his phone ping.

"The one I just sent out to everyone," I reply. Opening a portal, I step through and he follows.

When we step out the other side, he gives a little shudder. If there's one place an Underworlder doesn't like, it's the land of the Fae, especially the light Fae. Everything is superficially bright and unsuspectingly deadly. Without warning, the prettiest flower can turn carnivorous and chase after you, especially if you are not light Fae.

"You might want to look away," I remind him before turning up the summer side of my heritage and dimming my winter side. Holding my hands out in front of me, I watch while they turn from pale white to bronze with beams of light shining out of them. It's my least favorite form, but it's better to be the lion than the mouse in the light Fae kingdom.

We head toward the nearby village, where my records show one of the MacAllister witches lived shortly after the massacre. Even though Arden's other half is Elven, there's always a chance the witch moved there after she lived here, so it's better to check out every lead and rule it out.

Finding the inn, I leave Daire outside while I ask the innkeeper a few questions. Nobody is going to answer my questions with the prince of death and doom at my side, especially when he's constantly smiling. It's unnerving.

Thankfully, longevity of life means long memories, but it didn't even take the Fae more than a minute to recall the witch.

"Sima moved here a little over twelve hundred years ago. She was a nice young witch, not like most, and we welcomed her into the village. She would often bring cakes and other sweets to the market and sell them for money. She was an outstanding baker," he says fondly, patting his stomach. "We started placing orders for her to supply the inn with her goods, and she usually came into town once a week to deliver. One day, she met another Fae named... Hold on, let me think." He scratches his head and stares off into the distance. "I think his name was Rivan. Anyway, they fell in love not long after. She seemed happy, until one day, we heard a boom and smoke started rising from the trees. When we got there, the entire place had been blown apart. We found pieces of her in the rubble. Given she was human, we buried her and put up a marker." His voice is gruff when he gets to the end.

"When did this happen? And what happened to Rivan?" I ask suspiciously. I've met one Rivan in my life, and he serves the Queen of the Light Fae. He arrived sometime close to this period, if I recall. Does the queen know about his past?

"Probably about a year after she arrived. He was gone. We assumed he blew up too, but weren't sure," he answers, shaking his head like something bothers him about that fact, then he gives me directions to her grave.

"If you find out who did this, make sure they pay, will you?" His voice is hard when he asks. "She was the nicest young woman I've ever met and the best baker. She deserved better."

My voice is soft when I reply, "They all did." He gives me a puzzled glance, and I nod in agreement.

Stepping outside, I notice Daire is surrounded by Fae males with scowls on their faces, and I laugh.

He snarls. "It's not funny. You took your damn time." He moves to the side to let me step up beside him. When the Fae see me, they slowly back away. They probably don't get many Fae lords in these outskirts, maybe just the few who stay the night at the inn.

"Come on," I tell him, motioning for him to follow. A couple of miles outside of town, I find an old marker with the name "Sima" on it, red roses growing wildly around it. It's not a flower found in Fae, so I have to guess Rivan planted it.

I tell Daire the story the innkeeper told me. "Rivan showed up to work for the queen not too long after. I don't know if he's hiding or if he drifted there after she died, but I find it suspicious. I'll send a text to Solandis and see if she can make discreet inquiries."

"It does sound odd, but I wouldn't dismiss it. Alain taught me betrayal can come from those closest to you," he murmurs. "Before we go, I thought you might want to know something." He turns to face me. "After flying, we were headed to my room when Arden insisted on stopping by the lounge. She wanted to check on you. When she saw you slumped down on the couch asleep, she used magic to remove your waistcoat and shoes, then covered you with a blanket. She muttered something about you working too hard. She cares about you, a lot. Don't let all of this" —he waves his hands around— "get in the way. She might want answers, but she needs you."

Startled, I blink. Daire usually doesn't offer his opinion on personal matters. A smile breaks free at the thought of her interrupting their date to check on me. "Thank you."

Dipping his chin, he smirks. "Let's go. I can't stand to be here any longer," he drawls, strolling by me to create a portal.

LATER IN THE CONFERENCE ROOM, I walk through the findings of my research. "Of the five young women sent out by the MacAllisters, two were found dead not far from the Kingdom of Dragons. The other three went to the kingdoms of the light Fae, light elves, and dark elves."

Valerian, on the screen, nods. He'd found the two who died close to his kingdom by having village elders search through their records.

"This morning, Daire and I went to the light Fae to search for Sima MacAllister." I stop and flash Arden a look to warn her. "We found out she was killed about a year after she left."

Sadness fills her face. "How did she die?"

I repeat the innkeeper's story. When I get to the part of Rivan, her eyebrows rise in astonishment.

"Rivan, the one who put this tattoo on me?" she asks, her fingers finding the rune on her neck. "He always seemed sad when I was around him. Maybe that's why."

"I'm going to ask Solandis to make a few very discreet inquiries," I inform her. "We need to know all of our enemies going forward. There's a bigger picture we're missing, and I'm not sure if it has to do with the...Primary or something else."

"Great idea," she states. "And the other two witches? We know I'm Elven, so I'm guessing it has to be one of them?"

Fallon interjects, "Let's check out my kingdom first. Hopefully, we won't even have to go to the dark Elven territory." His compressed lips show his distaste for his dark brethren. "My father's been wanting to meet you, and we can accomplish two tasks with one visit."

"I don't want your father to know about the MacAllisters," Arden states firmly. "My mother was very clear about the danger, and I don't know him." She holds his gaze steadily until he agrees. "Also, I still want to check out the witch who went to the dark Elven territory."

"Why?" Fallon asks, his voice hard. "I can't escort you into their territory."

She raises her eyebrows at his reaction. "Because in order to tell their story, I need to know what happened to every single one of them. And if you can't escort me, that's fine. I'll find someone else. I know you've got a painful past with them."

I can tell he's torn when he hears her reply—the prince in him respects her answer, but the man whose mother was killed by dark elves wants to bar her from going. He finally dips his chin in acknowledgement but says nothing.

"Valerian, can you come back for a couple of days to go with us?" I ask.

"Things are going well, so I can spare a few days," he confirms. "And it will give me a chance to see Arden." He winks at her.

She blushes. "You don't have to come back, I can..." Her voice trails off when she sees us all shaking our heads.

"Astor and Daire can't accompany us. The light Elven king hates the dark and everyone associated with it. He tolerates me, but only if I use my summer form. He actually likes Valerian, which always helps," I explain, watching her eyes widen with every word. "Fallon's father is a bastard who doesn't like anyone. You're an unknown, and he'll single you out and drill into you the first chance he gets. We're going to make sure he doesn't get the chance. Right, Fallon?" I give him a hard stare.

He runs a hand over his face. "He's right, it's never pleasant visiting with my father," he admits. "And he's not been...well."

"This should be fun," she gushes with mock cheerfulness. "You know, this group isn't doing too well in the parent department. Good thing we have Solandis, Vargas, and Lucifer to share. I can even throw a brother into the mix, although you all sort have it covered. And we can add Meri as a sister. One big happy family." She grins and dusts her hands off. "Done."

Shaking my head at her antics, I barely hold in my smile. "We'll leave tomorrow afternoon when Valerian gets here."

I wait as everyone files out and catch Arden's arm. "A moment?"

THIRTY-FIVE

P ulling her around, I cage her between me and the wall. "A certain vampire told me you tucked me in last night?"

She gives a delightful blush. "You looked uncomfortable. And you've been working so hard on the search for Agnes and now my ancestor. It's the least I could do."

"So it's something a friend would do for another?" I ask her intently.

She snorts. Leaning into me, she places her mouth by my ear and whispers, "You always have my attention. Whether you're organizing a trip to the Kingdom of Dragons, making reservations for a delightful dinner, or staying up all night searching for my ancestor, I see you. When you're not in sight, I wonder what you're doing, and sometimes, I worry about you." She kisses the corner of my mouth. "And yes, you're my friend, but goddess, you're...so much more."

She throws my own words back at me, but they sound a hell of a lot better coming from her. I still, barely breathing, waiting for her next words

Her eyes stare intensely into mine. "Friend, warrior, icy winter Fae, warm summer Fae, member of the Imperium Cadre. They are all facets of you, and I want all of them." Cupping my jaw with her hands, she continues, "You've been a commanding presence in my life since the moment I arrived, but all that pales to how I *feel* around you. I live to see the tiniest change in your expression or the tapping of your fingers. When you ditch your formal attire for jeans or grace me with a full-blown smile, you leave me breathless. But nothing compares to seeing your violet eyes filled with turbulence and desire for me." She pauses. "Because then I know how much I disturb you. I know the desire you feel for me is real, and it makes me burn with the need to have you inside of me."

When her words crash into me, I savor each and every one, and the formidable control I've held onto for so long shatters. I lean into her body, spear my hands through her hair, and bring my mouth crashing down onto hers, taking and claiming everything she has to give. I'm relentless, refusing to give her time to think or walk away. Not this time.

Not content to be passive, she demands more, her lips sucking and tugging on mine. Her hands tighten around my neck, and she rubs against me. "Theron," she gasps. "You'd better not walk away."

"Never," I promise. "You ripped into my heart and tore down all my barriers. Goddess, I need you." My hands roam over her delectable body, trying to learn how close my dreams match reality. Using magic, I remove her shirt and groan when her luscious breasts fall into my hands. Ever since I saw her in the towel the first time, I've ached to see and touch them. Skimming over them lightly, I watch her dark pink nipples pucker.

She moans and arches up, pulling my head down to her breast.

Latching onto her nipple, I alternate between sucking and flicking before releasing it for the other. Back and forth, I worship each one with my mouth and tongue. The tug of her hands in my hair and her moans make me groan with satisfaction.

"Theron," she rasps. Her hand reaches down and grips my cock, and it's my turn to thrust up. She slides her hand down and back up again, and I swear.

Using magic, I remove my pants, needing to feel her hand wrapped tightly around me. When it does, I have to lock my knees to remain standing.

Swearing, I pull her leg up and around my hip, then thrust into her, only to find the barrier of her leggings. We both moan. The mere thought of a single layer being all that separates us is torture.

This time, she uses her magic to remove her pants, and next time I thrust against her, her wet body slides against mine like silk. I rub back and forth, breathing harshly, but I stop myself from entering her. Looking into her glazed eyes, I capture every detail, so I can savor it later .

Her hands grip my shoulders, and she arches into me. "Now, Theron."

Seizing her mouth with mine, I kiss her deeply and slide into her warm, tight body. Feeling her sweet heat wrapped around me makes me want to explode. "Wrap both your legs around me."

When she locks her heels behind me, I sink all the way into

her, and she moans and swivels her hips, grinding down on me. Gritting my teeth, I hold on to the edge for a minute, then start thrusting furiously. Our harsh breathing fills the air, along with the sounds of her moans.

Feeling myself near the edge, I reach down and find her slick nub with my thumb. I circle it, bringing her to a peak, and when she tightens around me, I let my remaining control go and fall over the edge with her.

Breathing rapidly, I lay my forehead against hers for a second to catch my breath. Glancing around the conference room, I chuckle. "Not quite what I planned for our first time." I brush her hair from her face. "But I'm adaptive." Swinging around with her in my arms, I head toward my room.

When we enter, she whistles. "Someone likes his creature comforts," she teases me, peering around at the furnishings. "Daire should have asked you to redesign his room."

Shrugging, I barely give the room a glance and stride straight through to the shower. Turning on the water to my pre-set temperature, I step in with her and let her slide to her feet. When I reach for the soap, I find she's already beat me to it.

Her soapy hands have barely begun to wash me, and I'm already hard again. Locking my jaw, I stand perfectly still and impassive while she teases me. When her hands wrap around my cock, I can't help thrusting forward. As if it's her cue, she slowly glides her hands from the base to the tip over and over, keeping me hard and on edge.

"Who's teasing now?" I raise my eyebrow a millimeter, knowing it drives her crazy. Pulling back, I rinse off and take the soap from her. She pouts, but I shake my head. "My turn." Paying attention to every detail of her delectable body, I catalog it and store it in the back of my mind for later. When my fingers glide over her sweet core, I can't help but linger, playing and thrusting into her until she comes around my fingers.

Moving away from her wandering hands, I chuckle and step out of the shower, leaving her in there to finish.

A minute later, she drifts into the bedroom wearing a towel, and I groan. "You've figured out my secret, haven't you?"

A wicked smile graces her face. "Sit down," she orders me huskily, pointing to a nearby club chair. When she sees my hard cock standing at full attention, she licks her lips and climbs on top of me. "Towel on or off?" she asks, maneuvering until I'm inside of her.

"On," I say gruffly, heat stealing across my face. My hands move toward her waist, but she shakes her head and places them on the arms of the chair.

Lifting up, she slides to the tip and back down again. Then, she leans forward to position her hands on the back of the chair. Setting an easy pace, her body is tight and wet as it glides up and down, pulling every sensation from me. "How does this feel?" she asks, her breath catching on the way down.

"My dreams are never going to be the same." My hands grip the chair tightly as I grit the words out. She looks so fucking good in the towel, her face and the top of her chest flushed with desire, and my head drops back to watch her need build with every stroke.

After a few minutes, she pauses, and I can feel the first quivers.

"Do you want me to take over?"

She nods, so I hold her tightly to me as I stand. With just a couple of steps, I lay her on the bed and stare down at the sight before me. Finally. It feels like I've been waiting forever to see her in this exact spot, her body flushed and her eyes filled with passion. For me. Still joined, I slowly slide in and out several times so I can watch her body react to mine. She's so damn beautiful. I want to stay like this but when she calls my name, my control starts to waver.

"Theron," she murmurs.

"Unwrap the towel," I demand, picking up speed again. She slides one side of the towel off slowly, then the other and I groan at the sight of her luscious body, but I don't stop. When she whimpers, my fingers find her core, and I bring her over the edge. Her release triggers my own, and I thrust hard and come.

Dropping my hand to the bed, I work to catch my breath. When her fingers run through my hair, I look up. "What the hell was I waiting on again?" I muse. I know though. After seeing her full of passion and in my arms, why would I settle for anything less? The reward is indescribable.

"Maybe they're right," she muses, her eyes dancing with laughter. "You plan too much."

THIRTY-SIX

FALLON

Dressing in my official Elven prince attire the next morning, I contemplate the possibilities of this visit going well. My father isn't known for his generosity of spirit, but he's my king and father so I've always excused it. Unfortunately, for the past fifty years, he's gotten progressively worse. I don't even recognize him most days.

When I walk into the lobby a minute later, Valerian and Arden are kissing. I stop, not wanting to intrude, and turn toward the kitchen. When I hear her moan, my body tightens, and it's all I can do to keep walking. Theron is standing by the coffee machine when I enter the kitchen, and I wince. He's almost blinding in his summer Fae form.

"Is the coffee fresh?" I ask, watching him stare at the pot. Picking up a mug, I walk over and grab it from the burner.

"Yes. I've already had mine, but I needed to get out of the lobby," he mutters. "Valerian arrived a few minutes ago."

Slapping him on the back, I laugh. "I was doing pretty well until I heard her moan," I remark. We linger in the kitchen for a few more minutes until I finish my coffee. "Ready?"

Instead of answering, he stalks toward the lobby, and I follow. "I'd like to go to the village first. Then, if your father isn't in a good mood, we can leave directly from the palace and come home."

It's a good plan. "I agree."

When we walk up to Arden and Valerian, she's leaning into him, listening to a story about Glynnis. "As a councilwoman, she's giving those men hell," Valerian says, laughing. "She's a great addition."

Arden's eyes widen when she takes in my uniform, and she twirls her finger, demanding I show her the whole thing. I turn in a tight circle, showing her the lightweight green wool trousers and jacket. It has a few medals and jewels on it, but not much.

I roll my eyes. "It's a uniform, and it's the least formal one I own," I remark self-consciously. "Why the surprise? I'm sure you've seen them when you've visited the light Fae queen with Solandis, and theirs are extremely ostentatious."

She lifts a shoulder. "They weren't you, but you're right— the Fae live for formality and ostentatious displays." She tosses a wink at Theron, then gestures to her own clothing. "Will this be okay to meet your father?"

She's wearing black slacks, a green silk blouse, and silver heels. "Since we're meeting him during the day, it will be fine," I tell her. "You look stunning."

"This reminds me of the first time we met," Theron murmurs, gesturing to her clothes. "We're going to the village first, then the castle."

When we step into the village a minute later, we find it teeming with life. It's market day, so everyone is out visiting with each other and shopping, while kids run around and play. I smile.

When the crowd sees me, everything stops. The village elder walks over to me and bows. "Prince Fallon, it's so good of you to visit us. I'm Elder Lo. Is there something I can do for you?"

"Hello, Elder Lo. Pardon our intrusion, but we're looking for information," I reply, motioning to Theron to step forward and explain.

"We're searching for a witch who might have lived here a little over twelve hundred years ago. Her name might have been Fiona," Theron tells him.

He studies Theron for a second before his eyes move to Arden. "She was here for about five years and a very sad young woman when she came to us. It took me a long time to get her to open up. She explained her family had been massacred and she was in hiding. She became my friend, so I helped her stay hidden. Whenever someone asked about her, I lied and told them no witches were living in our village." His eyes are filled with sadness as he recounts her story. "Unfortunately, when I was away visiting my family in a nearby village, they came again, and someone told them where to find her. I came back to find her dead."

My heart stutters. If she died, it means Arden is dark Elven. My head swirls, and my heart thumps hard in my chest. Wanting to roar in denial, I clench my fists to maintain my control. Theron gives me a sharp glance. He knows what this means too.

Arden steps forward and takes his hand into hers. "Thank you for helping her. I'm sure it meant the world to have you as a friend. Can you tell us anything about the ones who came looking for her?"

"They were from different races. Witches mostly, but other supernaturals too. Dark Fae, light elves, and dark elves, if I recall correctly. I wasn't here for the last inquiry, though," he informs us.

"Do you mind if I ask where she's buried?" Arden questions softly.

"Not at all," he replies, motioning for Arden to follow him. "She said someone would come searching for her one day, but the years went by and nobody came. I didn't realize it would be so long." He pulls out a medallion from his shirt and shows it to Arden.

When we stop in front of a house, I raise my eyebrows in surprise, but when he takes us through to the back garden, I realize it's his house. There, in the corner of his garden under a willow tree, lies a simple gravestone. "Fiona, Friend and Proud MacAllister Witch" is engraved on her tombstone, along with the date of her death.

Arden smiles at the elder. "I'm so glad she found you," she murmurs. "And I thank you for honoring her and keeping her secret."

"She said you would tell their story," he replies. "I hope you tell it well."

"I will," she promises him.

After thanking him for his time, we walk back to the market. Arden is biting her lip and giving me worried glances, but I can't assure her everything's going to be fine. My hatred for the dark elves is deep, cultivated by my father and fed frequently by us both for years. Raising my hand, I massage my temples. My head pounds with the knowledge of her heritage. They killed my mother, and I'm not sure forgiveness is in me, but my heart argues Arden's case, reminding me what she means to me. Taking a few deep breaths, I turn to her when we get to the portal.

"We can talk later, but we need to meet my father right now," I state softly, avoiding her gaze.

Theron and Valerian are torn between wanting to be there for me and protecting Arden, but I ignore them and lead us all directly to the castle.

My father is waiting for us in the throne room when we arrive. "Father," I say, greeting him with a bow. "You know King Valerian and Lord Theron." My eyes dart to the sides of the room, and I realize it's empty of everyone but us. Thankful for this small mercy, I steel myself to introduce Arden to him.

My father inclines his head to them, then peers past me to Arden. Narrowing his eyes, he looks at me with incredulity. "You dare to bring dark Elven to my home?" His voice is whisper quiet as he stares at her, and I can see his anger building with every second that ticks by on the clock. He probably hasn't even been this close to his enemy in over a thousand years. His lip curls as he tilts his head to study her like she's a bug under his boot.

Standing, he walks closer to Arden and reaches for her shoulder. "Maybe we can use this to our advantage. Let me see your mark. I want to know if you're worth ransoming or if I should kill you immediately." His voice is clear and reasonable, as if he's discussing the weather instead of her death.

Arden tenses and steps back, shifting into her battle stance, while Valerian moves in front of her and Theron slides closer to her back.

I pivot to stand in front of my father. "Arden was raised as a witch her entire life. She knows nothing of dark elves." Laying my hand on his sleeve, I turn him away from her. "And you can't kill her." Keeping my voice even, I work to control the fury running through my veins.

"I'm the king!" he roars. "I'll damn well do as I please. Guards!"

Garrett comes running, sword in hand, when he hears my father's shouting. When he finds me with him, he waits for a sign on what to do. I give a small shake of my head, silently telling him to stand down, and he sheathes his sword.

"Arden is on the witches' council, and she is King Valerian's mate. You cannot kill her without starting a war," I state firmly. "I apologize for bringing her here. We'll leave immediately." Taking a step forward, I wave a hand toward the portal.

"Stop," my father demands. I tense, waiting for his next move. "There's something else." He walks around Arden, his brow furrowed in contemplation. Stepping close, he holds his hand out in front of her, palm forward, and freezes. "The Fates have betrayed me again!" Enraged, he reaches out to grab Arden's arm, but Valerian steps in front of her.

"You will not touch her," he states, his voice hard as granite. "We're leaving, Fallon. Now." Shielding Arden, we start walking back to the portal with Arden in the middle.

"Fallon, you will not mate with her," he screams. "I forbid it."

Dread curls in my stomach. I turn to him, my mind churning with the thought of him knowing she's my mate. "My mate?" I question him, sounding vague. "I told you she's Valerian's mate."

"Don't lie to me. I feel your essence and power mixed with hers, and I know those fate bastards have been searching for a way to get back at me." He laughs maniacally. "Well, they've found it, but I will not have it. Do you hear me, Fallon? If you walk out that door with her, I'll disown you and both of you will regret it." His voice is determined, and from past experience, I know he's serious. When he's like this, he finds a way to get what he wants, even if he has to sell his soul. With his eyes narrowed on Arden, I know he's planning something nasty for her.

My eyes drift to her, and I hate what I have to do next. I've been ignoring my father's deteriorating state for a while, and it's time to deal with it. Plus, if I don't stay, I won't be able to neutralize him and protect her. When she looks at me, I turn my back on her. "Valerian, get her out of here," I command. "I'm staying. Theron, I'll call you later." Signaling to Garrett, I grab my father's arm and walk him in the opposite direction of Arden.

THIRTY-SEVEN

<u>ARDEN</u>

Waking the next morning, I pull the pillow over my head, bury myself in the covers, and decide to spend the day in bed. I didn't get much sleep last night, and I'm exhausted. For hours, my mind wouldn't shut off, replaying the scenes from yesterday over and over. My dreams were filled with Fallon's palace, his father, symbols, an old crumbling castle, and the elder. I'd hoped Fallon would text or call and explain or even call to yell, but he didn't.

When we connected the other day, I felt the deep well of hatred he holds for dark elves. It's a pitch-black, never-ending hole he's worked hard to feed regularly, and after meeting his father, I know it's because he wants Fallon's hatred burning bright.

Everyone said the king was an asshole, but they never

mentioned he's quite mad too, as in actually crazy. It was apparent from the moment I saw his eyes. When I questioned Theron and Valerian, they were as surprised as me. He's always been an asshole, but the last time they'd seen him, fifty years ago, he'd displayed his usual keen intelligence. Fallon never said a word to anyone about his mental decline.

Does he not realize his father is mad?

And now the crazy king knows Fallon has a mate. From the very first moment our hands touched and sparked, I'd thought it meant something, and after our deep connection the other day, I knew without a doubt. He did too, or so I thought, but now I'm worrying about his hatred of the dark elves and whether he'll be able to overcome it and accept me. Throw his father in the mix, and it's even worse. Mates are given to us by the Fates, but we don't have to accept them. I shudder to think of Fallon rejecting me.

A reminder sounds on my phone, and I drag myself out from the covers to read the notification. Witches' council meeting, three p.m. *Fuck.* Dropping it back on the bed, I contemplate whether to go or not. My eyes automatically drift to the MacAllister grimoire on my desk, and I know hiding isn't even a choice. Telling their story starts today, by getting the council to acknowledge they lived.

Sending the notification to Theron, I wait for him to respond, which he does immediately, stating he'll escort me to Witchwood. Thankfully, I have several hours until I have to get ready, and I'm going to spend them sleeping and hiding.

WHEN I STEP out of my room, Theron is waiting for me in the elevator. His eyes sweep over my face, assessing my state of mind. He must not like what he sees, because his fingers start tapping his jean-clad thigh.

Every time I see his tell, it makes me smile and feel warm and gooey inside. Leaning in close, I capture his lips with mine and kiss him until I feel the tension ease from his body. "Have you been able to locate the village where my ancestor lived?" I purposely distract him with the search, not wanting to talk about my emotional state.

His voice sounds frustrated when he answers. "She moved around quite a bit when she arrived, so it's made it more difficult to pinpoint her final stop. I'll find it, but it might take me a few days."

My dreams from my nap earlier today pop into my mind. "I've been seeing an old stone castle in my dreams. Is there a village with one? It's crumbling, and I don't think it's been used in a while."

"Seer dreams?" he questions.

"I think so," I answer hesitantly. "I'm not sure how to distinguish them from actual dreams, but I've seen a castle for a couple of days and I've never been to it." Shifting the grimoire in my arms, I study the dark circles under his eyes. "I'm not the only one who isn't getting enough sleep. We don't have to find my ancestor today."

"I wouldn't be able to sleep knowing we were so close anyway," he says, running a hand over his face. He places a hand on my lower back to escort me out of the elevator and to his car in the garage. His eyes dart to the grimoire. "Should I be worried about fireworks today?"

"No, this should be a reasonably friendly visit," I reply with a chuckle. "Although Meri wants you to video the reaction on

Caro's face when I show her the grimoire and prove my heritage."

He raises one eyebrow a millimeter and gives me an incredulous look.

Laughing, I hold up a hand before he can jump into a tirade. "Caro doesn't allow video recordings of the council meetings anyway, and honestly, she knows the MacAllisters were real because she found those documents for us. I think she'll be shocked to see how far back their lineage goes and the sheer number of witches."

After he opens the car door, I settle in the seat with the grimoire on my lap. He slides into the driver's seat, and in seconds, we're shooting out of the garage to Witchwood.

Gazing out the window, I watch the scenery go by. Theron's hand slides over and grasps mine. "Fallon will figure things out. His father—" he begins.

Cutting him off, I interject, "Theron, I appreciate all the things you are going to say about one of your closest friends, but you don't need to fix everything. Time might be the best solution in this instance. Today, I'm with you, not Fallon, and I want to be with just you." I lace my fingers through his. Theron's my rock, but it's too easy to rely on him for comfort and planning and all the things he does well. I want him to know how much I desire his company.

His violet eyes widen at my direct approach, and he clears his throat. "I guess my plan is working," he jokes. Lifting my hand, he places a kiss on the inside of my wrist. "And I definitely want to be with you. Here and now, tomorrow, whenever."

"This evening? After the council meeting?" I ask, flirting with him.

"That can be arranged," he replies, his voice cool, but desire flares in his eyes.

Roaring up the driveway at Witchwood, we find Henry standing at the foot of the entrance. After he opens my door, I get out and give him a peck on the cheek. "I'm so sorry I forgot to text you in advance."

"I'm sure Miss Caro will be delighted to see you, Miss Arden," he greets me loudly, throwing me a wink. I'm guessing she's nearby.

Taking Theron's arm, we ascend the steps.

"Lord Theron. Surely Arden can drive herself to Witchwood? You don't need to drive her every time." Her voice is sugary sweet as she addresses him in front of the coven.

"She insists," he replies smoothly, "and I serve at her pleasure." He gives Caro his most haughty look.

At my pleasure? I ask him silently.

His mouth skims up my throat to my ear. "Undoubtedly," he replies huskily.

Caro clears her throat loudly. "The council meeting is ready to start. Are you joining us, Arden?"

"Yes, absolutely," I respond. Squeezing Theron's arm, I leave him and follow her to the seats allotted to the council leaders. As I sit down, I see I'm on the very end, with An Lee on my left and Santiago next to him. Obviously, lines are being drawn.

After wading through the usual minutia, the meeting opens for new business. Unlike the first time, there are only a couple of witches with requests, and they finish quickly. When they're done, I stand to catch Caro's attention.

"Per your request, I have proof of the MacAllister bloodline and my right to sit in this council seat." I pass the grimoire to An, who glances through it, finds my name, and passes it down to Santiago. As it makes its way to Caro, I state clearly, "It's the MacAllister grimoire, and within those pages, it lists every single witch within our bloodline.

According to the dates, they were the first to be called witches."

Shocked gasps and cries of outrage fill the meeting hall.

Ignoring them, I raise my voice. "Unfortunately, a little over twelve hundred years ago, almost every single living MacAllister witch was massacred or murdered. Hundreds of witches lost overnight," I continue, wanting everyone to know what happened to this once mighty bloodline. "My ancestor was the only one to ultimately survive."

Caro grabs the book from the person closest to her and opens it. When she sees the dates of the first pairing, her lips compress into a straight line. She flips through the pages of names until she comes to the last one, where my name is listed.

"It doesn't state your father's name," she points out snidely.

I raise an eyebrow at her tone. "But it does state mine," I reply clearly. "And it proves I'm a MacAllister." It feels so weird to say it aloud. My eyes find Theron's, and he gives a satisfied nod.

Santiago interjects, "I motion for Arden to be recognized as the permanent leader of the MacAllister bloodline and council seat. The temporary status shall be removed."

An Lee and several other members second his motion, and with a sour expression, Caro bangs her gavel and approves it.

Walking over to her, I pluck the grimoire out of her hands. I don't trust her with it for more than a minute. Once I'm at my designated place, I remain standing. "I motion for the removal of the 'pure' classification. I believe all witches should be allowed to test for affinity and placement in the coven."

Santiago and An second the motion, but nobody else supports it. Nico stands and makes a motion to table the discussion until a future date and the rest of the council agrees.

I exhale slowly, keeping a tight rein on my temper. "I'll only make this motion one more time," I warn them. "If you do not have an answer, then I'll take your silence as the final answer. This council and the coven itself will not survive without this change, but don't worry, I won't let all witches go down with your ship." I pause to let those words sink into their brains. My patience is at an end today. "Please excuse me. I have another very important appointment."

With the grimoire in the crook of my arm, I step down and walk over to take Theron's hand. "Ready to go?"

Pride and delight shines in his eyes. "Absolutely," he replies.

When we reach the car, a hand stops me. "Be careful, Miss Arden," Henry whispers. "I saw Miss Caro on the north end of the property two nights ago. She was talking to a shifter, a wolf." He steps back and tips his imaginary hat. "Good evening, Miss Arden."

After we drive off, I search the countryside, and sure enough, a wolf is running parallel to the car, tracking us.

"Did you ever get a reply back from the alphas?" I ask Theron, pointing to the wolf.

"One alpha claimed the wolf as his, but he isn't able to call him back to the pack," he answers, his sure hands easily controlling the powerful car as he takes the next turn faster.

"Hmm, that's interesting," I muse. "I wonder what makes a wolf able to resist their alpha's call?" Picking up my phone, I text Astor. I'm sure he knows a wolf or two he can ask or torture.

CHAPTER
THIRTY-EIGHT

Yawning, I make my way from Theron's room to mine and think about Valerian's return to The Abbey. According to my phone, he should be here in an hour or two. When I talked to him on video conference yesterday, he walked me through all the changes he'd made to his kingdom.

There's a new council in place, with two elders leading it. The elders voted for two new positions to be instated and held by younger members to balance out the representation of the people. One of the new elders is Glynnis, and one of her grandsons is representing the younger population. All of the laws were reviewed and voted on by the people. Plus, Valerian made sweeping changes to the guards and implemented a new training regimen for all dragons.

Training is desperately needed. With Valerian in charge, the kingdom has experienced an unprecedented period of peace. When he fought the dissenter, he was appalled at how inept he was and wants to be sure his people can protect themselves from threats.

His eyes shine with determination and power, and his people are responding to it. He was worried about telling me his plans to regularly visit in the future, but I assured him we'd make it work. I'd go with him when I could, but I had responsibilities and other individuals to consider. With a glint in his eye, he chuckled and casually referenced the other four individuals who also had a claim on my time. I blushed but didn't contradict him.

Getting up, I dress in workout clothes. It's been a couple of days, and I've missed training. Opening the door, I almost run into Meri, who is standing in front of my door.

"Surprise!" she shouts, pulling me into a hug. "Daire graciously helped me set this up."

I spy Daire in the elevator with an amused smirk on his face. Winking at him, I turn to Meri and pull her into my room.

She waves a hand over her face. "Seriously, I'd do him in a second." She peeks over at me. "Have you?"

"It's interesting how you pick men. Would you do any of the others?" I'm curious to hear what she thinks about the cadre, and I want to avoid answering her question. Daire and I are too new to discuss without Meri going overboard.

Pondering the question, she answers, "They're all hot as hell, but I have to say only Daire is my type—sinfully seductive and powerful." She shivers. "Theron's too formal and icy, Valerian's a beast but he's too nice, Astor is dark and moody, too similar to the men in my neighborhood, and Fallon, he's too focused on doing good deeds. I like my men kind of bad, a lot arrogant, and with a couple of questionable morals."

"Interesting," I murmur. On the surface, they're pretty

accurate descriptions until you get to know them. "Is Cormal your type?"

She wiggles her eyebrows. "Cormal definitely falls into the category of hell yes, but he's more interested in running the criminal kingdom he's built." She sighs and licks her lips. "I'd do him in a heartbeat, though."

"So he is the man Fallon knows," I exclaim. "I wondered when I heard you say his name the other day. I'd ask how you know him, but I have a feeling you won't tell me."

"It's for the best," she says, giving me a pleading look. "I dropped by with some news. According to my guardian's information, the Primary is a supernatural who's chosen by the primal source of all magic for a specific task. The last known Primary was chosen over four thousand years ago. She doesn't know who it is, but four thousand years is a long time, so they're pretty fucking old and powerful. My guardian thinks the timing is odd, so she's still searching for information. She's all in and running me ragged. Believe me, I'm leaving here to go get another book."

"It does seem like a long time has passed if they were chosen to complete a task," I murmur, my thoughts wandering to my attempted assassinations. With my living almost a hundred percent at The Abbey, there hasn't been one in a while, which is a huge relief. "Thanks for letting me know. And, Meri, if the task gets dangerous at any time, back off. You're more important, okay?"

She shrugs and avoids my eyes. "Everything's a little dangerous," she remarks. "What's been going on with you? Did you show the grimoire to the witches' council?"

"Yes, but Caro's reaction was pretty subdued," I tell her. "She already knew the MacAllisters existed, but she didn't know they were the first witches, a little known fact that blew everyone's mind." I chuckle.

"I bet it did. Hard to feel superior when you're not first," she says snidely. "How did the visit to the light Elven kingdom go?"

My smile dims, and she frowns. "Not great. My ancestor is probably dark Elven. Fallon is my mate, but he's not exactly happy about my background. His father is mad, crazy not angry, and he's flipping out about me too. Fallon hasn't called or texted in days. I'm trying to give him space to handle his father, but I'm getting kind of pissed he hasn't reached out. It's a mess."

"Asshole," Meri mutters. "He needs to let go of his rose-colored glasses and deal with his father."

Shrugging, I agree, but I'm willing to give it some time. "I was heading down to grab a coffee when you arrived, do you want one?"

"No," she replies, wrinkling her nose. "I've had three cups already, and I'm bouncing off the walls. I wouldn't mind some water, though."

It takes me a few minutes, and when I get back, I hear her talking on the phone. Reaching for the knob, I freeze when I hear the word "journal." Putting my ear to the door, I listen in on her conversation.

"It's a journal by a witch named Agnes MacAllister... It's a story of their origins and information about the massacre. I don't know." I hear her sigh. "Hold on... It says something about a stone powered by blood and flame. That's what it says. It's hard to read. No, I'm not going to steal it. She would miss it and know it was me. I'll take a few pictures."

Angry tears fill my eyes. *Who is Meri? Why is she spying on me?* I decide to keep listening.

"There's a small chest with a tree on it," she mentions to the person on the phone. "I don't know, I can't open it. Stop. I can't open it. There's a grimoire. I can take pictures of it," she says, then silence.

"Fuck!" I hear her exclaim. "I don't know why the box won't open. It's not like I have any powers to open it. Care to share yours?"

Hearing enough, I grasp the knob and slowly open the door. Meri is standing by the chest, taking pictures of it. "You won't be able to open it because you don't have the special key," I explain softly.

When she turns to me, I see a red welt across her cheek. "She's back," she spits into the phone and hangs up. Crossing her arms, she stands there defiantly, saying nothing.

"What did you tell the person on the phone? Did you send them pictures?" I ask angrily. When she continues to be silent, I plead with her. "Who are you? Are you my friend, or are you only using me to find information? Talk to me. Please." My voice rises as I panic. Was it the Primary?

Her mouth compresses into a straight line, and she remains mute.

Setting the coffee and water on the desk before I throw them, I take a deep breath. "The cadre can help you," I tell her. "Please tell me something."

She snorts and looks away.

My hands start shaking as the anger builds in me. "I know you," I say, my voice breaking, "and I know you wouldn't do this if you had another choice. If you don't want the cadre to help, what about Callyx?" I know they text each other regularly.

Her eyes are angry, and she scoffs. "You know nothing about me, only what I've chosen to tell you. A few truths and lies. Our friendship is built on air." She throws up her hands. "Even if you knew the real truth, you wouldn't understand it. You've lived this remarkably sheltered life, and I both envy and pity you for it. Would you even be able to make it in the real world without the cadre? You lived in a bubble for a few hundred years and traded it for another bubble—The Abbey."

She laughs. "Me? I'm a survivor, and for almost a thousand years, I've survived the worst of the worst. You think I need your help? It's worthless, like your friendship. I need friends like Cormal, who know how to get their hands dirty." She strides to the door. "I'm glad my secret's out. If I had to hear more of your pathetic whining about the cadre and this destiny of yours, I'd seriously consider cutting my ears off. We've all got a destiny, Arden. Maybe now I can start searching for mine." She strolls out the door, and I let her.

My chest feels tight with anger, and I'm having a hard time breathing. Magic builds inside me like a wave. I swipe at the tears on my face, but they keep coming. The edge of my control slips, and I panic. Racing through the door, I head toward the gym, praying I'll get there in time. I pass Daire and Theron, who stare after me, but I don't stop.

Slamming through the door of the gym, I run to the side where we train with magic. Daire and Theron are right behind me. "Stop!" I shout to them. They pause, and I bolt through the magical barriers. When I get to the middle of the room, my control shatters and my magic explodes. Wave after wave rolls out of me as I scream, my anger bottomless, continuously feeding my magic. The building sways, and Theron scans the walls with concern. Bringing the phone up to his face, he calls someone. Valerian comes into the room, but I turn away, not wanting him or any of them to see me lose control. I'm crashing, my anger is overwhelming, and my throat is so tight, I can't breathe.

Astor comes running through the door at full speed. Stepping through the barrier, he saunters slowly to me, holding up his hand. "Hell, gorgeous, you've been holding out on me.

All this lovely power, and you couldn't share some with me?"
He braces himself when a wave of magic pulses out of me.
"Fuck, that's painful. Now why don't you tell me what this is
about?"

I clench my fists and try to hold back the next wave, but it
rolls out of me anyway. He winces again.

"Go away. I don't want to hurt you," I scream at him. My
anger rises higher.

"Is this about Fallon?" he asks. "Theron said he's dealing
with his father, and—"

"He called Theron?" I yell angrily. "Of course he did. He
can't call me, his mate, or even send me a fucking text, but he
calls Theron?" I tilt my head at Theron. "How many times?"

"There are things he has to take care of that he can't share
with you yet. He's trying to make it safe for you," Theron
explains, defending Fallon.

"How many?" I repeat. When he holds up the number
three, I lose it. "Between him and Meri, I don't know who I'm
pissed at more."

Astor lifts his head. "Meri was here? Why are you angry at
her?"

"She left," I snarl at him, and then I cry. "And she won't be
back."

Astor scoots closer to me, and his fists clench when another
wave hits him, but he doesn't stop until he's by my side. "Did
you two have a fight?"

"When I came back to the room, she was talking to
someone on the phone, telling them about the journal and the
rowan chest," I explain, sniffing. "She sent them pictures of
everything. The person on the phone was furious when she
couldn't open the chest, and I heard her cry out. So I stepped
into the room and confronted her."

The anger is turning to hurt, and the waves are finally softening. I hear Astor sigh with relief. "Apparently, everything was a lie," I tell him, finally sliding to the floor.

He gathers me in his arms and rocks me. "Tell me what she said," he demands.

I start at the beginning and tell him everything. "Some of what she said hit home. She's right. I've been sheltered my entire life. Could I even survive on my own?"

"I don't doubt it for a second," he assures me. "Besides knowing how to fight and how to wield magic like a badass, you're pretty resilient. You might make a few mistakes, but we all do. Hell, I'm the poster child of screw ups. I've been on my own since I was nine, and yet I still manage to make colossal mistakes." He sweeps my hair out of my eyes. "And I like your innocence, it's refreshing. This world needs more of it, along with a good dose of your kindness. Meri is a product of her background. You don't need to be like her." He kisses my temple. "Never let anyone change you to fit their mold."

I listen to him intently. Gripping his arm, I ask him the most important question. "Do you think it was all fake?"

"No, I'd know if I heard a lie, right?" he reminds me. "It sounds like she had a pretty rough childhood, similar to mine, and when people like her and me are confronted, we tend to lash out. If something hurts us, we lash out hard, tearing into their weaknesses and shoving them away so we can later reassure ourselves we're better off."

Blinking at him, I realize I've never gotten his story. "That's terrible."

He exhales loudly and gives me a grim smile. "Sometimes, the past isn't pretty, but thankfully, I'm a long way from that boy."

"I'm sorry." My fingers caress his face, wanting to pull the hurt from him, and I sigh. Playing the scene with Meri in my head, I sift for clues, but nothing jumps out. "I've never been this angry. I think it hit me harder today because I've been upset with Fallon and trying to hide it, along with the pressure over the whole dark Elven ancestor thing. I lost it when Meri added her betrayal on top of it all. She certainly knew what buttons to push." I peek around at the men standing on the other side of the barrier. "I probably seem like a crazy person."

"They've seen and done worse," he assures me. Peering into my eyes, he wipes the tears away. "Don't give up on Fallon just yet. Maybe he's trying to find a way forward like I did, but no matter what happens, we'll be here with you."

THIRTY-NINE

ARDEN

For the next week, I train harder than ever, pushing my body and mind to its limits, eliminating thoughts or feelings before they have a chance to form. Valerian, Astor, and Daire set up a rotation to train with me, but judging by their expressions, their frustration with my lack of communication and my unrelenting need to keep going is hitting its peak.

Valerian stormed out five minutes ago, roaring his refusal to watch me drive myself into the ground. Without stopping, I sheathe my sword and decide to throw knives for a while.

I think it's about ten minutes later when Theron strides into the room with a tray of food. He sets it down and motions for me to come eat.

"I'll eat in a minute," I call out. "I want to finish practicing."

"You've been throwing knives for three hours, Arden," he

informs me. "You haven't eaten at all today. Daire even went out and picked up your favorite food from the Italian restaurant." He folds his arms and waits for me to join him.

Three hours? Shocked, I waver, but I don't stop. If I stop, I have to think and feel, so I don't. I hear a door slam and find Theron has left the room.

Five minutes later, the door slams open, and Theron stands there in training clothes—loose black pants and a tight-fitting black shirt. His feet are bare, and he's holding a magnificent sword. Intrigued, I stop throwing knives and meet him in the middle.

"If I win, you eat," he proposes, calmly walking over to the mat. "You stop training for a couple of days and let us help you."

"And if I win?" I ask, biting my lip.

"What do you want?" he asks, separating the sword into two. He swings them both with expertise.

"I want you to set up a meeting with Fallon," I state firmly.

"Done," he agrees and attacks.

Where Valerian is brute force and strength, Theron is supple. He moves fluidly around me, giving me no room to maneuver, his swords easily dominating mine. My bursts of magic are quelled quickly without pause, and my swords don't even get near him. Unlike the others, his impassive face makes him impossible to read or predict.

After three minutes, I'm regretting the hours I spent throwing knives. My arms are quivering, and in a split second, he takes advantage of my weakness and easily disables me. Bringing his swords up in a crisscross, he lays them on each side of my neck. He won in less than five minutes.

Shocked, I stand there, chest heaving and body shaking. Maybe I have worked out too long. I sway, and the sharp blade slices my neck. His violet eyes grow stormy when he sees the thin rivulet of blood.

"Are you done?" His voice is quiet but rough, his emotions barely contained.

"I'm done," I concede.

He slides the two swords back together and sheathes it in the strap on his back. Yanking me into his arms, he ignores my stiffness and holds me tightly. Running his hands down my back, he commands, "Let it go, Arden. I've got you."

Breathing in the smell of chocolate and peppermint, I close my eyes and let it all go, my body folding into his. Reaching up, I fist my hands in the back of his shirt and hold on with everything I am. After a few minutes, he picks me up and takes me over to the table.

Sitting me down, he hands me a fork and motions for me to eat.

I take a bite absentmindedly. "Clearly, I should be asking you for sword training. Is everyone holding back?" I ask, my brow furrowed. Normally, I wouldn't question my ability, but my confidence seems to have taken a hit with Meri's words.

"No. You're a worthy opponent—unpredictable and kind of a wild card. They work hard when they're fighting you, and when you beat them, it's real. And humbling, I hear," he replies, amused. "But we've been fighting for a long time, so we've learned a few things, and none of them can beat me with a sword," he concedes.

He sweeps the hair back from my face.

"When I won the Gathering of the Light, I thought for sure my father would acknowledge me. The single reason I entered was because I knew he was going to be there to watch his other son compete. I thought if I could win, it would show him I was worthy, and he would see me differently." His voice is low and modulated while he tells the story, but his violet eyes reflect the hurt he'd felt. "After winning, I was at the banquet, getting crowned, when I saw him. He looked directly through me like he didn't even know me. I was devastated and angry, so I decided to confront him." His mouth compresses. "Only to find him fucking my lover in the hallway, in front of everyone, including his other son. The Fae certainly love a good scene, and he gave them one. This time, he looked directly at me and sneered. It was the last time I saw him."

When I finish my food, he hands me a glass of water. "Instead of fighting and training, I spent the next hundred years as a wastrel—drinking, gambling, and...other things. At least you chose a better escape than I did, but unlike me, you have five men who refuse to stand by and watch you destroy yourself. We need you."

Picking up the tray, he motions for me to follow him. Valerian, Daire, and Astor are standing in the hallway outside the gym. He hands the tray to Valerian and places a hand on my back while he escorts me to my room.

"I'm close to finding your ancestor. Get some rest, and I'd better not see you in the gym tomorrow," he warns me. "I know you don't want to hear it, but have some faith in Fallon." He kisses me hard on the lips and waits until I'm in my room to walk away.

Relieved, I take a long, hot shower and fall into bed.

CHAPTER
FORTY

I spend the next day in bed getting pampered. First thing in the morning, Theron comes by and brings me coffee and a banana. He stays for a while, walking me through every piece of information he's uncovered about my ancestor.

When he leaves, Astor joins me. He pulls up unique blood magic spells in the MacAllister grimoire, and we discuss the merits and difficulty level of each spell.

After Astor leaves, Daire brings me lunch and reads to me, which is a huge surprise. Apparently, he's a voracious reader, and I find it incredibly sexy.

Finally, Valerian comes by to take an afternoon nap with me. When I try to turn our nap into something more, he pins me down. "As much as I'd love to sink into you, we all agreed you needed rest. I'm here to nap—that's it," he informs me.

Hmm, I'd wondered why none of them had made a single move, I muse.

Sighing, I snuggle into him and drift off to sleep, my dreams full of the usual odd things like castles and symbols. After waking, I get up, take a shower, and get dressed. I'm packing a bag when Theron arrives.

"Seer dreams again?" he asks, although he already knows the answer. He kicks the bed, waking up Valerian. "It's time. Call Cormal."

Surprised, I watch Valerian pick up the phone. "It's Valerian," he says curtly. "Yes, Valerian, King of Dragons. I need a favor. We need an escort into the dark Elven kingdom. Do you have someone?" He listens for a second. "That sounds reasonable. We'll see you there in..." He raises an eyebrow at Theron, who holds up one finger. "An hour."

Hanging up the phone, he stretches and slides out of bed. "He'll meet us at the northeast corner in an hour. He asked for a blood-red ruby. I agreed." Leaning down, he gives me a quick kiss and leaves to get ready.

"Should I bring anything with me?" I ask Theron.

"Bring your sword and the Killian blades," he orders me. "It's not the scenic scene we experienced in the light Elven kingdom." He glances at his phone. "I'll see you downstairs in fifty minutes." Then he, too, walks out.

Exactly one hour later, we're standing at the dark Elven border when a startlingly handsome, well-built man walks up to us. He has dark hair and skin with bright blue eyes, and he flashes a speculative glance toward me. "So you're the witch stirring the supernatural pot." He assesses me from head to toe, lingering for a minute on the Killian blades strapped to my thighs, then dismisses me.

"Where are we going?" He directs his question to Theron, but his eyes constantly sweep the area around us.

"The old king's village," Theron replies, stepping up to hand him a small velvet bag. "We need safe passage in and out. Undetected, if possible."

The man pulls a large egg-shaped ruby from the bag and examines it. Valerian snorts. "You should know by now, Valerian, I trust very few people," the man reminds him. Satisfied with the gem, he gestures to the path. "Okay, let's go."

"You're escorting us?" Theron asks curtly. "I thought you'd send one of your men."

"Not for this little bird," he tosses over his shoulder. "I've lost too many men lately, and all because I made inquiries into her assassination attempts. I refuse to lose any more."

Interesting. This must be the infamous Cormal. If there was anyone with questionable morals, it would be this man. He feels like a predator, and even the air around him is menacing and lethal. I'm not sure what Meri sees in him. A pang of sadness hits me when I think of her.

We travel the rest of the day until late evening. Finally stopping, we make camp but don't light a fire. The forest is dark, but instead of finding it scary, my skin is buzzing with energy.

I'm chewing on a few bites of jerky when I feel a sting on my shoulder. Squirming, I try to pull my shirt back to see if something bit me, but I can't quite see. I move over to the lantern, peel it back, and see a dark smudge.

"Theron, can you come here for a minute?" I murmur, not wanting to disturb the others. When he gets close to me, I angle my shoulder toward the light. "Can you look at my shoulder? I think something bit me."

He grabs the neck of my shirt and pulls it down in the back, then he freezes. "It's not a bite," he whispers. "Don't show anyone else. I'll explain later."

Worried, I glance up at him. His mouth is compressed into a straight line, and he's wearing his thinking face. Straightening my shirt, he escorts me back to my sleeping bag and waits while I get in it, then he lies down behind me. A second later, Valerian drops down in front of me, sandwiching me between the two. Astor and Daire have first watch, while Cormal sits with his back to a tree, watching everyone and everything.

It's still dark when we rise. We walk all morning and finally come into a village about noon, but there isn't a castle in sight. After stopping to get food and drinks, we quickly head out into the forest again. When we stop that night, I'm exhausted.

We're deep into the forest, but we still don't light a fire. I study Cormal, trying to understand what makes a man choose to be king of the supernatural criminals. Was he born into it? Did he fight his way to the top?

Cormal's staring at his phone. "Don't you have enough men catering to you?" he asks snidely, his piercing blue eyes coming up to meet mine.

"I'm curious about you, but not in that way," I reply, amused by his arrogance. "Meri mentioned you the last time we spoke."

He sits up straight. "When did you last see her?" His voice is deadly as he asks, and Theron and Daire step closer. "She was supposed to meet me two days ago, and I haven't heard from her. It's not like her. If she tells me she's going to meet me, she does or she sends a text, and she's not answering any of my messages."

"She went to find a book," I recall from our last conversation. "And maybe her honor." My voice is bitter when I throw it out.

Quick as lightning, he wraps a hand around my neck and picks me up from the ground. Equally fast, Theron lays his sword on Cormal's neck and Daire grips his wrist. They order him to let me go, but he ignores them.

Feeling his hand tighten around my neck, I smile.

"Let me go, or you'll be of little use to any woman, or man, in the future," I demand, flipping my wrist sideways.

He looks down and finds my Killian blade against his dick. Laughing, he tilts his head and drops me. "Touché, little bird." He leans into my face. "But if you speak badly about Meri again, I'll kill you."

"Meri betrayed me," I retort curtly. "Instead of being a true friend, she's been spying on me since we met."

"Explain," he demands, then listens intently while I walk through everything. "Damn it, what is she doing?" Pacing around the camp, he mutters to himself for a minute. "I won't give up Meri's background, but if you caught her in the act, she meant for you to find out. She's been taught by the best of the worst, and she can't afford to fail. Failure results in extreme punishment, and letting you discover her is tantamount to failure. Fuck." He shoots off a few texts. "Do you have any idea where she was going to get the book?"

"No, but I might have someone who can help search for her," I volunteer.

He tenses. "Who?"

"Callyx Karth, my brother," I tell him. "Him and Meri text regularly. I'll send him a message." Picking up my phone, I send Callyx a text, letting him know Meri is missing. I also tell him to proceed with caution because she's been spying on me.

"Callyx Karth. Hmm...you get more interesting by the minute," he comments in a mocking tone.

Theron gives me a pointed look. I get his silent message. It's not good to be interesting to a man like Cormal.

My phone pings. "Callyx says he's on it," I inform Cormal. "He'll text when he has any leads."

I watch Cormal dip his chin in acknowledgement and go sit against the tree. I'm guessing he won't sleep at all while he's traveling with us.

Lying down on my sleeping bag, I watch the stars and think about his words. Could Meri have been doing me a favor? Truth and lies, she said. Which is it?

We rise early and start our final trek. Astor is traveling beside me today. "Why couldn't we portal to the village?" I ask him tiredly.

"Each kingdom has alerts set to monitor any portals. If they detect visitors from other races, they usually intercede. It's why Valerian had to alert the council when we visited his land and why Fallon opened the portal to his kingdom," he explains.

"Interesting," I mutter. I never realized it, since Vargas or Solandis usually created the respective portals to Underworld and Fae, but I guess it makes sense. "Does that mean we'll need to trek back out of here too?"

"Cormal's using someone from his network, a villager, to create a portal to get us back," Astor murmurs. "We should start seeing the castle soon."

After walking another ten minutes, a large, crumbling grey castle comes into view. It used to be magnificent, with several turrets and a moat, but it's been a ruin for a long time now, as evident by the lack of a roof and a few walls.

When we walk into the village, we're met with sullen stares. Unlike the last village we entered, these people seem defeated and the village is run down, with several homes and shops in complete ruin, much like the castle.

Theron and Cormal walk over to talk to a man and woman standing by the well.

After a minute, the woman comes up to me and grabs my hand. She pulls a medallion from her dress and shows it to me. It matches the one Glynnis and the elder from the light Elven village were wearing. Her eyes dart around as if expecting to be caught, but no one approaches us.

"Theron." I barely finish saying his name before he's beside me. "She's wearing the medallion." I smile at the woman.

We follow her to the castle grounds. She points at me, then to the castle.

I glance at Theron, then turn back to the woman. "I'm sorry, I don't understand. Did you know Catriona?"

She nods her head yes.

"Did she live here?"

She mimes something, but I can't tell what she's trying to get across.

Cormal slides up to us. "No one in the village can speak. The current dark Elven king cut out their tongues and had a warlock spell them so they wouldn't heal." He signs something to the woman, and her face shines with relief, then she nods.

Shocked, we stare at him. "Why?"

"They wouldn't tell him where to find the old king's son," he explains after the woman signs the answer. "The old king was murdered, and the son disappeared. When the villagers refused to give up any information, he decided they should lose their right to speak."

The woman points at me and signs something new to Cormal.

"She says her name is Liana and Catriona MacAllister was her friend. She hid here for several years." He pauses while he waits for her to sign more. "They both worked in the castle and lived in the village, until Catriona met the king's son, who was her mate. When his father, the old dark Elven king, was murdered, they left." He looks at me speculatively.

"Where did she go?" I ask her.

She shrugs, then signs something.

"They took the name of the castle's blacksmith, but I don't know where they went. She gave me this medallion to remember her and told me someone would come searching for her one day," Cormal says, translating for her.

Smiling, I clasp her hand. "Do you know the name?"

She shakes her head no, then her hands fly while she signs to Cormal.

Cormal waits until she finishes signing, then states, "She says the old steward would have written it in the castle records, but the records were taken to the new king's castle."

Theron steps up beside me. "We'll have to petition the new king to see the records. His archives are not open to everyone."

I catch Astor's eye. "Is there anything you can do?"

He shakes his head sadly. "I'm sorry, no."

Reaching out, I hug the woman. "Thank you for wearing the medallion and remembering her. It means more than you know."

She pats my hand and smiles.

Stepping close to Cormal, I murmur, "If I gave you payment, could you find a way to ease their lives?" It's heartbreaking how they've been treated for their loyalty.

Cormal gives me a hard stare before turning to view the devastated village. "Yes." He ushers us back to the square. "We've stayed too long. If we don't leave now, we'll miss our portal." He signals to the villager in the square to open a portal.

Waving to the woman, I step through the portal and walk out in front of The Abbey.

Cormal quickly creates his own portal, but before he steps through, he jerks his chin at me. "Send me the payment, and I'll make sure they get supplies. Don't forget what I said about Meri, and if you hear from Callyx, tell him to text me."

I indicate my agreement and watch him leave. "He's one scary man," I muse softly. After all, who knows if he has any spies nearby. "And unfortunately, he's now aware I'm a royal descendant and a MacAllister witch, which is very dangerous information for him to know."

The cadre says nothing, but their expressions tell me they agree.

FORTY-ONE

ARDEN

After stripping off my shirt, I peer in the mirror behind me, trying to catch a glimpse of the Elven symbol tattooed on my shoulder. The thick line looks like an exaggerated seven, with another line crossing through the middle and a small circle above it. Theron told me all high Elven families, both light and dark, have a unique symbol which magically appears as a tattoo and signifies their heritage. Now I know what Fallon's father was referencing when he tried to look at my shoulder and it's a good thing I didn't have it at that time. And given my heritage is a dead king, I should probably keep it hidden.

Theron sent off a petition to the current dark Elven king to request access to his archives. He explained he was researching changes in monarchies over the last five thousand years and wanted to get an idea of the roles and responsibilities of the servants in those households. This would ensure we would get access to the right records.

After grabbing a shower, I lie on my bed, thinking about the most recent revelations. If Catriona mated with the old king's son, would she have told his father about the MacAllister massacre? Is that what prompted his letter to the dark Fae king? Did the Primary find out and make a deal with the current dark Elven king to kill the old one? Or did she try to make a deal with the old Elven king and he refused, which led to his death? Alain said she was making deals right and left during this time, but with whom?

From my father, I inherited two dead but powerful lineages—the MacAllisters and the old dark Elven king's royal line. Frowning, I pick up my phone and send a text to Theron. He replies back immediately with the name Balinor. The MacAllisters and the Balinors. This is the second secret my father was hiding, which is why my mother bound my powers. By hiding my other half, she prevented the dark elves from finding me.

I dart a glance at the Killian blades hanging on the wall. Remembering what the woman in the village said, I wonder if the blacksmith was indeed the old king's son. But if so, why did he create the blades? Blowing the hair out of my eyes, I realize I don't have enough information to answer all the questions yet, but the picture is forming.

Someone knocks on the door, and I get up to answer it, only to find Astor standing in the hall with his blood magic kit in his hands. His eyes light up when he sees me in my tank top and briefs.

"Hello, gorgeous. It must be my day to be tortured," he jokes, but his eyes devour me. "We received permission to search the archives. Given how dangerous it is for you, I don't suppose you'd consider staying here? I'll stay with you."

I tilt my head and cock my eyebrow. "Good try." I prefer to know my enemies and look them in the face.

"I didn't think so," he says, shrugging. "On the bright side, I get to experiment with a new blood magic concealing spell." He holds up the kit. "We need to make sure your tattoo isn't detected. Mind if I come in?"

He scans the room and grimaces.

"The desk would probably work best." Setting down the kit, he motions for me to take a seat sideways in the chair to allow him access to my back. "Do you mind pulling your hair to the side? And slide your strap down?" His voice is gruff when he makes the requests.

Pulling my hair to the other side, I slide my strap down to my shoulder. "Is this okay?" I ask, laughter in my voice.

"Minx," he chides. Picking up the knife, he slices his palm and drops blood into the bowl. He dips his finger into the bowl and brings it up to my shoulder, where he lightly traces over the tattoo while murmuring the spell.

His fingers skim my shoulder, and I shiver. He's not the only one this is affecting.

"It worked," he informs me. "I don't think it will hold for more than a few hours, but Theron doesn't think we'll need much time."

When I look over my shoulder in the bathroom mirror, I see a few smears of blood, but the tattoo is gone. Surprisingly, it makes me a little sad and anxious. What if it doesn't come back? Astor's hand comes down on my other shoulder, and I peer into the mirror and meet his eyes.

"It will come back," he promises huskily. Grabbing a wash-cloth, he gently wipes the blood off my shoulder and drops a kiss on top.

Turning back around, I lay my hand on his cheek. "Thank you," I whisper, reaching up to give him a soft kiss, then another, my lips lingering on his. It's been so long since I tasted him, and every time I do, I need more. Desire swirls in me as I pull his lower lip between mine and slide my tongue over it.

"Arden." His voice is strained as he drawls my name. "I'm hanging on by a thread."

"Kiss me," I demand, wanting it more than I want to breathe.

The thread snaps, and his lips descend on mine, claiming and owning them. They devour, pulling every bit of response from me, while ripping apart my world. Moaning my surrender, I kiss him back, needing him to know how I feel. The kiss slows for a second, as if he's going to stop, but he groans and deepens it again. Lost to everything, it takes us a moment to realize the phone is ringing.

He pulls back and places soft kisses on my lips. His hand is wrapped around my jaw, while his thumb caresses my cheek. I grip his wrist and try to catch my breath.

"I've been dreaming of that kiss for weeks," he admits. "But nothing could have prepared me for the reality." His brown eyes are dark with emotion. "Tell me you don't regret it."

"I don't regret it," I tell him, stroking his wrist. The phone stops ringing, then starts up again. "Do we need to go?"

He drops a kiss on my lips. "Yes, we were supposed to be downstairs five minutes ago. It's court, so you'll need to wear something dressy. I'll wait for you in the hall."

Pulling the sleek purple tailored dress out of the closet, I decide it will have to work and pair it with black heels. Using magic, I dry my hair and pull it into a sleek bun to match, then add some makeup. My lips are puffy from the kiss, but the rest of me is sleek and sophisticated, so I grab my phone and run out the door.

"Purple, nice choice. Theron's going to love it," he teases me.

"It's not as if I have many clothes right now," I remind him. If this dress hadn't been at the dry cleaner when Amelie broke into my hotel room, I'm sure she would have destroyed it too.

He runs a finger down my spine, giving me goosebumps. "Always gorgeous," he assures me.

"Hmm, you don't look too bad yourself," I tell him, studying his black button-down shirt and pants, which he's topped with a sharp blazer.

When the elevator stops, I step out and find Theron pacing and Daire leaning against the wall.

"What took you so lon—" Theron stops talking when he sees me in the purple dress, the one I wore the first time he and I went to Witchwood.

Daire glides over and picks up my hand. "Stunning," he murmurs, placing a kiss on my palm. He walks over to the portal and goes through, with Astor following him.

"Where's Valerian?" I ask Theron, who's staring at me intensely.

"The dark Elven king isn't a fan, so Valerian left to check on his kingdom, but he'll be back later today." Theron's voice is hoarse when he answers. "Goddess, what I wouldn't give to sweep you away right now." He rubs his thumb over my puffy lips.

Licking my lips in anticipation, I assure him, "Soon."

Arriving at the current dark Elven king's castle, I find it light and airy, its architecture modern, and the furnishings luxurious. It's the antithesis of what I expected. We're greeted immediately by the queen herself. Unfortunately, the king is away right now.

Bending my knees in a curtsy, I let Theron introduce me to the beautiful, petite woman. With dark brown hair and gorgeous green eyes, she's the epitome of Elven royalty. He introduces me as his friend and explains we're researching a project together, but his stance and the hand on my back tells her I'm under his protection.

"A mysterious dark Elven woman under your protection?" Her voice is dry and amused, and she waves a hand to a nearby servant. "Would you like some refreshments?"

Knowing it's impolite to refuse, we accept and sit down across from her. Theron and she engage in the usual small talk, while I skim the room. There are several portraits on the walls, but it's the stunning woman with the green eyes and black hair that catches my eyes.

The queen follows my gaze and smiles. "She's my sister," she explains.

I feel Theron stiffen beside me. "She's stunning. Are you close?"

Daire coughs, and I glance over at him. He shakes his head.

"Please don't," the queen implores him. "It's refreshing to run into someone who isn't aware of the story." She turns to face the painting. "We were only a couple of years apart and very close, so we did everything together. Until she was murdered."

Startled, I raise a hand to my chest, now understanding why Theron and Daire tried to warn me. "I'm so sorry."

"It was a long time ago," she murmurs. "She had an affair with the light Elven king, and he quickly became obsessed with her. Even though they weren't mates, she became pregnant, and a son was born. When she couldn't stand his behavior anymore, she broke it off, but it did no good. He continued to hound her night and day. She wanted nothing more to do with him, but they shared a son, and she wanted him to know his father. One day, she took their son, Fallon, and went to meet him. We found her remains a couple of days later." Her voice breaks as she remembers that day. "And we never saw Fallon again."

Shocked, I realize she's speaking about Fallon's mother, and I compare it to the version Fallon told me. "Fallon thinks you murdered his mother. He's filled with hatred because of it." Theron and Daire are restless as they watch this unfold, while Astor is his usual enigmatic self.

Outraged, she stands and walks over to the painting. Her voice is raw as she points to the painting and screams, "Never! I could never hurt her. I swear this on my life. I loved her more than anyone else in this world." She paces back and forth. "I can't believe he thinks *we* murdered her." She mutters a few words about the light Elven king. "Do you think Fallon would come talk to me?"

Theron speaks up quickly. "I'll send him a message and let him know what you said. Beyond that, I can't guarantee he'll visit."

She clasps her hands together and pleads with him. "Please, I'll owe you a great favor." She looks sadly up at the painting. "I've been racked with guilt all these years because I let that bastard take her child, but I couldn't do anything without causing a war. To hear he thinks we killed her? I can't let it stand. I won't."

Slumping into her chair, she waves a servant over and commands him to take us to the library. "If you'll excuse me, I'm feeling quite worn out," she says softly.

We follow the servant out of the room, but when I glance

back, she's staring sadly at the painting of her sister. She looks devastated.

"The archivist is not here right now," the servant tells us. "But all of the old king's archives are in this room." He opens a small door in the middle of two shelves. "If you don't find what you're searching for, please leave a note for the archivist on the desk over there and he'll address it when he returns." He gives us a short bow and walks out.

For the next couple of hours, we search through the old steward's ledgers, but in every instance, the blacksmith's name is blank. I drop my head in my hands. "It's not here." Agreeing with me, they begin to put the books back on the shelves. "What do you think I should leave in the message?

"Keep it simple. Explain we're searching for ledgers with information on servants who worked on the grounds of the castle—stable hands, blacksmiths, and such," Daire suggests.

After writing the letter, I drop it on the desk.

CHAPTER
FORTY-TWO

Two days later, we get a message from the archivist. He's returned from his travels and can help us find what we need. Thankfully, I've had time to purchase another dress, a dark red fitted sheath with black accents, which I pair with the black heels.

Astor gives me a long look when he sees the dress. "Mmm, I love this color on you. You look positively sinful, and it makes me want to devour you."

"One day, when you take me to dinner, I'll wear it for you," I promise him. "And if you're very, very lucky, it will find its way to the floor."

His eyes widen, and he throws his head back and roars with laughter. "I will indeed be a very, very lucky warlock, even if dinner is the only thing on the menu."

When Daire and Theron arrive, we quickly make our way

through the portal. When we arrive this time, a tall handsome man with dark black hair and intense green eyes is waiting for us. He scrutinizes each of our faces as if searching for something.

He inclines his head and introduces himself. "I'm Torin, the chief archivist. Please follow me."

When we get to the library, he heads toward the little room we were in the other day. Pointing to the books on the table, he informs us, "I believe you will find what you need in those books."

Frowning, I lay my hand on his arm. "We read through those books the other day. They seemed to be missing key servants typically found in royal households, such as stable hands, blacksmiths, and others who might have worked outside."

He gives me a wry smile. "Really? That's strange. I read them myself this morning and found several listings." He glances down at my hand on his arm.

Lifting my eyebrows, I jerk my hand away from his arm and shrug. Maybe we missed a book. I watch him walk over to his desk and leave us with the ledgers. Striding over, I pick one up and skim my fingers down the listings. "Blacksmith—Keir Balanthir" jumps out at me, and I stop and turn the ledger toward Theron.

Intrigued, he pulls the other books toward him, and we find the same name several times. We glance at each other and the door. This name wasn't in the ledgers two days ago, and now it's suddenly listed? Is this the queen's doing?

Astor takes a picture of the ledger, and we stack the books in a pile on the table. Stepping out from the little room, we find the archivist waiting for us.

"Did you find what you need?" His question is innocent, but his tone seems to suggest something else.

Daire steps forward, shielding me from his gaze. "We found the information we needed to complete our research. Thank you for your time." Turning, he places a hand on my back and escorts me to the hall. Theron and Astor trail behind us, and the archivist behind them.

At the portal, we turn and thank the archivist again. Before I step through, I watch him make a sign with his hand, but I can't tell what it means.

Theron and Astor are beyond excited when we return. Keir is the name of the blacksmith who created the Killian blades long ago, although nobody had a last name to go with it. If he is my ancestor, maybe he chose Balanthir because it's relatively close to Balinor? We don't have proof yet, but we have a name and a place to start.

Picking up my phone, I send Fallon a text to let him know what we found, although I don't give him the actual name. He hasn't sent me any replies, but I've been keeping him in the loop.

"Theron, did you send the dark Elven queen's message to Fallon?" I ask lightly.

"I did," he answers. "Fallon is going to schedule a visit with her. He has specific questions about her activities that day, and Astor is going to help him sort the truth from the lies. It's definitely odd to have such two distinctly different stories."

"I think it will be good for him to find out, one way or another," I state. "Before you all disappear to your respective rooms, why don't we take the night off and celebrate? We can always look for Keir tomorrow."

Daire's sexy smile convinces me it's a great idea. Theron looks torn, but when Astor asks him if he's going to turn down a beautiful woman's invitation to dinner, he looks at me sheepishly and agrees to go.

Piling into Daire's SUV, we head to a new Asian fusion

place close by. According to Daire, the food is delicious, with new twists on the traditional fare.

Both Astor and I place a shield around the place to protect us, then we settle in with a couple bottles of wine and various dishes. While eating and drinking, I listen to them tell stories from their decades together. They know each other so well, and I only hope I'm here in another five hundred years to listen when they tell stories about me.

For the first time in a couple of weeks, I feel lighthearted and at ease with myself. Smiling at the three sinfully delicious males with me, I count every one of my blessings. I only wish Fallon and Valerian were here with us.

With my arm in Theron's, we're strolling toward the vehicle when a portal opens near the SUV. We freeze, watching the scene unfold.

"Daire!" Theron shouts.

"No." I countermand his order. "We leave together, or we fight together."

Theron tosses me a hard look but agrees. Tense, we use magic to pull our weapons and wait. A man in a hooded cloak steps out of the portal, along with a beautiful woman with red hair and bright green Elven eyes. She's carrying a gleaming mahogany box in her hands. He stands by the portal, sword in hand, while she walks calmly over to us.

Her intense eyes sweep over me, taking in every inch, from my heels to my sword. Extending the box, she waits for me to take it.

Wary, I glance down at the box, and my eyes widen. Sheathing my sword, I take it from her. "Who sent you?" I question, my voice hard. "Did the queen send you?"

She shakes her head. Scrutinizing each of the men with me, she smiles and nods as if giving her approval. "Your father sent me. It's not safe for you to visit the dark Elven kingdom. Word about your visit to the old village has made it to the king, and he's hunting for information about the visitors. It's imperative he does not find you. Your father will reach out to you when it's safe. For now, this is what you need to continue your journey." Dipping her head, she walks slowly back to the portal. The two stand there staring at us for a brief second before stepping through and disappearing.

Stunned, I grip the box while my mind plays her words over and over in my head. *Your father sent me.* Could it be true?

A hand tightens for a brief second on my back, then everything blurs, and I find myself sitting in the back seat. Daire's icy blue eyes search mine before he closes the door and gets in the driver's seat, Theron and Astor close behind us.

Before driving off, I turn on the overhead light and put the box on the console for everyone to see. Burned into the wood is the same symbol as the one on my shoulder, the one signifying my royal Elven heritage. It's the reason I took the box from her. Very few people know about this symbol.

Fiddling with the latch, I raise the lid and find a dark brown leather journal, identical to Agnes', with the name "Catriona MacAllister" engraved on it—my ancestor who survived the massacre. This is hers. The second journal foretold by my mother's letter.

THANK YOU!

Thank you for reading. I hope this second book took you on a fantastical journey with Arden and her cadre. I love writing this world and these characters, and I'm hard at work creating book three.

Creating characters and worlds in your head, trying to get them cohesively on paper, then putting them out there for the world to view is daunting. Whether it's "give me more," or "I think this character needs more love," reviews help me write the next story. Please consider leaving one for this book.

*If you find an error, please feel free to email me at Stellabrie@stellabrie.com.

The journey comes to a conclusion in The Rowan's Destiny.

To get a free eBook copy of my first book, My Salvation, just subscribe to my newsletter.

Website: https://www.stellabrie.com/my-salvation

Acknowledgments

Huge thanks to everyone who made this book possible! Both, my husband and mom, who listen to my incessant plot and character discussions. Thanks for all your support!

My beta readers, who catch so many big and little things! I know this book is a thousand times better because of your feedback. Thank you, Nia, Bianca, Iliana, Melissa, Rachel, and Debbie for all of your feedback!

My gorgeous cover is by Mayflower Studio. Amala does fabulous work! Check her out.

Rockstar editing and proofreading by two lovely ladies, Meghan at Bookish Dreams Editing and Jess at Elemental Editing & Proofreading.

About the Author

Stella Brie lives outside of Nashville, TN, with her husband. After mentioning her desire to write a book a million times to her husband, he challenged her to sit down one day and write a paragraph. Instead, she wrote her first book, *My Salvation*.

She decided to trade in her career in digital marketing, working on big brands, for this wildly creative one. Armed with a notebook and crammed full of ideas, she's constantly thinking about bold heroines, sexy men, and HEAs. Whether it's a paranormal book full of creatures and magic or a contemporary romance full of heat and drama, she's always thinking about how she can bring her books to life.

Latest News and Updates:
Facebook Group: Stella's Stalkers
TikTok: @stellabrie_author
YouTube! Playlists (all books): @authorstellabrie
Instagram: @stellabrie_author
Website: Stellabrie.com - Exclusive sneak peeks, cover reveals, giveaways, and more!

facebook.com/AuthorStellaBrie
instagram.com/stellabrie_author
goodreads.com/stellabrie

BOOKS BY STELLA BRIE

PARANORMAL WHY CHOOSE

KILLIAN BLADE SERIES

The Rowan (1)

The Rowan's Stone (2)

The Rowan's Destiny (3)

Spin-offs:

Wicked Savior - Lucifer's story (MF Romance) - Book 3.5

The Light Falls (4) - Meri's story

The Dark Rises (5) - Meri's story

CONTEMPORARY WHY CHOOSE

THE SAVAGES SERIES

Savage Traitor (1)

Savage Ruin (2)

Spin-off:

Lethal Vengeance (Standalone)

My Salvation (Standalone)

To get a free eBook copy of my first book, My Salvation, just subscribe to my newsletter.

Website: https://www.stellabrie.com/my-salvation